JUST
LIKE
THAT

SCHMIDT

JUST LIKE THAT

CLARION BOOKS
Houghton Mifflin Harcourt
Boston   New York

Clarion Books

3 Park Avenue

New York, New York 10016

Copyright © 2021 by Gary D. Schmidt

Clarion Books is an imprint of Houghton Mifflin Harcourt Publishing Company.

hmhbooks.com

The text was set in Fairfield LT Std.

Cover design by Sharismar Rodriguez

Interior design by Sharismar Rodriguez

Library of Congress Cataloging-in-Publication Data is available.

ISBN 978-0-544-08477-3

Manufactured in the United States of America

DOC 10 9 8 7 6 5 4 3 2

4500819960

For David and Taylor,
with a father's love

JUST LIKE THAT

Summer 1968

ONE

IN JUNE—THE JUNE BEFORE MERYL LEE KOWALSKI'S eighth-grade year—she watched the evening news reports from the Vietnam War. Twenty-three American soldiers in a CH-46A Sea Knight had helicoptered in to evacuate Marines not far from Khe Sanh, South Vietnam. Their helicopter was hit by enemy fire and went down. Half the men were killed.

No one who loved those Marines had a chance to say goodbye.

Meryl Lee watched the story with her hands up to her face.

In July, Meryl Lee watched the evening news report about the American Marines on Hill 689, who killed three hundred and fifty North Vietnamese soldiers. They weren't going to leave the hill, they said, until every North Vietnamese soldier was dead.

They didn't.

And no one who loved those soldiers had a chance to say goodbye.

Meryl Lee watched that story, crying.

Then in August, Meryl Lee's best friend—her very best friend who had once handed her a rose, who had danced with her at Danny Hupfer's bar mitzvah, who had listened with her to the sound of a brand-new bottle of Coke when you pry the lid off and it starts to fizz—her very best friend was sitting in the back of his father's Mustang on the way to a movie, a stupid movie, a stupid

stupid movie, when they were rear-ended and Holling Hoodhood's head snapped back.

Just like that.

Meryl Lee did not make it to Syosset Hospital in time to say goodbye.

For Meryl Lee Kowalski, everything in the world, absolutely everything in the world, became a Blank.

The service was at Saint Andrew Presbyterian Church. It was packed. Men in black suits, women in dark dresses. Everyone from Camillo Junior High—the principal, Mrs. Sidman; Holling's teachers; his friends Danny Hupfer and Mai Thi. Cross-country runners from Bethpage and Farmingdale and Westbury and Wantagh, wearing their uniform shirts. Mr. Goldman from Goldman's Best Bakery, sitting in the back, bawling. Mercutio Baker holding a new white perfect baseball he had wanted to throw with the kid, and Lieutenant Tybalt Baker in his dress uniform. The priest from Saint Adelbert's. The rabbi from Temple Beth-El.

His seventh-grade teacher, Mrs. Baker, spoke the eulogy, holding a single chrysanthemum. She did fine until she got to the end: "Fear no more the heat o' th' sun," she said, "Nor the furious winter's rages; / Thou thy worldly task hast done, / Home art gone and . . ." She could not finish. She tried, but she could not finish. She went back down to her seat. As she walked past the casket, she laid the chrysanthemum oh so gently upon it.

So the pallbearers came to take Holling, and his father stood—they all stood—and when Holling passed him, his father put his hands on the casket and began to howl. Horrible, horrible hollow howls that could not be stopped, because there was no comfort.

The pallbearers stood still. They waited a long time.

Even through the Blank, Meryl Lee heard the howls.

She thought she would hear them the rest of her life.

She thought they would echo in the place where her heart had been, forever.

She did not go to the graveside. She could not go to bear those last words, to bear that thud of earth, to see Holling . . .

She could not go.

Her parents drove her home.

In the next weeks, Danny Hupfer and Mai Thi came over, and Mrs. Baker, and some of the other teachers from Camillo Junior High, and even Mr. Goldman, but Meryl Lee did not leave the house much that whole month. Everything she saw was without Holling, and the howls echoed in her empty chest. She could not go onto his block, she could not pass that Woolworth's and its lunch counter where they had had a Coke, she could not walk down Lee Avenue, and she could not could not could not go near Camillo Junior High. She could not.

Because if she did, then the Blank would change. It would become a hole, a dizzying white hole, and she would fall into it, and she would be the empty hole where the howling echoes rolled around, and she had already come close, very close, to falling in.

So in September, her parents made phone calls to St. Elene's Preparatory Academy for Girls. She would have a new start, her parents said. A whole new routine, her parents said. She would meet so many new friends. She would become so Accomplished. That's what the headmistress had promised. Meryl Lee would become so Accomplished. And she had never before lived so close to the sea. The Maine ocean would be beautiful, they said.

And Meryl Lee knew that Holling Hoodhood had never been to the coast of Maine. He had never been there. And nothing familiar would be in Maine. Not Lee Avenue. Not Camillo Junior High.

Not Goldman's Best Bakery. Not . . . anything. Maybe that was where she should go.

Her mother packed her clothes for her.

Her father packed some books for her.

They bought her St. Elene's regulation uniforms: six white shirts, three green and gold plaid skirts, two green and gold sweaters, and two green blazers with the gold St. Elene's cross insignia. They packed them all carefully into her suitcase.

Then on the day, they packed her into the car.

On the ride up to St. Elene's Preparatory Academy, it rained all across New York. And the whole way through Connecticut. And every mile of Massachusetts. New Hampshire and southern Maine were nothing but gray drizzle.

They stopped at a hotel in Brunswick overnight, and it poured.

The next morning, Meryl Lee leaned her head against the hotel window and stared at the blurred world outside.

None of them spoke.

TWO

1967–68

No ONE ON THE PENINSULA KNEW HOW LONG MATT Coffin had been around. A year? How old was he? Hard to tell. Thirteen, fourteen? He was that kid who lived down by the shore, that kid who never went to school, that kid who skipped rocks into the waves at sunset, that kid who was always by himself.

That kid who never let anyone get near him.

He did live by the shore, in an old lobster shack left behind by Captain Cobb after he died. When folks saw smoke meandering out of its stone chimney, they figured some grizzled tramp had moved in, even though the place was falling down from rot and gravity. But fall came and went, and winter came and went, and the old shack still stood, and Matt Coffin lived like a seal near the ocean: he'd be standing by the water, and then he'd slip away and be gone.

The town did try twice to force Matt Coffin into Harpswell Junior High, but both times he quit after a few days, and neither his teachers nor the principal were inclined to bring him back. So he spent his days clamming, or fishing, or tending the rows of beans he planted in the spring behind Captain Cobb's shack, bush beans in rows straight enough and pole beans on posts sturdy enough that folks said he'd do as a gardener if he put his mind to it.

Things might have gone on this way for a very long time, except one early spring evening, when the orange sun was low and the shadows of the pines long, Mrs. Nora MacKnockater came down the steep ridge to the shore beneath her house and settled her substantial rump on a smooth rock large enough to hold it. She watched a flat stone skip in the trough between the low waves—the tide was heading out—turned, and saw Matt Coffin brush back his hair, pull his arm to toss the next stone, see her, and stop.

"Five skips," she said, "is a creditable throw."

Matt Coffin jerked out the T-shirt looped around his belt and turned toward the pines.

"Is that the best you can do?" said Mrs. MacKnockater.

He turned back to her, pulling the shirt over his head.

"Five?" she said.

His head popped out. "Seventeen," he said.

Mrs. MacKnockater looked around her, rose, maneuvered about the rock, stooped, and picked up a stone. She steered her large self down toward the water as Matt Coffin stepped away—but he still watched.

Mrs. MacKnockater pulled her arm back and threw.

She turned to Matt Coffin. "Eight," she said.

"Seven," he said.

"You miscounted," she said.

"It doesn't count when the last one goes into the wave."

"That is hardly charitable arithmetic," said Mrs. MacKnockater.

Matt Coffin came down to the shore beside her, stooped, and picked up two stones. He handed one to her. Until it got too dark to count, they threw stones into the water and watched them skip over the outgoing tide, away into the lowering dark orange.

Mrs. MacKnockater was back at the next sunset.

So was Matt Coffin.

"Eleven," he said.

"What happened to the rule about the last skip going into the wave?" she said.

"I didn't count that one."

"You most certainly did," said Mrs. MacKnockater, and she threw her stone.

"One," Matt Coffin said, "counting the skip into the wave. How's that for charitable arithmetic?"

"Do you like franks and beans?" said Mrs. MacKnockater.

He looked at her. In the low light, she couldn't quite tell what he was thinking—and she was good at telling what people were thinking.

"Sometimes," he said.

"It would only take a moment to warm them up," she said.

Matt Coffin threw his last stone into the trough.

"Three," she said.

"Okay," he said.

It took more than a moment to warm up the franks and beans, and to set out the brown bread with raisins, and to lay a line of cinnamon over the applesauce, and to put out the dish of dill pickles, and to pour the ice cold milk, and to light the two tall candles that threw their lovely glow up to the ceiling beams.

Matt Coffin ate everything on the table, stopping only once, then twice, to look at the rows of bookshelves that lined the walls of the parlor beyond.

"Are those reading books?" he said.

Mrs. MacKnockater nodded and moved the plate of brown bread closer to him. She scooted the plate of butter beside it.

"You read all those?"

"Every one," she said. "Do you have a favorite writer?"

He took another slice of brown bread, dipped it into the applesauce, and ate it.

It rained the next day, and Mrs. MacKnockater did not go down to the shore. But at suppertime, when she could hear the waves at low tide, she stepped out onto the porch and Matt Coffin was standing by the rhododendrons, one hand in his pocket, one hand holding a half-full pillowcase over his shoulder, his hat drawn low and dripping.

"Eighteen," he said.

"Meatloaf," she said, and he came inside.

"You can leave your bag in the parlor," she said.

He sat down, laid the pillowcase on the floor, and kicked it well underneath the sofa with his heel. He could already smell the meatloaf.

"We're ready," Mrs. MacKnockater called from the kitchen.

He picked out as many onions as he could, then ate almost the whole meatloaf by himself, stopping only to spread tomato ketchup over it. Mrs. MacKnockater watched him the whole time.

Later, after two apple dumplings, he walked back into the parlor and looked at the rows of books.

Mrs. MacKnockater followed. She drew out *Treasure Island* and showed it to him.

"What's it about?" he said.

"A boy named Jim," she said. "The sea. A search for buried treasure. Pirates. Captain Flint and Black Dog and Billy Bones and Long John Silver."

He took the book and flipped through it. "The pictures look pretty good," he said. He handed the book back to her.

"You know, Matthew, I've always enjoyed reading aloud. I used to do it when I was a teacher, but now I've no one to read to. Would you mind terribly if I read the opening chapter to you?"

Matt shrugged. "If you want to," he said.

Later, when Dr. Livesey had stared down the Captain and Mrs. MacKnockater had finished the first chapter, Matt said, "Why do you talk so funny?"

"Funny?" said Mrs. MacKnockater.

"Yeah, funny."

"I grew up in Edinburgh," said Mrs. MacKnockater. "A long, long way from here, across the wide ocean."

And Matt suddenly grew quiet, very quiet, and he looked at her, then he looked out the window into the dark, and he wondered if that would be far enough.

On sunny days after that, Mrs. MacKnockater went down to the shore and skipped stones with Matt. And when they both got hungry—that is, when Mrs. MacKnockater got hungry, since Matt was always hungry—they climbed the shore ridge to her home and ate supper, and afterward Mrs. MacKnockater read *Treasure Island*. On rainy days, Matt just came to her house when it was suppertime.

When he did not come, Mrs. MacKnockater understood that he was out on the water. At dusk on those days, she stood on her porch and held up her binoculars to watch the fishing boats and the lobster boats come in, and Matt would be standing on the deck of one, waving at her, and she would be surprised at the way her heart filled.

Once she asked him about school.

"I thought you weren't a teacher anymore," he said.

"No teacher ever really stops being a teacher. I'm the headmistress at St. Elene's Preparatory Academy for Girls."

"What does a headmistress do?"

"I ensure that the school is run properly."

"How do you do that?"

"With guile. Matthew, you should be in school."

"I tried that. Twice. I'm not going again."

"Whatever happened before, it is not inevitable that—"

"Are we going to read tonight?"

"Matthew . . ."

"Are we?"

So they ate supper together that night—slabs of white scrod with lots of tartar sauce—and then they read, and they read through the heat of July, and through the firefly nights of August, and into the first cool days of September when the maples looked as if they had tipped the edges of their leaves in pirate blood. They finished *Treasure Island* a few nights before St. Elene's Preparatory Academy for Girls would open its doors to the new fall term, with the voice of Captain Flint squawking in the parlor: "Pieces of eight! Pieces of eight!"

Mrs. MacKnockater looked down at the book. "Mr. Stevenson certainly knows how to tell an adventure," she said.

Matt was quiet, and then he said, "It's like Long John Silver is a jerk, but it's also like he's Jim's father. Sort of."

Mrs. MacKnockater looked at him. "I suppose that's true, but Jim is certainly glad to be rid of him."

Matt reached over and closed the book in her hands. "I guess," he said. "But still, he hopes he's okay at the end."

"Perhaps," Mrs. MacKnockater said quietly. Then, "Matthew, do you know where your father is?"

Something shattered in the room like old glass. Matt Coffin looked at her as if betrayed. He stood up.

"I don't mean to pry, Matthew."

The screen door slapped behind him as he left the house.

"Matthew," she called.

He did not come the next evening. Mrs. MacKnockater wrapped the meatloaf without onions in tinfoil and put it away in the refrigerator.

Three days later, when Mrs. MacKnockater went to preside over the opening ceremony of St. Elene's Preparatory Academy for Girls, the missing Matthew Coffin was all she could think about.

FALL SEMESTER
September–December 1968

OBSTACLES

THREE

WHEN MERYL LEE AND HER PARENTS DROVE ONTO the grounds of St. Elene's Preparatory Academy that first morning, girls in regulation green and gold school uniforms were holding dark umbrellas and pointing the way to the dormitories. They smiled in the rain as if they were the happiest girls in the world, and they waved as if Meryl Lee were a long-lost friend finally come home.

Meryl Lee did not wave back.

Her father followed the signs to Margaret B. Netley Dormitory, where portly Mrs. Kellogg, who was the dorm matron and looked exactly like what a dorm matron should look like, was waiting beneath the overhang on the front porch. While the Kowalskis stood with Mrs. Kellogg, two girls in black dresses and white aprons—they didn't have dark umbrellas and they weren't smiling—unloaded Meryl Lee's suitcase and two shopping bags. The shopping bags, Mrs. Kellogg said, were to be taken up by Alethea, the suitcase by Bettye. They were to carry everything to Miss Kowalski's room: Netley 204.

Meryl Lee watched them go.

"We're so glad to have you here," said Mrs. Kellogg.

"Thank you," said Meryl Lee. She did not believe that Mrs.

Kellogg, who sounded as if she were reading her lines from a script, was really all that glad to have her there.

"We hope that you'll be very happy at St. Elene's," said Mrs. Kellogg.

Meryl Lee didn't believe that either.

If Holling had been there, Meryl Lee would have turned to him and said, "See what I mean?" and Holling would have said, in some sort of robot-y voice, "We are so glad to have you here, Meryl Lee. We hope that you will be very happy at St. Elene's, Meryl Lee. The girls of Margaret B. Netley Dormitory are eager to meet you, Meryl Lee, Meryl Lee, Meryl Lee."

Then Mrs. Kellogg shook Meryl Lee's hand and said, "The girls of Margaret B. Netley Dormitory are eager to meet you, Meryl Lee."

Really, she said that.

Holling would have been rolling on the ground, holding his stomach, laughing.

"I think it's time," said Meryl Lee's father.

She felt as if someone—maybe Mrs. Kellogg—had punched her in the stomach.

Her mother hugged her and her father kissed her on the top of her head, and suddenly Meryl Lee knew it was really going to happen. They were going to leave her at St. Elene's Preparatory Academy for Girls and Holling wasn't there and she would be very, very alone.

The Blank.

The howling echoes in her empty chest.

She followed them to the car and stood beside it. In the rain. Without a dark umbrella.

Her parents got in. They closed the doors.

Her mother rolled down her window.

"Mom," said Meryl Lee.

"It will be all right," said her mother.

"You are not leaving me here," said Meryl Lee.

"Meryl Lee, this is a new start. It will be all right."

"No," said Meryl Lee. She put her hand on the back door handle. It was locked.

"Meryl Lee, you'll be used to all of this in a day or so. You will. I promise."

Rain coming down harder. Meryl Lee wiping at her eyes.

She looked over the car at the clapboard buildings of St. Elene's Preparatory Academy for Girls. She looked at the white chapel across the commons, more gray than white in the rain. She looked at the steps of Margaret B. Netley Dormitory, where the waiting Mrs. Kellogg, standing strategically under the porch roof, purposefully wound the watch dangling from a dark braid from around her neck. She looked at the green and gold uniformed girls walking in and out of Margaret B. Netley Dormitory in umbrellaed groups, smiling as though they had been walking in and out of Margaret B. Netley Dormitory in those same umbrellaed groups together since, oh, first grade. Smiling with friends they had known all their lives.

Oh, smiling with friends they had known all their lives.

The two girls in the black and white uniforms had come back and were standing behind Mrs. Kellogg. They were both very wet. They both looked down at the ground.

"You are not leaving me," said Meryl Lee.

Her father leaned across the car seat toward her. "Meryl Lee, we've been over this. There will be wonderful opportunities here, and new people, and new friends. St. Elene's is one of the finest academies in all New—"

"Do you see that brick wall?" said Meryl Lee, pointing. "Do you know why it has iron spears on top?"

"That's wrought iron on top, Meryl Lee."

"So if anyone tries to get out, she'll fall on the spears."

"It's time to go," said Meryl Lee's father.

"And do you see the ivy climbing the brick wall?"

Meryl Lee's mother began rolling up her window.

"That's poison ivy."

"It is not poison—"

"No, it really is. And if you touch poison ivy that thick, you know how infected you'll get? Do you really want to leave me in a place surrounded by a brick wall with spears on top and covered with poison ivy?"

"Meryl Lee," said her father.

"This is a big mistake," she said.

"Meryl Lee," said her mother, "you're going to love St. Elene's. And you're going to love Dr. MacKnockater. In every call we've had, she's assured us that St. Elene's will be just what we hoped for. A month from now, St. Elene's will feel like another home."

"Who knows if I'll be here a month from now?" Meryl Lee said.

"Of course you'll be here a month from now," said her mother.

"Holling isn't."

The Blank.

Her mother got out. She took Meryl Lee's hands. "No, he isn't. And we all miss him. And we'll always remember him. But you are here. You are. And now it's time to live your own life, because you must."

Meryl Lee knew her mother was right. She must. What else could she do?

"And you're going to make the most of this new beginning. And we're going to be so proud of you."

Meryl Lee could not speak.

"We already are," her mother said.

Meryl Lee nodded, and she tried to smile—because her mother wanted her to smile.

Her mother got back in. Her father put the car in gear.

"We love you," said her mother.

"Don't get too close to that poison ivy," said her father.

They waved, and she watched them drive down the road toward the main gate—which also had spears on top—the dark wet gravel crunching under the tires. She watched the brake lights come on for a moment—"Please, please," she whispered—and then the car pulled out of St. Elene's and was gone.

The edges of the Blank blurred.

Rain misted around her, so that Meryl Lee almost looked as if she was crying.

Mrs. Kellogg finished winding her watch. She called from the steps of Margaret B. Netley Dormitory, "Miss Kowalski, being late for your arrival hardly grants you the privilege of being late for the opening ceremony as well."

Meryl Lee took a deep, solidifying breath. One last look down to the main gate—just in case—and she turned to Mrs. Kellogg, who stood as straight as an exclamation point. Then Meryl Lee pushed back the Blank and walked up the porch steps, wishing beyond all wishing that she was not a new student at St. Elene's Preparatory Academy for Girls, wishing beyond all wishing that she was at Camillo Junior High, wishing beyond all wishing that Holling, oh that Holling was coming up the main staircase with that worn-out black and white jacket he always wore and he would give that shy sort of wave he does—did—from his hip.

"Your luggage has already been taken to your room, where you should have been some time ago," said Mrs. Kellogg. "Students—even new students—are expected and required to don the St. Elene's Academy uniform for all school activities and events—especially the opening ceremony."

Meryl Lee looked at the two girls standing under the porch roof, one still looking down, one now staring at Meryl Lee.

"Alethea," said Mrs. Kellogg sharply.

Alethea looked down.

"Please follow me," said Mrs. Kellogg.

Meryl Lee followed her.

But she had seen Alethea's face before she looked down.

Alethea was not smiling.

Alethea was definitely not smiling. And somehow Meryl Lee knew that Alethea did not care at all whether Meryl Lee would be happy at St. Elene's or not.

She went to don her regulation St. Elene's Academy uniform.

FOUR

THE SOAP-SMOOTH WOOD FLOOR OF MARGARET B. Netley Dormitory was to be trod upon only by the upper school girls of St. Elene's Preparatory Academy; the boards resounded with every single step Meryl Lee and Mrs. Kellogg took. Above them, aged dark beams crossed the ceilings—"Norman abbots once walked beneath these," said Mrs. Kellogg. On Netley's first floor, doors to the kitchen—"The refrigerator is well provisioned with snacks: cheese rounds, cut vegetables, assorted fruit juices, and bottles of Coca-Cola, the last supplied only if each girl, on her honor, pays twenty-five cents per bottle"—and to the laundry room—"Locked after nine thirty p.m. and packets of detergent available upon request, but to use only if needed, in between regular laundry days, when soiled garments are picked up in the morning and delivered back to your room by four o'clock"—and to the telephone—"No calls after nine forty-five p.m." On the second floor, doors to the girls' rooms, which were all open. Mrs. Kellogg made introductions as they passed, and Meryl Lee tried to listen: "Here are Elizabeth Koertge from Los Angeles and Julia Chall from St. Paul. Here are Ashley Louise Higginson from Brooklyn, New York, and Charlotte Antoinette Dobrée from Charlotte, North Carolina. Here are Marian Elders from Manhattan and Barbara

Rockcastle from White Plains. Here is Heidi Kidder from Rutland, Vermont. And here . . ."

Meryl Lee felt the Blank hovering.

"And here is your room," said Mrs. Kellogg. "You will be living with Jennifer Hartley Truro from Truro, Massachusetts." To make sure Meryl Lee understood, Mrs. Kellogg leaned down and said, "The town is named after the family." This door was closed, so Mrs. Kellogg knocked and opened it. "Miss Truro? Here is your new roommate, Miss Meryl Lee Kowalski, from . . ."

She turned to Meryl Lee.

"Hicksville, New York," said Meryl Lee.

"New York," said Mrs. Kellogg. "Miss Kowalski, Miss Truro."

Jennifer Hartley Truro slowly elevated from her bed, tossed her long blond hair back like a cape behind her, and floated cloudlike across the room. She extended her hand in a way that suggested Meryl Lee should bow down and do worship.

"Hey," said Meryl Lee.

"Good morning," said Jennifer Hartley Truro.

"Generally Miss Truro rooms with Stephanie DeLacy from Philadelphia," Mrs. Kellogg said. "But Stephanie's father is a United Nations diplomat and the family is living in Budapest for the next year. So the two of you will be rooming together. I'm sure you will get along well."

The whole time Mrs. Kellogg was talking, Jennifer was looking at Meryl Lee as if she had completely blundered into the wrong room and there was no reason in the whole wide world that they would ever get along well.

Then Jennifer pointed to a corner of the room, beyond Meryl Lee's bed and the mattress that lay naked upon it, where a suitcase held together with a leather belt and two wet shopping bags dripped.

"Those must be yours," she said.

Jennifer had obviously been in the room for several days—and it looked like she had brought her interior decorator with her. A green satin duvet covered her bed, and gold satin pillows lay strewn over it, perfectly placed as if they had been tossed there so very carelessly. A paisley cloth covered her dresser and cushioned the tray that held her set of tortoiseshell combs. Above them, a gilded mirror hung. On the wall above the green satin duvet, framed posters of Ringo and Paul and John and George, all signed in big felt-tip marker. "Love and kisses to Jennifer," said Ringo. "This night the stars were all in your eyes," said Paul. In the closet, her hangers were pink and plush. Meryl Lee turned away before she could see what they were holding.

This isn't going to work, she thought.

"You'll need to change quickly, girls," said Mrs. Kellogg. "The opening ceremony is in"—she looked down at her dangling watch—"eighteen minutes."

"I'll be ready," said Jennifer.

Meryl Lee lugged her wet suitcase onto the mattress. She undid the leather belt. The first thing she took out was a dried rose. She laid it carefully on the desk beside her bed. Then she took out her regulation St. Elene's uniform and looked around for the bathroom so she could be alone for a minute, just a minute, just one stupid minute—and then maybe she could hold back the Blank a little while more.

But there wasn't even time for that, since Jennifer made it to the bathroom first. She took twelve minutes—mostly, Meryl Lee figured, with her hair. Meryl Lee took two—mostly with her eyes closed, breathing slowly. Then, one minute after that, Meryl Lee was walking down the hall, three steps behind the blond hair of Jennifer Hartley Truro, the flowing auburn curls of Charlotte Antoinette Dobrée, and the chocolate-colored locks of Ashley Louise Higginson. The three were all wearing their regulation St. Elene's Academy uniform—except for Charlotte, who had substituted a blouse made of something that shimmered.

Charlotte's shimmering blouse fit her perfectly.

The regulation St. Elene's Academy uniforms that Jennifer and Ashley wore fit them perfectly too.

The sleeves of Meryl Lee's regulation St. Elene's uniform shirt—which did not shimmer—came down over her knuckles.

Of course.

"Maybe we can find some paper clips," said Ashley, looking back.

They paused on the steps of Margaret B. Netley Dormitory. The rain had stopped and the sudden sun was already steaming the puddles. Across the commons, Newell Chapel shone brilliantly white in the clearing air.

Suddenly, more than anything, Meryl Lee wanted to hear the sound of a bottle of Coke being opened. That wonderful fizzing sound that said something wonderful was about to begin. Something wonderful that was wonderful because you were sharing the Coke with someone you . . .

But all she heard was the sound of boots on the gravel path, the giggles of friends reunited after a summer, the light chimes of Newell Chapel, Mrs. Kellogg's matronly fussing.

This wasn't going to work.

They walked past the oldest part of campus—the long white steps and high wooden pillars of eighteenth-century Greater Hoxne

Hall, the shorter white steps and shorter wooden pillars of Sherbourne House, the diamond-windowed Putnam Library, the six-gabled Lesser Hoxne—and joined the current of girls (lower school first, then upper school) channeling into two lines beneath the high white steeple of Newell Chapel, which needled the newly blue sky.

Every regulation St. Elene's uniform in sight fit every girl perfectly—except Meryl Lee and, as it turned out, the girl beside her in line. Her skirt was a lot longer than it should have been. She kept hitching it up. Meryl Lee was afraid to look, but she thought the girl might be crying.

She knew how she felt.

She *really* knew how she felt.

Suddenly, at some cue Meryl Lee missed—maybe it was the organ starting to play, or maybe it was a glance from Mrs. Kellogg—the girls quieted, then marched side by side through the high doors of Newell Chapel. They marched beneath the ancient school banners of St. Elene's Preparatory Academy for Girls, and Meryl Lee looked up. *Those banners must be a hundred years old,* she thought. They marched up the center aisle between the black-robed academy teachers, who stood at attention by the end of each of the pews. *Some of them must be a hundred years old too,* thought Meryl Lee.

When they had all moved into the pews—Meryl Lee stood in the pew behind Jennifer and Ashley and Charlotte since they hadn't left room for her beside them—the organ shifted from its slow processional into something a little more rousing, paused dramatically, and then boomed into what Meryl Lee figured was the school song—which she did not know, but everyone else seemed to.

Hail to thee, St. Elene's.
I pledge my heart to you.
Hail to thee, St. Elene's.
I pledge my two hands too!

Meryl Lee thought the school song used the word *hail* a little too much.

Hail to thee, St. Elene's.
The stars shine down on you.
Hail to thee, St. Elene's.
To you we will be true.

Definitely too many *hails*. If Holling heard this song, he would be on the floor again, laughing like a dog. He would laugh and laugh and his hair would be all messed up and his eyes would be bright and . . .

The organ went back to being solemn, and then Dr. Nora Mac-Knockater, the headmistress of St. Elene's lower and upper schools, and Mr. Lloyd C. Allen, the chairman of the St. Elene's board of trustees, together slowly processed down the main aisle, then up the stairs to the plush red chairs upon the podium, where Mr. Allen sat in Regal Ease, and where Dr. Nora MacKnockater stood in Awful Dignity and gazed at the girls—sort of like a searchlight scoping out the incarcerated in a dark prison yard. When Meryl Lee saw the headmistress's gaze looming toward her, she looked down and waited until she knew it would be past. Then she looked up again.

But her timing was off: Dr. Nora MacKnockater was gazing directly at her.

Quickly Meryl Lee clasped her hands behind her back and held her breath.

The gaze lingered, lingered, lingered—and moved on.

Meryl Lee breathed again.

When the organ finally stopped, a minute of terrible silence stuffed Newell Chapel until Dr. Nora MacKnockater spoke: "The Faculty"—she paused—"may be Seated."

It seemed to Meryl Lee that Dr. MacKnockater spoke in Capital Letters.

The collective sound of the faculty being seated. The strain of the pews. Adjusting of long robes. A few light coughs.

"Returning Girls"—Dr. Nora MacKnockater paused—"may be Seated."

More pews strained. A few quick laughs, quickly stilled.

Meryl Lee looked around. Almost everyone in the chapel was now seated. Except the lower school's youngest girls. And Meryl Lee. And the girl whose regulation St. Elene's uniform skirt was too long and who was definitely crying.

"I would speak first to the New Girls of St. Elene's Preparatory Academy," said Dr. Nora MacKnockater.

And she did.

She spoke about Obstacles that come to everyone in life. She spoke about the Resolution we need to face Obstacles. She spoke about how Resolution leads to Accomplishment. She spoke about the Accomplishments of the Students of St. Elene's: Jennifer Dow currently had a still-life painting in a youth exhibition at the Museum of Fine Arts in Boston, where Marian Elders had three art pots she had thrown during the summer also displayed. Stephanie DeLacy had two short stories published in a

New England literary journal. And Elizabeth Koertge had won a science fair competition hosted by Harvard University for her project on light fibers.

Meryl Lee thought, *Light fibers? Harvard University?*

Then Dr. MacKnockater spoke about the Accomplishments of the Faculty of St. Elene's: Mrs. Connolly and her new book of poems that Houghton Mifflin would publish next fall. Mrs. Mott and the acquisition of her most recent landscape painting by the Portland Art Museum. Mrs. Bellamy's paper in *Nature* on new dissection techniques for earthworms, frogs, and fetal pigs. Mr. Wheelock's conference presentation in Prague during which he had successfully disproved a theorem that mathematicians had accepted as axiomatic since it was proposed in 1927. At St. Elene's Preparatory Academy for Girls, said Dr. MacKnockater, we become our Best Selves, our most Accomplished Selves.

And Meryl Lee began to feel—it was hard to find the word—a little filled. Maybe that was the word. *Filled.*

Obstacles, and Resolution, and Accomplishment?

Was it really possible?

She could hardly remember what it felt like to live without the Blank.

Could she be filled with Accomplishment?

Dr. MacKnockater leaned toward them.

"The girl who lives purposelessly, looking only to the past, lives a wasted life. And a wasted life honors no one and gilds no one's memory. Girls of St. Elene's, this year, what will your Resolution be?" Another long pause. "What will your Accomplishment be?"

And Meryl Lee felt herself leaning toward Dr. MacKnockater, and she wondered, what would her Accomplishment be?

"How will you become your Best Self?" said Dr. MacKnockater.

And Meryl Lee, still leaning forward, wanted to know. She desperately wanted to know.

"At the end of the year, where will you find—" Dr. MacKnockater stopped. Everyone looked at her. She swallowed and held herself still. Then, "Where will you be found?" she said, her voice not quite so strong.

Ahead of her, Meryl Lee saw Ashley turn toward Jennifer, yawning. Maybe she had heard all this before. Maybe she had heard all this at the beginning of every school year for eight grades. But Meryl Lee had not, and still standing before the Awful Dignity of Dr. MacKnockater, still filled with the solemn moment, Meryl Lee felt that the Blank might be a little further away, and she was not far from tears.

Then across the aisle from Meryl Lee, the girl whose skirt was too long hiccupped twice and threw up.

Marian Elders, who was sitting directly in front of her, was the unfortunate full recipient of what the girl evacuated.

Her pew evacuated too.

Meryl Lee watched. She figured that most of the lower school at least would have run screaming from the chapel except they were probably terrified of Dr. MacKnockater.

On cue, she sat down. She didn't follow all of the next flurried moments, since suddenly she was trying to not throw up herself. But she saw Mrs. Kellogg lead the girl whose skirt was too long out of the chapel by a side door. And she saw Bettye, who had schlepped Meryl Lee's luggage, appear with a very large towel, which she wrapped around Marian Elders, who was covered with . . . well . . . and who was now crying herself—with pretty good reason, thought Meryl Lee. Then Alethea appeared with a pail and mop.

And though Mr. Lloyd C. Allen, chairman of the board of trustees, rose to speak his welcome to the girls of St. Elene's Preparatory Academy, and though he hurtled his voice toward the rows and pews as if he were speaking from the other side of the campus, he did not receive everyone's full attention.

FIVE

At five o'clock in the morning on the day when Mrs. MacKnockater would greet the new girls of St. Elene's Preparatory Academy for the first time, Matt Coffin was down below Harpswell, walking out onto the docks.

In the purple light before dawn, Captain Willis Hurd of the lobster boat *Affliction,* his blue cap pulled down low, did not see him. The Captain had two dozen lobster traps to stow on board, and the day before, Jonathan Buckminster—his crew entire—had boarded a train down to Mississippi, of all places, drafted into the war. And now the Captain's back was doing what it always did on cold mornings: seizing up like a broken piston. He stepped sideways into *Affliction.* Dang, how was he going to get all those traps aboard?

Captain Hurd listened to the creaking of the mooring lines and the collapsing of the low waves. He closed his eyes and smelled the sea-washed boards and the tar of the dock and the piney breezes that came down from the ridges. He felt the give of *Affliction* as the tide began to urge inward.

He thought of young Buckminster, just a boy, hefting the weight of a rifle. Aiming it at some other young boy who—

He opened his eyes, and there was this scrawny kid on the dock, handing one of the traps down to him.

Captain Hurd looked at the kid, grunted. Then he reached out and took the trap.

And the next one.

And the next.

The kid was good. He kept up. Actually, Captain Hurd had to keep up with the kid, scrawny as he was.

When it came to the last trap, the kid climbed aboard with it himself and stowed it. Then he looked at the Captain as if he expected something. And he did. Questions. Questions like "What do you want?" and "Where are you from?" and "How old are you?" and "Why aren't you in school?"

And "Where are your parents?"

But Captain Hurd didn't ask any of those questions. Instead, he asked, "Can you tie a buoy hitch?"

Matt nodded.

The Captain looked at him a long time, then threw him a rope. "Show me," he said.

Matt did.

The Captain nodded. "Okay," he said. "Okay, I'll give you fifteen percent of the profits since it's my boat. You can have one of the tuna fish sandwiches I made and I hope you like tomato and pickle and mayonnaise because I do. There's some brownies but I made them too so don't expect much and they don't have any nuts because I hate nuts. I'm laying four six-trap strings down below where the New Meadows empties. Mile and a half out. Boots are over there. You tie up the traps on the way. After that, gloves are over there. No, over there. Pay attention. So that's it. Come if you want to."

Captain Hurd fiddled with his cap and turned to the engine.

Matt went over to put on the boots.

"Take care of the stern line," Captain Hurd called back.

Matt took care of the stern line.

"And the bow line."

Matt went forward and took care of the bow line.

"Push off," called Captain Hurd, but Matt was already pushing off the dock.

And that was, pretty much, the last time they spoke until mid-morning.

Affliction sputtered along the coast as the sun was almost peeking. If Matt had looked up the ridge toward Mrs. MacKnockater's house when they passed by, he might have seen the lights on and maybe Mrs. MacKnockater out on the porch with her binoculars, watching—but it was too dark, and she wouldn't be able to make him out. *Affliction* chugged by with its neatly stowed traps, the engine missing occasionally—she was an old trawler. Matt tied hitches between the traps and the buoys, and they came past the end of the peninsula and out into the long swells of the Atlantic, where the air was cold and the spray sort of moderate. The sun was barely full up, and the water was blue-black.

They worked as though they had been working together all their lives. Matt tied the lines to each of the traps, and then he put on the yellow gloves and baited the traps with herring while the Captain slowed the trawler and brought her around to face into the breeze. When the Captain nodded, Matt made sure the buoy hitch was tight and slid the first of the traps over the stern, and then the second trap, and then the Captain came to help lay the next four as the sea pulled and the line got heavier. Back at the wheel, the Captain brought *Affliction* around and chugged out into the waves, turned her toward the breeze again, and they laid the next six-trap string.

It was past ten o'clock when they finished, and the Captain came back to the stern, sat down, and stretched out his legs. "You know the bay?" he said.

Matt nodded.

The Captain drew his blue cap down low over his eyes. "Don't hit anything. Take us around some."

And Matt did. Around Chebeague, and then up to Little French, and Bustin, and past the Sow and Pigs since it wasn't yet high tide, and over to Upper Goose and then back out to sea past the Goslings, then the long stretch to Whaleboat Island, and then Stockman Island, the water so blue and the sky bluer, and if the Captain had raised his cap and seen Matt's face, he would have seen something close to happiness.

They anchored off the lee shore of Stockman and *Affliction* lay smoothly on the low swells. The Captain opened his cooler and took out the tuna fish sandwiches—Matt opened his and threw the tomato and pickle overboard, and he tasted right away that the Captain really did like mayonnaise. Afterward they shared the bottle of water—which Matt drank the most of because the brownies were pretty terrible, not at all like Mrs. MacKnockater's.

The thought stung him.

And that was when they saw the whales.

Or heard them, first.

There were four, five, or maybe six. Seven. Swimming over toward Chebeague, riding the currents below the surface in long and slow curves, spouting their mist high into the air, as calm as if they were feeling the earth rotate slowly beneath them, as unconcerned as if there were nothing else on the planet except for this blue day, these green islands, those gray shores.

They watched until the whales moved off around the island, then sank away, Matt leaning over the side of *Affliction* the whole time.

He could have watched them for days.

The Captain, too.

"Only God sees them now," said the Captain, as quiet as a ripple. Then, "Best get your gloves back on," and the Captain headed the trawler around toward the first trap.

But Matt kept his eyes on the ocean beneath which only God could see.

He wished he could too. See what God could see, that is.

Captain Hurd didn't hurry. They rode the troughs that Matt might have skipped stones in—Matt and Mrs. MacKnockater. Another pang. They slowed as they passed each island, as if to enjoy the light glinting off the mica in the rocks. So they didn't reach the buoy of the first string until around 2:30, and when they pulled them up, the traps were disappointing: no lobsters at all in the first four, three total in the last two. Matt banded the lobsters and dropped them into the live tank. The second string of traps had no lobsters at all. The third was better: four in one, three in another, all legals. But the fourth string! The fourth had five lobsters in the first trap! And all the others had three or four, all good size, all legals.

"Guess we know now where we should have put all the strings," said Captain Hurd.

While Matt stowed the traps and ate the last of the terrible brownies, they headed back to the Harpswell docks.

The sun was lower now, and the sky had begun to take on that yellow color that it takes in fall afternoons. Soon everything would be washed in gold—the rocks along the island shores, the high pines, the higher clouds, and even Mrs. MacKnockater's house, where she was standing on the porch, looking out through her binoculars as the trawler was chugging past. She waved.

Captain Hurd waved back.

Matt did not.

"Wave to Mrs. MacKnockater," said the Captain.

Matt looked at him.

"Wave to her."

It had been a long time since Matt Coffin had done something that someone told him to do—except maybe Mrs. MacKnockater. He looked up at her. She was still waving, still watching through her binoculars.

He guessed he might as well wave.

"And that house there. Green shutters. Down the ridge from Mrs. MacKnockater's? That's mine. Just so you know if you need something."

"Like what?"

"Just so you know."

At the docks, Matt and the Captain tied *Affliction* securely, bow to stern. They unloaded the live tank and flushed out the seawater. They secured all the traps, washed down the bait bucket, stowed the buoys, and flushed the engine. It was almost suppertime, and Matt was hungry. Terrible brownies and one tuna fish sandwich with too much mayonnaise weren't a whole lot.

"I'll get these weighed and sold," said the Captain. "Be here tomorrow morning and you'll get your fifteen percent. Meanwhile"—he reached into the swarm of banded lobsters—"take these two to Mrs. MacKnockater."

"Why?"

"To apologize for being a rude jerk. Someone waves, you wave back. Maybe she'll be in a forgiving mood and boil one up for you—but don't count on it. I wouldn't if I were her."

Matt took the two squirming lobsters, one in each hand.

Not much later, Mrs. MacKnockater heard someone kicking at her back door. It was more than a little annoying, the kicking. So when she pulled open the door, she was ready to point out that even someone with quite low intelligence should be able to manipulate a doorbell, and there was Matt, with his two squirming lobsters.

"From Captain Hurd," he said.

Mrs. MacKnockater nodded. "Come in," she said. "I'll put the water on to boil. They'll be done in no time."

Matt looked at her. "No time?"

"Poetic license," said Mrs. MacKnockater, and turned to find her lobster pot.

And it wasn't no time, but Matt thumbed through the illustrations in *Treasure Island,* and when Mrs. MacKnockater told him to, he went and washed up, and she didn't ask him anything about where he'd been—probably since she knew she shouldn't—and she handled the lobsters as well as Captain Hurd did, in and out of the boiling pot, and onto the plates, and onto the table, a small pot of melted butter next to each of them.

"It looks like you two must have had a good haul," she said.

Matt nodded.

"He usually does," she said.

Matt nodded again and opened up the first claw.

He ate quickly.

He paused at his second claw. "You know the Captain?"

Mrs. MacKnockater, halfway through her first claw, paused

too. "We've known each other for quite a long while," she said, and smiled when she turned back to her claw.

Matt watched her.

"I'll go get some more butter," said Mrs. MacKnockater, and she went into the kitchen.

He wondered about Captain Hurd and Mrs. MacKnockater as he headed down the steps of Mrs. MacKnockater's front porch that Friday night. He wondered as he walked the pathway down the ridge and into the dark pines. He wondered as he walked down toward the shore and Captain Cobb's old fishing shack.

He wondered as he got inside, and closed the door behind him, and lit the lantern, and lay down, so very alone.

SIX

WHEN MERYL LEE GOT BACK TO MARGARET B. Netley Dormitory after the opening ceremony, she found Jennifer combing Charlotte's hair in her room, and Ashley sitting on the floor, and all of them laughing, laughing, laughing.

Until she walked in.

Then, quick silence.

She looked at the suitcase she had left open on her mattress.

Not everything in it was folded as neatly as it had been.

"Is your name really Kowalski?" said Ashley.

"Yes," said Meryl Lee.

"Really? Because I'm not sure I've ever met someone from Eastern Europe."

"I'm from Long Island."

"Oh," said Ashley.

"Aren't you going to unpack?" said Jennifer.

Ashley stifling a laugh.

Meryl Lee looked at the closet, filled with Jennifer's blouses and dresses and regulation St. Elene's Academy white shirts and green and gold plaid skirts and green and gold sweaters and green blazers with the gold St. Elene's cross insignia—eight of each—all on their pink plush hangers, with lavender, pale yellow, and light blue sweaters on the shelf above.

"Not just now," Meryl Lee said.

She decided to make up her bed, even though she hadn't packed anything like a green satin duvet. She put her suitcase on the floor and took the bedclothes out of one of the shopping bags, and while she stretched the slightly damp sheets over the mattress, Jennifer and Ashley and Charlotte talked about Stephanie, about how wonderful Stephanie was, about how Stephanie knew everyone and had even once met Ringo like Jennifer had, about how Stephanie always knew exactly what to wear and how she had the nicest clothes and how she would never be caught dead in a public school sweatshirt like some girls wore, about how they wished Stephanie was back from Budapest.

Meryl Lee tried to come up with some smart and beautiful and wonderful thing to say. Something like how someday soon she was going to Budapest and she would do the same things in Budapest that Stephanie was doing, whatever they were. But she couldn't come up with anything smart and beautiful and wonderful to say, and she wasn't going to Budapest anytime soon, and she *did* have a public school sweatshirt in her suitcase, and it was her favorite thing to wear mostly because she'd worn it when she and Holling . . .

She took a long time making her bed while Jennifer and Ashley and Charlotte talked about Stephanie, who had been to Brussels with Jennifer twice, and how they had shopped all around La Grand-Place and how maybe next summer they would go to London together after Stephanie got home from Budapest because they loved going to Europe together.

Meryl Lee tucked in the corners. She thought about the lunch counter at Woolworth's. She pushed away the Blank.

When Meryl Lee finished, she said, "I'm going to go for a walk to explore."

"Don't you have a duvet for your bed?" said Jennifer.

Meryl Lee shook her head.

"So your bed is going to look like that all the time."

"I guess so," said Meryl Lee. She tried to say it with a little laugh.

None of the girls said anything.

"Anyone want to explore with me?" said Meryl Lee.

"I'd—" Charlotte began.

"I suppose not," said Jennifer.

"We've been at St. Elene's together forever," said Ashley. "Why would you think there's any place left for us to explore?"

"Maybe there's something you haven't seen before," said Meryl Lee.

"There isn't," said Ashley.

Meryl Lee knelt and tried to slide her suitcase under her bed. It didn't quite fit, and she felt their eyes upon her as she struggled, then forced it under.

"Unless you find St. Elene's Arm," said Jennifer. "No one's seen that before."

Meryl Lee looked up at her. "St. Elene's Arm?"

"It's hidden somewhere on campus. Her mummified arm. Only the Knock knows where it is."

"The Knock?"

"MacKnockater," said Ashley, as if Meryl Lee was such a dope.

"It's not just her arm," said Jennifer. "There's a ring on each of her fingers: a diamond ring, a ruby ring, a sapphire ring, and a pearl ring. And whoever finds the arm gets to keep one of the rings. That's the school tradition."

"So has anyone—"

"No. I told you: no one has ever seen it. But maybe you'll find it while you explore."

Ashley began to laugh.

Meryl Lee's face reddened.

"I'll keep my eyes open," she said.

"Do that," said Jennifer. "And if you find it, maybe we can each choose one of the rings."

Ashley and Charlotte were both laughing now.

Meryl Lee left. Laughter followed her under the dark beams and along the soap-smooth wood floor and down the white hall, where all the doors were open and all the rooms were filled with groups of girls on their beds and on their floors and on their window seats and on their toes, holding transistor radios and dancing.

She walked past Greater Hoxne and Lesser Hoxne and past Sherbourne House, sometimes jostled by groups of girls who straddled the sidewalks and did not even see her, it seemed. She walked past Putnam Library, and past smiling Julia Chall and Barbara Rockcastle and Elizabeth Koertge—who probably smiled because they had been going to St. Elene's together forever and who wouldn't smile about that?

Meryl Lee walked alone, without a whole lot of Resolution.

Except she had resolved not to cry.

She walked beyond Newell Chapel and past the commons behind Newell, and past three white barns and past a couple of sheds and through a line of shady maples, and suddenly St. Elene's was all behind her and she was out by an open field, woods beyond, and between them lots of long painted fences. Unseen, a crow was cawing, cawing, cawing, but other than that, it was quiet and still. She walked past the long fences, then steeply down a footpath that led straight toward a stand of birches, as white as the fences. She ran her hands along their papery bark until she came into a grove of firs where thin branches brushed against her on both sides.

And then, suddenly, the firs curtained open and revealed the blue waves and the green islands and the white gulls and that white and red sail scudding along and the gray rocks a-tumble down to the water and the bleached driftwood upon them.

She sat down, and even though she could feel the Blank lurking behind her, it was a little easier without Jennifer and Ashley and Charlotte from Charlotte lurking in front of her.

Meryl Lee got back to her room just before dinner at noon; Jennifer and Ashley and Charlotte from Charlotte were gone. Quickly she knelt and dragged her suitcase out from under the bed. She looked into the closet and decided she wouldn't hang up what was in her suitcase next to Jennifer's blouses and dresses on pink plush hangers—even if there had been room. So she stuffed everything into her dresser drawers—including her Camillo Junior High sweatshirt—and tried to fill herself with the Resolution she knew she would need to face the meal.

But when she walked into Greater Hoxne, she knew that she would need a whole lot more Resolution than she had imagined.

Orange and yellow floral arrangements. White linen tablecloths on round tables. White linen napkins. White china plates with a pale floral design. Heavy silverware. Heavier crystal. Bettye and Alethea lined the walls with other girls wearing bright white aprons over their black dresses—all of them looking down at the floor. The tinkling of glasses, the scraping of chairs. Warm Parker House rolls on the tables. Small square pads of white butter by each plate. Tiny bowls of salt with tiny silver spoons.

Upper school girls on the north side. Lower school girls on the south.

Meryl Lee sat beside Jennifer—because who else was she going to sit next to?—and Jennifer sighed and scooted her chair a little closer to Ashley and Charlotte. Jennifer wore a string of pearls. The kind of pearls that blond demigoddesses wear whenever they want. Their luster glowed like the luster of Jennifer's blond hair.

Meryl Lee looked around Greater Hoxne Dining Hall.

Probably all the smiling girls here had sat beside all the other smiling girls for forever.

Probably all their smiling mothers knew one another.

And their smiling grandmothers, too.

Then the double doors to the kitchen opened and Bettye and Alethea each pulled out a silver cart with chilled fruit cups on white linen cloths to serve the eighth-grade upper school girls of St. Elene's Preparatory Academy.

Ashley was the last one at their table to be served—by Bettye.

"Town girls are so slow sometimes," she said.

Bettye leaned down and placed a chilled fruit cup in front of Ashley.

"And they don't even know to serve from the right," said Ashley.

Meryl Lee felt Bettye stiffen.

"That's because they grew up on farms," said Charlotte.

"I went down to the shore this afternoon," said Meryl Lee.

Bettye stood and looked at Meryl Lee.

"You didn't find St. Elene's Arm?" said Ashley.

Jennifer fingered her pearls. "I'm missing the spoon for my fruit cup," she said.

Immediately Bettye turned and went to fetch the spoon. When she brought it back, she did not look at Meryl Lee again. She didn't look at anyone at the table again.

And for the rest of the meal, Jennifer and Ashley and Charlotte talked about Stephanie DeLacy and how they wished she wasn't in Budapest.

Which was probably why Meryl Lee did not want to go back to Netley right away after dinner was finished, and the white china dishes had been taken away, and Mrs. Hannah Adams Mott, Associate Headmistress of St. Elene's Preparatory Academy for Girls since Genesis, had given the announcements regarding the first day of classes on Monday. Arm in arm, the girls left Greater Hoxne Dining Hall in their smiling groups, but Meryl Lee wandered alone down to the main gate, walking on the loose gravel until she reached the gate and turned back toward the school; she was almost startled by how beautiful St. Elene's looked in the long September light. The buildings glowed softly, their windows reflecting the solid yellow. Sunlight ribboned around the steeple of Newell Chapel, then bore off into the trees, where an early afternoon breeze was taking a few leaves off their branches to twirl down to the perfect trim of the green lawn.

Meryl Lee wondered if there might come a time when she would feel a part of this school. Or if she even wanted to.

And then, unaccountably, she thought of Bettye.

SEVEN

THREE DAYS AFTER MATT'S LOBSTER DINNER WITH Mrs. MacKnockater, late at night, Matt found his way to Captain Cobb's shed, limping. His hand held his back, and his face was white enough to be seen even in the pale light of a quarter moon. He crawled inside. He pulled himself toward the water pump. Then he took two steps toward his bed. Then he fell to the floor, bleeding along the new slash that opened to his low ribs.

His left arm twisted strangely beneath him.

When Matt woke up, he was bouncing up and down in the darkness.

Bouncing up and down—and it hurt like hell.

He tried to yell, but his mouth wasn't working. His eyes either, or at least, his left eye. His right opened a little bit, and he could see he was moving past dark pines. He thought that it might be nighttime.

"Georgie?" he got out.

Wheezing came back at him. Someone really old, wheezing.

Not Georgie, then.

He was being carried.

His left arm lay across his stomach, sort of held against his body. His right arm hung down, and he raised it up to push against whoever was carrying him.

"Lie still."

"Get . . ."

"I said, lie"—there was a long pause, and more bouncing up and down, with lots of wheezing—"still."

Matt tried to open his right eye wider, but it hurt like hell too.

"Where's Georgie?"

They were going slower. Uphill. More wheezing. Matt closed his eye. Uphill very slowly. They stopped, and Matt felt whoever was carrying him sink down. Kneeling, maybe.

The breathing was so heavy.

"For such a scrawny kid . . ." whoever was carrying him said.

When he heard a car coming, Matt opened his eye and saw the headlights. And he saw who was holding him in his arms.

"I can tie a buoy hitch," he said.

"Shut up," Captain Hurd said. Matt heard the car stop. A door opened. He heard someone call, "Captain." And he heard, "Help me. For God's sake."

Then everything was dark again, and Matt felt himself falling into deep water, deep water, deep water, where only God could see him.

He woke up. He hurt. A lot. He decided that the deep water was better, so he let himself sink down. He looked around for whales and thought he saw one swimming toward him.

Then it was dark.

He woke up again. He still hurt, but maybe not as much. Well, maybe as much. He could open his right eye most of the way, and without turning his head, he looked around the room, which was humming. Or something in the room was humming. Or maybe it was snoring—or both, since there was Mrs. MacKnockater, sitting perfectly straight in a chair—as she did—wearing her hair in a bun—as she did—except that the bun was mostly coming apart, which hers would never do. At least, it never did when Matt was around. She was sleeping. And snoring.

The hum grew louder, sort of like the ocean when it was calmest and just swelling a little bit.

He closed his eye.

And it was dark.

He woke up again. He opened his right eye and let his head turn a little. A window, and the night sky. He let his head turn the other way. A lit hallway. He looked above him. A soft light—the humming he'd heard before, and now.

He thought he should get up and pee. He wondered what he was wearing. He looked down.

Oh, man.

Then he wondered why he didn't have to pee too bad, and he explored.

Oh, God.

He closed his eye.

Dark.

The next time, his right eye opened, and some of his left. It took him a little while to figure out how to make the two of them work together, partly because someone was standing right over him and it was hard to focus.

"Matthew," the someone said, "wake up now."

He looked at Mrs. MacKnockater.

"Wake up," she said.

He closed his eyes. "Why?"

"Matthew, it's time to open your eyes and wake up."

Eyes closed.

"Listen, you scrawny deckhand. Open your damn eyes."

Matt opened his eyes.

Captain Hurd stood next to Mrs. MacKnockater.

"You . . . dotard. That language!"

"It worked, didn't it? He opened his eyes."

"This is a hospital. And he's a boy."

"You think he's never heard anyone say 'damn' before?"

"Hurd!"

"Damn. Damn. Damn. Damn."

Matt started to laugh. He was amazed at how much it hurt to laugh. He was amazed at how many places it could hurt when he laughed.

"Matthew, are you awake?"

"He's awake. He's laughing. You don't laugh when you're not awake."

"Matthew," said Mrs. MacKnockater, "are you hungry?"

"He hasn't eaten in three days. Of course he's hungry," said Captain Hurd.

"Will you shut up?" said Mrs. MacKnockater.

Matt looked at them. He tried to keep his left eye open, but it was starting to close down again.

"Three days?" he said.

He felt Mrs. MacKnockater's hand touch the side of his face. That hurt too, but it had been so long since someone had touched the side of his face *like that,* he didn't say anything.

"He probably has to pee, too."

"Hurd, if you won't stop . . ."

"Don't you?" said Captain Hurd.

Matt shrugged. That hurt too.

"We'll go get the nurse," said Mrs. MacKnockater. And with his right eye, Matt watched them go off together, and he wasn't at all sure what it was he felt then. Whatever it was, it didn't hurt.

But he fell asleep before the nurse came back.

Over the next two days, Matt's hospital room was filled with Captain Hurd and Mrs. MacKnockater—mostly Mrs. MacKnockater. Matt figured the Captain had to be out in *Affliction* during the day, probably needing him. But, as the Captain pointed out, what with Matt's left arm being in a sling, he wasn't going to be tying buoy hitches and laying traps anytime soon. Mrs. MacKnockater, meanwhile, was reading him *The Jungle Book,* which, she said, was a whole lot better than Mr. Disney's cartoon—which Matt hadn't seen anyway, so it didn't matter.

The Jungle Book was okay.

But there were a lot of other people in the room too.

The nurse who kept waking him up to change the dressings on his face, his chest, his back, and who kept reminding him that he really needed to be resting on his side—which, if you do that for a couple of hours, is really hard to do.

The cop who had lots of questions, like "Who did this to you, kid?"

Matt didn't say.

"You trying to protect someone? Who are you trying to protect?"

Matt didn't say.

"He could have killed you, you know."

Matt let his left eye close.

"Did you get a shot at him?"

"I broke half his ribs," said Matt.

The cop looked at Matt's left hand. At the split knuckle there. "That why he broke your arm?"

Matt let his right eye close.

"I'm just trying to help you, kid. All I got to go on right now is a guy with some broken ribs."

Matt snored.

The cop wasn't the only one who wanted to help. Miss Phyllis, a social worker, wanted to help too.

"Matthew, we need to contact your family. Can you tell us where they are?"

Nothing from Matt.

"Can you tell us their names? Do they live in Maine? In New England?"

He had no idea.

Matt didn't even try to keep his eyes open for those questions.

Two days of all that, until his doctor—who was a good guy and only asked where it ached and who always told him when he was about to do something that he knew would hurt—told him he could go home on Sunday.

Miss Phyllis was in the room when the doctor told him that. "We still haven't found a placement for him," she said.

Mrs. MacKnockater was in the room too.

"He'll come to live with me," she said.

"We are legally required to send him to an approved place- ment," Miss Phyllis said.

Mrs. MacKnockater allowed her considerable bulk to arise.

Miss Phyllis said that exceptions could be made on the occa- sion of an emergency.

When the doctor and Miss Phyllis left, Mrs. MacKnockater sat down to read. "We'll finish these last few pages, then pack everything up so you can come home in the morning," she said.

Matt looked at her a long time.

"Okay, Long John," he said.

Mrs. MacKnockater looked at Matt a long time.

"That reference," she said, "is both to the wrong novel and of the wrong gender."

Matt looked at her again, his left eye only a little closed. "So maybe something from *The Jungle Book,* then. Like Bagheera."

"That would be unnecessary," said Mrs. MacKnockater.

"Bagheera. Bagheera works."

"Bagheera is a black panther, which I am not. And the gender referent is still incorrect," Mrs. MacKnockater said.

But she smiled and began to read.

EIGHT

THE NEXT MONDAY, AFTER A WEEKEND OF ENFORCED
bonding activities that would have left Holling rolling in laughter
on the ground and that exhausted Meryl Lee in her fight against
the Blank—really, a fashion show by the senior students? really?—
classes at St. Elene's Preparatory Academy for Girls began.

Meryl Lee—who had lived eight minutes from Camillo Junior
High if she walked and four and a half minutes if she ran and so
had been used to getting up eleven minutes before she had to be at
school—found out that a lot happened at St. Elene's between waking up and sitting in a classroom.

None of it made her happy.

First, breakfast at Greater Hoxne Dining Hall. Meryl Lee had
skipped breakfast every school day since fourth grade. Now, an
assigned table and an assigned seat with assigned Jennifer and four
other assigned girls and one assigned teacher. A huge glass of fresh
grapefruit juice beside her plate—also assigned, she guessed. A
platter of scrambled eggs with cheese and bacon—Meryl Lee hated
cheese in her eggs—and her table served by Bettye in her assigned
black dress and starched white apron. Toasted English muffins.
Small dishes of marmalade to be scooped with a pewter spoon that
was way too small.

And all this was for Meryl Lee to eat before eight o'clock—except for the marmalade, which she was supposed to share with her assigned teacher: Mrs. Saunders.

Mrs. Saunders. Whom Meryl Lee feared.

When Mrs. Saunders's head moved, it pivoted slowly above her shoulders, like an owl's. And her eyes, dark and darting, saw everything. Mrs. Saunders saw Meryl Lee sit down and she said, "The rules of polite society dictate that the spine of a young lady should not touch the back of her chair." Mrs. Saunders saw Barbara Rockcastle reach for her fork and she said, "A young lady starts with the fork farthest to her left." Mrs. Saunders saw Marian Elders—the girl who got evacuated upon and didn't look as if she had quite recovered—Mrs. Saunders saw Marian Elders about to eat and she said, "The neck of a young lady is not to bend when she takes up her scrambled eggs with cheese."

It made breakfast sort of nerve-racking. *Suppose I burp?* thought Meryl Lee. What would the rules of polite society say about that?

If Holling were there, she thought, he would say, "Suppose you fart?"

At that, she almost snorted fresh grapefruit juice out her nose—which she was sure the rules of polite society would have something to say about.

Mrs. Saunders also believed breakfast was the perfect place to teach the intricacies of the English language. So she kept a dictionary beside her on the table. A dictionary that weighed about what she weighed—which is saying something. If one of the girls used a word incorrectly, Mrs. Saunders would say, "Please rise and consult *Funk and Wagnalls.*"

By the end of their first breakfast together, Meryl Lee had risen and consulted *Funk and Wagnalls* for *neither,* which was no longer acceptable as an intensive terminal (who knew?), and for *dollop,* which was colloquial and so, Mrs. Saunders said, vulgar.

Meryl Lee decided not to say very much at breakfast.

Meryl Lee was pretty sure Marian Elders would decide on the same strategy. When Mrs. Saunders told her that a young lady should abstain from a too-great indulgence in bacon and she should rise and consult *Funk and Wagnalls* about the meaning of *abstain,* Meryl Lee thought Marian was going to faint face first into her scrambled eggs with cheese.

But slowly, properly, the girls finished their breakfast, and slowly, properly, Bettye came to carry their crystal glasses and heavy silverware and china plates away, even Meryl Lee's plate—which was still filled with a dollop of scrambled eggs with cheese.

"I hate scrambled eggs with cheese," said Meryl Lee.

"Me too," whispered Bettye.

Meryl Lee nodded. "Do you live near St. Elene's?"

"Down by the shore," said Bettye. "I think I saw you there."

"I went a few days ago."

"I go almost every day," said Bettye.

"Finish clearing, please," called Mrs. Saunders, and Bettye wheeled the plates away.

After breakfast, the girls of St. Elene's went to Morning Chapel, where Dr. MacKnockater was waiting to read an Uplifting Passage from the classics to both the lower and upper schools. In Latin.

Or maybe it was Greek.

Meryl Lee couldn't be sure, but it didn't matter because she did not understand a single word of Latin—or Greek. Looking around, she wondered if she was the only one in Newell Chapel who didn't understand a single word of Latin—or Greek.

Then Mrs. Hannah Adams Mott glided to the podium and told the girls to rise for the singing of the school song. They did, to the booms of the organ. And after all the *hails* were done, Mrs. Hannah Adams Mott told the girls to sally forth and enter the world of the Liberal Arts. "Grow in wisdom and knowledge. Resolve and Accomplish. Find your Best Selves so you may take your proper place in the world!" she proclaimed.

Meryl Lee wished she felt the same Resolution she had felt at the opening ceremony. But she did not. She had been rooming with Jennifer and her green satin duvet for four days now. It was hard to sally forth after rooming with Jennifer and her green satin duvet for four days.

And all that fresh grapefruit juice made her want to go to the bathroom.

Classes started right after Chapel, beginning in Lesser Hoxne Hall, which, though Meryl Lee looked very carefully, appeared to have no bathrooms on the first two floors. Which was annoying.

In fact, she thought the decision to place the only bathroom in Lesser Hoxne on the third floor—which she discovered after her first class—and at the extreme southern end of the hall, with a lock to which the key was kept in the administrative office on the first floor—to which Meryl Lee had to descend before she could rapidly reascend with the key hot in her hand—was inscrutable.

Talk about sallying forth!

Tomorrow, she would plan better.

In each of her classes, Meryl Lee knew at least one girl enough to say hello to—but this made her about as happy as not having a bathroom on the first two floors of Lesser Hoxne.

Meryl Lee sat next to Charlotte from Charlotte in American

Literary Masterpieces for first hour, and in Life Sciences for second hour—right across from Marian Elders. Mrs. Connolly taught American Literary Masterpieces, and during that first class she asked them each to write a brief paragraph identifying the author whose work they would like to study on an independent basis during the coming school year in order to develop taste and discernment. Life Sciences was taught by Mrs. Bellamy, who smelled of formaldehyde, and who promised that before September was out, they would all smell of formaldehyde too. Charlotte from Charlotte raised her hand and said that she would not, could not, get formaldehyde on her pale skin—it was a medical condition—and Mrs. Bellamy said that perhaps her lab partner would take on most of the formaldehyde duties. When Charlotte from Charlotte asked who her lab partner would be, Mrs. Bellamy consulted her roster and announced that it would be Meryl Lee Kowalski.

Of course, thought Meryl Lee.

Rolling eyes from Charlotte from Charlotte.

In third hour, Meryl Lee sat in front of Ashley in Famous Women of History with Mrs. Saunders, who on the first day assigned ten-minute oral reports on famous women to be performed in pairs, and who chose Meryl Lee and Ashley to deliver the report on the Empress Joséphine, born Marie Josèphe Rose Tascher de La Pagerie. "Just saying her name will take up half the time we have for our presentation," Meryl Lee whispered to Ashley.

Ashley lowered her face so that her chocolate-colored hair covered it.

Fine.

Dinner was precisely at noon, and while the girls ate in Greater Hoxne Dining Hall, mail was sorted into little mailboxes off

Greater Hoxne Hall lobby. All the girls—except Meryl Lee—knew this was happening. So after dinner was done and Mrs. Hannah Adams Mott had delivered the St. Elene's midday announcements, the girls processed out of Greater Hoxne Dining Hall in the calm and dignified manner that befitted their station in life—then took off at a sprint for the lobby. They mobbed the little mailboxes.

Blood could be spilled, thought Meryl Lee, who stood back for a bit, then made her way around the fringes and dove in behind Barbara Rockcastle, who was taller than most of the girls so able to navigate through the masses. Meryl Lee twirled the little knob on the little door into her mailbox and reached in sort of hopelessly. And she was right. Nothing.

But when Jennifer reached into her little box, she pulled out a letter. And Jennifer squealed a high squeal because she was holding another letter—she sniffed it—another scented-with-his-after-shave letter from Alden, dear Alden, and she wished she could read it out loud for everyone, she really did, but Alden, sweet Alden, would never want her to share their secrets.

All the girls who wanted to be Jennifer Hartley Truro more than they wanted their next breath began to squeal too, and wasn't Jennifer lucky to have a boyfriend like scented Alden, and was it really true that his family owned estates and manors all over Scotland? And that they even had their own tartan?

But Jennifer only held her letter to her heart. She smiled and did not tell. Alden would never want her to share their secrets, she said. He's *that* kind of a boy.

"Has he ever sent you flowers?" Ashley asked.

Jennifer looked at her with the disdain of a demigoddess. "Of course," she said. "Roses. Dozens of roses."

The Blank, immediately in front of Meryl Lee.

She tried to shake it away. She looked into her mailbox again. Perhaps she had missed something.

She hadn't.

And as the girls gathered around Jennifer—wouldn't she tell them just the eensiest, teensiest bit?—Meryl Lee went to her fourth-hour class.

By herself.

Meryl Lee sat behind Heidi Kidder and ahead of Jennifer in Algebra with Mr. Wheelock for fourth hour, and behind Jennifer and ahead of Heidi Kidder in Domestic Economy with Mrs. Wyss for fifth hour. Meryl Lee was not sure what Domestic Economy was supposed to be about, but Jennifer, who was still vibrating over Alden's letter, seemed to know. She whispered to Barbara Rockcastle next to her that she did not need a class with Mrs. Wyss because someday she'd have a staff of Scottish maids and cooks and they could worry about stupid domestic economy for her.

Jennifer would not even look at her, so Meryl Lee did not ask why all the maids and cooks would be Scottish. She was afraid Jennifer would think she was such a dope.

And she still had no idea what Domestic Economy was about. Cooking? Then why didn't they call the class Cooking?

She'd had a lot to figure out, and the day wasn't even over.

After fifth hour, the girls of St. Elene's were free to "engage in meaningful activity," as Mrs. Mott put it. So Meryl Lee headed over to Putnam Library to find something about Empress Joséphine, born Marie Josèphe Rose Tascher de La Pagerie. The wind on the commons was swirling, stirred up, perhaps, by Mrs. Connolly, who was carrying a briefcase and strutting quickly along the sidewalk, parting girls from the lower school like Moses at the Red Sea. But when she saw Meryl Lee, she billowed sharply right to intercept her.

"Miss Kowalski," said Mrs. Connolly.

Meryl Lee had already lived long enough at St. Elene's to know how to reply.

She forced the Blank away from her—but it hovered nearby.

"Good afternoon, Mrs. Connolly."

"Good afternoon. I had hoped to see you after dinner."

"To see me?"

Mrs. Connolly zipped open her briefcase and rummaged inside for a moment. She drew out Meryl Lee's paragraph identifying her chosen author for American Literary Masterpieces. "You write here that you would like to study John Steinbeck to develop taste and discernment," she said. "That is impossible."

"Impossible?"

"Impossible. He has none."

"I'm so sorry, Mrs. Connolly. He has no what?"

"Taste and discernment."

Meryl Lee's eyebrows moved sharply upward and held steady—which is what they always did when she was surprised. Holling said it made her look like a startled chipmunk. Holling *used* to say it made her look like a startled chipmunk.

The Blank so close.

"I thought I would read *The Grapes of Wrath*," she said.

Mrs. Connolly did this thing with her nose, breathing in quickly as if in great suffering. "John Steinbeck," she said, "is a lewd writer. No student of mine who hopes to develop taste and discernment would ever read anything written by that Communist. Find someone else, please."

Meryl Lee's eyebrows were still pretty chipmunk-y.

Mrs. Connolly did the thing with her nose again.

"Charlotte Dobrée will be reading the poetry of Henry Wadsworth Longfellow, a wise and sensitive choice. I'm sure she would be delighted to help you to find another author." Mrs. Connolly smiled sweetly, as if the name Charlotte had brought her a deep happiness. Then it passed, and Mrs. Connolly looked hard at Meryl Lee. "Failing that, I will assign you a suitable author."

"I'll talk to Charlotte," Meryl Lee said.

"Very well," said Mrs. Connolly. She handed the paper back to Meryl Lee. "I'll be waiting for the rewritten paragraph."

She zipped her briefcase.

Meryl Lee's eyebrows came back down.

"And one more thing, Miss Kowalski. A word of caution, actually, from an observation this morning at breakfast."

Meryl Lee's eyebrows went back up.

"It is never wise to speak overmuch with the staff. You have come to St. Elene's to study and to learn. The girls on staff have been hired to serve the students and faculty of St. Elene's. They are not here to be associated with. You attend to your studies. Let them attend to their work. Is something wrong with your eyes?"

"No, Mrs. Connolly."

"Have I made myself understood?"

"Yes, Mrs. Connolly."

"Then I'll see you in class tomorrow. I look forward to the semester with you, Miss Kowalski. I can see from even that short paragraph that your writing style has potential—yet another reason to avoid the infection of a lesser writer such as John Steinbeck."

"Thank you," said Meryl Lee. "I am looking forward to a semester with you as well, Mrs. Connolly."

And as Mrs. Connolly left, the wind brisking and swirling around her, Meryl Lee thought, *I've just flat-out lied to a teacher.*

She had.

Because she *was not* looking forward to a semester with Mrs. Connolly.

She decided that she'd go to Putnam Library later, and instead Meryl Lee walked out past the open field and the woods beyond and down through the birches and the firs to the open blue shore, and she went out on the warm rocks and closed her eyes and listened to the waves—that sound that never stopped—and she listened a long time.

And when at last she walked back to St. Elene's, she found that the birches had startled into a bright yellow—or perhaps it was the slant of light that shone on them. Now they looked like torches lighting the way.

They did all that this afternoon, she thought. *Just like that, everything can change.*

NINE

Back at Netley, after evening meal, Meryl Lee put on her Camillo Junior High sweatshirt to do homework. She still had to figure out how to shorten the sleeves on her regulation St. Elene's uniform, but right now, somehow, she could still hear the lovely sounds of the waves, and she did not much care what she wore.

Then Jennifer put on her lavender silk robe. "From Brussels," she said.

The sounds of the waves vanished and Meryl Lee thought, *It's Monday night and it's time to do homework and she's wearing a lavender silk robe from Brussels.*

She took off her sweatshirt and put on her new best blouse. The pale yellow one. And Jennifer said, "Your Woolworth's tag is showing."

"I'm just trying it on for size," said Meryl Lee. "I'll probably return it."

"Then probably you don't want to try it on inside out," said Jennifer.

Meryl Lee put her Camillo Junior High sweatshirt back on. She went to Putnam Library to find an author for Mrs. Connolly's class—which was not something you would do if you were wearing a lavender silk robe from Brussels.

But at Putnam Library, she got distracted.

First, because Mrs. Hibbard sat by the reference desk, knitting what seemed a very complicated pattern, and clicking her needles like an industrial machine.

Second, because the reading room of Putnam Library glowed with sunset light coming through stained glass windows taken from a manor house in East Anglia—windows that were ancient when Henry VIII looked at them; at least, that's what the plaque beneath them said. The room was dark wood and huge beams and thick rugs and marble floors and a curling wrought iron staircase and long tables with green glass lamps across from each chair. On the walls, thick paneling behind the portraits of the eighteenth-century sea captains who founded St. Elene's. Gold frames around them all. Eighteenth-century tapestries hanging above the card catalogue.

And third, she got distracted because the first book she saw in the fiction section was *The Grapes of Wrath*. Really. It was.

And even though she knew she should be looking for an appropriate and not lewd author for Mrs. Connolly, she did want to read *The Grapes of Wrath*—and so she pulled it off the shelf. She sat at one of the long tables and put her Domestic Economy book within reach to cover *The Grapes of Wrath* in case Mrs. Connolly was on patrol. Then she quickly thumbed through to see if she could find the lewd parts. She couldn't, so she turned to the first page and fell into the red and gray country of Oklahoma.

Everything else vanished.

The reading room.

St. Elene's Preparatory Academy for Girls.

Time.

The Blank.

So when Mrs. Hibbard came to tell her that Putnam Library was closing soon and she might begin to gather her books, Meryl Lee looked up, startled. The truck was just about to hit the turtle. Would Mrs. Hibbard mind if she—

"Of course not," said Mrs. Hibbard. "Finish the chapter. Wait until you see what happens."

That night, Meryl Lee lay in bed, thinking about what happened at the end of the turtle chapter. And she thought about Holling, and what Holling would have said about the turtle. About the stupid second driver. About what happened to the turtle.

Then the Blank came.

The stupid driver.

The stupid stupid stupid stupid driver.

She tried not to let Jennifer hear her crying.

At St. Elene's midday announcements on Tuesday, Mrs. Mott said that each of the new girls—which, in the eighth grade, was only Meryl Lee, since the girl with the regulation St. Elene's uniform skirt that was too long had not been seen since the evacuation—was required to participate in one of St. Elene's team sports, teamwork being a means by which individual girls might elevate themselves into something larger and more Accomplished.

The fall semester team sport for all eighth-grade students of St. Elene's Preparatory Academy for Girls was field hockey, commanded by Coach Rowlandson, who was a dragon.

Or could have been if she tried.

Coach Rowlandson was interested in Accomplishment too. She held her field hockey practice every Tuesday and every Thursday afternoon. Rain or sun, snow or light breezes, gray sleet or blue skies, monsoon or blizzard or tidal wave or tornado or thunder and lightning or general apocalypse consuming the planet, field hockey practice was still on, every Tuesday and every Thursday afternoon.

The upper school field hockey team for St. Elene's Preparatory Academy for Girls was called the Lasses. So was the upper school soccer team.

What Holling would say about that!

At practice, the girls wore regulation physical education uniforms—bright white tops and short green and gold striped skirts. And they carried lethal-looking sticks as they sprinted back and forth between the chalk lines of the circles, and the whole time they quaked for fear of Heidi Kidder, who was the goaltender for the Lasses.

Wearing her pads and holding her own much larger stick, Heidi did not smile. She did not joke. She looked as grim as the guy who hauls the axe at a beheading. During the first practice, she hollered the whole time. She hollered in high decibels while waving her field hockey stick too close to people's faces and while girls with smaller but still very hard sticks were thwacking at Meryl Lee's legs while she was trying to dig out a ball buried in the grass and they were all yelling but not as loudly as Heidi Kidder, who said things like this:

"Clear to the side! Kowalski, clear to the side!"

"Out of the circle! Out of the circle, Kowalski!"

"Sweeper! Sweeper! Where's my sweeper! Kowalski!"

"Kowalski! Only people with hemorrhoids run like that!"

Everything she said on the field hockey field had an exclamation point. It did not even matter if you knew what she meant or not. You just knew you'd better Do Something Right Away.

Meryl Lee was terrified of Heidi Kidder.

During the second practice, Coach Rowlandson decided to try Meryl Lee as a midfielder. "Do you know what a midfielder does?" she asked Meryl Lee.

"Is a midfielder closer or farther away from the goalie?" said Meryl Lee.

"Farther away."

Good. This sounded promising.

"What does she do?" said Meryl Lee.

"A midfielder runs back and forth across the field hockey field until she dies," said Coach Rowlandson.

"Until she dies?"

"Go on out and give it your best," said Coach Rowlandson.

Meryl Lee did.

Here is Meryl Lee's conversation with Coach Rowlandson after her second practice. She was a little bit out of breath.

Coach Rowlandson: Kowalski, are you putting all you've got into this?

Meryl Lee: (Nods. She cannot speak just yet.)

Coach Rowlandson: Can you keep your stick on the ground?

Meryl Lee: (Nods. She still cannot speak. She is not sure she will ever speak again.)

Coach Rowlandson: Show me how you do that.

Meryl Lee: (Shows her.)

Coach Rowlandson: Kowalski, you think that's going to stop a shot?

Meryl Lee: (What was she supposed to say? She thought it would.)

Coach Rowlandson: Sticks down! Try again. No, sticks down! Sticks down!

Meryl Lee: (Thuds her stick into the ground.)

Coach Rowlandson: Maybe we need to toughen you up with some wind sprints.

During the third practice, Coach Rowlandson had the whole field hockey team run up and down and up and down and up and down the field as fast as they could.

Heidi Kidder lapped Meryl Lee twice.

Most of the other girls lapped her once.

Here is Meryl Lee's conversation with Coach Rowlandson after her third practice.

Coach Rowlandson: Kidder is right. You run like you have hemorrhoids.

Meryl Lee: Maybe . . . I need . . .

Coach Rowlandson: I'll tell you what *I* need, Kowalski: a midfielder who can stay in the game. And right now, that means you. So how about you start to show some Effort?

Meryl Lee: Effort?

Coach Rowlandson: (A stony stare at Meryl Lee.)

Meryl Lee: Okay . . . Effort . . . But . . . I think . . . I'm . . . done for the . . . day.

Coach Rowlandson: You haven't worked with a coach before, have you, Kowalski?

Meryl Lee: (Shakes her head.)

Coach Rowlandson: The coach decides when you're done for the day.

Meryl Lee: Then . . . can . . . I have a . . . sip . . . of water . . . first?

Coach Rowlandson: And throw up all over my grass? Get on over to the goal and we'll do some more wind sprints. Effort, Kowalski. Effort.

Coach Rowlandson was not a comforting presence.

During the fourth practice, Meryl Lee decided she would show Effort. She stayed up with Heidi Kidder for the first two wind sprints, and even though Heidi later lapped her, no one else did. Meryl Lee tried to run like she didn't have hemorrhoids.

She wielded her field hockey stick so widely that most of the girls cleared away from her.

And she blocked most of the long passes that came within reach.

Except the six that went through her legs.

Here is Meryl Lee's conversation with Coach Rowlandson after her fourth practice.

Coach Rowlandson: You weren't as terrible as usual, Kowalski.
Meryl Lee: (Nods her head.)
Coach Rowlandson: I saw a whole lot more Effort out there.
Meryl Lee: (Nods her head.)
Coach Rowlandson: Maybe if you keep your eyes on the ball, you'll make a half-decent midfielder.
Meryl Lee: I . . . hope so.
Coach Rowlandson: Who knows? Miracles can happen.

Meryl Lee scored a goal during the first field hockey team scrimmage—but not for her side. She was defending, which is not easy because so much happens so fast, and because whenever the ball was anywhere near the circle, Heidi Kidder was screaming her head off. So when Heidi told Meryl Lee to block block block block, Meryl Lee stuck her field hockey stick down and Julia Chall's clearing shot ricocheted off it and up into the goal. The way Heidi Kidder went on, you would have thought this was Meryl Lee's fault and they'd just been eliminated from the Olympic trials, and even though Meryl Lee still wanted to be Accomplished, she didn't really want to be Accomplished in field hockey.

But everyone on her side was mad at Meryl Lee because they lost and had to run laps and Coach Rowlandson said she hoped Meryl Lee had gotten *that* out of her system because we wouldn't want something like *that* to happen during a real game, and so Meryl Lee went back to her room because there wasn't anything else to do and when she got there Jennifer was holding out Charlotte from Charlotte's scarf and saying, "Oh, Charlotte, nobody wears an orange scarf with a peach blouse."

And Charlotte—who was indeed wearing an orange scarf with a peach blouse—was looking pretty pouty until Jennifer opened a drawer and pulled out a light green scarf. "This will be perfect with your eye coloring," she said. Then Charlotte smiled and Ashley said Jennifer ought to know since she's traveled so much in Europe and Jennifer smiled—"Don't make me blush," she said—and she wrapped the scarf around Charlotte and they all giggled and hugged. And then Jennifer said she was dying, just dying, just absolutely dying, to tell Ashley and Charlotte about Alden and maybe, since she couldn't reveal their secrets, she could tell them instead about what they were all going to do at Christmas. Would they like to know?

The three of them held hands and giggled.

Meryl Lee thought she might throw up.

"Why don't *you* have to go to field hockey practice?" she said.

They looked at her as though she was such a dope.

"Because we have been excused," said Ashley.

"Why?"

"Because," Jennifer said, "girls should never have to sweat. Didn't you know that?" Then she turned to Charlotte from Charlotte and said, "My sister called and she's going to Vienna with her fiancé for Christmas and they want me to come along!"

And Charlotte from Charlotte said, "Vienna! I've always wanted to go to Vienna!"

And Ashley said, "Can you imagine? Floating in a gondola. With someone who adores you. With a gondolier singing about love in Italian from some opera." She held her hands together over her heart.

And Jennifer said, as if engineering a conspiracy, "Do you think I should ask Alden to come with us?"

And Charlotte from Charlotte said, after a lot of giggles, "Do you think he would?"

And Ashley said, "Maybe he would ride in the gondola with you!"

More giggling and holding of hands over hearts, and then Meryl Lee, who had been looking for a clean towel all this time, decided to offer a point of cultural observation: "Gondolas are in Venice, not Vienna."

Silence in the room.

Charlotte from Charlotte adjusting her light green scarf quietly on the green satin duvet.

"I think I'll ask Alden," Jennifer said.

And Ashley said, "Maybe the gondolier will take a picture!"

Then Jennifer took out the two photographs of handsome, sweet-smelling Alden in his kilt, and Ashley and Charlotte both began to sigh. Jennifer let them each hold a photograph tenderly, and Ashley asked if it was true that underneath their kilts boys don't wear . . . and Jennifer put her finger up to her lips and smiled.

Talk about secrets, thought Meryl Lee.

She found a towel and went into the bathroom and turned the hot water on and she remembered last summer's walks with Holling, and how they talked, and how she could say anything, and how sometimes they didn't need to say anything, and the yellow light yawning and going to sleep and the night air up in the maples cooling and the sounds of the peepers, the smell of the petunias, the quiet of their steps.

She turned the water on harder. Hotter.

When she came out, Jennifer was putting away her laundry. "Yours is outside," she said.

Meryl Lee opened the door and picked up the basket. Everything folded, cleaned, pressed. And a note from Bettye on top of her regulation uniform shirts: "I've shortened the sleeves a little bit," the note said. "I hope you don't mind. I thought you might be more comfortable."

By the last week in September, Meryl Lee had decided that field hockey was really really really not what she was going to become Accomplished in.

This was mostly because during Tuesday's practice that week, she broke Marian Elders's pinky.

Marian considered herself more than a little put upon.

Meryl Lee had not intended to break Marian's pinky, but Heidi Kidder was hollering, "Clear! Clear! Clear!" and "Swing at it! Swing at it! Swing at it!" and when Meryl Lee swung at it! swung at it! swung at it! she did not know Marian was right behind her. When she hauled back, her stick snapped the little bone above Marian's pinky's knuckle and Marian screeched out a note two octaves higher than any note she had ever rendered before.

So it wasn't going to be field hockey.

That evening, Meryl Lee went back to Putnam Library, waved to Mrs. Hibbard at the reference desk—Mrs. Hibbard's needles were still clicking like an industrial machine—and sat down. She still hadn't handed in her author paragraph to Mrs. Connolly, and Mrs. Connolly was not being patient about this. Meryl Lee really did mean to write it. She really did. But she was on her second reading of *The Grapes of Wrath*—she hadn't found the lewd parts on the first—and now Tom Joad was about to be in a whole lot of trouble, and Meryl Lee felt it coming closer, and then the trouble was right on him, when suddenly there was a sort of looming presence right across the table and Meryl Lee jumped and she didn't have time to grab her domestic economy book to cover *The Grapes of Wrath*.

She looked up.

It was Heidi Kidder.

Heidi took the book from Meryl Lee's hands and looked at the title page. "Have you gotten to the lewd parts yet?"

And Meryl Lee said, "I couldn't find any."

Heidi said, "I couldn't either. Let me know if you find them."

Meryl Lee said, "I'll do that."

Then Heidi nodded the kind of nod you would give if you'd been lifting weights with your neck all your life, and she went over to another table, took out a book, and began to read.

Meryl Lee had to know. She had to know. She waited a little bit, then went over.

"What are you reading?" she said.

Heidi Kidder showed her.

"*The Wonderful Wizard of Oz?*" said Meryl Lee.

"I've always wanted to be Dorothy," said Heidi.

Meryl Lee sat down next to her.

That night, under her duvet-less covers, Meryl Lee lay in the bed and looked out at a half moon stroking its silvery light onto St. Elene's. *It's hard to figure out how a friendship begins,* she thought. *Maybe sometimes it's because someone you thought you knew—and that you didn't really—turns out to be a whole lot more like a friend than you ever guessed.*

I guess it can happen just like that, she thought.

Meryl Lee drew her blanket up to her chin and lay back, covered in white moonlight.

TEN

THIS IS WHAT MATT'S ROOM ON THE SECOND FLOOR
of Mrs. MacKnockater's house—which Captain Hurd helped him
up to that first day out of the hospital—looked like:

A bed, with a pretty hard mattress and a pretty hard pillow, and
a beige wool blanket that said U.S. NAVY on it tucked in with severe
hospital corners, and a blue and white quilt folded at the foot.

A round rag rug, mostly browns, ovalled beside the bed. Wide
pine planks for the floor.

White walls. Two framed pictures by a guy named Claude
something. Matt couldn't make out the last name, but since the
pictures were dumb—and the guy obviously not any good because,
I mean, just look at them—it didn't matter.

A smooth pine ladder nailed to the wall underneath a chute.
Matt stood and, holding on to a rung, looked up. The ladder led
past a cabinet door and all the way up to a skylight. From there,
he guessed, it would lead out onto the roof. He'd explore that later.

A short pine dresser with three drawers.

A pine wardrobe with a mirror on the front. Inside were white
and blue shirts and dark ties and two tweed jackets. And a navy
pea jacket. It was a little big, but it would do. And he didn't have
anything else to wear in the cold.

A pine chair pulled up to a pine desk. *Treasure Island* leaning against the lamp on the desk.

He put his stuff away in the pine dresser. It took one drawer.

He picked up *Treasure Island* and made his way through the first couple of pages. He stopped after about ten minutes when his left eye started to close a little bit.

Then he looked out the window—at the September light slanting beyond the wooded ridge and stroking its soft hands upon the darkening sea. If he could keep his left eye open, he could probably see the tide coming in. Maybe, in the right light, he'd be able to see the currents left by the whales as they moved their way through the ocean, under God's eyes.

If Georgie could see him now. Safe and warm. A room of his own. The ocean.

If only Georgie could.

In the mirror, Matt twisted to look at his back, still bandaged along the low ribs. Then he lay down on the bed. Below him, he could hear Bagheera clattering around in the kitchen. "Dinner will be ready in a moment," she had said.

He turned the pages of *Treasure Island* again until he felt himself falling asleep. He tried to stay awake, but finally his left eye closed, and then his right, and so Georgie appeared to him in his dreams, as usual. His guts blown out, as usual. All that blood.

Matt gasped.

Georgie.

He clutched at the sheets.

Georgie.

Then the two men coming out of the Alley.

And him walking down into it.

That blood pooling toward him.

And Georgie's eyes still open, even if whatever made Georgie *Georgie* was already gone.

All that blood.

Then, "Matthew!"

"Matthew!"

He woke up, panting.

"Matthew!"

Mrs. MacKnockater. It was only Bagheera calling.

She was still in the kitchen when he came down, but he sat at the dining table, where Mrs. MacKnockater had laid out brown beans and brown bread with raisins. And a green salad that Matt knew he wouldn't touch but she probably would. And chocolate milk. And he smelled something apple-y still baking in the kitchen. He leaned back in his chair.

"Matthew," Mrs. MacKnockater said, coming in with the ham steak, "we will be observing some decorum. And you're perspiring. Are you all right?"

He looked at her.

"You need to wear a shirt when we come to the table."

"Why?" he said.

Mrs. MacKnockater set the ham steak down on a trivet. "Matthew," she said.

He went back upstairs. He looked inside the wardrobe. He put on a white shirt—he let the left sleeve hang over the sling and cast—a broad maroon tie that he kind of wrapped around his neck, and one of the tweed jackets—he let the left sleeve hang on that, too. He went back down to the dining table and sat.

"Honestly, Matthew," said Mrs. MacKnockater.

"You know how hard it is to put on a tie with one hand?" said Matt.

"You seem to have made that point."

"The beans will get cold if I have to change again, Bagheera."

She passed him the beans.

They ate quietly together. Through the open windows—maybe the last open windows of the fall, since the frosts were coming and already the night air was starry cold—through the open windows came the eternal sounds of the waves against the rocks, and they both imagined the dark pines leaning over to listen, and the frothy water swooshing up and drawing back, dragging the pebbles of the shore with it.

If only Georgie . . .

"Matthew," said Mrs. MacKnockater, "tomorrow we start with lessons."

"I'm not going back to school."

"No," said Mrs. MacKnockater, "you are not. You'll be under my tutelage, which, I promise you, will be much more rigorous than anything you might experience at Harpswell Junior High School."

Matt put his fork down. He looked at her. He almost told her how long it had taken him to get through the first two pages of *Treasure Island*.

But he didn't need to.

"I know," said Mrs. MacKnockater.

"I'm not any good at—"

"I'll teach you," she said.

He picked up his fork and started in on the ham steak.

They began the next morning. They began with the vowels.

After a week, they started in on the consonants—the stops first.

Then the fricatives.

Then they put them together. The *ng* together with the /o/ in

Long. The fricative /j/ together with that /o/ sound again in *John.* The short /i/ in *Silver,* and "Do you see how the sound varies with the placement of the tongue?"

And that's how Mrs. Nora MacKnockater, headmistress of St. Elene's Preparatory Academy for Girls, and Matt Coffin, late of Captain Cobb's fishing shack and now settled into the seaside home of said Mrs. Nora MacKnockater, spent their mornings, after which Mrs. MacKnockater walked over to St. Elene's and Matt read his assigned pages beside the bay window nearest the parlor wood stove.

He had never read a whole book by himself before.

And this one he was reading for the second time, if you counted Mrs. MacKnockater reading the book aloud as the first time.

And while he read, the bruises on his face and on his chest healed. He began to wake up and have no trouble at all opening both his eyes. The bandages came off as the cuts across his back knit and faded. And Dr. Pulsifer, who visited every couple of days, said that his arm was doing fine, his fingers were nice and pink, and he wasn't going to have any trouble with that shoulder.

"Better not," said Captain Hurd, when this was reported at supper one Friday night. "I need a deckhand who can pull his weight."

"I can pull my weight," said Matt.

The Captain looked at him. "Scrawny as you are, that's not saying much. Knockater, you'd better pass him some more of those brown beans."

Meanwhile, the maples passed into their brightest reds, the birches to their quick yellows, the oaks to their brown garb. Some mornings the windowpanes in Matt's room were webbed with frost, and Matt could see his breath in the room and would hurry downstairs, where Mrs. MacKnockater was "merrying up" the embers in the wood stove. And there would be the smell of bacon from the kitchen, and the sweet scent of burning applewood, and the sounds of the house creaking to its new warmth. And together they would watch for the passing of *Affliction* and they would wave at Captain Hurd, and Matt would wish that he were on that deck, tying buoy hitches.

And aside from those days when Lieutenant Minot—who had been assigned to the case, he said—came to ask the same questions, or Miss Phyllis's office called to arrange visits that Mrs. Mac-Knockater never could seem to fit into her schedule, Matt realized that he was, for the first time in a very long time, maybe safe.

Still, truth to tell, on those long afternoons when Mrs. Mac-Knockater was off being a headmistress, he was a little bit lonely.

And every night, there was always Georgie, and all that blood.

And the two men who came out of the Alley.

And that blood.

ELEVEN

Soon, every morning had its frost, and now Matt got up before Mrs. MacKnockater to coax the wood stove into red life. Mrs. MacKnockater, who was hardly eager these days to kneel and blow on the embers, was more than a little grateful that Matt would. When she came down, she would smile at the warm rooms, at the crackling of the wood, at Matt sitting close to the warmth and flipping through the pages of *Treasure Island,* and she would go into the kitchen to make oatmeal.

But Matt was starting to feel housebound, and after lessons, when Mrs. MacKnockater left for St. Elene's and before he began the assignments she had set him, he would go for walks through the pines and hemlocks above the ridge, and then past those and across the two-lane by St. Elene's—the campus carefully guarded by the brick wall with the spears. Some pine-strewn paths that hunters had probably left meandered through the woods beyond the school, and he tracked those as if he were Ben Gunn, mapping out the island on which he was stranded.

On colder, stormier days, when the waves were high and the clouds weighted low, Captain Hurd, who didn't feel like braving *Affliction* out on the Atlantic today, thank you very much, would find Matt out on the rocks below Mrs. MacKnockater's house, and they would sit there, both huddled in pea jackets, watching the wind slice off the frothy tops of the waves, and they would eat the terrible brownies that the Captain brought.

They didn't need to talk, and didn't much.

By now, Miss Phyllis had pretty much given up on making headway with Matt—or maybe she felt that Matt was in a secure place. Or maybe Miss Phyllis was just afraid of Mrs. MacKnockater. But Lieutenant Minot had not given up, and now he started a new campaign: on Tuesday, he was at Mrs. MacKnockater's house at breakfast time, and he was loud. In the kitchen, Matt could hear him as if he were right next to the lieutenant, who said to Mrs. MacKnockater, "Enough is enough." And he said, "I've waited longer than I should have." And he said, "It's not his arm I need to get to work. It's his mouth." And he said, "I'll see him now, Dr. MacKnockater. Here, or down at the station. Either one."

After a few moments, Lieutenant Minot came into the kitchen.

Mrs. MacKnockater came in behind him.

Matt stood and carried his bowl of oatmeal to the sink.

"Matthew," said Lieutenant Minot, "it's time to answer some questions."

Matt didn't turn around.

Lieutenant Minot sighed. "What is it with you two? Listen, I'd rather ask these questions here. But like I said to Dr. MacKnockater, it can be at the station, too."

Matt walked back to the table and sat down. "What do you want to know?"

"I want to know who beat you up. I want to know who broke your arm. I want to know who bashed your face in." Lieutenant Minot sat down at the table with him. "I want to know who cut you to the ribs. Matthew, I want to know who almost killed you."

"I don't—"

"And I want to know why you're protecting him."

"Look, it was just some guy."

"Did you have something he wanted?"

"How should I know?"

"Did he tell you his name?"

"You think someone who's beating you up stops to tell you his name?"

"Had you seen him before?"

"I told you, he was just some guy."

"Who wandered into a fishing shack."

"I guess."

"And who waited for you."

"Maybe."

"And then beat you up."

"Yeah."

"Why was he waiting for you?"

Matt shrugged.

"Did he get what he wanted?"

"I guess."

Lieutenant Minot leaned back against his chair. "You're a whole lot of help. Did it even happen in the shack?"

Matt shrugged.

Lieutenant Minot leaned back into the table.

"Who's Georgie?"

Suddenly Matt was staring at Lieutenant Minot. He did not move at all.

"You called for him all the time in the hospital. Did he get beat up too?"

Nothing from Matt.

"Because if this guy beat you up for no reason at all, and if he beat up Georgie, too, he could do it to someone else—maybe for a reason."

And at that, Matt's eyes flicked up toward Mrs. MacKnockater and back—and Lieutenant Minot suddenly knew.

"Dr. MacKnockater," he said, "would you mind letting me and Matthew here talk by ourselves?"

"Yes, I would mind," said Mrs. MacKnockater. "The boy's a minor and I'm his guardian."

"No," said Lieutenant Minot. "The boy's a minor, but scaring off his social worker doesn't make you his guardian. I'm investigating an assault, Dr. MacKnockater—maybe an attempted murder. You need to let me do my job."

Mrs. MacKnockater looked at Matt.

"It's okay," he said.

She waited a moment. "I'll be in the parlor," she said. She turned to Lieutenant Minot. "And if you—"

Lieutenant Minot held up his hands. "Gentle as a lamb," he said.

Mrs. MacKnockater left the kitchen. She kept the door to the kitchen open.

Lieutenant Minot waited, and then he said, quietly, "You're afraid he's coming back."

Matt didn't move.

"Maybe he wanted something you had. Maybe he didn't. Maybe he got it. Maybe he didn't."

No move from Matt.

"Maybe he wanted to teach you a lesson."

No move.

"Maybe he wanted *you*."

No move.

"And he hurt Georgie, didn't he? Maybe he did it, or maybe someone who worked for him did it." Matt staring at him. "And now you're not just afraid he's coming back. You're afraid he's going to hurt Nora MacKnockater."

This time, Matt did move.

He put his hands up to his eyes.

"But you don't have anywhere to go. And what's more, maybe for the first time, you don't want to go."

Matt looked at Lieutenant Minot. "Not the first time," he said.

"Okay, not the first time. Listen, Matt, I can't help you if you don't tell me who he is."

"Don't you think I know that?" said Matt. If Mrs. MacKnockater hadn't been in the house, he would have screamed it.

Lieutenant Minot sat back.

From outside, Matt could hear that wild squawky call that seagulls make, and he let himself go to *Affliction* out on the water, tying the line of traps, letting them slide below the surface with that splash until only God could see them, and then later, when the sun was lower, pulling them back in, full of lobsters. And Captain Hurd smiling the way he did, with the ends of his mouth pulled down, and maybe laughing through his nose—the way he did.

"You know," said Lieutenant Minot, "I'm pretty good at what I do."

And then Matt wasn't on *Affliction*. He was in Queens. In that Alley that no one went down because everyone knew what happened in that Alley.

He looked at Lieutenant Minot. "It doesn't matter," he said. "No one's good enough."

That afternoon, Matt lay in his bed instead of doing Mrs. MacKnockater's punctuation lesson at the dining room table—as if anyone ever used semicolons. The day was warmer than it had been, and he lay with the window open so he could hear the sea. Maybe that's where he should head again, he thought. It had worked for a while before. No one looks for kids on fishing boats.

Maybe he should go.

He'd moved the pillowcase from under the sofa to the convenient cabinet built into the chute out to the roof. He still had almost everything he'd stuffed into it.

Maybe he really should go.

He tried to stretch his left arm over his head. He couldn't get it up that far.

He couldn't handle himself in a boat yet.

He'd have to give it another week.

When he and Georgie used to talk about getting out, they'd dream about the West. They'd get jobs as cowboys and ride horses, and drive cattle, and do whatever else cowboys do. They'd brush off the city like they brushed off dirt, and they'd ride all day and into the night, and they'd camp by a fire and its sparks would light millions of stars. That's what they'd do when they got away.

That's what they'd have done.

TWELVE

MERYL LEE DECIDED SHE SHOULD GO TO PUTNAM TO try—again—to find her classic American author for Mrs. Connolly. When she passed Marian Elders's room, Marian was wearing a cast on her pinky that looked a lot bigger than it had to be, and she looked up at Meryl Lee sort of accusingly.

"I'm so sorry, Marian. Does it hurt?" said Meryl Lee.

Marian grimaced. "Sometimes it throbs and I can feel it all the way up my arm."

"At least it got you out of field hockey practice," said Meryl Lee.

"I love field hockey practice," said Marian, and lifted her hand to wipe away an incipient tear.

Meryl Lee decided that Marian Elders was inclined to drama.

After she got to Putnam—where she should have been looking for her classic American author—and after she waved at Mrs. Hibbard at the reference desk, she decided to read just a few pages of *The Grapes of Wrath* to get her started, and she put her domestic economy book close by—just in case. Like before, it took only a couple of pages to put her on the highway with the Joads. Looking for work. Looking for food. Looking for a camp to stay in but they were turned away from everywhere. And the oranges were burning. And Ma Joad was keeping them together but only just. And the bosses didn't care who lived and who died and they were hollering at the Joads, "Is that book for my class?"

Meryl Lee looked up.

It wasn't the bosses hollering.

It was Mrs. Connolly.

Meryl Lee stood.

Several lower school girls at a nearby table quickly packed up and fled.

"You don't have to stand, Miss Kowalski. I was merely wondering if that book is for my class—particularly since you have yet to turn in your author paragraph. May I see it?"

Meryl Lee handed *The Grapes of Wrath* to Mrs. Connolly, who opened it and slowly turned past the title page and through the opening of chapter one. Then she set it down on the library table. "Since this is a book by John Steinbeck, and since I have been very clear that John Steinbeck is not an acceptable writer, I must assume this is *not* your book for my class."

Meryl Lee nodded. "No," she said.

"And so I am led to ask the next, rather obvious question: Whose work will you be studying this year?"

Meryl Lee felt the name of every writer she had ever known seep out of her brain cells.

"You have had more than enough time," said Mrs. Connolly.

Then, miraculously, like a gift, a name bobbed up into Meryl Lee's memory.

"Have you consulted with Charlotte Dobrée, as I suggested?" said Mrs. Connolly.

Meryl Lee grabbed at the name as if grabbing at a paper cup bobbing in the deep end of the ocean.

"Miss Kowalski?"

"The Wizard of Oz," Meryl Lee said in sort of a rush of breath.

Mrs. Connolly did that breathing thing with her nose. "You wish to study the writings of the Wizard of Oz?"

"No, no. To read *The Wizard of Oz.* I mean, I wish to read *The Wonderful Wizard of Oz* and to study it as my classic American book."

"I see," said Mrs. Connolly.

"It's really good. Have you seen the movie?"

"You feel *The Wonderful Wizard of Oz* is a work of such literary merit that it might be called a classic?"

Meryl Lee nodded.

"And you feel this is a book to help you to develop taste and discernment?"

Meryl Lee nodded again.

"Judging from the film, I doubt that very much. Do you know the name of the author?"

Meryl Lee raised her eyebrows to chipmunk-y level. "Oz?" she said.

Mrs. Connolly sighed. "You have a great deal of work to do." She did that thing with her nose again. "I am not completely sure you are equipped for success."

"Me either," said Meryl Lee.

"You have not made a good beginning. Developing taste and discernment through reading L. Frank Baum's *The Wonderful Wizard of Oz.*" She shook her head. "You may try, but I would advise you to consider the plight of the Scarecrow." She turned and left.

Meryl Lee watched her strutting backside leave the library. If Holling had been there, right then, he would have tried doing that nose thing that Mrs. Connolly did. Or maybe the strutting backside thing. She might have tried too—at least the nose thing. She wasn't sure she would have gotten it, but Holling would have.

But now she wondered if Mrs. Connolly was right. Could she become Accomplished by reading *The Wonderful Wizard of Oz*?

Maybe not.

And not field hockey either.

So what could she be Accomplished in?

The Blank started to form in front of her, but then, suddenly, she wondered what Mrs. Connolly had meant by mentioning the plight of the Scarecrow. That he was missing his . . . hey . . . and Meryl Lee's eyes narrowed on the retreating backside.

But after Famous Women of History on Monday morning, Meryl Lee wasn't thinking very much about Mrs. Connolly and *The Wonderful Wizard of Oz* by L. Frank Baum.

After Famous Women of History that morning, Meryl Lee had other things to think about—mostly homicidal thoughts about Jennifer and Ashley and maybe Charlotte too and the problem of finding a place to hide their bloody bodies. And if by chance their bloody bodies were found, any jury would declare their deaths to be justifiable homicides.

Meryl Lee would tell the jury that for almost three weeks, she had been researching and writing her oral report on the Empress Joséphine, born Marie Josèphe Rose Tascher de La Pagerie, which she was to present with Ashley.

For the same almost three weeks, Ashley had sat in her room—or Meryl Lee's room—doing her nails and sighing over Jennifer's kilted Alden.

Meryl Lee would tell the jury that when she asked Ashley how she wanted to divide up the work for the project, Ashley said, "Oh, let's just both give our impressions."

Meryl Lee would tell them that when she finally finished her report and put it together in a bright yellow plastic binder, she had left it on the corner of her desk, underneath the dried rose, until class on Monday.

She would tell them she had been ready when Mrs. Saunders called on them in class on Monday, but Ashley got up to read her report first.

Then Meryl Lee would read to the jury—who would be hanging, aghast, on her every word—she would read the opening of her report on the Empress Joséphine, born Marie Josèphe Rose Tascher de La Pagerie:

> When the Empress Joséphine was still very young, she met a fortuneteller who said to her, "Listen: you will be married soon: that union will not be happy; you will become a widow, and then—then you will be Queen of France! Some happy years will be yours; but you will die in an hospital, amid civil commotion."

Then she would tell them she thought that was a pretty good opening, and the jury would nod, their mouths open in agreement, agog at Meryl Lee's startling prose and clever handling of a quotation from a primary source.

Then Meryl Lee would tell them that Ashley obviously liked her opening as well, because here's what Ashley read aloud in Mrs. Saunders's class before Meryl Lee stood up:

When the Empress Joséphine was still very young, she met a fortuneteller who said to her, "Listen: you will be married soon: that union will not be happy; you will become a widow, and then—then you will be Queen of France! Some happy years will be yours; but you will die in an hospital, amid civil commotion."

And the jury's faces would turn to ashen fury and they would cry to heaven for vengeance. Or something like that. Because after Ashley had finished giving Meryl Lee's whole report, there was nothing left for Meryl Lee to say. Not a single thing. So when she stood up for her turn, she sounded as if she was making everything up on the spot.

Because she was.

"Empress Joséphine, born Marie Josèphe Rose Tascher de La Pagerie," Meryl Lee had said, "was someone who, uh, had a really long name. It would have taken her servants a long time to announce that she was coming into a room. Because she had a really long name." Meryl Lee had paused. She grasped again. Maybe something about *The Wonderful Wizard of Oz*? Probably not. She took a deep breath. "Part of her name sounds, uh, like a flower," said Meryl Lee. "And the first syllable of *Josèphe* rhymes with *rose,* which may be why her parents named her *Josèphe*—which is a long name just by itself."

And, agonizingly, more like that until she sat down—wondering whether Ashley had stolen her report herself or if Jennifer had given it to her.

Either way, the jury would say it was definitely justifiable homicide, and Meryl Lee would walk.

Mrs. Saunders, who was obviously not on the jury, asked her to stay after class.

When all the reports were finished, Mrs. Saunders announced that since most of the girls had done so well—especially Miss Koertge's report on Eleanor of Aquitaine, which showed both discernment and eloquence—she was going to assign a second oral report on more of history's famous women. "This one will be a little longer and you will be preparing the reports in pairs again. But for a challenge, I would like several girls to volunteer to do individual reports. Each of these girls will receive extra credit. Do I have any volunteers?"

When Meryl Lee raised her hand, Mrs. Saunders said, "I was hoping some of our stronger students would volunteer to work alone."

Ashley Higginson raised her hand.

Despite the furious protests of the jury, Mrs. Saunders picked her.

She assigned famous women of history to all the girls until only Meryl Lee and Marian Elders were left. Marian was holding her pinky and looking apprehensive. Mrs. Saunders was looking apprehensive too. Meryl Lee understood why. Marian Elders might like high drama, but she hadn't exactly won Most Promising Orator of 1968 with her report, which she had delivered in a voice so quiet, only angels could have heard it.

"Well," said Mrs. Saunders, "there is nothing else to do, I suppose."

She assigned them Mary Stuart, Queen of Scots.

After class, Mrs. Saunders told Meryl Lee she should resolve to put more Effort into her work if she was going to become an Accomplished student at St. Elene's Preparatory Academy for Girls. Mrs. Saunders was willing to excuse this one disaster because

Meryl Lee had spent her early education accustomed to the standards of a public school and so deserved some accommodation.

Meryl Lee, who was feeling some high drama rising in her, too, said, "Accommodation?"

"Do you need to consult *Funk and Wagnalls*?"

"No, Mrs. Saunders."

"Do you understand that you have used up your one pass?" said Mrs. Saunders.

"I understand," said Meryl Lee.

"I certainly hope so," said Mrs. Saunders. "Marian Elders has fine research and writing skills, but she is very quiet. I am hoping that some of your . . . *energy* may rub off on her."

Meryl Lee nodded.

"And Miss Kowalski," said Mrs. Saunders, "Mary Stuart, Queen of Scots, is an important figure in English history. I would expect a proper report on her Accomplishments."

"I understand," said Meryl Lee again.

Justifiable homicide, she thought, all the way back to Netley Dormitory. Definitely justifiable homicide. With a wrench. Or a candlestick. Or a rope.

But when she got back to Netley, no one was in her room.

A good thing.

Jennifer did not seem to notice that Meryl Lee was purposefully ignoring her and her pearls at dinner that afternoon.

Jennifer was too excited to notice, because her birthday was a week from Saturday and guess who was coming to visit her from his Scottish manor house? Alden! Yes, Alden! Kilt and all. He was taking her to the Parker House hotel in Boston for an early supper and then to the Boston Symphony and then afterward to a secret place that he wouldn't reveal just yet. Alden!

Meryl Lee played with the small crème brûlée that Bettye had placed on her dessert plate.

She didn't tell anyone at the table what she had suddenly discovered.

She and Jennifer had the same birthday. Two weeks from Saturday.

No one at the table knew that she and Jennifer had the same birthday.

There are thirty eighth-grade girls living in Margaret B. Netley Dormitory, she thought. *Thirty. And not a single one knows that we have the same birthday.*

If Holling were coming, he . . . and there was the Blank. She hadn't seen it for a few days, but there it was again, blocking everything out, starting to lean into a long hole, starting to . . .

She pushed it back, almost crying, but the Blank followed her out of the dining hall and past her empty mailbox and alongside Newell Chapel.

Still, when the hour chimes struck, they sounded so sweetly that Meryl Lee stopped and looked back toward the chapel, and to Greater Hoxne beyond it, and she saw Bettye just coming out, a bag of garbage in each hand, lugging them to a waiting small truck. She slung them in, one at a time, and the first landed fine but the second must have been heavier. The bag hit the top of the pickup bed and it ripped, and the lousy remnants of din-ner—potato peels and carrot greens and chicken carcasses and leftover crème brûlée—slopped down the pickup's side and onto the asphalt.

The driver of the pickup stood over Bettye while she scooped it all up with her hands.

Meryl Lee almost went to help her—until she saw Mrs. Connolly walk out onto the commons.

When the pickup drove off, Bettye stood, looking at the lovely ivied buildings of St. Elene's, and Meryl Lee fled behind Newell Chapel, hoping Bettye hadn't seen her.

After Domestic Economy, Meryl Lee went to Putnam, where Mrs. Hibbard said that she looked awfully morose and was she feeling well? And Meryl Lee said she was fine and where could she find books about Mary Stuart, Queen of Scots? And Mrs. Hibbard, who was tiny, with a tiny nose, and tiny ears, and tiny hands and feet, and a tiny smile and a tiny voice that you had to listen to carefully, held her by the arm and said, "My dear, aren't you still reading *The Grapes of Wrath*?"

Meryl Lee nodded.

"I'm so glad," said Mrs. Hibbard. "It is my very favorite novel."

"Really?" said Meryl Lee. "What about the lewd parts?"

"Are there any?" she said.

"I think so," Meryl Lee said.

"Let me know when you find them," Mrs. Hibbard said, and she smiled—Meryl Lee smiled too—and she took tiny steps away toward the 900s and came back with three books about Mary Stuart, Queen of Scots.

Meryl Lee wanted to kiss her.

She sat beside one of the green-shaded lamps and opened all three books.

In her portrait—the same one in the front of each of the books—Mary Stuart, Queen of Scots, looked like she used hot rollers in her hair—which is something that Jennifer did all the time. But unlike Jennifer, Meryl Lee read, Mary Stuart, Queen of Scots, "wrote and spoke Latin with great ease and elegance, and had a taste for poetry. She played well on several instruments, danced gracefully, and managed a horse with dexterity: she also spent much time in needlework."

Now, that *is Accomplished,* thought Meryl Lee.

She figured she had better get busy if she was going to be Accomplished too.

She waited for Resolution to fill her.

She waited some more for Resolution to fill her.

It didn't.

When Meryl Lee got to her room with the three books, Jennifer was stretched out on her duvet. She had—no kidding—hot rollers in her blond hair. Meryl Lee wondered if Jennifer ever missed an opportunity to put hot rollers in her hair. If atomic bombs fell and all western civilization was destroyed, Jennifer would be okay as long as there were hot hair rollers beside her in the underground bunker.

Meryl Lee put the books on her desk.

"If you're going to study," said Jennifer, "do you think you could find someplace else? I'd like to take a nap."

"I'm just reading," said Meryl Lee.

"And I'd like to take a nap," said Jennifer.

"You can't take a nap while I'm reading?" said Meryl Lee.

Jennifer raised herself slowly on one elbow. "No, I can't."

Meryl Lee left the three books about Mary Stuart, Queen of Scots, on her desk. She had barely enough time to get down to the shore and back before the light was gone, and so she hurried past the gate and along the fence and down the footpath by the birches and the firs and then out onto the rocks—almost crying again.

"Geez," said a voice.

A boy. His left arm in a sling.

"What?" she said.

"So, is the whole world coming down here now?" he said.

And Meryl Lee had sort of had it. It had been that sort of day.

"Yup," she said, "the whole world is coming down here now. There are three and a half billion people lined up behind me."

He looked back to the water and threw a stone.

"What are you doing?" she said.

"Practicing."

"For what?"

"The Olympics. Look, I don't mean to be a jerk or anything, but I used to be able to come down here and be by myself."

Meryl Lee walked down toward the water and picked up a stone. She threw it out as far as she could. "It must be tough, having to share a whole beach with another person."

The boy picked up a handful of stones. "You know what? I know an old lady who can throw better than that."

"You know what else? You *are* a jerk."

The boy paused for a moment, and then he threw one of the stones, and Meryl Lee watched it skip, and skip, and skip, and skip, and then shimmy into a whole lot of tiny skips until it nuzzled itself into a wave.

"Okay," said Meryl Lee. "That was kind of amazing. But you're still a jerk."

The boy looked out to the water. Already it was starting to get dark, and the outlines of the islands were merging into the waves.

"Sorry," the boy said.

"What?" said Meryl Lee.

The boy walked across the rocks to her. "Sorry. My best friend used to tell me I was a jerk all the time."

"He was right."

"Here." He handed her a flat stone. "Throw it like this."

Meryl Lee took it and threw.

"Try again. Keep your arm lower."

She did try again, and she kept her arm lower.

It was a terrible throw, but the boy didn't say anything. He handed her another stone.

"You throw it."

He did. Three skips.

"That's not bad," she said.

He turned to look at her. "It's pathetic," he said.

"What happened to your arm?"

"Never play checkers," he said. "It's way too dangerous."

It was exactly what Holling would have said.

Exactly.

Meryl Lee got up to seven skips that afternoon—not counting the one that went into the wave, which he wouldn't give her, no matter what she said. And for the first time that day, and maybe for the first time in many days, Meryl Lee did not feel the Blank behind her. All she wanted was to be thinking of nothing else except throwing flat stones into the waves with this boy, to count the skips, to imagine the stones slowly sliding through the cold water to the bottom and resting.

And something familiar came to her, as if she could remember how it felt to have her heart inside her chest.

THIRTEEN

1959–66

THE NIGHT AFTER HE MET MERYL LEE, MATT COFFIN lay on his bed and thought about the only photograph he had had of his family.

He didn't have it anymore, and probably by now it would have been folded into oblivion anyway. But he had had it during the years with Leonidas Shug.

It was black and white, of course. They were on a beach. On a blanket. A toy shovel and bucket beside him. He was, maybe, four years old. He sat between his mother and father, though most of his father was beyond the frame. Matt was reaching past the edge of the blanket toward the sand. His hand was open, his fingers splayed out. He was smiling, and his mother was smiling, and probably his father was smiling too. Behind them was the ocean, calm and quiet, only a ripple of a wave showing. Seagulls above, just barely in the picture—like his father.

He had kept that picture in his back pocket, and at night he would take it out and stare at it. He would wonder what their names were. He would wonder which beach it was. What had happened to the toy shovel? Where did that blanket get to?

He would stare at that picture and try to summon up more memories—what happened at that beach, the sound of his father's voice, the feel of his mother's hand, where they might have lived. He would try to remember something that he had once owned beyond the shovel and blanket, and sometimes there would be a hint of a memory—and then it would dissolve.

He remembered being alone. He didn't know why he was alone, but he was.

He remembered walking past buildings.

He remembered he was cold.

He remembered he turned into that Alley to get out of the wind, and when he had turned, it was suddenly very still and quiet.

He remembered the group of men, the quick looks, the Small Guy who had scampered away, the Big Guy who had strolled past him.

The man lying on the ground.

Then Leonidas Shug.

Shug, who had come up and loomed over him. "And who are you, little man?"

"I'm lost," he had said.

Shug had reached out a long arm and put his hand on Matt's shivering shoulder. "Do you want to come with me?" he said. "It will be okay."

Matt had nodded.

"Bingo," said Shug.

After that, nothing was ever okay again.

There had been a bunch of boys, all of them much bigger than he was. They kept moving, and sometimes they were all in one room, sometimes two. Since he was the smallest, the boys made him sleep closest to the window—if there was a window—when it was cold. He quickly learned to fight for what he ate, or he wouldn't eat. And since he was the smallest, he didn't eat much for a while. Finally he got so hungry that he didn't care if he got hurt or not—he'd fight like crazy until the other kid did care.

All this Leonidas Shug watched as if he might eat *them*.

And Matt Coffin was a quick learner. Once you didn't care, everything else was easy. You didn't care about the drunk whose pockets you emptied. You didn't care about the lady whose purse you stole—anyway, she'd been carrying it like she wanted to have it stolen. You didn't care about the addict you cheated, about the jerk Shug bumped into so you could slip his wallet, about the drug runs, about the store owners you collected from because they were too frightened to report on Shug and his boys, or about the houses you broke into because you were the smallest and could scamper through an open window like it was a door wide enough for a parade.

You cared only about making the other kid care enough so you could eat.

And you never, never asked what went on in that Alley.

And you never let yourself wonder about . . . stuff.

And so Matt Coffin turned six, seven, then eight, then nine, and ten and eleven—though he couldn't say exactly when his birthday was. The summer? And even though he figured that someday he might disappear with Shug down that Alley too—like some of the boys had—he stayed, because where else was he supposed to go?

Where else?

And then one frigid winter day, he met Georgie, who was standing over a heating vent, trying not to cry in its steam. Georgie was almost as big as Shug. He was starting a mustache, for crying out loud. But his eyes were wide, and the way he looked at Matt told him that he'd never have to fight this kid for food. Dang, this kid would probably give his food away.

"That steam is poison," said Matt.

"Don't be a jerk," the kid said. "If that was true, I would have died a long time ago."

"You're going to die if you stay out in this cold," Matt said.

"Maybe," the kid said. Then he opened his jacket and drew out an orange. He threw it to Matt. "If I'm going to die tonight, you may as well have this."

I knew it, thought Matt.

Matt went over to the vent and stood with Georgie in the poisonous steam. He peeled the orange and they shared it.

"I know a place," said Matt—even though he almost didn't want to tell him, because of that Alley. But it was so cold! "And there's food. Sort of."

So they went, and when they walked in together, Matt could tell right away that Shug didn't like Georgie. And he could tell right away that he was about to get smacked. But when the kid stood between them and Shug backed off, Matt could tell that things were about to change.

And they did.

A little.

Georgie wouldn't let anyone fight for food anymore. Especially the smaller kids.

Georgie made sure that everyone had a coat and that no one took what wasn't theirs.

And Georgie slept by the window, and the smallest kids by the far wall—or wherever was warmest.

When Matt told him he had to be careful around Shug, Georgie said Matt was a jerk and shouldn't worry.

And when Shug was about to smack someone, Georgie was there. Always.

That spring, Georgie took Matt all over New York City—not for jobs, but just to see New York. He took him to Central Park, to the lions by the New York Public Library, to Rockefeller Center and to Radio City, where they snuck in to see the Rockettes—who were worth what the ushers said to the boys when they were caught. They went to Flushing Meadows and climbed the Unisphere until the guards told them to get the heck out of there! They went to the Metropolitan Museum of Art, and Georgie told him he was a jerk because he liked the Egyptian stuff a whole lot more than the medieval armor. They went to Lincoln Center, and Georgie told him he was a jerk because Matt couldn't figure out why someone would like music without any words. They went to the UN and Georgie told Matt he was a jerk because he didn't know that "UN" stood for "Unified Nations."

And if Shug was ticked off that Matt had missed a job because he was standing in front of some painting or climbing on the Unisphere or something, Georgie was beside him, and Shug would say what he had to say, but he would never smack Matt.

Georgie.

In the summer when Matt was twelve—they figured—Georgie said he wanted to give him a birthday present. He asked Matt if he'd ever gone anywhere outside the city, and Matt said he hadn't even thought about it. "You jerk," said Georgie. So the next day they went to Grand Central Station. They boarded a train for anywhere north. It was easy to keep moving from train car to train car, or to pretend they were with a family, or to hide in the bathrooms—the conductor never said a thing. Maybe he didn't want to fuss with the trouble it all might bring. Or maybe he'd boarded a train without a ticket once when he was a kid. Anyway, they rode for a couple of hours, and when they got off, it was into a different world. Trees everywhere. They'd never seen so many trees. A river broader than a city block. Broader than two city blocks. Three! The air clean and bright with sunlight. Houses made of wood, painted clean, and people push mowing their lawns and walking with their dogs. Smiling like it was real.

They slept that night in a shed that someone hadn't even locked. "You can always find a shed when you need it," Georgie had said. It smelled like Matt imagined deep woods would smell.

And they talked about being cowboys and it always being like this—except there probably weren't so many trees out West. But wouldn't it be fine, out under the stars, riding horses, rounding up cattle and roping them, riding during the day, sleeping by the fire at night. The stars. Wouldn't it be fine?

Neither wanted to go back. Ever. But what else could they do? They'd wait a couple of years, until Matt was older, and then they'd head West. They'd be cowboys. Horses, stars, cattle, sunlight. They'd be cowboys.

Shug didn't say anything to them when they got back. Just nodded, told them to go to bed, he had a job for Matt tomorrow. Better get some sleep after being out so long.

It was all a little spooky. And it didn't help that the other boys looked at them like they knew something.

Matt and Georgie slept late, and when they got up, Shug told Matt he should go check out the winos over in Times Square. He handed him the change for the train. "Don't get caught," he said. "I'm not going to bail you out if you do. And if you do, you keep quiet, like I told you a hundred times. Remember, I got boys all grown up and serving hard time who would eat you if I told them to."

He leaned closer to Matt.

"I got boys . . . everywhere."

Matt nodded. He believed him. And he wouldn't get caught.

And he didn't. There were enough winos in Times Square that day to make it worthwhile. One even had four twenties on him. Matt splurged at a hamburger joint, then got on the train. It wasn't a fantastic haul, but it was better than you'd expect from the winos of Times Square.

When he got back, he saw them again: the Small Guy who scampered, the Big Guy who strolled. They were standing at the end of that Alley, the Big Guy wiping his knife off on the Small Guy's shirt, then laughing, then combing back his hair. They looked at Matt and separated and walked their own ways—scampering, strolling. And Matt—with a heart that had stopped beating—went into that Alley.

What he saw there, what he saw there, made everything that had ever happened to him *Before,* and everything that would ever happen to him *After.*

What he saw there, what he saw there, made Matt kneel down and whisper, "You jerk, you jerk, you jerk."

Then he went upstairs as if in a dream, as if he could not see to see, as if he could never care about anything ever again. He opened the door as if his hands were not his own. Shug was not there. Matt opened all the drawers in Shug's desk and threw them to the floor. He opened all the drawers in his dresser and threw them to the floor. He looked in the closet and pulled everything out. He looked under the bed and dragged everything out. Then he walked back to the closet and stepped on a loose floorboard.

That's where he found what he knew would hurt Shug most. That's where he found what, if it went missing, might even get

Shug taken into the Alley himself. It was in a white pillowcase—all hundreds.

He did not take anything else. He left the building. He walked to Grand Central Station, sweating under the hot summer sun. He knew which train to take and how to get aboard without the conductor seeing.

He headed anywhere north.

FOURTEEN

By MIDMORNING ON HER BIRTHDAY, MERYL LEE WAS waiting by the poisoned wall with spears, shoulders huddled against the cold, as her mother drove up.

"It's October nineteenth!" Meryl Lee hollered when the car stopped.

Her mother rolled down the window. "So it must be someone's birthday," she said.

"It's mine!"

It was what they had been saying to each other on Meryl Lee's birthday since she was four years old.

"Where's Dad?"

"I'm sorry, Meryl Lee. He wasn't able to come."

"He wasn't able to come?"

"So what shall we do today?" said her mother.

Meryl Lee got in the car and they drove south and Meryl Lee breathed in the smell of her mother's lily of the valley perfume. She had not realized how much she missed that smell. Along the way, her mother tried to catch her up on what was happening back home. Jerusalem Avenue was being repaved again. A model Florida condominium had been built a few blocks away and they had painted the cement grass green! Goldman's Best Bakery had bought the clock repair shop next door to expand, probably because developers were thinking of building an indoor mall nearby, but honestly, no one was happy about the idea.

Meryl Lee listened to her mother's voice. She listened and listened and listened. She closed her eyes. It was wonderful.

Did Meryl Lee know that Mr. Collins next door was retiring from the school? Her mother had had no idea he was ready for retirement. He looked so young still. And the Caseys were converting their garage into an apartment for their daughter and new son-in-law. And down on the corner, that green house, it was being painted yellow. And the Hoodhoods—

Her mother's voice went silent for a moment.

"The Hoodhoods are moving farther out on the Island. They'll put the house up for sale in the spring."

Meryl Lee tried not to cry.

They were in Portland a little before noon. They drove along the waterfront, got lost twice, went past the same burned-out wharf three times, and finally found a deli in a neighborhood where all the roads were cobblestones and went every which way. The smells of good bread and sweet cakes and honey and cinnamon billowed at the doorway.

They ate chocolate éclairs. The éclairs were fine. Afterward they stood by the harbor and watched the shipping. Fine. It was a perfect October day, with the sky a perfect blue, and the cool breezes perfect, but both of them sort of quiet, as though they were thinking of things they didn't want to say.

It got colder in the afternoon, and they had watched enough lobster boats. They went back to the car by the deli and her mother gave Meryl Lee her present: a Wedgwood pendant. Meryl Lee fastened it around her neck.

"How does it look?" she said.

"Fine," her mother said. Then after a minute, "Are you getting to know many of the girls?"

"Some," Meryl Lee said.

"Are they friendly?"

"Some," Meryl Lee said.

They drove back to St. Elene's quietly, and it was almost dusk when they parked beside Newell Chapel. Meryl Lee's mother said, "Honey, I was hoping to talk with you about something."

Meryl Lee looked at her. "I miss Holling," she said.

"I know," said her mother.

"I miss him every day."

"We all do," said her mother.

"No," said Meryl Lee. "Not like this."

They held each other until Meryl Lee sat back, feeling the weight of the Blank flat against her. "I never knew how much I would miss him," she said. Then, after another long time, "I'm sorry. You wanted to tell me something?"

Her mother looked out the car window.

"You know, Meryl Lee, it's not so important. We'll talk about it another time. This is your birthday and it's supposed to be a happy day." She patted Meryl Lee on the leg. "The pendant looks so lovely on you. Happy birthday. Happy birthday, Meryl Lee."

She was waving when she drove off past the poison ivy, and Meryl Lee was waving. The car turned out of the main gate, and Meryl Lee thought, *What did she want to tell me?* And beside her, the Blank hovered. It moved with her across the commons, and to Netley, and then, later, to Evening Meal, where Meryl Lee was more than a little surprised. Actually, a whole lot more than a little surprised.

Because Jennifer was sitting at the table.

Jennifer, who was supposed to be at the Parker House hotel in

Boston, and then at the Boston Symphony, and then at the Secret Alden Destination.

But Alden—they learned this between bouts of tears—wonderful Alden, divine kilted Alden, couldn't come because he had to fly to Stockholm to visit his great-aunt who was dying and entrusting her vault of jewels to his care. Jennifer held her napkin to her eyes and Mrs. Saunders said, "Indeed," and Jennifer sent her salad back with Bettye and then her soup and then her entrée because how could she possibly, possibly eat halibut fillets when she was distraught, and she knew that Alden couldn't eat either because he was distraught too, and didn't anyone understand that?

"I think we do understand," said Mrs. Saunders.

Then the doors from the lobby opened and Bettye came into the dining hall with yellow roses wrapped in white paper and Ashley called out from her table, "Are those from Alden?" but it wasn't really a question because Ashley knew they were and some of the girls started to squeal with delight because they knew they were too and wasn't Alden wonderful, even if he couldn't come to see Jennifer at St. Elene's?

Except they were not from Alden.

And they were not for Jennifer.

They were for Meryl Lee. From Mr. and Mrs. Hoodhood. For her birthday.

It got pretty quiet in Greater Hoxne Dining Hall when Bettye walked by Jennifer and laid the yellow roses in front of Meryl Lee.

"How lovely," said Mrs. Saunders after a moment. "Bettye, can you bring a vase and water, please?"

Bettye turned to find a vase and water as the Blank fell upon Meryl Lee like a granite slab.

FIFTEEN

1966

THE DAY HE RAN FROM LEONIDAS SHUG, MATT MADE it to the train station in New Haven, Connecticut, where he was discovered by an annoyed conductor who didn't want any trouble or any paperwork or any official fuss and who did not did not really did not want Matt on his train anymore.

So Matt got off and slept the rest of the night on a high-backed wooden bench in the station.

The next morning he walked to the bus station and decided that this time, he'd better buy the ticket. So he pulled out a hundred-dollar bill and waited in line for the sleepy guy in the ticket booth.

"Where to?" the sleepy guy said.

Matt looked at the possibilities on the DEPARTING TO sign above him.

"New Bedford," he said.

"Ticket for one?" he said.

"Yes," said Matt.

"Return?"

"Nope," said Matt.

The ticket guy looked at him.

"Aren't you a little young to be traveling by yourself?" he said.

"I've been with my aunt," Matt said. "My parents will be waiting for me at the New Bedford station."

"Huh," said the ticket guy.

Matt handed him the hundred.

The ticket guy turned it over, then held it up to the light. "So," he said, "you carry a lot of these?"

Matt held up the pillowcase. "I got a whole bag of them."

"Sure you do," said the ticket guy. He pulled the ticket out of its slot and punched it. Then he leaned forward and handed it to Matt. "Should I think twice before giving you this ticket?" he said.

Matt almost said yes. He almost handed the ticket guy the whole pillowcase. He almost asked to come inside the booth and curl up under the counter like a little kid might—maybe even go to sleep.

He almost did.

"Nope," said Matt, and he took the ticket and left.

He stayed in the men's room, standing on a toilet, the door locked, until it was almost time for the bus to pull out. Then he boarded and settled on a seat near the back of the bus, sitting beside a black guy in a suit who hummed "Leaning on the Everlasting Arms" like a lullaby until Matt fell asleep to it, wondering where he had heard that song before, wishing he could remember, thinking it might be important, wishing he knew what it would feel like to be safe and secure from all alarms.

He slept all the way to New Bedford, and woke only when the bus hunched its hulking self to a stop and passengers began to stand up.

And when he woke up, Matt realized right away that he had been leaning against the guy in the suit while he slept.

He sat up. "Sorry," he said.

"That's all right," said the guy. "You meeting someone here?"

Matt nodded.

"No, you're not," said the guy.

"My aunt and uncle are . . ."

The guy shook his head. "A young puppy can't never fool an old dog." He leaned down close to Matt. "Son, are you in any trouble?"

And because a young puppy can't never fool an old dog, and because you can't lie to someone who's been singing you a lullaby all the way from New Haven to New Bedford, Matt nodded.

That night, Matt stayed in the home of Pastor Darius Malcolm and his wife, Sophia.

"It's just a tiny house," said Sophia.

"But there's plenty of room for you," said Pastor Darius.

"Yes, there is," said Sophia, "but the bedroom upstairs is kind of cold."

"There's Milly's quilts put away," said Pastor Darius. "He could use them."

"He could," said Sophia, "but I hope you won't mind that the bathroom is behind the kitchen and you have to be sure to jiggle the handle once you're done."

"He won't mind," said Pastor Darius.

"But he's a boy, Darius, and he needs to run around, and—"

"He won't mind."

And Matt, who thought this was the most beautiful home he'd ever been inside, did not mind.

He fell asleep under Milly's quilts and slept almost a whole day. When he woke up, Pastor Darius and Sophia stuffed him with scrod, and sweet potatoes, and buttered peas, and blueberry buckle with vanilla ice cream. Then he went back to sleep under Milly's quilts, remembering somehow what it used to mean to be home.

He stayed with Pastor Darius and Sophia Malcolm for the whole summer.

He was the happiest he could remember being.

Pastor Darius was the minister of the Second Baptist Church of New Bedford, Massachusetts, which meant that he preached and prayed and baptized, and Sophia did all the rest. They were, they liked to say, poor as church mice but blessed beyond Solomon in all his glory, and Matt could see that at least the first was true. It didn't take him long to realize that the scrod dinner he'd had that first night probably took most of the cash they had in the house. He didn't know how they would ever get by without the casseroles and pies that parishioners brought in—some of which were pretty good. (Not Mrs. Nielson's Brussels Sprouts Surprise.) Matt would watch the faithful bring their meals while he set up the chairs for Wednesday night prayer meeting, or when he swept the sanctuary of Second Baptist on Saturday afternoons, or when he picked up all the broken crayons in the primary kids' Sunday school rooms on Mondays.

He also didn't know how they got him the clothes they did, and even though the clothes had once belonged to some other kid, Sophia made sure that the other kid was exactly his size, and the clothes came to him clean and folded and smelling like the warm dryer they'd just been in.

And no matter if they were as poor as church mice, Pastor Darius and Sophia hosted the Second Baptist Church's Tuesday and Thursday community lunches; on those days, the white steeple that rose high, high above anything else in the neighborhood, rallied the hungry, who lined up by ten o'clock and waited quietly outside Second Baptist until Pastor Darius sent Matt to open the doors up. Matt did not know where all the food came from—and he sometimes wondered if even Pastor Darius knew. When Pastor Darius preached one Sunday morning about the loaves and the fishes and the five thousand, he seemed to Matt to be speaking from personal experience. But every Tuesday and Thursday, Matt stood in the kitchen assembly line to make who knows how many ham and cheese sandwiches—some with mustard, some with mayo—and he mixed enough lemonade to quench the thirst of all New Bedford. And afterward, he wrinkled his hands in the hot water of the great steel sinks of Second Baptist, then went out to help take down the tables and sweep the floors.

He had never been so happy.

Ever.

By the end of the summer, Sophia Malcolm began to talk to Matt Coffin about school, which Matt figured he might be able to give a shot. She wondered if he remembered ever going to school, and he did—a little. Kindergarten, he thought. Maybe first grade, but probably kindergarten. She thought that maybe she and Pastor Darius might teach him a bit before September—not math, but the more important stuff, like reading and writing, and Matt figured she could try that. She wondered if he could show her how well he could read, and Matt showed her with this book about a pig that had a pretty good opening, but after three or four pages he told her that he'd better get over to Second Baptist. It was a Tuesday morning, and somehow Pastor Darius had got hold of three cartons of hot dogs. Matt thought he'd better bring the butter over so they could fry them up.

And so the summer came to an end, and the days began to get noticeably shorter, and one afternoon Pastor Darius took the bus to the New Bedford Correctional Facility to visit with the son of Mrs. Nielson, and Matt went along to keep him company. He sat in a metal chair at the back of the visitors' room and watched Pastor Darius pray with the guy on the other side of the glass, who was crying. Pastor Darius put his hand up on the glass, and so did the other guy, and Matt would not have been surprised if they could feel each other's hands—because it was Pastor Darius, who did not seem to Matt to be beyond a miracle.

But he was surprised when the guy next to Mrs. Nielson's son suddenly sat up straight and looked straight at him.

Straight at him.

It was the guy from that Alley.

The Small Guy.

The Small Guy, who looked at Pastor Darius, then at Matt, then back to Pastor Darius, then back to Matt.

The Small Guy who slowly lifted his arm up and pointed at Matt, and then pulled his finger back like he was cocking a pistol.

Matt lowered his face, stood, and left the visitors' room.

He waited for Pastor Darius outside the prison door.

He was shaking.

"You all right?" said Pastor Darius when he came out.

Matt nodded.

"You sure?"

"Let's go," said Matt.

He thought about leaving New Bedford that night. There wouldn't be much to pack. The pillowcase with the bundles of hundreds. Maybe some of the clothes they'd given him—he hoped they wouldn't mind. That was it. There had to be another bus from New Bedford heading anywhere north.

But the Small Guy was in prison. It wasn't like he was going to come after him. Maybe he hadn't even recognized Matt. Maybe he was just being a jerk to a kid.

Matt thought for a while.

The Small Guy had recognized him.

He knew it.

Matt pulled Milly's quilts over his face and tried to sleep.

The next Saturday, when Matt had finished sweeping the sanctuary and everything was all set for Sunday morning, Pastor Darius asked Matt to sit down in the front pew with him.

"A gentleman stopped by the church yesterday," he said. "Sort of a scary man."

Matt waited, but he knew.

"His name was Mr. Leonidas Shug, and I don't think he has visited many churches lately," he said, almost smiling.

Matt still waiting.

"He was looking for a boy. A runaway. His son. He said a friend had seen him with me."

Matt felt everything emptying out. "What did you say?" he asked.

"Oh, preachers have to learn to dissemble," said Pastor Darius. "He's not your father, is he?"

"No. What else did he say?"

"Words that preachers tend not to use."

"He threatened to do something to you, didn't he?"

"Nothing worse than what I've heard before, and from scarier men than him."

Matt stood up.

"You're going to run, aren't you?"

"Pastor Darius, you—"

"You've been going to run since we got home from the prison."

Matt nodded.

"Here." Pastor Darius reached into his pocket. He pulled out a few bucks and some change. "It's all I've got. Matthew, if I knew how to keep—"

"It's okay."

Pastor Darius stood up and he wrapped Matt in his long arms. "You have been a blessing to us. You have been a blessing to us. We love you. We love you more than we can tell you how. And wherever you are, you should know that the door of our house is always and forever open to you."

He began to sing softly—a lullaby, or maybe a prayer.

Matt turned and ran out of the church before he would fall on the ground and cry. But the words clung to him like a blessing: "What have I to dread, what have I to fear, / Leaning on the everlasting arms?"

Matt stopped at the house and grabbed the pillowcase. He took five of the bundles out and left them on the dresser. Then he stuffed the pillowcase with what clothes he could fit inside.

He was at the bus station in time to catch a ride to Portland.

SIXTEEN

BEGINNING IN OCTOBER, THE TEACHERS OF ST. Elene's Preparatory Academy for Girls hosted afternoon Tea and Biscuit Conversations on current national and international events. It was an experiment, Mrs. Mott explained, since part of learning to be an Accomplished student at St. Elene's Preparatory Academy for Girls meant engaging with interesting current national and international events.

The Tea and Biscuit Conversations were mandatory.

And all students were expected to wear the regulation St. Elene's uniform.

At dinner, Mrs. Saunders handed out the Tea and Biscuit Conversation assignments to the girls at her table: Meryl Lee, Marian, and Jennifer would be meeting with Mrs. Mott in her rooms at Sherbourne House on Monday, October 21, at 3:50 p.m. "Does everyone know where their assigned rooms are?" asked Mrs. Saunders.

Meryl Lee did indeed know where Sherbourne House was.

But Meryl Lee completely forgot about engaging with interesting current national and international events—until 4:00 p.m., when Meryl Lee, who was wearing her Camillo Junior High sweatshirt and her ratty red sneakers, was wondering why it was so very quiet in Netley.

Then she remembered.

She ran out of Netley. She ran past Newell and across the commons. She ran to Sherbourne House, a building she had never entered. She had no idea where Mrs. Mott's rooms were.

On the way she saw Alethea, who was pushing a silver cart from Greater Hoxne—a heavy silver cart loaded with metal thermoses and pots, a heavy silver cart with a right front wheel that turned sideways and kept shoving the thing off the path and onto the lawn.

"Alethea," said Meryl Lee, "do you know what floor Mrs. Mott's rooms are on?"

Alethea shoved the cart a little harder.

"Now, how would I know that?" she said.

"I was hoping maybe you'd been there."

"You think town girls get invited to Tea and Biscuit Conversations?"

"I meant . . ."

"You don't even know what you meant," said Alethea. "Town girls don't count. They just exist at St. Elene's because they need the money that rich families have lying around. And that's why you can treat them like . . . like they don't count."

She wrestled the silver cart past her.

Meryl Lee looked at her back. "I'm sorry," she said. She didn't quite know why.

Alethea never turned around.

When Meryl Lee finally found Mrs. Mott's rooms in Sherbourne House, she was a little late—a lot late—and everyone looked up from their chairs when she walked in, sort of panting, and all she had to see were Jennifer's pearls to know her Camillo Junior High sweatshirt and ratty red sneakers were not what she was supposed to be wearing. But what could she do? She sat down.

Mrs. Mott handed her a cup of tea.

Tea and Biscuit Conversations are not easy. You have to hold a teacup and saucer made of china as thin and delicate as an eggshell. You have to hold a cookie in a napkin so tiny it wouldn't do a whole lot if you really did have to wipe your mouth with it. (Holling would have been so happy to point this out.) You have to lift the delicate teacup from the delicate saucer every so often to drink the tea—which starts out way too hot to drink anyway. You have to pass a bowl by its tiny handles without letting the little cubes of sugar drop to the floor. And you have to pass a little pitcher of cream with a handle smaller than your pinky—especially Marian Elders's pinky, which was still in a cast. And Meryl Lee had to do all of this without any part of her touching the chair except the very edge of her behind. And her ratty red sneakers had to stay flat on the floor, out in front of everyone, right beside Jennifer's toeless black heels.

This would not have been a problem for Dorothy, who after all had the silver shoes of the Wicked Witch of the East to walk around in instead of ratty red sneakers.

And this might not have been a problem for Mary Stuart, Queen of Scots, either, because she probably didn't own anything that was ratty.

But it was a problem for Meryl Lee, who shuffled her feet back under her chair as far as they could go and still stay flat.

And this wasn't the worst of it.

Later, when Alethea—who did not look at Meryl Lee—brought another hot pot of tea into Mrs. Mott's rooms, Mrs. Mott asked Meryl Lee if she would like to pour, and Meryl Lee said, "Yes, I'd love to," because she couldn't exactly say, "No, it's the last thing on the planet I want to do," even though it was. So she took the teapot from Alethea—who still did not look at her—and started to pour, but the spout didn't work right, so when she poured for Marian

Elders, a little bit of the hot tea went into the cup—but most of it ran down the spout and onto Marian's lap.

It probably was pretty hot, but even so, Meryl Lee thought Marian Elders really didn't need to make that much of a fuss.

After Mrs. Mott came back from taking Marian to Miss Ames—and it was fortunate that the infirmary was on the first floor of Sherbourne House—no one wanted Meryl Lee to pour tea into their cups and so Meryl Lee poured some into her own but the stupid spout still didn't work and tea filled up the saucer. So Meryl Lee stuck a biscuit into the saucer to soak up the tea and it did, except when she picked up the biscuit, the soggy half dropped off and splatted onto Mrs. Mott's antique Persian carpet from Mashhad.

Meryl Lee tried to hide the splattered biscuit with her ratty red sneakers.

And that was all before the conversation.

Which started when Mrs. Mott said to Jennifer, "Would you like to present the first current event, Miss Truro?"

And Jennifer said, "Thank you, Mrs. Mott. I'd be very pleased to do so. I would like to consider what the election of Richard M. Nixon as our next president might mean for the involvement of the United States in the Vietnam War."

That's really what she wants to talk about? Meryl Lee wondered.

But it turned out that everyone in the room seemed to have considered what the election of Richard M. Nixon as the next president might mean for the involvement of the United States in the Vietnam War. And they all had something to say about it.

Everyone except Meryl Lee.

When that was finished, Mrs. Mott turned to Marian—who had come back, a little bit scalded and kind of twitchy and glaring at Meryl Lee accusingly again—and asked for her current event.

And Marian said, "Thank you, Mrs. Mott. I would like to consider the benefits to the United States of a moon landing by the end of the decade." And it seemed to Meryl Lee that everyone had been considering the benefits to the United States of a moon landing by the end of the decade for quite some time.

Everyone except her.

Then Mrs. Mott asked, "Would you like to present your current event, Miss Kowalski?"

Meryl Lee was forced to improvise—but it helped that she knew what Holling would have been thinking about in October.

She said, "Thank you, Mrs. Mott. I would like to consider what trading with the Mets for Tom Seaver might mean to the possibility of the New York Yankees winning another World Series by the end of the decade."

Everyone looked at her as if she had upchucked next to the splattered biscuit on the antique Persian carpet from Mashhad.

And Mrs. Mott said, "I wonder, Miss Kowalski, why you might find this to be of interest in a conversation about current national and international events."

It sure would have been of interest to Holling, she almost said. But she didn't.

Mrs. Mott waited for a moment, then turned to the girl beside Meryl Lee. "Miss Tuthill, would you like to present your current event?"

Lois Tuthill was moved to consider which foreign policy alternatives toward China would be most effective in opening that country up for trade opportunities.

Meryl Lee decided that probably she would not become Accomplished in current national and international events.

<hr />

On the way back to Netley, Meryl Lee passed Alethea on the path again, still with the heavy silver cart, the right front wheel still shoving the thing off into the grass.

Meryl Lee stopped and helped her pull the cart back.

Then, "You could have told me what floor her rooms were on," Meryl Lee said.

"You found out for yourself. Was that so hard?"

"You could have told me."

Alethea shoved against the cart and moved a couple of feet ahead before it leaped toward the grass again. She must have felt Meryl Lee come toward her, because she turned back and said, "I don't need your help."

"I could just—"

"I don't want help from you."

"You don't even know me," said Meryl Lee.

"I know you," said Alethea. "I've been knowing you ever since I got to St. Elene's Preparatory Academy for Girls four years ago. And now I have to bring tea and biscuits to Sherbourne House while you talk about current events like they even matter to you. You think anyone ever asks if they might matter to someone else?"

"Of course they matter to me."

Alethea looked at Meryl Lee like she was—well, like she was such a dope.

"What did you talk about?"

"Vietnam."

"You know anyone in Vietnam right now?"

"Not personally," said Meryl Lee. "But I know Mrs. Bigio, and her husband—"

"Then it doesn't matter to you and maybe you should stop talking."

"Do you?"

"Do I what?"

"Know someone in Vietnam right now?"

Alethea shook her head as if Meryl Lee really, really was such a dope. Then she turned back to the cart and shoved it ahead.

That night, Meryl Lee lay on her bed, reading *The Wonderful Wizard of Oz* again, wondering if she would ever figure out what she could become Accomplished at. Wondering what would ever fill the Blank. She had no idea. She sort of felt like the Joads, driving and driving without ever getting closer to anything. Or like Dorothy, walking on the yellow brick road to the City of Emeralds, walking forever, not really knowing what was in front of her.

Maybe, Meryl Lee thought, she shouldn't be figuring it out. Maybe she should just wait and the answer would come upon her, like a surprise, completely unexpected, something she could never have planned for, something she could never have predicted.

Maybe it would come just like that.

Of course, maybe it would never come to her and she would never be Accomplished at anything.

Probably that.

On Wednesday, Meryl Lee and Marian worked on their Mary Stuart, Queen of Scots, presentation.

Marian, for some reason or other, was keeping her distance.

"It needs some drama, some panache," said Meryl Lee.

"Panache?"

"Like this." Meryl Lee stood up. "As Mary Stuart, Queen of Scots, was led to her execution, she looked askance at her massive murderer and said,

'Accept this handkerchief! With my own hand
for thee I've work'd it in my hours of sadness
and interwoven with my scalding tears: with
this thou'lt bind my eyes.'

And so the burly executioner tied the veil around her eyes, and unseen, he lifted his axe, its sharpened edge stained with the blood of earlier beheadings, and holding it high aloft, he plummeted it against her fair flesh."

Meryl Lee glanced at Marian. She looked a little pale. She was moving even farther away across her room.

"'The blood of earlier beheadings'?" said Marian.

"It's got panache," said Meryl Lee.

Marian swallowed. Her eyes seemed to have forgotten how to blink.

They decided that after the opening scene with panache, Marian would talk about how Mary Stuart was queen of France for a year until her husband died. Then Meryl Lee would talk about how Mary Stuart was married to her cousin until he was killed in an explosion. Then Marian would talk about how Mary Stuart was forced to abdicate. Then Meryl Lee would talk about how Mary Stuart was arrested by Queen Elizabeth and tried for treason. Then together they would act out her beheading, which took the executioner two tries.

"If we used some fake blood," Meryl Lee said, "everything would be a lot more dramatic. I mean, talk about panache."

"Blood?" Marian said.

"There would have to be enough for two tries. Maybe Miss Ames has some real blood we could use."

Marian pale again.

"I could be the executioner," said Meryl Lee. "You can't lift an axe because of your pinky. Or maybe we should get Heidi to play the executioner. *That* would have panache. Have you seen how Heidi slashes her field hockey stick? If I was Mary Stuart, Queen of Scots, and I wanted to get my beheading over with, I'd pick Heidi Kidder as my executioner. It wouldn't take two tries."

Marian said they had better stop since it was almost time for Evening Meal.

She backed out of her room.

Evening Meal was stuffed pork chops and three-bean salad and carrots in light brown sugar. Dessert was lemon cheesecake—a specialty of Mrs. Wyss, who would perhaps share the recipe with the eighth graders later in the semester during Domestic Economy. Polite conversation going on—except Ashley kept calling over to Jennifer and Charlotte from Charlotte from Mrs. Bellamy's table until Mrs. Saunders politely asked Jennifer Hartley Truro to rise and consult *Funk and Wagnalls* on the word *decorum*. The tinkling of forks on plates. Candles on tables. Linen napkins on laps.

The serving girls were in their black dresses and white aprons. Alethea served Meryl Lee's table, her eyes mostly on the floor. Meryl Lee wondered who Alethea knew in Vietnam. Maybe she felt the Blank too, thought Meryl Lee.

Then Alethea leaned down and asked if Miss Kowalski would like her to take her plate. And Meryl Lee felt . . . well, she wasn't sure what.

But she didn't have time to say anything, because Jennifer tapped her glass and Bettye, who was standing by the water pitchers, came over to pour. "From the right," said Jennifer. "Do we have to teach you everything? You pour from the right."

"Yes, Miss Truro," said Bettye. "I'm sorry."

Meryl Lee watched as Bettye moved to Miss Truro's other side and poured from the right.

Shame. That's what Meryl Lee felt. It was shame.

It bothered Meryl Lee more than she could stand that she sat while Bettye and Alethea brought the dishes in and took the dishes out and brought the dishes in and took the dishes out and all the time they were not supposed to meet anyone's eyes and they weren't supposed to speak unless spoken to and they had to say, "Yes, Miss Truro," or "No, Miss Dobrée."

It really bothered Meryl Lee more than she could stand to hear Bettye call Jennifer "Miss Truro" and Charlotte from Charlotte "Miss Dobrée."

It was even worse when Bettye called her "Miss Kowalski."

So Meryl Lee stood. She picked up her tall crystal glass.

And Mrs. Saunders said, "Miss Kowalski?"

Meryl Lee said, "I'm thirsty. I'll just be a second."

Mrs. Saunders said, "One of the servers will bring the water to you."

"I'm fine," Meryl Lee said.

"Miss Kowalski," said Mrs. Saunders.

Meryl Lee thought she saw Mrs. Connolly turn her way, but she walked over to the table where the water pitchers were anyway.

In Greater Hoxne Dining Hall, polite conversation stopped. The tinkling of forks ceased. Meryl Lee could feel eyes all over her.

She walked to the table. Bettye was standing beside it, her eyes on the floor until Meryl Lee came close.

Meryl Lee picked up a pitcher and Bettye whispered, "What are you doing?"

"I'm thirsty," said Meryl Lee.

"I'll bring you the water," said Bettye.

Meryl Lee looked at Bettye. "I'm right here," she said.

Bettye looked at her as though she was afraid.

Meryl Lee filled her glass and put the pitcher down and walked back to her seat.

No one at her table spoke during the rest of the meal. When the upper school students of St. Elene's were dismissed, no one except Heidi said anything to her.

Heidi said, "Sticks down."

"Is a glass of water so important?" said Meryl Lee.

"It's not about the glass of water," said Heidi.

But Mrs. Connolly stopped Heidi and Meryl Lee in Greater Hoxne lobby. "We won't speak about this tonight," she said. "But we will tomorrow morning. Before Chapel. In my office."

"Meryl Lee didn't do—"

"Miss Kidder, please join Miss Kowalski in my office. Eight o'clock."

That night, Meryl Lee laid her head against the windowpane and looked out. She could feel the cold through the glass. The bare trees were black.

Did a glass of water matter so much?

The next morning, a note from Mrs. Connolly had been slid under Meryl Lee's door, notifying her of the appointment with Mrs. Connolly at 8:00 a.m. precisely.

Heidi got one too.

As if they might have forgotten.

So at 8:00 a.m. precisely, they knocked at Mrs. Connolly's door, and when they heard "Enter," they opened it slowly.

Mrs. Connolly was standing behind her desk. The office walls were bright white. The carpet was office gray. A gray file cabinet close behind her. Her glass desktop completely swept—not a book, not a pen, not a single piece of paper.

Mrs. Connolly gestured to two chairs.

Meryl Lee and Heidi sat down.

Immediately Meryl Lee felt her toes starting to lose all feeling.

Mrs. Connolly sat behind her desk. "Miss Kowalski, do you know what rule you violated last night?"

This seemed like a trap, but Meryl Lee said, "I stood up and got a glass of water."

And Mrs. Connolly said, "I did not ask what you did. I asked what rule you violated."

"She got a glass of water," Heidi said.

Meryl Lee coughed a little to warn Heidi, but Heidi didn't want to be warned.

"You violated a social rule," said Mrs. Connolly. "You were shockingly rude and completely careless of the codes of St. Elene's Preparatory Academy for Girls."

"Mrs. Connolly," Meryl Lee said.

"Excuse me," Mrs. Connolly said. "I understand that in this day and age, it seems that authority is to be ignored completely. Your generation calls this 'freedom.' It is not. You are here as a student. Bettye Buckminster is here as a member of the staff. Alethea Browning is here as a member of the staff. You have your place. They have their place—though you have now jeopardized it."

"Their place?" said Meryl Lee.

"They know it and you know it, so do not be impertinent, Miss Kowalski. This is not a state university where the faculty may be cowed by students in beads and blue jeans. This is St. Elene's. Those unable to abide by its code of conduct will be dismissed. And in this case, I promise you that your dismissal would be accompanied by that of Bettye Buckminster and Alethea Browning."

Meryl Lee felt as if she were in a play.

She also felt Resolution.

She stood.

Meryl Lee: That would be unfair, Mrs. Connolly.

Mrs. Connolly: That is not for you to judge.

Meryl Lee: Isn't being at St. Elene's all about learning to decide for ourselves?

Mrs. Connolly: Continued impertinence impresses no one, Miss Kowalski. And you are confusing independence with license.

Meryl Lee: Isn't being at St. Elene's all about deciding what we believe in, and overcoming Obstacles, and becoming Accomplished?

Mrs. Connolly: Within sanctioned limits.

Meryl Lee: And after deciding what we believe in, shouldn't we be acting out of those beliefs?

Mrs. Connolly: Not when those beliefs violate the school's code of conduct.

Meryl Lee: Then maybe the school's code of conduct needs some work.

Heidi: (Coughs a little loudly.)

Mrs. Connolly: (Stands to match Meryl Lee.) As may the character of those who willfully violate it.

Meryl Lee: (Puts her hands on her hips, sort of like Mary Stuart, Queen of Scots, but refusing to bow her head to the block.)

Mrs. Connolly: (Puts her hands on her hips too, sort of like
the executioner eager to lift the axe.)
Heidi: (Coughs a little loudly again.)

But suddenly, as if this really were a play, there was a dramatic knock on the door, and Dr. MacKnockater entered and spoke her lines.

"I'm terribly sorry, Mrs. Connolly, but I have need of both Meryl Lee and Heidi. Are you finished with them?"

Mrs. Connolly's eyes did not leave Meryl Lee's eyes and Meryl Lee's eyes did not leave Mrs. Connolly's eyes. Hands at hips.

"I do not believe we have come to complete understanding," said Mrs. Connolly slowly.

"It is in regards to the vice-presidential luncheon," said Dr. MacKnockater.

"The vice-presidential luncheon is in the spring," Mrs. Connolly said.

"So there is no time to lose," Dr. MacKnockater said. "I hope you don't mind. Reaching complete understanding can take awfully long. Thank you." And she held out her arms to Meryl Lee and Heidi.

As they left, Mrs. Connolly didn't say anything. Meryl Lee didn't say anything. Heidi didn't say anything.

It was pretty quiet.

Meryl Lee walked out with her arms straight down and her fists clenched. If she had been holding Heidi's field hockey stick— forget the glass-top desk. Entire corridors at Lesser Hoxne Hall would now be impassable with rubble.

They walked to Dr. MacKnockater's rooms at Sherbourne,

and while they walked through the cold morning, whenever Meryl Lee or Heidi began to speak, Dr. MacKnockater held up her hand to stop them. She had to hold up her hand several times.

When they reached her rooms, Dr. MacKnockater closed the door and immediately Meryl Lee said, "It's so unfair—" and Dr. MacKnockater held up her hand again and said, "I think a cup of tea. Miss Kidder, if you would get the teacups, and Miss Kowalski the tea bags—just there, in that cupboard—I will put the kettle on."

And ten minutes later, over steaming Earl Grey, Dr. MacKnockater suggested that change comes slowly but inexorably to people of goodwill, that it is possible to be right but to be right at the wrong time and place, that those who have the skill and wit and desire to bring about changed hearts will learn to do it by small and peaceful acts with accumulated power that would be greater than a revolution. And, she pointed out, when all the risk is being taken by Bettye Buckminster and Alethea Browning, maybe we should hold back a little and wait for St. Elene's to catch up to the rest of the country—which, she said, is heading in the right direction, even if it is not heading there very quickly.

"It isn't, is it?" Meryl Lee said.

"No, it isn't," she said. "But it's still the right direction."

Meryl Lee told her she would think about this.

Dr. MacKnockater said she would pour again.

And then, with their second cup of tea and calm spirits, Dr. MacKnockater told Heidi Kidder and Meryl Lee Kowalski that they were now appointed to the organizing committee for the vice-presidential luncheon. "I would rather not have it appear that I deceived Mrs. Connolly," she said.

———※———

Meryl Lee wasn't exactly in the mood for field hockey practice that afternoon, Coach Rowlandson could tell. "Meryl Lee Kowalski, you run as if about to commit homicide."

"I might," she said.

"You can't," Coach Rowlandson said.

"Why not?"

"Because it would be against the laws of God and man, and they'd send you away to Sing Sing, and I am considering you for right wing next season."

"Right wing?"

"And not only that, but what will happen to the revolution at St. Elene's?"

Meryl Lee looked at Coach Rowlandson.

"What do you mean?"

"I mean the rise of the proletariat. Imagine, girls pouring their own water. What will come of that? Girls making their own beds? Girls earning their own money for their own pearl necklaces? Girls thinking of getting jobs?"

"I wasn't thinking of starting a revolution at St. Elene's."

"What you did was brave and heroic and full of heart, and maybe a revolution wouldn't be such a bad thing. But you should still run with your hands unclenched."

Meryl Lee kept her hands unclenched, and when practice was over and she was about to head back to Netley, Coach Rowlandson said, "Sticks down, Kowalski."

And Meryl Lee thought, *Maybe Coach Rowlandson is a good egg.*

The last week of October, and now the sun was rising up in a fog just before breakfast and setting in long yellow shadows before Evening Meal. The leaves of the St. Elene's maples were mostly gone and the grass was turning that gray-green color that means it's done for the year. Dr. MacKnockater had been patrolling the wall with two gardeners, setting burlap over the azaleas, pruning the hydrangeas back, turning the soil around the perennial beds.

She finished just in time. That same week, a cold, drizzly, almost icy rain settled over St. Elene's Preparatory Academy for Girls and decided it would stay for a few days, so that the girls scurried back and forth across the campus hidden by umbrellas and hoods, and sometimes by the notebooks they held over their heads. The rain pulled all the color out of any leaf still hanging on, and then drearied the clapboard buildings with a patina of gray and chilled everyone straight to the bone—to the bone!

And maybe that's why everything that happened that week was so bleak and cold.

On Monday the students of St. Elene's Preparatory Academy for Girls received their first quarter evaluations—which weren't all bleak for Meryl Lee, but didn't quite warm her heart. Some of the comments were okay—"Miss Kowalski shows creditable skills in Algebra; I anticipate a strong year for her," wrote Mr. Wheelock—and some of the comments were not really okay—"Miss Kowalski has yet to show the kind of discernment that will lead to success in this course of study," wrote Mrs. Connolly—and some were impossible to figure out—"Meryl Lee is just a cupcake to have in class," wrote Mrs. Wyss.

On Tuesday, it was so drizzly and dreary that Meryl Lee hoped that field hockey practice would be called off—but drizzles and dreariness didn't matter to Coach Rowlandson. It would have to be a whole lot drizzlier and a whole lot drearier before she'd call off a day of field hockey practice. So when it was finished, Meryl Lee and Heidi were looking pretty drizzly and dreary themselves, and they were coming back to Netley carrying the huge canvas bag with the extra field hockey sticks and maybe they were not looking as young ladies should, which is probably what Mrs. Kellogg thought, since when she saw them she said that tours for prospective students and their parents were heading to Netley Dormitory right then and could Meryl Lee and Heidi enter through the back instead of through the lobby? So they lugged the canvas bag all the way around to the back and there was Alethea, just coming out of the dorm to get her ride home on the train.

And Meryl Lee thought *she* looked drizzly and dreary and exhausted.

But Alethea pulled open the back door and stood holding it for them. The whole time, she looked down at the ground.

Meryl Lee was ashamed.

"Thank you," she said.

Alethea did not answer.

She only looked down at the ground.

Meryl Lee walked in like she was supposed to.

But she was still ashamed.

The door closed behind them.

Then on Wednesday afternoon, Ashley and Charlotte from Charlotte came into the room and Jennifer announced that the Knock might be on her way out. How did Jennifer come upon this information? Because her father had read a letter protesting the Vietnam War that appeared in the *New York Times,* written by one Dr. Nora MacKnockater, Headmistress of St. Elene's Preparatory Academy for Girls.

At this news, shrieks of horror from Ashley and Charlotte from Charlotte.

And, Dr. Nora MacKnockater said Hubert H. Humphrey—the

Democrat!—was the candidate best suited to get the United States out of the war.

More shrieks of horror.

And, Dr. Nora MacKnockater said the draft was immoral, almost as immoral as the war itself!

Even more shrieks of horror.

So, said Jennifer, her father was going to speak with Mr. Lloyd C. Allen to see what could be done, and what he wanted done, she said, would get done.

Meryl Lee said, "The United States Constitution grants us freedom of speech. Dr. MacKnockater has the right to say what she wants."

Jennifer and Ashley and Charlotte from Charlotte looked at her, then looked back at one another.

"Maybe the Knock will be gone by Christmas," said Ashley.

Charlotte from Charlotte shook her head and her auburn curls flounced.

Meryl Lee decided to go to Putnam. But the whole time there, she couldn't stop thinking about Dr. MacKnockater.

Then on Thursday—still drizzling, still dreary, as if it might always be drizzling and dreary, forever and ever—Meryl Lee and Marian Elders presented their report on Mary Stuart, Queen of Scots. They had been practicing swinging an executioner's axe (really a shovel, but if they hid it until the last second, they figured no one would notice), and they were ready to perform the great execution scene. Here's what Marian Elders as Mary Stuart, Queen of Scots, was supposed to say with panache:

As a sinner, I am truly conscious of having often offended
my Creator and I beg Him to forgive me, but as a Queen

and Sovereign, I am aware of no fault or offence for which I have to render account to anyone here below.

It was not exactly what Mary Stuart, Queen of Scots, said *right* before she died, but Meryl Lee thought it would be dramatic and heart-rending—which anyone should appreciate when panache is shouting at you like that.

Then Marian was supposed to kneel and bare her neck and Meryl Lee was supposed to raise the shovel and hack away. Twice.

Except when Marian was supposed to say the lines—and they'd practiced a million times, and she really did have panache—Ashley raised her hand and said out loud, "So, Mary Stuart had acne all over her face? Is that true, Mrs. Saunders?"

Complete silence, and everyone looked at Marian Elders— who did have acne all over her face—and then everyone except Meryl Lee started to laugh, and Marian turned red and redder, and so everyone laughed more and more, until Mrs. Saunders said the class had to come back to order and she told Marian to continue, please.

But Marian couldn't. She put her hands over her face and Mrs. Saunders said, "Miss Elders, please continue," and then, "Miss Elders, you really must continue now," but Marian kept her hands over her face and finally Mrs. Saunders said she and Meryl Lee had already given sufficient information and "You may both take your seats," and they did.

But Marian kept her hands over her face the rest of the hour.

And Meryl Lee thought, *I am truly conscious of having often wished to grind Ashley into the muddiest patch of our hockey field and it would be no fault or offense for which I have to render account to anyone here below.*

That afternoon, as October thought about lugging its drizzly, dreary self into November, Jennifer got another letter from Alden, and she was still not willing to share any of dear Alden's secrets, except that every letter he sent she held to her heart and she told Ashley and Charlotte from Charlotte that Alden said he adored her and he was so looking forward to Thanksgiving and then Christmas by the Scottish loch and then spring when she could come to Brussels and he knew the best cafés in Brussels since he'd spent so much time in Brussels and like many of the aristocracy he had a mole shaped like a fleur-de-lis (*What is a fleur-de-lis?* Meryl Lee wondered) and it was on a special place on him. Then Jennifer started to giggle and she said he showed her once and she couldn't tell anybody about it but he was wearing a kilt when he showed her, and then Ashley and Charlotte from Charlotte giggled so hard they had to hold pillows over their mouths.

Meryl Lee wished Jennifer would stop not sharing their secrets.

It was said of Mary Stuart, Queen of Scots, that "her charms of beauty and genius, that made her such a fascinating woman, unfitted her for the throne of a rude nation." Meryl Lee thought she knew how Mary Stuart, Queen of Scots, felt.

The beginning of November was still drizzle and drear, but a few days in, the drear was all wiped away and the sky was a polished blue without a single streak. Not a cloud anywhere. The sun strong and warm, and the trees, even though they had lost their leaves and were dark with the wet, leaned into the light and stretched.

Meryl Lee could hardly wait for the afternoon.

Past Newell Chapel and past the commons, past the three white barns and the sheds and the shady maples and the rows of painted fences. Then steeply down the footpath and through the birches and firs.

Then, just as suddenly as before, the shore.

She didn't expect the boy to be there. After all, she didn't even know his name—or where he lived—or anything except that he liked skipping stones.

So she was surprised when she went down to the shore and found him, wrapped tightly in a pea jacket.

Sitting on the cold rocks.

Crying like the whole world was wrong.

Crying . . . as if he saw the Blank too.

When he saw Meryl Lee, the boy didn't say anything. Nothing at all. He just stood, wiped his face, and scrambled up the shore ridge.

Meryl Lee watched him, then turned and headed back to St. Elene's, trying to figure out why she felt as if she'd just been kicked in the stomach.

SEVENTEEN

1966–67

WHEN MERYL LEE CLIMBED DOWN TO THE SHORE that early November afternoon, Matt was remembering his year in Portland.

He was remembering walking out of the bus station late that first night, alone, and being passed by all the other passengers who had been on the bus and who were now laughing and holding hands with the people who had been waiting for them, and he came out onto a street he'd never seen before and headed in a direction that led to he had no idea where.

That fall, that winter, that spring, he did exactly what Leonidas Shug had trained him to do. Even though he had the stuffed pillowcase, he did it to stupid tourists and filthy drunk lobstermen and gift shop owners from away and even once to a reporter working on a story about the homeless in Portland. He lived in doorways and small abandoned mills and in a junior high over Christmas break and in the public library on Sundays because they always left that one basement window unlocked. Usually he was alone, but sometimes he huddled with others against the cold—and when he went out for food, they were always surprised at how much he brought back along with the sweatshirts and scarves and hats and gloves that he said he'd lifted.

Until a late spring night when that cop started walking after him, then running after him, then sprinting after him, and Matt—carrying the pillowcase, since he'd been looking for a new spot—headed downhill since fat guys couldn't run downhill and he dodged into thin streets toward the water. Already every shop was pretty much closed, with shop owners locking their doors and getting ready to head home. Matt turned down Commercial Street and found a chowder house that was about to lock up too, and the owner didn't look too pleased to see a kid come in just before closing. But Matt sat down with his back to the window and the owner served up a plate of fish and chips with a bowl of chowder thrown in—since the chowder wouldn't be any good in the morning anyway, he said—and he watched the kid eat as if he were in a race.

"You can slow down," he said. "I'll stay open till you're done."

Matt nodded and kept on.

"You from around here?" the owner said.

Matt looked up at him.

"I'm just asking, kid. It's not like I'm a cop or anything."

Matt wasn't worried about him being a cop.

"Okay. You don't have to tell me. It's none of my business anyway."

"I'm from New Bedford," Matt said.

The owner smiled and gave a low laugh. "Sure you are. Listen, you wipe down the tables and help me do up the dishes, and we'll call it even."

"I can pay," said Matt.

"No one said you couldn't."

That night, Matt wiped down the tables and helped do up the dishes—of which there were plenty—and he carried the garbage out past the waiting seagulls, and he helped set all the chairs up on the tables and swept the floor, and when they were finished, the owner, whose name was Mr. Tush—"Really?" Matt said, and "Shut up, kid. You don't know how many people got broken noses making a joke about my name"—said, "I've got an apartment upstairs. That's where I sleep. There's a rollaway in the storeroom down here if you want it, and maybe a job as kitchen boy starting tomorrow morning if you want that."

Matt did. Both of them.

"It depends on if the Myrnas like you, though."

"The Myrnas?" Matt said.

"Myrna One's the real cook around here. Do what she says, don't mess with her knives, keep things clean without her asking, and she'll give you a pass. But, kiddo, mess with her knives, and you'll be lucky you don't get one stuck in your rear."

"And Myrna Two?"

"She'll come down to check you out when she feels like it." Then Mr. Tush turned out most of the lights and went back into the kitchen. Matt could hear him take the stairs, and then he heard every creak of the wide floorboards above him as Mr. Tush settled into his apartment.

Matt waited for Myrna Two for a while, wondering, and then he pulled out the rollaway and stuffed his pillowcase at the back of the storeroom behind sacks that looked like they hadn't been moved in a very long time. He pushed the bed in front of the sacks and below the window, which was open to the harbor. Through it, he could hear the low moaning of the tide, the bumping of boats against the tires strung along the docks, the straining of ropes, the quiet plashing of sluggish waves against hulls.

Matt lay down; he took off his shirt but nothing else since Myrna Two might come in at any moment—even though the sounds from the creaking floorboards above had stilled. He waited, and waited, and the sea's moaning was so quiet and calm, and far away a buoy sounded and sounded and sounded with the coming in of the tide, and then something jumped up on Matt's legs and he screeched and pulled them up and when he looked down, there was a tabby, sitting at the end of the rollaway, licking her left paw and watching him as if she had been there the whole time.

"Myrna Two?" said Matt.

She put her paw down. She waited a moment, then stood, held her tail straight up, and walked onto Matt's chest. She lay down and stretched her nails into him a little bit, like cats do. Then she held her head up, waiting to be scratched—which Matt did until she'd had enough, and she closed her eyes and fell asleep on him.

Matt didn't want her to leave.

He didn't move the whole night.

In the morning, Matt woke when someone kicked the end of the rollaway.

"Your bed is blocking my way to the flour," she said.

Matt sat up, blinking. "Huh?"

She looked at him.

"Lay back down," she said. She went toward the kitchen and came back with a small red bottle and a wet towel. "You never know where Myrna Two's been," she said, "and if you don't get something on those scratches, they could get infected." She took the stopper out of the red bottle and approached.

"Wait a minute," said Matt. "Isn't that going to—"

It did: it stung like anything. But Myrna One told him to stop being a baby and so he stopped but every time she dropped the iodine onto his chest, he squirmed more than a little. And when she was done, she threw him the wet towel—which was cold—and told him to get washed up and they had the chairs to take down and the tables to wipe and set and the menus to put out and when did he plan to move that dang bed so she could get to the flour?

"When the sun comes up," said Matt.

Myrna One looked at her watch. "It's up over the Azores, so let's get going. Breakfast crowd doesn't like to wait."

That morning, while Myrna Two patrolled around the legs of the breakfast crowd, Matt washed and dried more dishes than he had used in his whole life, and when he wasn't washing dishes, he was hauling them in from the dining area and wiping down tables and sometimes, when Mr. Tush couldn't keep up or when he had to cook the hash—which only he could do right, according to the breakfast crowd—Matt even took orders:

"Scrape three, kid."

"Huh?"

"Scrape three"—spoken more slowly.

"Um—"

"Just tell Myrna One that Darryl wants his regular."

"Okay."

And after the breakfast crowd there was the brunch crowd—which Myrna One didn't like much. Neither did Myrna Two. They were mostly tourists who wore the bright shirts and stupid hats they'd just bought in gift shops and they were loud and eager and liked to order cinnamon buns, which Myrna One didn't think were real food. After the brunch crowd was the lunch crowd, who were still mostly tourists and who ordered mostly hamburgers even though *it's the freaking Chowder House!*—as Myrna One pointed out to Matt. And then there was a break until the supper crowd, a lot of whom were the same as the breakfast crowd, who had been out fishing and lobstering all day and who needed some good thick chowder to stick to their ribs.

Myrna One loved these guys. She called every one by name when they came in.

Myrna Two loved them too—maybe because they let her jump up on the table and lick their chowder spoons and sometimes the bowls.

Mr. Tush joked around with the supper crowd like he'd been a fisherman himself—which, Matt found out later, he had been—and they pointed at the scrawny kid helping him and told him they could use that guy for bait and Mr. Tush said they couldn't have him and Matt hoped they really were only joking.

That night, Myrna One told Matt he'd done all right for a scrawny kid, and then she said, "Let's get some more iodine on those scratches."

"I can do it," said Matt.

"I know you can do it," said Myrna One. "The question is whether you will."

"Promise," said Matt.

She handed him the bottle. "If you don't take care of those, then they'll start to ooze and pus and you'll die an agonizing death and it'll be your own stupid fault."

"I said I'd do it."

"I'll check in the morning. And, kiddo, in case you die from infection overnight, you should know you didn't do so bad today."

She patted him on the cheek. "See you tomorrow." She pointed at the iodine. "Take care of those scratches"—and Matt watched her go out the door.

Later, when the tables were wiped and the chairs put up on them and the floor swept and all the dishes done, Mr. Tush said, "The Myrnas like you."

Matt reached down and picked up Myrna Two. He held her against his chest and stroked her gray fur as she purred and purred.

"I guess you can stay, if you want," said Mr. Tush, and he headed upstairs.

That's pretty much how every day went that whole summer—breakfast crowd, brunch crowd, lunch crowd, supper crowd again—except for Sundays, when Mr. Tush closed the Chowder House and took Matt and Myrna One and Myrna Two out in his trawler, *Iodine.* ("Guess where that name comes from," said Mr. Tush, and Myrna One hit him.) They chugged out beyond the pilings and along the coast and around the islands, stopping in the calm to fish and lay a string of lobster traps—just one string, since Mr. Tush didn't have a license and technically shouldn't have been laying any traps at all. He taught Matt how to tie a buoy hitch, and how to be careful laying the line since the sea could pull the last traps down, and how to handle the lobsters—"Stroke them right here, underneath, and they'll be calm as clams"—and how to band their claws. He taught Matt when to lay in the troughs and when to head the bow into the waves and when to speed up in the rougher water so as to give Myrna One a scare. Mr. Tush showed Matt how to read the sea but to remember that the sea was as changeable as a cat—"Present company excluded"—and could betray you when she felt like it and maybe that's why he loved her so much.

Dang, thought Matt, *Georgie would have loved this.*

How he would have.

It turned out that there were a bunch of kitchen boys on Commercial Street—Davey from the Brothers' Fish and Chips, Lew from the Green Apple, Donny from the Clam Shack, Chad from the Lobster Company, Jesse from Shrimp 'n Stuff—and they all came in one afternoon and Mr. Tush threw them some root beers and told them to take the scrawny kid down to the harbor. They did—and after that they all met up down there on their two o'clock breaks. They showed Matt the best place to dive in and how to do a flip, the safest place to skinny-dip, the boat that the girl lived on that Chad was going to marry someday (and they waited for her to come on deck but she never did), the back door to the Biggest Dip (with an owner who gave free cones to local kitchen boys—but only single scoops), the alley where they could run bases, the best place on the shore to find flat rocks that they could skip out into the harbor (Davey was the best one at that), the orchard where Mr. McBride grew his sweet apples (he didn't care if local kids picked them). It was the first time Matt had been with a group of boys he didn't have to fight.

The two o'clock break hours would go by like lightning.

So did August.

And when August was almost at an end, Mr. Tush and Myrna One began to ask the questions Matt knew they would ask. And he hated like anything to tell them he had an aunt down to New Bedford and she'd wanted him to have an adventure and so she'd given him a ticket to Portland to let him make his own way for the summer and how his school back home didn't start until the end of September and maybe it was even the beginning of October and it was a vocational school for boys who wanted to learn how to man a fishing boat and maybe he could stay a while beyond the end of September or the beginning of October and do, like, a vocational sort of program with Mr. Tush.

Mr. Tush would look at him.

Myrna One would look at him.

"How much of that malarkey is true?" Mr. Tush would say.

Matt would shrug.

"So what's the name of the school?"

"New Bedford Junior High."

"What's the name of your aunt?"

"Helen."

"What's her last name?"

"I don't remember."

"You don't remember your aunt's last name?"

"We never use it."

"It's not Coffin?"

"Something else. I can't remember."

And Mr. Tush and Myrna One would look at each other, then at Matt.

"We could just beat it out of him," Myrna One would say.

"I don't know. All that chowder this summer, looks like it's put some meat on his bones."

"We could still beat it out of him," Myrna One would say. "I'd hit him with a chair first."

"We'll do it after the supper crowd," Mr. Tush would say. "Have the iodine ready."

With September, the brunch crowd and the lunch crowd got smaller and smaller—the tourists were going home—and some of the boats were pulled up into dry dock, including the one that Chad's future wife lived on. Then the restaurants began to shut down—first the Green Apple because it had a stupid name, then the Brothers' Fish and Chips, then the Clam Shack, then Shrimp 'n Stuff, then the Lobster Company. Davey, Lew, Donny, Jesse, and Chad started team practices at school and weren't around much— and the water was getting way too cold to skinny-dip. The Chowder House stayed open because, Myrna One said, every fisherman in town would have their heads if they dared to close, but by Labor Day there wasn't much at all to do between the breakfast crowd and the supper crowd.

And then, late one night, after the chairs had been put on the tables and the floor swept, Mr. Tush and Myrna One sat him down. Matt took Myrna Two onto his lap and stroked her as she purred. And Myrna One said quietly, "Matt, it's time to tell us the truth."

But he knew that if he did, if he did, Leonidas Shug would find out where Matt was. Somehow he'd find out.

He'd find Mr. Tush.

He would find the Myrnas.

"I'll tell you everything in the morning," Matt said.

"Everything?" Myrna One said.

"Everything."

That night, he packed what he owned into the pillowcase. He slept a couple of hours, and then he gathered Myrna Two off his chest, dressed, and walked to the Portland bus station.

He bought a ticket for anywhere north.

He was gone before the sun was up over the Azores.

—— »« ——

That's what he was thinking about down on the shore when Meryl Lee found him.

He missed Mr. Tush and the Myrnas like he'd miss his eyes—which were crying, but so what?

When he saw Meryl Lee, he stood, wiped his face, shrugged his pea jacket up, and climbed the shore ridge—all without a word.

EIGHTEEN

ON THE SECOND MONDAY OF NOVEMBER, MRS. MOTT
held her next Tea and Biscuit Conversation.

The afternoon before, Meryl Lee had asked Bettye to help her
practice pouring tea in Netley's kitchen—because, said Meryl Lee,
she was petrified about what could happen.

"This sort of worries me," said Bettye. "You poured from that
pitcher, and guess what almost happened."

"I know. I'm sorry," said Meryl Lee. "It's just that I'm desperate."

"Let me see you pour," said Bettye.

Bettye watched the hot tea running underneath the spout, then
splashing to the floor. "Everyone in the room should be petrified,"
she said. "I'll show you—for safety's sake."

She did, and by the morning of Mrs. Mott's November Tea and
Biscuit Conversation, Meryl Lee was pretty sure she was prepared.

Current national or international event: Ready. The likely
effects on the Vietnam War if Hubert H. Humphrey were elected
president of the United States (it seemed appropriate for Veter-
ans Day).

Required St. Elene's Academy uniform since this was an official school activity: Ready.

Non-ratty non-red shoes: Ready.

Strategy for pouring tea: Probably okay because of Bettye's lesson, but maybe she wouldn't have to. In fact, the more she thought about it, the more unlikely it seemed that Mrs. Mott would ask her to pour the tea.

Strategy for the teacup: Ready. Have it filled only halfway.

Strategy for the biscuit: Ready. She wouldn't take one.

Everything was ready.

But as Dr. MacKnockater says, sometimes in life there are Obstacles.

Late that afternoon, back at Netley, Meryl Lee told Bettye that usually her hiccups lasted only a couple of minutes. Never as long as they had lasted at Mrs. Mott's November Tea and Biscuit Conversation. And never that loud before.

And it had been bad luck hiccupping when she was passing a cup to Marian Elders, and so a drop or two might have fallen on her and probably because Marian remembered what happened last time, you can understand why she stood up like that and the teapot got knocked out of Meryl Lee's hands and the tea went a little over Lois Tuthill but mostly over Marian.

It was too bad the teapot was so full. But it showed foresight that Mrs. Mott had thought to allow the tea to cool a bit before letting Meryl Lee get her hands on it.

Two weeks before Thanksgiving break, Mrs. Connolly decided to give her students an Obstacle. They were to study and memorize a passage of no fewer than two hundred and fifty words from the book they were currently studying in order to develop taste and discernment. Then, they were to present those two hundred and fifty words interpretively in front of the entire middle school. "This will not only teach you how to read attentively and choose judiciously," said Mrs. Connolly, "but it will also develop poise."

But when she heard what Marian and Heidi were preparing, Meryl Lee wondered about the assignment leading to apoplexy more than poise.

Marian was preparing the climax of *Oedipus Rex* because it was so bloody and had panache.

This surprised Meryl Lee some.

Heidi was preparing the scene in *Moby-Dick* when the white whale smashed the *Pequod* to bits. "It's the best part of the whole six hundred pages," she said.

This did not surprise Meryl Lee at all.

Meryl Lee wasn't sure the Tin Woodman scene from *The Wonderful Wizard of Oz* would hold up. The most exciting part was when Toto bit the Tin Woodman, but even then, Toto hurt only his teeth. And the whole business of the Tin Woodman groaning for a year and no one ever coming to help seemed sort of pale next to the *Pequod* getting smashed and sinking beneath the waves.

She decided to look for a more profound passage.

She tried to do this at night in Putnam Library, but it was difficult since she was struggling to find a way of sitting that didn't hurt quite so much. The reason she was trying to do that had a lot to do with the very last field hockey scrimmage, when Heidi, determined to do her all at the end, swung her very large stick and flat out walloped Meryl Lee in a very unfashionable place.

The next morning, Meryl Lee's very sore unfashionable place was a whole spectrum of bright and dark colors that she was glad no one else could see, and she was walking around like an unoiled

Tin Woodman since every left step hurt like anything. When Heidi saw her, she hugged her and wouldn't stop saying how sorry she was. When Bettye saw her, she offered to bring over a hot water bottle. When Mrs. Saunders saw her, she told her to "straighten up, young lady."

Meryl Lee did the best she could.

From Jennifer, no response to her suffering. Meryl Lee figured that if she came in with blood erupting out of her eyes, Jennifer would hardly notice. And if she did, she'd worry only about blood getting all over her green satin duvet.

Latest conversation in their room:

Ashley: Jennifer says when Alden comes to visit her for Thanksgiving, he's going to give her one of his great-aunt's jewels!

Charlotte: (Squeals, then places hands over her heart.) I can't believe it!

Jennifer: It's a ruby ring that's been in his family since Mary Stuart, Queen of Scots.

Charlotte: It's almost like you're engaged.

Meryl Lee: (Rolling her eyes.) It doesn't mean they're engaged. It's just a gift.

Jennifer: Do your eyes always roll around like marbles?

Meryl Lee: Only when they need to.

Jennifer: "Only when they need to." How clever.

Meryl Lee's spectacular colors lasted almost a week; the soreness lasted a little bit longer. But you can put up with a lot if you know escape is imminent. They were only days away from Thanksgiving break. Just days! Soon, her mother and father would come to St. Elene's to pick her up, and they would drive away through the main gate, past the wall and its poison ivy vines, and they would head back home to Long Island.

She didn't even care that Jennifer would be riding in her family limousine.

Meryl Lee was going home.

On Wednesday, the day before Thanksgiving break, Mrs. Connolly's students gave their oral recitations of two-hundred-and-fifty-word passages. Mrs. Connolly was in a happy mood; she had been in a happy mood for the past three weeks, because the election was over and Richard M. Nixon would be the next president of the United States of America and in Chapel she announced that he would be the savior of our nation to boot. Truth and righteousness, she said, had triumphed.

Meryl Lee thought that Dr. MacKnockater had not looked convinced.

So Mrs. Connolly was smiling as the entire upper school of St. Elene's Preparatory Academy for Girls gathered in Lesser Hoxne Recital Hall, where tradition coats the paneled walls. Dr. MacKnockater and Mrs. Connolly sat in two upholstered chairs on the stage, and one by one Mrs. Connolly called the presenters down. "Poise, girls," said Mrs. Connolly. And they were all poised, especially when they walked from their seats to the podium, because the floor was polished wood and sort of steep and everyone could hear every step.

As each girl positioned herself behind the podium, she handed Mrs. Connolly her book with the passage marked, and Mrs.

Connolly turned the pages and studied the passage as if she had written it herself, and then she set the book on her lap, looked over her glasses, and said, "Begin, please."

Meryl Lee wondered if everyone wanted to throw up—like she did.

Heidi was positioned before Marian and Meryl Lee, and she got her reading perfect—except Mrs. Connolly arched her eyebrows at Heidi's obvious delight in destruction, which, she said after Heidi finished, had made her sound inappropriately mannish, and she wished that Heidi had brought the piece to her for approval.

"I'm sorry, but was that on the list of requirements?" said Heidi.

Silence in the room.

"Courtesy should have been enough motivation," said Mrs. Connolly.

Then Mrs. Connolly called Marian, who forgot to hand Mrs. Connolly her copy of *Oedipus Rex* and Mrs. Connolly was already annoyed so she said, "Pay attention, Miss Elders," and that made Marian nervous and she dropped the book and then she bent to pick it up again and her glasses fell off and she bent again to pick them up and Mrs. Connolly grabbed at the book but the marker had fallen out and she said, "What page will you be reciting from?" and Marian didn't know the page number so Mrs. Connolly handed the book back and Marian put on her glasses and found the page and she handed the book back and by then everyone was laughing and Mrs. Connolly did her studying-of-the-passage thing and said, "Begin, please," but Marian was so nervous now that she didn't hear her and so Mrs. Connolly said, "Do you want to pass this course or not, Miss Elders? Begin, please."

Marian was about to cry.

But she looked out and saw Meryl Lee—who winked—and Heidi—she winked too—and Marian took a deep breath and began.

It was bloody.

It was really bloody.

But it had panache.

Even Mrs. Connolly clapped.

Marian almost danced off the stage.

Then Mrs. Connolly called out, "Miss Kowalski," and Meryl Lee walked up to the podium and handed *The Wonderful Wizard of Oz* to Mrs. Connolly, who held it at a distance as if it were infectious, and Meryl Lee waited to be told that she should begin, and just when she began with "All the same," a marble began to roll down from the top of Lesser Hoxne Recital Hall.

Really, everyone could hear it on the steep, polished wood floor. Meryl Lee stopped. The marble hit a chair leg, bounced off, hit another chair leg and poised there a moment before starting down again, and it rolled, bumping against chair legs, and stopped somewhere halfway down, probably stuck. People were trying not to laugh, but it was kind of hard.

Meryl Lee thought about executioners' axes and two tries, but Mrs. Connolly said, "Poise, Miss Kowalski," and "Continue, please."

Meryl Lee took another deep breath and started again—"All the same"—but she didn't finish the sentence before the marble came unstuck, and it rolled down, and rolled down, and the girls started to laugh, loudly now, and Meryl Lee glanced at Heidi—who was looking very grim about the mouth—and Mrs. Connolly said loudly, "Please, Miss Kowalski. Poise," again, and Meryl Lee tried, but finally the marble smacked into the stage and stopped and the girls clapped and laughed.

Heidi stood and looked back at the top row.

Meryl Lee thought that if Heidi ever looked at her the way she was looking at the top row, she would definitely head for Canada.

"Miss Kidder," said Mrs. Connolly, "you are to sit down, please."

"You don't think that was done on purpose?" said Heidi.

"I do not. Miss Kowalski," Mrs. Connolly said, "I remind you that this performance is not insignificant in regard to your quarter's grade. Please begin."

Heidi sat down like a cannon resting before a blast. And Meryl Lee looked at Mrs. Connolly, who sat as if nothing at all had happened. Then she looked up at the top row, where Jennifer and Ashley and Charlotte from Charlotte smiled oh so sweetly, and there was the Blank, coming down the rows toward her, and then onto the stage, and then to the very podium, and Meryl Lee turned to look at Dr. Nora MacKnockater, who sat forward in her chair, almost as if she would stand but not quite, and who was watching her carefully.

And suddenly Meryl Lee knew exactly what to do. Exactly. She felt Resolution come into her. Moving as if in a dream, she parted the Blank like a thick sea fog, and she stepped through, and she began.

"All the same," said the Scarecrow, "I shall ask for brains instead of a heart; for a fool would not know what to do with a heart if he had one."

"I shall take the heart," returned the Tin Woodman; "for brains do not make one happy, and happiness is the best thing in the world."

Dorothy did not say anything, for she was puzzled to know which of her two friends was right.

She spoke on, and it was quiet in Lesser Hoxne Recital Hall. Quiet as Meryl Lee finished. Quiet as Meryl Lee walked back up to her seat. And quiet until she sat down, when there was quiet clapping.

At the end, Mrs. Connolly came to the podium and she thanked the girls for their hard work and wished them all a happy Thanksgiving holiday and then dismissed the upper school. Dr. Nora MacKnockater went to the recital hall door first, and as the girls walked by, she congratulated them on their good work too. As Meryl Lee walked toward that door, it seemed to her that again and again Dr. MacKnockater's gaze would come over the heads of the other girls and fall fully upon her. And the gaze felt heavier and heavier as Meryl Lee came nearer and nearer the door. And when she got there, she looked up, and the Awful Dignity *was* looking at her, looking right at her, and Dr. MacKnockater said, "Would you please wait outside for me, Miss Kowalski?"

So Meryl Lee waited outside the auditorium while Heidi and Marian walked on to Netley, looking over their shoulders to see what disaster was about to befall Meryl Lee, and then Meryl Lee was walking slightly behind Dr. MacKnockater to one side of Lesser Hoxne's lobby while all the girls looked at her as if *she* had caused a whole lot of commotion. But Dr. MacKnockater looked around in all her Awful Dignity until the girls fled and then she said, "Miss Kowalski, your presentation was powerful. Thank you."

"It's just *The Wonderful Wizard of Oz*," said Meryl Lee.

"Good books have questions for us to ponder. That is what all good art does. So, for example, in your passage, which assessment is correct? That of the Scarecrow or that of the Tin Woodman?"

Meryl Lee thought. "Right now, I guess I think it's Dorothy's," she said.

Dr. MacKnockater considered this. "For the present," she said finally, "that is a good answer. But only for the present."

"How will I know when I have the right answer?" said Meryl Lee.

"Is there only one right answer?"

"Isn't there always one right answer?" said Meryl Lee.

Dr. MacKnockater shook her head.

Meryl Lee considered this. "There can be more than one right answer?"

Dr. MacKnockater smiled the Awful Dignity smile. Then, "I have something to tell you," she said, "that will be a disappointment. I have received a call from your mother, who informs me that she and your father have scheduled legal appointments that they absolutely must keep, and they will be unable to come to St. Elene's to pick you up for Thanksgiving."

Meryl Lee looked at Dr. MacKnockater. "You mean they're not coming?"

"I'm sorry, yes. That is what I mean."

The Blank, right there, without warning.

Right there.

"I don't understand," said Meryl Lee.

"The heart is more difficult to understand than the brain," said Dr. MacKnockater quietly. She took Meryl Lee's hand in her own. "Miss Kowalski, as your plans have unexpectedly changed, may I ask this? It would give me great pleasure if you would come to my house tomorrow afternoon and share Thanksgiving dinner with me."

"You're inviting me to Thanksgiving dinner?"

"I am."

"Are my parents all right?" Meryl Lee said.

"You will see them at Christmas. They will explain everything."

Meryl Lee looked through the glass doors of Lesser Hoxne. The clouds of the morning had been sheared away, and across the commons, the girls of St. Elene's were skipping in the sudden sunlight. Just outside the doors, Heidi and Marian were waiting for her.

"This is an Obstacle, isn't it?" Meryl Lee said.

Dr. MacKnockater nodded. "It is."

Still holding the Awful Dignity's hand, Meryl Lee felt a small, small bit of Resolution remaining, that same Resolution that had stayed her so well on the stage. She decided to use it all in one shot: "I should love to come to Thanksgiving dinner with you, Dr. Mac-Knockater," she said.

"Four o'clock, then," said Dr. MacKnockater, "unless you come early, in which case we shall mash the potatoes and cream the onions together."

Then, the Resolution expended, and the Blank not too far away, Meryl Lee ran out onto the commons.

Without a word, she walked back to Netley with Marian and Heidi. And when they got to Heidi's room, they sat on her bed and Meryl Lee, exhausted, let any small wisps of Resolution flow away and she said, "I . . . I'm . . . my . . ." and that was all.

And because Heidi Kidder and Marian Elders knew that the Tin Woodman is usually right, they held on to Meryl Lee as she stared into the Blank, and wept.

NINETEEN

1967

At NIGHT—EVEN ON COLD NOVEMBER NIGHTS— Matt would climb up the ladder in the chute, past the cabinet where the pillowcase was stored, and open the skylight and go out onto the roof to watch stars so close he could almost inhale them.

Sometimes, he'd shiver in the cold.

Sometimes, he'd shiver, remembering.

Matt had left Portland on the earliest bus out of the city, long before the sun was shining over the Azores. He might have fallen asleep—but he didn't, because whenever he looked up toward the bus driver, the driver was watching. He'd seemed suspicious from the moment Matt had boarded the bus. Maybe it was the pillowcase. Maybe it was because he got on the bus so early. Maybe it was because Matt took a seat at the very back. Maybe it was because he was alone. Maybe it was because, when the bus driver asked where he was heading, Matt had to look at his ticket to be sure. Or maybe, somehow, the bus driver just knew what it looked like when you ran.

Matt watched the dawn come up as they stopped outside of Yarmouth. While the bus idled in its schedule, the driver came back and nodded at Matt. "You okay, kid?" he asked.

"Yup," said Matt.

"You sure?"

"Yup," said Matt.

"Tell me where you're heading, again."

Matt looked at his ticket again. "Augusta."

"You got business in Augusta?"

"My Aunt Helen lives there."

"I live in Augusta. What's your aunt's last name?"

"I'm really tired," said Matt, and laid his head against the side of the bus.

The bus driver came back again while they idled in Freeport.

"You remember your aunt's name yet?" he said.

"Helen."

"Helen what?"

"Tush."

"Tush?"

"Tush." Matt laid his head back against the side of the bus.

The driver came back again while they idled in Brunswick.

"I never heard of any Tushes in Augusta."

"People don't have tushes in Augusta?" said Matt.

"Don't be smart, kid."

The driver came back again while they idled in Bath.

"You know," said Matt, "I'm getting off here."

"I thought you were getting off in Augusta."

"I meant Bath."

"Bath's a long way from Augusta and your Aunt Helen Tush."

"Thanks for the ride." Matt stood and shouldered his pillowcase.

The bus driver put his hand on Matt's arm. "You don't know a guy named Leonidas Shug?" he said.

A moment passed, and Matt pulled his arm from the bus driver's hand. "Nope," he said, and headed down the aisle of the bus.

"You sure?" the driver said. "Because he's looking for someone a lot like you."

"I hope he finds him," said Matt, and made himself move slowly down the steps, slowly across the lot, and slowly into the bus station. He made it into the bathroom and into a stall—which he locked—before he let his arms clench his shivering body.

He stayed there until he thought the bus had probably pulled out for Augusta.

Matt ate three hamburgers and a chocolate shake at a diner, sitting as far from the windows as he could. Then he found a route out of the city, staying close to the river. He was an idiot, he thought. He should have waited until the weekend. A kid traveling alone, in September, on a school day—he was pretty obviously up to something. Every other kid his age would be in school for another couple of hours, and here he was, walking with a pillowcase over his shoulder.

So he headed toward the water, and it wasn't long before the streets grew narrower, the houses less frequent, the cars going by fewer. He passed a woman putting up laundry on clotheslines, and an old guy scraping paint off the hull of a boat pulled up on shore. Matt kept walking until the hamburgers and shake were only a memory, and still he kept going, until there were hardly any houses at all, and then it was dusk and past dusk, and he knew he'd need a place to sleep. He took a dirt road that led sharply down to the shore, and there he found a shack that wasn't locked because there wasn't anything worth locking up: an old wood stove, a rusted lantern, a wire bed with no mattress except a sheet of plywood, a water pump in the sink that worked, sort of. But the shack was sturdy enough, and when the rain came later that night, he stayed dry, pretty much. He'd seen some shingles stacked against the outside walls when he came in. He'd fix the roof tomorrow and call it good.

The next morning he hid the pillowcase under the floorboards under the wire bed, washed himself down by the river—Pastor Darius would have said that the water was cold as sin—and then Matt walked back to the outskirts of Bath. He found a diner— "Scrape four," he said, and they did—and then he found a hardware store and bought a hammer and nails and a sleeping bag they had on sale and a small cast-iron fry pan and six white candles and a box of matches. Then he went to an A&P and bought eggs, bacon, milk, a couple loaves of bread, Concord grape jelly, peanut butter, three cans of tomato soup, and three boxes of Fig Newtons. He walked back to the shack with the bags at his sides; he had never known how heavy a cast-iron fry pan could be after a couple of miles.

For the next week, Matt made this trip every day unless it rained. At the hardware store, he bought the essentials: a couple of plates, a bowl, two knives and forks and spoons, two glasses, a scraper that he really needed for the cast-iron fry pan, a hatchet to cut up branches for the wood stove, some duct tape because there's not a day that goes by when you can't use duct tape, some TP and a shovel for related needs, a flashlight and extra batteries, some fishing line and hooks, a Buck knife. The store was run by Evelyn, who smiled across the counter as if she were about to hand you a homemade cherry pie. "You're one of my best customers," she said one afternoon, "and I don't even know your name."

"Tush," Matt said.

"Tush?"

"Yeah."

That was all. Matt knew what could happen if he got to know someone.

At the A&P, he bought food—and the inessentials: soap, a toothbrush, tooth powder, a towel, a postcard of Commercial Street in Portland that showed a corner of the Chowder House, dish detergent. After a raccoon began to show up, scratching at his door once the sun went down, he bought dog biscuits, too. It was good to have some company, and the raccoon was as faithful as the tide, which Matt could see rising and falling along the rocks a few steps from the shack. And the raccoon didn't ask his name.

He called the raccoon Georgie.

Sometime toward the end of September—he couldn't be sure, since a calendar was really an inessential, he figured—he came home with his bag from the A&P (sausages, cooking oil, a fryer, a bag of carrots, and a bag of potatoes) and his bag from the hardware store (a sharpening stone, some more cedar shingles he could nail around the leaky windows, some caulking, and a Phillips screwdriver to tighten the clasps on the stovepipe), and he found four boys sitting in his shack, smoking cigarettes and eating his Fig Newtons.

"Who are you?" one said.

"I live here," said Matt.

"No one lives here," said the boy.

Matt put his bags on the ground. "Look around you, doofus," he said.

The boy snuffed his cigarette out on the wall.

"It's ours," he said. "We come when we want a smoke. Thanks for fixing it up so nice. And thanks for the Fig Newtons. You can go now."

The other boys laughed. One snuffed his cigarette out on

Matt's sleeping bag. Another knocked the two glasses off their shelf and they shattered on the floor. "Sorry," he said, and laughed again.

There were four of them, prep-school boys, two of them a little bigger than Matt.

But they were in his house.

He hit the first one square in the face, as hard as he could, hoping he could break his nose and scare them with the blood. But the guy fell back onto the bed, and the three others came at Matt, who learned pretty quickly that these guys might have been in school fights before but probably never in a fight they really, really had to win, a fight where losing meant you got hurt so badly you might die.

So they were pretty surprised when Matt got on the first guy—who was still on the bed—and pounded his eyes shut. And when they pulled Matt off, they were pretty surprised when his teeth drew blood, and when he kicked the guy who snuffed his cigarette on the sleeping bag hard and several times in a place he'd never been kicked before, and when he picked up a shard from a shattered glass and held it so tight to the neck of the guy who'd knocked the glasses down that a thin line of blood oozed out.

"You're crazy," the guy who'd been bitten yelled. "You hear that? Crazy!"

Matt stepped toward them again, holding the broken glass out in front of him, and they backed out of the shack, the one who'd been kicked sort of hobbling.

"You're nuts! You think this is over? Nuts!"

Then they were gone up the dirt road, the one boy well behind the others, still bent over.

Later, Matt sat on the rocks above the water, trying his first cigarette from a pack left behind. He gave it a couple of drags, decided he didn't like it, and threw the cigarette and the pack into the water, where they drifted away. For a while he went down to the shore and skipped stones, but the water was too choppy for it, and he climbed back up, lay against the rocks, and watched the sun turn yellow, orange, red—then disappear. The stars began to announce their visit, and Matt headed back to the shack.

Georgie would be there soon.

A few days later, Matt asked Evelyn what the date was. She was surprised he was speaking to her.

"The date?" she said. "October 1, 1967."

"Thanks," said Matt.

"Is there anything else I can help you with?"

He shook his head. "Just these," he said, handing her some candles. Then he went to the A&P and bought a small cake. Chocolate cake with chocolate icing.

He figured he'd missed his birthday over the summer.

He figured he was something around thirteen—give or take a year. He might as well celebrate now.

So he ate the whole cake.

TWENTY

1967–68

A WINTER IN MAINE, BY YOURSELF, IN A LOBSTER-man's shack that had never even thought about being insulated, will teach you a lot about cold.

Matt learned the rules quickly.

Never let the fire go out.

Pine boughs around the foundations of the shack—such as they were.

Never let the fire go out.

Keep the well pump working so it doesn't freeze up.

Never let the fire go out.

Shovel snow over the pine boughs.

Never let the fire go out.

Stuff the cracks, especially around the windows, with all the socks and underwear you're not wearing right now.

Never let the fire go out.

Sleep in two sleeping bags, one inside the other.

Never let the fire go out.

Keep the clothes you're going to wear the next day in the foot of the sleeping bags.

Never let the fire go out.

Hang a blanket over the closed door, with rocks on the bottom to keep the wind from blowing in.

Never let the fire go out.

Never, ever let the fire go out.

That winter in the lobsterman's shack was long and dark.

So spring was as welcome as daylight. Matt almost kissed the first golden buds on the maples. He could taste the air when he pulled his socks from the window frame and pushed open the glass. The snow melting quickly, the scent of dark earth and pine, the unrolling of fiddleheads, the bright green of the moss, the stretching of the leaves, the love calls of the birds and the peepers, the ballet of the deer he watched from the doorway—they were all as welcome as daylight.

That early spring, bathing in the cool waves in the morning, skipping stones in the dusky evening. And then, suddenly, Mrs. MacKnockater with her strange name and stranger accent. And that summer, being out on the water again, a hand on any boat a lobsterman would let him get on. Then in the fall, meeting the Captain and *Affliction*. He actually didn't mind winter that much, but the seasons between winters were heaven.

And Matt was beginning to feel that he had always been here, in this shack, above the sea and its longings, the scent of the pines always around him, the seasons coming and going. It was as if he had never been anywhere else.

But, of course, he had been anywhere else. And he thought often, late at night, of Pastor Darius and Sophia, and the Second Baptist Church of New Bedford, and Milly's quilts, and even Mrs. Nielson's Brussels Sprouts Surprise. "The door of our house is always and forever open to you," Pastor Darius had said. Always and forever is a really long time, but it had already been a long time, and Matt felt the need deep inside to go see them.

A little bit more than a week into September, a couple days

after a lobster dinner at Mrs. MacKnockater's house, he decided to go. He put a sweater on over his T-shirt, and a sweatshirt on over the sweater—it would be colder by nightfall—and headed out.

In Bath, he purchased a round-trip ticket to New Bedford.

"Do you always walk around with hundred-dollar bills?" said the ticket man.

"It's from my aunt," said Matt.

The bus left at 10:06 in the morning. He slept most of the three hours to New Bedford but woke up when the bus began to move slowly into the city, into places he knew well.

It wasn't a long walk from the New Bedford bus station to Second Baptist's neighborhood, maybe twenty minutes. Maybe less. And as he got closer, Matt found himself starting to run and grinning like a loon—but he didn't care.

Always and forever.

It was a Monday. Pastor Darius would just be finishing the cleanup after yesterday's services.

Closer now, and Matt watched to see the white steeple fingering up into the sky.

Looked up.

Looked up.

The steeple was gone.

He stopped. He stepped into the road to angle himself toward where he knew it had to be.

Gone.

He walked slowly the rest of the way, keeping himself close to the buildings as if to stay in their shadows, until he turned the corner and saw the blackened wreck of New Bedford Second Baptist Church.

He heaved everything inside his stomach right into the street.

It was hardly remarkable that it was Mrs. Nielson and her son who found him on his hands and knees, the two of them carrying bags of donated day-old rolls for the Tuesday lunch. They told him about that night. Two, some said three, men broke into the church. Pastor Darius practicing Sunday's sermon. Beaten to within an inch of his life. Second Baptist set on fire, but by a miracle, Pastor had managed to crawl out, even after the rafters burned through and the steeple dropped into the sanctuary. No one could understand how. "Safe and secure," was all he'd said.

But now, he was blind.

And he was still insisting on the Tuesday and Thursday community lunches. Imagine that, she said.

Matt had no trouble at all imagining that.

Mrs. Nielson said he should come home with her. She'd call Pastor Darius. He'd be so glad to see Matt again.

See me again, Matt thought.

Matt said he couldn't. He couldn't. This was his fault. He couldn't. Mrs. Nielson's son started to help him up from the sidewalk.

"It's not your fault," said Mrs. Nielson.

Then, "It looks like it's true," said a voice behind them. A voice that sounded like cool and satisfied Hate.

Matt looked up.

"They always come back to the scene of the crime."

The Big Guy from the Alley.

"You just have to wait long enough."

Matt thought he was going to heave again.

"Who are you?" said Mrs. Nielson.

The Big Guy looked at her. "The Devil," he said. "You better go away."

"I've never been afraid of the Devil," said Mrs. Nielson.

The man stepped closer. "You should be afraid of this Devil," he said.

Mrs. Nielson sniffed. "You wear too much cologne," she said. "It stinks."

It was probably not what the guy from the Alley expected.

Matt stood. "Mrs. Nielson," he said, "you'd better—"

"You got no business here," said Mrs. Nielson's son.

"This boy's my business," said the Big Guy from the Alley. "And you don't want to get between me and him."

But Mrs. Nielson's son did. He turned to Matt, mouthed, *Run, kid*, looked once at his mother, and then threw himself against the Big Guy. But Mrs. Nielson's son was a lot smaller than the Big Guy from the Alley, who tossed him into the street, reached into his coat, and drew a knife as wicked as his grin. Matt broadsided him, but the guy didn't go down. A couple of quick slashes tore through Matt's sweatshirt. "Matt, get out of here," he heard, and he turned, saw Mrs. Nielson's eyes wide and her mouth open, and he felt a quick and deep line of narrow heat slash low across his back, felt his left arm jerked behind him, felt it twist cockeyed off his shoulder, and then suddenly he was knocked to the ground and Mrs. Nielson's son was pounding the Big Guy's face.

Matt staggered up, holding his arm—which hurt like anything.

"Matt, go," he heard Mrs. Nielson cry, and he ran, sprinting away, trying to cradle his arm, looking back at the corner to see the Big Guy from the Alley down on the sidewalk with Mrs. Nielson's son still pounding at him, and he crossed the road and headed toward the bus station.

He stopped to check the time and platform for the Bath bus.

He had an hour and a half to wait.

He ran into the men's room, into an empty stall, pulled the door closed, locked it, and sat with his feet up on the toilet.

He noticed that he couldn't move his left arm.

Then he noticed the drops of blood that he'd left behind on the floor, leading right to where he was.

He came out of the stall again, looked around. No one. He took off his sweatshirt—this was hard to do—and held it against the cut along his back as he wiped up the blood spots with paper towels. Then back into the stall, door closed and locked, feet up on the toilet, still holding the sweatshirt against his back, which was starting now to ache.

He waited, listening, for an hour and twenty-five minutes, his heart stopping every time someone rattled the locked door, his left arm screeching with pain. Then he opened the stall and looked around the bathroom. No one. He threw away the sweatshirt, took handfuls of paper towels and stuffed them at his back inside the sweater, and tried to walk to the bus as if he couldn't care less whether he made it to Bath or not—and as if his back wasn't aching like all get out, as if his eyes weren't starting to close.

And he tried not to look as if he was looking around.

He made it to the bus and showed the ticket to the driver—"Hey, you only had about thirty seconds to spare, kid. You okay?"—and took a seat in the last row, where he lay down, pressing himself against the seatback.

That's how he stayed all the way up to Bath, his eyes closed, hoping the other passengers thought he was sleeping, really hoping he wasn't bleeding too badly, trying not to jostle his arm.

When the bus finally reached the station, he didn't turn around to see how much blood he'd left on the seat—probably plenty. He wondered whether he should leave his sweater behind but figured that the blood would show worse on his white T-shirt, so he waited until everyone got off before he came up the aisle, his hand on his back, and quickly went down the bus steps and into the station, staying close to the walls.

No one seemed to notice him.

Out of the bus station and into town, thankful that it was close to dark. Through the streets of Bath and out onto the peninsula, the ache like hell now, his hands bloody, his legs feeling like they didn't belong to him, his eyes focusing badly, the way home a lot longer than it should be.

He fell once on the path down to the shack, and he almost decided not to get up. But he did, and fell again against a stand of pines, their branches so sharp at his back that he almost screamed—or maybe he did scream.

He crawled the rest of the way to Captain Cobb's shack, pushed open the door, let it close behind him, tried to pull himself up to the pump to get some water, and finally collapsed.

That night, Mrs. MacKnockater, who hadn't heard from Matt for long enough that she was worried, told Captain Hurd to get off his duff and go check on the boy.

TWENTY-ONE

MORE THAN A YEAR HAD PASSED SINCE MATT HAD come to the coast, and now, with Thanksgiving close, Matt did something he had never done before: he went to Breck's department store and bought a bright yellow button-down shirt. He kind of guessed at the size. Then he bought a tie. Red. Sort of fire engine red. Actually, red like the center of a cooling star. Then he bought black dress pants. At home, when he tried the shirt on, twisting his back so that he could see the wicked scar along his low ribs in the mirror, it turned out that the shirt was a few sizes too big; he'd have to roll the sleeves up over his elbows and tuck the tails deep into his black dress pants. He figured Mrs. MacKnockater wouldn't care. He knew Captain Hurd wouldn't care.

And Matt knew something else.

His left arm was fine, and his back no longer hurt, not even when he twisted it. He knew he should go now. Staying more than a year in one place was really dumb. It was only a matter of time before Leonidas Shug sent someone else to find Matt and what he had taken—and probably do something a whole lot worse to him.

And to anyone who helped him.

He knew he should go.

Everything in him told him he should go.

But something had happened. Something he never expected.

He'd found a home.

And maybe it wasn't like most homes. Maybe it wasn't what it would have been if his parents . . .

But it was still a home. In the evenings when Mrs. MacKnockater came back from St. Elene's, they ate dinner together—and she wasn't a terrible cook, even though she sure did like to boil anything she could fit into a pot. Then they'd go through the lessons he'd done that day, mostly literature and history. She'd given him Ernest Hemingway's *The Old Man and the Sea,* where, she said, "the two disciplines coalesced," and he was working his way through it sort of slowly. But it was okay. He liked Santiago well enough.

Usually sometime around seven thirty, Captain Hurd would stop by, and he'd fuss at Mrs. MacKnockater about the way she didn't keep the damper right on the wood stove and how the headmistress of St. Elene's never could learn the first thing about real life, and then he'd trounce Matt at one or two games of checkers, and then they'd all three talk, quietly enough to hear the waves in the dark, frothing into the shore.

Matt couldn't bear to leave again. He'd found a home.

Maybe if he talked with the lieutenant. Maybe if he told him everything.

But Matt knew that wouldn't help. Nothing would help.

So how long could he dare to stay?

That's what he was wondering on Thanksgiving afternoon, long before Captain Hurd would be arriving, when he went upstairs to try on his new black dress pants—which turned out to be so long that they covered his feet, so he took those off to figure out how to cuff them so they wouldn't unroll, or he would wear his jeans—and meanwhile he put on his bright yellow button-down shirt and his red-like-the-center-of-a-cooling-star tie—and how was he supposed to know that you couldn't use a buoy hitch on a stupid tie?—and that's when his heart stopped completely because he heard someone knock at Mrs. MacKnockater's door and he knew it would be just like Leonidas Shug to send a guy on Thanksgiving afternoon.

Then he heard Mrs. MacKnockater's high-pitched, surprised voice.

Matt let every instinct catch him up. It was for this reason that he had carried his hatchet from the shack to Mrs. Mac-Knockater's house.

He reached under the bed, grabbed it, and banged out of his room and took the stairs three at a time.

Meryl Lee did decide to come early to Dr. MacKnockater's home to help mash the potatoes and cream the onions. She had spent rather a long time dressing—since this was not a school event, she didn't want to wear her regulation St. Elene's Preparatory Academy uniform. So she had chosen her very best, and borrowed a garnet necklace from Marian, and shined her black pumps, and come well before time, figuring that it was better to arrive early to help than to come on time to be served. Somehow, she didn't want that.

At the door, Dr. MacKnockater was surprised and genuinely pleased to see her. She welcomed her in, wished her a most happy Thanksgiving Day, told her that if she would wait right there she would run and fetch an apron so that Meryl Lee wouldn't get her pretty dress floured, and bundled back into the kitchen.

And that was when Meryl Lee heard something like a scream and turned to see the boy, wearing a bright yellow button-down shirt and a red tie the color of the center of a cooling star on top, and nothing but his boxers on bottom—the boxers were red too—thumping down the stairs and toward her with an upraised hatchet.

It wasn't exactly what she had expected to see at Dr. Mac-Knockater's house.

She might have screamed. A little bit. She turned back to the door and reached for the knobbly walking stick that leaned against the corner. She whipped it in front of her and held its point against the boy's chest—actually, right on the cooling-star tie.

The boy was still holding the hatchet up. He looked sort of frozen, even though he was breathing heavily.

Meryl Lee was breathing a little heavily too.

And that was how Mrs. Nora MacKnockater saw Matt and Meryl Lee when she swung the kitchen door open.

This wasn't exactly what she had expected either. Slowly she walked toward them, holding the apron.

"I see you've met," she said.

There was a long moment, and then Meryl Lee slowly nodded. Matt lowered his hatchet.

"Matthew, this is Miss Meryl Lee Kowalski."

Matt nodded again.

"Meryl Lee, this is Mr. Matthew Coffin."

Meryl Lee nodded.

"If you would put your chosen weapons away," said Dr. Mac-Knockater, "I think we shall call a truce for Thanksgiving Day."

Matt stood back and held his hatchet down by his side. Meryl Lee lowered the point of the walking stick a little.

"Much better," said Dr. MacKnockater. She handed the apron to Meryl Lee. "Forbearing the obvious questions here, I will return to the kitchen and its relative peace. Matthew, I'll need your help in a few minutes to lift the turkey out of the oven to baste, and, Meryl Lee, if you'll help me prepare the onion mix for green beans, I think we shall be right on schedule."

Mrs. MacKnockater hustled back into the kitchen.

Meryl Lee looked at Matt, who looked at her.

"Sorry. I didn't mean to scare you," said Matt.

"Who's scared?" said Meryl Lee.

"You, for one," said Matt.

"I wasn't scared," said Meryl Lee.

Matt looked at her again.

"Okay, maybe a little startled. It's not every day that a boy comes at me with a hatchet."

"I thought you might be someone else."

"I wasn't."

"I know."

"Do you always run downstairs in your boxers?"

Matt looked down, then back up at Meryl Lee.

"I guess I'd better . . ."

"Yeah, I guess you'd better." Meryl Lee leaned the walking stick back into the corner. "Probably Dr. MacKnockater would . . ."

"I know," said Matt. "I'll meet you in the kitchen."

Matt went upstairs. He slid the hatchet—not too far—under the bed. Then he put on his jeans and tucked in the bright yellow button-down shirt as best he could. Then back downstairs and into the kitchen, where Meryl Lee was at the table, paring and slicing carrots, and Mrs. MacKnockater asked him to take out the turkey—a twenty-two pounder—and he set it on the table near Meryl Lee, and they watched while Mrs. MacKnockater basted it and its lovely smell filled the kitchen. Matt put it back into the oven, and then Mrs. MacKnockater gave them the cooked yams to scoop into a glass casserole dish and layer small marshmallows upon, which they did together, and Matt watched Meryl Lee while pretending he was not watching her and he thought, *This is the first time I've ever done something like this with a girl,* and he felt the heat of a cooling star inside him.

Well, maybe not a *cooling* star.

Later, after they creamed the onions and unmolded the Jell-O salad, they set the table in the dining room with Mrs. MacKnockater's Spode and Waterford. "We'll need five place settings," she said, and Matt didn't ask who the fifth person would be, and Meryl Lee didn't either, because Matt was trying to figure out what that heat inside him meant, and Meryl Lee was . . . confused? Because somehow, this boy, this boy who ran down the stairs with a hatchet to protect the Awful Dignity, who ran down the stairs in his red boxers and with a tie knotted into a disaster, who was setting knives and forks and spoons beside china plates with her and getting them all mixed up, had done exactly what she could imagine Holling doing. Exactly. And now, even now when she was thinking of Holling—when she was thinking of Holling!—the Blank wasn't there.

The Blank wasn't there.

This boy was.

Why wasn't the Blank there?

Later, Dr. MacKnockater lit a white candle and brought it into the dining room while Matt took the turkey out of the oven again. It was perfect. Meryl Lee spooned the stuffing from the turkey, and Mrs. MacKnockater asked Matt to cut long slices of white meat and some shorter slices of the dark meat—"No one likes the dark meat nearly as much as the white," she said—and he wasn't terrible at it, and while he did that, Mrs. MacKnockater made the gravy, and then it was four o'clock and a minute or so later Meryl Lee heard a knock, and while Matt watched carefully, she ran to open Dr. MacKnockater's door, where she found, standing on the stoop, the second person she had not expected that afternoon: Jennifer Hartley Truro, wearing her pearls.

At least Jennifer wasn't running at her with a hatchet.

"What are you doing here?" said Jennifer.

Well, maybe she *was* running at her with a hatchet.

"Having Thanksgiving dinner," said Meryl Lee. "Where's Alden?"

"As if it's any of your business," said Jennifer.

"Is that Miss Truro?" called Dr. MacKnockater.

"I'm here, Dr. MacKnockater," called Jennifer, pushing past Meryl Lee. "Is there anything I can do to help?" She pulled her blond hair back and looked at Meryl Lee as if she was about to stick her tongue out at her. Then she went into the kitchen, and there was a boy—an actual boy. His shirt was way too big, and it was bright yellow, and he was wearing jeans that he'd probably worn to play in the mud. He didn't say anything when they were introduced—he just mumbled. And look what he'd done to that turkey! A massacre! And sneakers? He was wearing *sneakers* to Thanksgiving dinner? And didn't he believe in a decent haircut? And okay, she didn't mean to laugh at what he'd done to his tie, but really, who would be able not to laugh at that?

She'd have a lot to tell Ashley and Charlotte about the kind of people the Knock invited to Thanksgiving dinner.

Captain Hurd arrived soon afterward—he didn't knock, he just came on in—and he greeted Meryl Lee in the kitchen and then he went out with Matt to fuss at the wood stove's draft until they got a steady blaze, and then they went into the dining room, where Jennifer sat across from the boy and as far as she could from the

Captain, who, she thought, smelled like fish. Mrs. MacKnockater sat at the head, and she told them to hold hands for prayer, and she let silence go on for a bit, and then she prayed: "Oh Lord our God, help us to be truly thankful for the innumerable blessings Thou hast bestowed upon us in this past year. Thank you for those moments of joy that enliven our hearts and souls. And when it may have seemed to us, your servants, that Thou hast held Thine hand back and allowed us to be troubled, help us to see even in that, Thy blessing meant for our good, though we may not know how it might be so. Bless us in the Unexpected. Amen."

And strangely, Meryl Lee found herself close to tears, and when she looked across the table at Matt, in the light of that white candle, he was looking at her, and she thought that he might be close to tears too.

Bless us in the Unexpected.

The Captain, though, was not close to tears. He was hungry and eager for turkey, and filled with stories of his friend Buckminster, the old coot, grandfather to those young Buckminsters, who couldn't manage a boat despite fifty years of life on the Maine coast. And Dr. MacKnockater was almost, well, merry, handing around the green beans and mashed potatoes with the gravy and sweet yams and onions and long slices of turkey and Jell-O mold—"We need to eat this before it starts to melt"—and opening the wine for the Captain—"You never could manage a corkscrew"—and bundling into the kitchen for the cold grape juice that would serve for the toasts "for the young ones in our midst" and coaxing Matt into the conversation, which the Captain did much better than she did.

But Meryl Lee watched Matt from across the table. The way, when he looked up, his eyes shone in candlelight. The way that he tried with his hand, sometimes, to hide the scar that went up his cheek. The way his left pinky was crooked, like it had been broken and not set right. The way his tie was knotted with determination. The way he handed Dr. MacKnockater a hot dish, waiting to be sure she had hold of it. The way he looked at the Captain when he spoke about their days on the water, and the smile that crossed his face—his whole face—and the one tooth missing as though it had been knocked out. The way he sometimes glanced across at her.

Because he did glance across at her, more often than Meryl Lee knew. At the way *her* eyes looked in the candlelight, the way she held her hands, the way she ignored stupid Jennifer's insults, the way she listened to the Captain's stories even though she had probably never handled a boat in her life, the way her head tilted and her hair hung and that funny way she laughed with her head a little back.

Jennifer might have noticed the glances. So she was wondering, she said, where Matt came from, and when Matt said, "Nowhere special," she would not let it go. "Everyone comes from somewhere," she said. "Is it a secret?" Matt looked at her. "I love secrets. Really, where are you from?"

And Dr. MacKnockater said, "Jennifer is joining us because her plans fell through at the last moment, much as yours have, Meryl Lee."

And Jennifer paused, took her linen napkin up to her eye, and explained: Alden, it turned out, dear Alden, was not able to visit the vast Truro family estates over Thanksgiving and hand over one of his great-aunt's rubies so he and Jennifer could be almost like engaged because, according to Jennifer, his family was commanded to have Thanksgiving dinner with the Windsors at Buckingham Palace. And no one, of course, can neglect royal obligations.

Dr. MacKnockater said, "You must be disappointed."

Jennifer dabbed an eye.

Meryl Lee almost threw up into the creamed onions.

"But we'll be in Austria together over Christmas," she said.

"That will be nice," said Dr. MacKnockater.

"We'll be boating in gondolas," said Jennifer.

"Then you'll be in Italy, too."

Jennifer looked confused.

"Yes," she guessed.

"Perhaps you might pass the yams, Miss Kowalski," said Dr. MacKnockater. "They're a bit too sweet, but it's Thanksgiving, after all. And do you like to travel as well, Miss Kowalski?"

"I've been to Quebec City," she said.

The look from Jennifer. *Such a dope.*

Dr. MacKnockater spooned some of the Jell-O mold onto her plate. "A lovely city, with a spiritually moving cathedral. But I understand a reluctance to travel, Miss Kowalski. When I was a girl your age, my parents took my brother and me on a tour of the great capitals of Europe. I suppose it was exciting. London, Paris, Madrid, Berlin. But when we got back, I realized that if I had seen one more cathedral—just one more cathedral—I would have turned atheist. All I wanted was to be home."

She ate a spoonful of the Jell-O mold.

"I wonder," said Meryl Lee, "if it's sort of like in *The Wonderful Wizard of Oz.*"

That look from Jennifer again.

"What do you mean?" said Dr. MacKnockater.

Meryl Lee thought for a moment. "I mean, Dorothy walked all that way to the Emerald City, but in the end, she really didn't need to go there at all. She just had to go back to a place she already knew."

Dr. MacKnockater put down her fork and took a sip of her dark wine. "Perhaps," she said, "the greatest journey might be the journey inward."

Meryl Lee shivered, because just like that, she felt herself wondering what that greatest journey might be like. And when she looked across at Matt, who was looking at her, she thought he might be wondering too.

"I think I may reread Mr. Baum's classic," said Mrs. MacKnockater. "There may be more to it than I have remembered. Perhaps in the spring. Spring seems the right time to read a fantasy, don't you agree?"

It was only later, after everyone had left, that Mrs. MacKnockater asked Matt about the hatchet.

"It wasn't anything," he said.

TWENTY-TWO

THE DAYS AFTER THANKSGIVING WERE PERFECTLY blue. High clouds, easy tides, a breeze shifting the tips of the pines, cold in the mornings but warm enough to let the wood stove go down to embers in the afternoon. Still, with all this, Mrs. Mac-Knockater was troubled. She could not help but think about Matthew rushing down the stairs with a hatchet—which, she had pointed out, he should keep outside and he promised he would, but she didn't believe him. What would make a boy rush down the stairs with a hatchet? Was he protecting himself?

Was he protecting her?

And from what?

She had wondered if the attack on him in September was isolated, something a lunatic had done out of malice. But was there more? And she wasn't blind. She'd seen the policeman drive slowly by the house often enough. There were few enough cars that went by that she couldn't miss him. Did Lieutenant Minot think there was more?

And now, Matthew had taken to calling out in his sleep for Georgie. He called out loudly, as if in a panic. "Georgie." Almost every night.

Should she take the initiative to speak to the lieutenant?

Should she ask Matthew who Georgie was?

Captain Hurd was no help when she asked his advice. "There's only two ways about it," he said.

"I suspect there are more than two, but which two are you suggesting?"

"Tell him to go on his way and take his trouble with him."

"I would hardly do that. Neither would you, you old coot. What is the other way?"

He looked at her. "What I've been telling you for years, Nora. Love him and all that comes with him."

"You are conflating two different things," said Mrs. Mac-Knockater.

Mrs. MacKnockater was very troubled. But she realized—as perhaps she had always known—that Willis Hurd was right. She knew what she had to do.

Truth be told, Matt was very troubled too.

He wanted to stay. He did. But how long could he? So Shug hadn't sent someone on Thanksgiving Day. So what? He could come any day. If he'd found Matt on the streets of New Bedford, he could find him anywhere.

And Matt really could go wherever he wanted. He had most of the money that had been in the pillowcase. He could go to China if he wanted. Australia. Edinburgh. Anywhere.

But even as he imagined boarding the ship that would take him to Anywhere, he couldn't imagine leaving Here.

He spent these blue days reading *The Old Man and the Sea* and studying the presidency of FDR and reading some of Darwin because Captain Hurd's friend Buckminster had been partial to Darwin and the Captain thought his book on coral islands was worth a read—even though Matt thought it was hard and kind of dull and the pictures were terrible. He hated the arithmetic lessons Mrs.

MacKnockater left him just because Mrs. MacKnockater believed he couldn't spend his life counting on his fingers—which he probably could. But he sort of liked the geography lessons Captain Hurd left him: plotting out a route to Easter Island and Madagascar and Hong Kong and Sydney. They beat out arithmetic every time.

Still, Matt Coffin was very troubled.

Meryl Lee was very troubled too.

After Thanksgiving dinner, she had walked back to Netley with Jennifer Hartley Truro, and Jennifer had talked of nothing but the boy. If it wasn't for Alden, she said, she might be interested in him. She'd have to clean him up and teach him how to look away from his mashed potatoes now and then—he ate like it was the last meal he was ever going to get—and she'd have to teach him how to talk since he obviously didn't even know how to be polite, and of course that was because he didn't have the kind of breeding that had been in Alden's family for generations. But his eyes were cute and if he got a good haircut he'd look . . . And so on.

His eyes.

That was it, thought Meryl Lee. It's what she saw in his eyes.

She was sure of it now.

He'd seen the Blank too. She could tell. He knew.

Matt had seen the Blank.

That's what she was thinking about when, at dinner on the Monday after Thanksgiving break, Mrs. Mott announced the annual St. Elene's Upper School Christmas Soiree. Meryl Lee did not know what a soiree was, but according to Mrs. Mott, they'd be soiree-ing three weeks from now, and they would be hosting students from St. Giles's Preparatory Academy for Boys for an evening of Yuletide cheer.

General applause and exclamations of joy and delight.

Then Dr. MacKnockater stood to announce what Meryl Lee was sure would be announced every day right up until the fateful night—that the girls of St. Elene's upper school were expected to be young ladies of polite society, that they must not giggle or flirt or act in any way unbecoming to the traditions of St. Elene's, that there must be at least a handbreadth of hem beneath their knees and a handbreadth of air between them and their dancing partners.

And there was the Blank, suddenly and unexpectedly, as large and consuming as ever. It was as if Absence had moved into the room and taken up all the air.

And it wasn't just Meryl Lee who acted as if all the air had been evacuated.

By Wednesday of that week, everyone at Mrs. Saunders's table had had to rise and consult *Funk and Wagnalls* several times; Meryl Lee had to consult *Funk and Wagnalls* for *distracted* and *woolgathering* [colloquial]. In Life Sciences, Mrs. Bellamy handed out freshly inked dittos and told them to fill in the work sheets on one-celled creatures and since filling in work sheets did not require talking, she expected silence. Absolute Silence. In Famous Women of History, Mrs. Saunders promised pop quizzes on every chapter every day that week because she was sure her students were not reading their history text attentively enough. And in domestic economy, Mrs. Wyss was cranky about wasting cake flour. "St. Elene's has to pay for these supplies," she said. "Don't repay generosity with waste."

By Friday, Meryl Lee thought it had been a very long week.

But on Friday, she figured out why all the teachers were the way they were.

At Evening Meal, Dr. MacKnockater stood up to address the students of St. Elene's Preparatory Academy for Girls. The Awful Dignity folded her arms across her chest, and her eyes glittered behind round glasses. She looked around, the searching gaze as fearsome as always. Then she began. Letters of complaint had been sent to the board of trustees of St. Elene's, she said, opposing her public support of Hubert H. Humphrey during the recent presidential campaign. She said she believed that the foundation of democracy was everyone's right to hold freely and to voice freely his own opinion, but members of the board apparently did not believe that the freedoms promised in our Constitution's Bill of Rights should be extended to headmistresses. So, after three decades of active service as headmistress of St. Elene's, she would be relinquishing that role. Hers had been a long and happy tenure, she said, and now she looked forward to new opportunities.

And then, Dr. MacKnockater lobbed the devastating bombshell: as Mrs. Mott had declined the opportunity to advance to the role of headmistress due to her own impending retirement, the trustees had chosen Mrs. Agatha Connolly to become the new headmistress of St. Elene's Preparatory Academy for Girls effective July 1, 1969. Dr. MacKnockater wanted to express her personal gratitude to Mrs. Connolly for taking up this burden and to thank the faculty for their support over these many years.

Meryl Lee looked around. All the other teachers were staring down at their tables, as if they were the ones about to take on burdens. Mrs. Saunders looked as if she wanted someone to stand up and consult *Funk and Wagnalls* but she didn't have the right word to assign.

"I am glad my successor is a colleague who will guide the students of St. Elene's in the traditions and ways that have always been a part of the school," said Dr. MacKnockater, "and

I hope every student will continue to develop her gifts into real Accomplishments."

Then she sat down.

Not a single teacher's face moved at all.

On Sunday afternoon, Meryl Lee felt the restlessness of the salt sea. It was almost as if she could hear the sounding waves in Netley 204. So she left Jennifer in her light blue blouse and cream cashmere sweater and found Marian and then Heidi, and together—sort of quietly—they walked down to the shore.

They found Bettye sitting on the rocks.

She was not in her black dress and white apron.

She was in jeans and a gray sweatshirt and boots and a heavy brown jacket—"my brother Jonathan's," she said. Her hair was down and blowing all around, and her face was red in the stiff wind, and she moved easily and surely around the rocks, as if she had known them all her life. As if they were dear friends.

It was very cold, and the water was gray. Even the fir trees seemed to be shivering. But they skipped some stones into the troughs—Bettye reached six—and Bettye showed them where the crabs scuttled, and where the clams dug into the mud flats, and where the seagulls dropped the mussel shells, and then, just before they left, Bettye asked, "So, Dr. MacKnockater won't be headmistress next year?"

"I guess not," said Marian.

"And Mrs. Connolly will be?"

Meryl Lee nodded.

"Then that's it," said Bettye.

"What do you mean?" said Marian.

"If Mrs. Connolly becomes headmistress, I'll be fired."

Heidi standing up, brandishing her arms as if slashing with the field hockey stick.

"Are you sure?" said Meryl Lee.

"Pretty sure."

"What can we do?" said Marian.

Then Heidi, with Marian and Bettye, looked at Meryl Lee. "What are we going to do?" said Heidi.

Meryl Lee felt the rush of the wind.

"We're going to watch for ways to change the world," she said. "And then we'll see what happens next."

She felt full.

That week, Meryl Lee wondered what she was going to do about Bettye and Dr. MacKnockater as she studied quadratic equations for Mr. Wheelock's final exam.

Meryl Lee wondered what she was going to do about Bettye and Dr. MacKnockater as she studied the life of Florence Nightingale for Mrs. Saunders's final exam.

And as she studied her dittos on one-celled animals for Mrs. Bellamy's final exam.

And as she memorized the patterns for fixed form poems for Mrs. Connolly's final exam.

And as Coach Rowlandson had her girls run wind sprints across the field hockey field in temperatures that absolutely should not be associated with wind sprints.

On Friday, Meryl Lee still didn't know what she was going to do about Bettye and Dr. MacKnockater.

But she was watching.

⟶»«⟶

"Edinburgh," said Mrs. MacKnockater.

"Edinburgh?"

"It's where my people are from."

"Across the wide ocean," said Matt in a whisper.

"Yes," said Mrs. MacKnockater.

"In Australia, right?"

"Scotland, Matthew," said Mrs. MacKnockater.

"You're going to Scotland?"

"*We* could go to Scotland. We could live there."

"The three of us?"

"Yes," said Captain Hurd.

"That's still to be decided," said Mrs. MacKnockater.

"And—"

Mrs. MacKnockater folded her arms across her chest. "And whoever is after you, Matthew, will never find us."

"Who said someone was after—"

Mrs. MacKnockater held up her hand. "They would never find us," she said slowly. "Never."

The Christmas Soiree was Friday night—the fall semester's final day. Meryl Lee wasn't sure she was going to attend. But a soiree was a soiree, and she had never been to one, and her parents weren't coming until Saturday afternoon, and Heidi and Marian were both going, and so that evening, a little late, the three of them walked into Greater Hoxne Hall, after all.

And Hoxne Hall was beautiful. On the tree, red glass bulbs sparkled and green glass bulbs glowed. Holly and fir boughs hung around the hall, and their crisp smell mixed with the waxy scent of the red and gold candles, which were flickering brightly. Music to dance to, and the floor cleared of most of its furniture. A table with a green cloth for the punch, three tables with frosted cookies and frosted éclairs and glass vases filled with peppermint sticks and plates with small square pastries decorated like Christmas presents and a chocolate cake and a white cake almost as big as the table. Another table with small meatballs steaming in a silver warmer and sweet breads and cherry tarts and apricot tarts and strawberry tarts and lemon tarts—all sprinkled with powdered sugar.

Across the hall, most of the pale boys imported from St. Giles's sat on chairs, talking a little to one another, holding their kilts down around their knees—really, they were all wearing kilts. It was pretty clear not a single one of them wanted to be there.

Or to be wearing a kilt.

Except maybe for the four guys surrounding Ashley and Charlotte from Charlotte and sad-eyed Jennifer, who seemed to be refusing to dance, probably since dear, dear Alden would be brooding alone in his cold Scottish manor by the loch, and she couldn't betray him by dancing with another boy. And Ashley and Charlotte from Charlotte were also looking sad-eyed, probably because they wouldn't want to cause Jennifer pain and suffering by dancing and having a good time themselves. So they were all standing with their sad arms crossed, their sad faces downcast, brooding like Mary Stuart, Queen of Scots, before her execution. But the music was playing and the decorations were glittering and the silver star atop the tree gleamed and the four boys were wearing kilts and frilly white shirts and the tassels on the high stockings were so cute and even as Meryl Lee watched, Jennifer gave in oh so reluctantly and one of the boys took her hand and led her out to the dance floor where there probably was not a handbreadth of air between them.

Ashley and Charlotte from Charlotte followed with two of the boys, and there probably was not a handbreadth between them, either.

The fourth boy stood holding the glasses of punch—which wasn't easy, considering how many he was holding.

Heidi took Meryl Lee and Marian by the arms and said, "Sticks down."

Marian said, "What are we going to do?"

Heidi said, "I don't know yet."

"Do we have to—" Marian began.

"Yes," said Heidi.

They walked across the open floor—Meryl Lee and Marian a little behind Heidi, who kept looking back to make sure they were coming—to the imported St. Giles's boys sitting together. The imported boys stretched their kilts over their knees a little more and watched them approach. They looked scared.

Then Heidi stood in front of one.

"What's your name?" she said.

His eyes widened.

"What's your name?" she said again.

"Adam," he said.

"Adam," said Heidi, "you are going to ask me to dance right now."

Meryl Lee thought she heard Marian beside her whimper a little.

The two boys on either side of Adam looked at him.

Adam looked at the other two boys.

"We don't really dance," he said.

The other two nodded.

"You came to a dance but you don't dance?"

They all three nodded, then stretched their kilts over their knees again.

Heidi smiled and leaned close in to him. "Adam," she said, "are you afraid of me?"

Adam's eyes got big—because he probably was.

"No," he said, shaking his head.

"Then prove it," said Heidi.

The other two boys looked at Adam.

He looked back at them.

Heidi turned to St. Giles's Boy #2. "Are you afraid of me too?" she said.

Adam stood up. He was really tall. Heidi's eyes were level with his Adam's apple.

Heidi took Adam's hand and together they walked out onto the dance floor.

Bing Crosby began to sing about a white Christmas.

One of the other boys stood. His eyes were pretty big too. He held out his hand and Marian took it. They walked out onto the dance floor.

Meryl Lee looked at the other boy.

He shrugged, and stood. "Is this how you always get guys to dance?" he asked.

And then, as if a buoy had sounded behind her, Meryl Lee turned to the door into the hall and saw it open.

She almost expected Holling to walk in. She really almost expected that.

But it wasn't Holling.

Matt.

He was wearing a white shirt that fit with some sort of frilly stuff at his throat. Jeans. Black sneakers.

He pulled at the frilly stuff as if it were going to choke him and looked around.

"Excuse me," said Meryl Lee to the boy.

And while Bing Crosby was wishing that all of Meryl Lee's Christmases would be white, she walked across the hall and up to Matt, who looked at her, still pulling at the frilly stuff.

"I like the shirt," she said.

"I hate the shirt."

"It is kind of frilly."

"Good job noticing," he said. "You should go into detective work."

"So why wear it?"

"Because Mrs. MacKnockater tried to get me to wear a skirt and this was the compromise." He pulled at the frilly stuff again.

"It's a kilt. The guys from St. Giles's are all wearing them."

"Yeah. Some party."

"It's a soiree."

"Okay."

"And you just saved me from having to dance with that boy over there." She pointed to the boy, who still stood, watching her. "He didn't really want to dance with me."

"Then he's an idiot," said Matt.

Meryl Lee looked at him. She thought that might have been one of the nicest things that anyone had said to her since Holling had . . .

"So, do you want something to eat?" he said.

"I think I'm okay."

"Me too." Then, "I'm glad you didn't dance with that guy."

And Meryl Lee thought, *Oh, Holling. Oh, Holling, I hope you don't mind.*

"I guess we should try," said Matt.

"I'm not very good at it," said Meryl Lee.

"And I don't know how to dance at all," said Matt.

She wasn't, and he didn't, but who cared? In the light of the flickering candles, Dr. MacKnockater watched them first hold hands, then come closer, then reach around each other, and it was as if she were watching herself and that old coot, a hundred years ago, and she felt herself beginning to cry, and she left Greater Hoxne to finish some end-of-the-semester paperwork, wondering if it was wise to go to Edinburgh after all, and filled with irresolution.

Meryl Lee did not see her go. She was dancing, dancing with this boy she hardly knew, and she was dancing with *him,* not just remembering Holling, but dancing with *him.* Matt Coffin.

And the Blank was behind her.

A long way behind her.

Then Matt was looking past her, over her left shoulder, and Meryl Lee felt a hand on her arm, and she turned.

Four boys.

They were looking at Matt.

She felt Greater Hoxne Hall suddenly get cold.

"It's Shack Guy," said the boy holding her arm, nodding toward Matt. "Listen, I don't even know you, but girls from St. Elene's shouldn't be dancing with guys like Shack Guy. He's crazy."

Matt didn't say anything.

"You still living out in the woods, Shack Guy? I'm surprised they even let you in here. It's, like, letting a dog come in or something." He sniffed the air. "Smells like it too."

"Stop it," said Meryl Lee.

"We're just having a little fun. He doesn't mind, do you, Shack Guy?"

"Take your hand off my arm," said Meryl Lee.

"In a minute," said the boy.

Meryl Lee's free palm came up flat against his nose, which drove his head back, so when Matt's right arm came at him like an arrow, Matt could grab the boy's neck above the frills. The boy's eyes grew wide, and he reached for Matt but couldn't pull his arm away. And just as Bing Crosby was hoping that everyone's days would be merry and bright, Matt pushed the St. Giles's boy backwards across the dance floor and out the door of Greater Hoxne Hall.

After a moment, the other three boys sprinted across and followed them out.

So did the headmaster of St. Giles's, along with two of the chaperoning teachers.

Some Christmas soirees are remembered for their food, some for their music, some for their decorated trees. But at St. Elene's Preparatory Academy for Girls, the Christmas Soiree of 1968 was remembered in later years for the remarkable amount of blood left behind on the tiled floor of Greater Hoxne Hall's lobby, the blood having flowed from the broken noses of the four boys from St. Giles's Preparatory Academy for Boys, one of whom would spend much of his Christmas holiday having dental work done. In the lobby of Greater Hoxne Hall, the tile grout would never be the same color.

At St. Giles's the Christmas Soiree of 1968 was remembered for the initiation of a boxing program in physical education, the headmaster having decided that personal defense was a remarkably understudied discipline.

In the apartment of Mrs. Connolly, the Christmas Soiree of 1968 was remembered as a social disaster—and likely the last time that boys from St. Giles's would visit—and when *she* was finally headmistress, things like this would never happen.

In the home of Dr. MacKnockater, downstairs, the Christmas Soiree of 1968 was remembered as the single most exciting Christmas soiree that St. Elene's had ever hosted, and Dr. Mac-Knockater could not help but smile at the image of the distraught St. Giles's headmaster.

Upstairs, in a bedroom in the MacKnockater home, the Christmas Soiree of 1968 would be remembered as the evening that Matt wept, because he had done for Meryl Lee what he had not been able to do for Georgie—but it wasn't enough.

And in Netley 204, while Jennifer prattled on about Peter Vaughn and how he was so funny and so sweet and so cute and so honorable and how he ran to rescue his friend from that wild boy, Meryl Lee knew she would remember the Christmas Soiree of 1968 as the beginning of something.

On Saturday, waiting for her parents to come pick her up for Christmas vacation, Meryl Lee wondered what she was going to say if her mother said, "So what have you become Accomplished in this semester?" because she wasn't sure she was even close to becoming Accomplished in anything and she still wasn't sure she could even imagine what it was she might become Accomplished in.

The second quarter evaluations did not help much. "Meryl Lee is both an attentive and eager student who shows promise in her scientific endeavors," wrote Mrs. Bellamy. "Meryl Lee seems utterly unable to grasp the meaning and purpose of a semicolon," wrote Mrs. Connolly. "Meryl Lee is the powdered sugar of Domestic Economy," wrote Mrs. Wyss.

The second quarter evaluations painted a sort of confused portrait, Meryl Lee decided.

While she waited, Meryl Lee watched St. Elene's Preparatory Academy for Girls empty out.

Jennifer had left first thing in the morning so she would be sure not to miss a minute of Venice—or Vienna—or wherever she would be with Alden. Meryl Lee helped her drag her two huge suitcases down to Netley's lobby, and when the limousine drove up and Charles got out—really, his name was Charles—Jennifer sparkled, "Hello, Charles!" and he held open the door for her and she got in slowly and then sidled over to the window while Charles loaded her luggage into the trunk and she looked back at Meryl Lee and smiled.

The yellow taxi came while Charles was still loading. Limoless Charlotte from Charlotte was mortified—but Jennifer smiled even wider. The taxi driver told Charlotte from Charlotte and Ashley to put their own luggage in the trunk—"I got a bum back," he said—and when he asked where they were headed, Ashley said pretty loudly, "The airport," but Charlotte from Charlotte said just as loudly, "But first we have to stop at the Greyhound bus terminal for Ashley." Then she smiled at Meryl Lee, and at Ashley, who did not smile back.

Meryl Lee figured that her parents were still at least an hour away, so she went back to Netley, where she found Bettye starting to mop the hallway for the holiday break.

She was crying.

When Bettye saw Meryl Lee, she tried to stop, but she couldn't—and Meryl Lee embraced her, gripping hard.

"It's Alethea's brother." Bettye took a deep breath. "She heard last night. He was out on patrol and . . . oh, Meryl Lee, he's dead."

They walked out through the cold and spitting snow. They walked down to the wall, where the last brown poison ivy leaves caught in the vines rustled with infection. Bettye was quiet now, but when Meryl Lee looked over, she was still crying.

"And we haven't heard a word from Jonathan," Bettye said.

Meryl Lee took her hand.

Bettye took another deep breath. "Jonathan is only eighteen. He's a kid."

The wind whipped one of the leaves on the poison ivy vines, and it skittered away across the frozen ground.

"He shouldn't be in Vietnam. He just shouldn't be there," said Bettye.

Then she couldn't stop.

Jonathan's hair was dark yellow most of the time, but it lightened after a summer out on the water, she said.

He was great with knots and could tie them blindfolded.

He cooked scrod like no one else could.

He ran like a lanky dog, all loose and half-jointed.

He knew the Gettysburg Address by heart and would recite it for you if you asked—and sometimes when you didn't ask.

He knew where the lobsters were going to be.

He liked to memorize the timing of the tides.

He was going to be an engineer and build bridges all over the world. And when he was done building bridges all over the world, he was going to come back to Maine to be a fisherman.

That's what he was going to do.

"But who knows if . . ."

After that, they were silent.

Because that's what the Blank does.

Later, driving out past the poison ivy walls, Meryl Lee's mother explained that her father hadn't been able to take time off to come pick her up. Actually, he wasn't at home at all. He was so busy these days. In fact, he was away for the holidays.

"Where is he?"

They'd talk about that later, said her mother.

Meryl Lee felt the Blank crowding into the car.

On the way home, Meryl Lee's mother did ask if she thought she was becoming Accomplished. Meryl Lee played with her Wedgwood pendant and she said, "I think I'm beginning to see the Obstacles." And then it began to snow—lovely, large flakes of twirling snow, so large you could almost see their shapes.

They got back to Long Island late.

It felt funny to come back after being away for so long. Small things had changed all over—a new lamp by her mother's living room chair, a new carpet running up the steps, a new sleeper couch in her father's study—all of these had happened without her. It seemed as though things should stay the same while she was away.

But they didn't.

Meryl Lee went up to her room. A new spread on her bed. Yellow. She hated having a new bedspread.

She looked out the window. The snow looked so . . . real. Like this had happened a million times before, and it would happen a million times again. No matter what Obstacles got in its way, snow would keep on.

Meryl Lee sat on her new bedspread. Yellow like the yellow tights Holling once wore on stage in *The Tempest*. Yellow as a yellow brick road. Yellow like the shirt that—

She thought about Matt. About Dr. MacKnockater. About

Bettye. About Alethea's brother. About Heidi and Marian. Even about Jennifer.

Holling.

She thought about the next semester at St. Elene's Preparatory Academy for Girls.

She thought about becoming Accomplished.

"I think I'm beginning to see the Obstacles," she had said.

She wondered what was next.

SPRING SEMESTER
January—June 1969

RESOLUTIONS

TWENTY-THREE

In 1968, THE YEAR BEFORE MERYL LEE KOWALSKI'S second semester at St. Elene's Preparatory Academy for Girls, sixteen thousand five hundred and ninety-two American soldiers died in Vietnam. Most of them were one or two years older than Alethea's brother. They had had their whole lives in front of them: meeting the girl they loved, sundaes at Woolworth's lunch counter, opening Coke bottles, dancing, getting married, having children. Everything.

Like Holling. Like Alethea's brother.

While she was home, Meryl Lee had almost gone over to see Mai Thi, and she had almost gone over to see Danny Hupfer, but every time she almost went over, the Blank stopped her at the door. She couldn't go. They hadn't any of them written, they hadn't any of them called. It was as if Holling's death had walled them off.

And right now, it was too much to even imagine being together. It would hurt beyond hurt.

Still, on the day before Meryl Lee Kowalski's return for the second semester at St. Elene's Preparatory Academy for Girls, Meryl Lee woke resolved. She walked to Holling Hoodhood's house. She stood in front of it, trembling. She stood in front of it for a long time. And then the door opened, and Holling's sister, Heather, came out. For a moment she was on the porch, her hands at her face, and then she ran to Meryl Lee, and they held each other, and they cried and cried and cried and cried, right out there on the sidewalk, cried and cried.

Just like that.

And for Meryl Lee, on that quiet sidewalk, there was the Blank again.

But maybe, something else too.

She would have to figure out what it was.

But that wasn't all she would have to figure out. Over Christmas vacation, Meryl Lee had learned what she did not want to learn when she went into her parents' bedroom and saw that everything that belonged to her father was gone—his suits, his ties, the photograph of the two of them in Quebec City he always had on his dresser—all gone, and she suddenly knew why her parents had not come up for her at Thanksgiving and why her father had not come up for her birthday and to bring her home at Christmas and what the legal appointments were about and why her father was away for the holidays.

When her mother had walked into the bedroom behind her and put her hands on her shoulders, Meryl Lee knew that everything she had figured out was true.

"We're calling it a trial separation," said her mother. "I'm moving down to Philadelphia."

"Philadelphia?" said Meryl Lee.

"A new start," said her mother. "It's for the best."

"You could have told me together," said Meryl Lee, "instead of letting me find out because of an empty room."

Her mother didn't answer.

Christmas was awful, even though her mother had tried to act like everything was fine. They took a hotel room for three days and shopped all over New York City until Meryl Lee had more new clothes than she needed or wanted.

And when they weren't shopping, her mother toured her around the city because, Meryl Lee figured, she thought they should stay busy. The Museum of Natural History, a Broadway matinee, Tiffany, the Christmas show at Radio City, St. Patrick's, Central Park. Lots of silent walking in Central Park.

After they got back home, Meryl Lee spent the rest of Christmas vacation in her room, as the sparkle and glow of the red and green bulbs of the St. Elene's Christmas tree faded, as the needles browned and dropped, and as she wondered how Matt had celebrated Christmas and if he had celebrated Christmas with Dr. MacKnockater, and where he'd grown up, and . . . *You know,* she thought, *I don't know anything about him.*

She wished she did.

On the day she was to return to St. Elene's, her father drove her up. They were going to stop in Portland so he could meet with a client, and Meryl Lee said she'd take the bus the rest of the way to Bath. It was only a short ride, and it would probably be good for her to get used to the bus system anyway.

Her father said that would be fine. He'd meet with the client, and then they'd get directions to the bus station. She only had the one suitcase. She'd find her way with no trouble. And he'd call the school to make sure someone could pick her up when the bus got in to the station.

One thing Meryl Lee did not know was that Matt had never cel-ebrated Christmas before—at least, he couldn't remember cele-brating Christmas before. He remembered walking through New York City at Christmastime, of course. The snow, the cold, the stupid tourists, jostling so close together they couldn't feel him lift-ing their fat wallets to bring back to Leonidas Shug. The windows decorated and more stupid tourists with fat wallets. The chestnuts burning on the street corners and even more stupid tourists with fat wallets.

He could remember all that.

But nothing like this. The boughs that he helped Mrs. Mac-Knockater put up over the bookcases so that the whole house began to smell like pine. The baking baking baking as if an army were coming to dinner. The cards from old students that she read again and again and kept in a wooden box beside the huge tree that he had dragged in, so huge he'd had to cut the stu-pid top off to get it to stand upright in the corner. The bright lights, the gold and silver ornaments so thin and fragile he had to hold them with two fingers—and even so he'd broken three. The tinsel that picked up the bright glow from the birch logs that burned in the fireplace. And the wrapped and ribboned pres-ents, some with his name on them, some with Captain Hurd's name. One had Bagheera's name on it—the one with the worst wrapping job.

Mrs. MacKnockater made Matt go to the midnight service at St. Luke's on Christmas Eve. She made him sit between her ample self and Captain Hurd, as if they were protecting him from the whole world—as if they could. And there was a little too much praying for Matt's taste, and a lot too much preaching, and he let the offering plate pass by even though he was tempted, but the singing was okay. It even felt as if he'd heard the tunes before—maybe.

And afterward they came out and it was past midnight, so Christmas Day, and the yellow lights of the church shone through the windows onto the soft snow that was falling, and Mrs. MacKnockater had turned to him right there in front of the church and done something she'd never done before: she kissed him on the cheek, and she whispered, "Merry Christmas, Matthew." And Captain Hurd had said, "And one for me?" and Mrs. MacKnockater had said, "Old coot," but she'd kissed him anyway, on the cheek, lightly and quickly, and he'd said, "Not your best effort," and she'd said, "How would you know?" and he'd said, "I remember," and they walked home through the soft snow, quiet after that.

The next morning, Matt opened his presents under the tree, as Mrs. MacKnockater and the Captain watched. A field compass from the Captain and a new slicker—"For squalls, because they can come up, you know." A tortoiseshell pen from Mrs. MacKnockater—"It's time you had a good one," she said—and two sweaters that were a little too big but "you'll grow into them." Some wool socks because everyone should get wool socks at Christmas—the Captain got a pair too. And then Mrs. MacKnockater opened her present from Matt: *The Strange Case of Dr. Jekyll and Mr. Hyde,* by Robert Louis Stevenson. "He's the guy that wrote *Treasure Island,*" said Matt. "And it's a lot shorter." He'd practiced the first chapter over and over, and they sat down in front of the fireplace and he read it to the two of them, word perfect.

He was sort of surprised when Mrs. MacKnockater cried. It wasn't the sort of thing she did.

So Christmas came to Mrs. MacKnockater's house, the happiest Christmas in a long time. And at the end of each of the days that followed, Matt lay down in his bed and thought about a day filled with good chores—keeping the wood stove going, splitting maple splints, repairing lobster traps. And he thought about going out on the bay on *Affliction,* sailing on calm days and chugging around the islands, coming back to read some more of *The Strange Case of Dr. Jekyll and Mr. Hyde,* eating the Christmas cakes that Mrs. MacKnockater would keep baking. At night, having climbed through the chute up onto the slate roof, he thought, *So this is happiness. This is what it is.* And he remembered Georgie. And he remembered Pastor Darius and Sophia, and Mr. Tush and the Myrnas, and even though he was a bit afraid of going down to New Bedford again, he figured there would be no reason that Leonidas Shug would be watching for him in Portland. And it was just a short bus ride, after all.

And so, that first week of January, Matt told Mrs. MacKnockater that he'd be going down to visit some people he knew in Portland. He'd take the noontime bus and be back not too late. He was pretty sure they'd feed him well enough. No, she didn't have to wait supper for him. No, he'd be fine. Of course he'd be fine.

On the day he left, he'd been gone only an hour or so—maybe he'd just arrived in Portland, thought Mrs. MacKnockater—when Lieutenant Minot came to the house again.

Mrs. MacKnockater was wrong about his getting down to Portland; he'd already been there twenty minutes. The bus trip had been faster than usual—it was freezing cold and snowing a bit, and even people who live in Maine don't always want to travel when it's freezing cold and snowing, so no one had been waiting at the bus stations—and Matt had already come down Commercial Street and was standing across from the Chowder House.

Or what used to be the Chowder House.

It, and the two stores beyond it, and the art gallery beside it were burned-out ruins.

Even the pier behind the Chowder House was mostly gone. Just three or four darkened columns led out into the harbor, one with a seagull standing atop it, its wings out, its head bobbing up and down, its mouth open to squawk.

As the new, soft snow gentled Portland, Matt could hardly breathe. He turned and went into the Odds and Ends Gift Shop, where the manager was packing Christmas away. Yeah, he said, the fire had happened six, maybe seven, months back—maybe more—he couldn't remember. Funniest thing, the fire had started in the art gallery, for no reason that anyone could find. It had spread right into the Chowder House, and Cyrus Tush had been plenty lucky to get out with his tush intact. The fire had run across the attics in the buildings, and the whole block was burning before the fire trucks had even gotten there. Too bad. Folks around town, especially the lobstermen, really missed the Chowder House. Didn't look like they'd be rebuilding anytime soon, though.

And Mr. Tush? And the Myrnas?

Cyrus had gone to Georgia, or some such southern place. Myrna—there was only one, you know—Myrna had gone out to her people in Alberta. Nope, he didn't know a thing about any cat.

The manager finished putting away the strings of lights. "You sound like you knew them," he said. "You aren't the kiddo who worked for them? I heard there was some kid that worked for them."

"No," said Matt. He backed toward the door. "I used to eat at the Chowder House when I came to visit my aunt."

The manager shook his head. "Sure is a shame," he said.

"Yeah," said Matt, and he backed out into the frigid air and the snow.

He looked up and down Commercial Street.

No one was out in this cold.

He walked across to the wreck. There was already enough new snow to whiten the timbers, and he reached down and let his hand rest upon them. Then he walked around and behind what remained and stood on the shoreline, looking out at what he had looked out at from the window where he'd slept for months.

He could imagine the Chowder House standing behind him.

But it wasn't easy.

He felt the presence of those charred beams as if he were carrying them on his back.

"Hey, kid," he heard.

He turned quickly.

"Kid, that's not a healthy place to be standing."

And Matt took off, clambering over the beams. He slipped a couple of times and tore his hand against a nail that stuck out, but made his way down to the pier, and then quickly up toward Commercial Street so that he wouldn't be trapped against the water. He headed down one side street and up another, slipping on the new snow, and turning to face away from the wind that was cutting through him now. Somehow, his face had gotten all wet. He slowed to a hunched walk so that no one would notice him moving through the streets, and kept the harbor to his right so that he could find the bus station.

He took off his hat and wrapped it around his hand, which was starting to throb.

Dang, it was cold.

He hurried toward the station, feeling the tips of his ears start to freeze.

"There's not much I can tell you," said Lieutenant Minot. "There was a fire down to New Bedford. A church burned—Second Baptist. It's pretty clear it was arson. And it happened a few weeks after a boy who was living with the pastor and his wife disappeared."

"That hardly represents conclusive evidence, Lieutenant."

"The way that people who worshiped at Second Baptist described the boy, he's a ringer for your Matthew. And the way the pastor and his wife stayed strangely quiet about what happened to him makes me wonder."

"Still, none of that—"

"Mrs. MacKnockater, there was another fire. After a boy who was living in a restaurant suddenly disappeared. And the owner of the restaurant isn't talking about him either."

Mrs. MacKnockater turned toward the windows and looked out at the ocean.

"That fire was in Portland," said Lieutenant Minot.

"Portland?" she said.

"You understand what that means? It means they're getting closer."

"And the 'they' that you refer to is who . . . ?"

"I don't know. But I think Matthew does. I think he's hiding from them. And I think they're very good at finding him."

Mrs. MacKnockater nodded.

"I need to talk to him right now," said Lieutenant Minot.

"He'll be back tonight," she said. "Probably on the seven forty bus."

Meryl Lee walked out of the Trelawney and Smollett Real Estate Offices and into the bitter cold welling up from Portland Harbor. *How do people live here,* she wondered, glad that she had decided not to pack all the books she had wanted to lug back to St. Elene's. Mr. Smollett had promised that the bus station was close: three blocks, then a right, and it would be on the next corner. Wavy wisps of snow blew down the street against her, and she kept her face covered with one mittened hand. She breathed through the wool, which quickly became wet and then icy. How could that happen so fast?

The drive up from New York with her father had been too quiet and too long. They had not talked about the trial separation, or about Philadelphia, or about anything much. When they veered toward her life at St. Elene's, it was a relief. They could act as if they both really, really wanted to talk about St. Elene's. She could talk about her classes, about the teachers, about Thanksgiving dinner at Dr. MacKnockater's home—though she didn't, for whatever reason, say a thing about Matt—about how nice the grounds were in the fall, and how lovely they were when snow-covered, and how wonderful it would be to see them in the warm spring, and so on, and so on, and so on, and so on.

They talked so they didn't have to.

"You're sure you can find the way?" her father had said at Trelawney and Smollett's. "It's pretty cold out there. And that snow is coming down harder."

"I'll be fine," she said. "Are you going to be okay?"

He looked at her. "I guess," he said.

"I guess I will be too, then," she said.

He held the door open for her and waved her out into the snow. And when the door closed, everything that was warm was gone—just like that.

She walked the three blocks, pulling her suitcase through the gathering snow, and then she took the right turn and the bus station was on the corner, just as Mr. Smollett had promised.

It wasn't a very big bus station, but it was warm. She bought the ticket up to Bath, sat on one of the long benches, and thought about *The Wonderful Wizard of Oz*. She wondered, *Suppose Dorothy didn't want to get back to Kansas? What then?* So she took out *The Grapes of Wrath*, which she was reading for the third time—because if there was anything lewd, she'd missed it entirely. What she'd found instead was one beautiful thing after another, especially at the end, when Rose of Sharon fed the old man. She thought it was the most beautiful thing she'd ever read.

She went out to the bus twenty minutes or so before it was due to leave. The bus driver saw her coming and motioned for her to put her suitcase in one of the open bins. She did, and climbed on board, and went to hand the ticket to him. "Put it under the clip on the seat ahead of you," he said. "I'll pick them all up when everyone's on board."

She took a seat about halfway back, put the ticket under the clip, then leaned back and looked out the window. The sky was darkening early; it really did look as though the snow was coming down a lot harder.

Meryl Lee did not recognize Matt when he boarded the bus at the last second—probably because he came down the aisle pretty quickly, and he was all hunched over, and he had his hood up and his face turned down. He might have walked right by, except he had to stop when the passenger across from her stood in the aisle to push a full shopping bag into the overhead, and they looked right at each other, and in his eyes was what had been in his eyes when he'd bounded down the stairs in his boxers, holding a hatchet.

"Matt?" she said.

He sat down next to her. He was breathing kind of raggedly. His right hand was hidden in his hat.

"What's wrong?" she said.

"Nothing's wrong."

She looked at him. "You are a stinky liar," she said.

He looked at her. "What are you doing on this bus?"

"Water-skiing. What are you doing?"

"Tickets, please."

In the front of the bus, the driver had stood and was slowly moving back, punching holes in the tickets.

Matt froze.

"Do you have a ticket?" said Meryl Lee.

"Of course I have a ticket."

"Put it under the clip."

"He'll see me."

The driver—the same one, the very same one whom Matt had seen before—moved closer.

Matt took the ticket out from his back pocket and held it.

"Who cares if he sees you?" she said. She took his ticket and slid it under the clip.

"He'll see you, too," he said.

"So?"

The driver was only a couple of seats in front of them now.

"Don't you get it?"

"No, I don't get it. What's the problem?"

The driver moved ahead toward them.

The driver who knew Shug.

The same dang driver.

Matt suddenly reached behind Meryl Lee's head and leaned toward her and kissed her. And kissed her. And kissed her. Meryl Lee could hardly breathe, and she didn't know what to do. Of all the times she had imagined kissing Holling, it was never like this— like someone kissing her as if his life depended on it. And all she could feel was this close presence of Matt, and his face against hers, and his desperate need, and she put her hand behind his head and held on, and she heard the chuckle of the bus driver and the clicking of his hole punch, and she sensed, more than heard, that he had moved on.

She let go of Matt and backed into her seat.

When she looked at him, she thought he was going to cry.

She thought she might too.

"What was that about?" she whispered.

"I can't let him see me," he said. "We should get off the bus."

"Oh, and he won't see you if we get up now?"

Matt slumped down. He gathered his hood closer around his face.

"Matt, you have to tell me what is going on."

And there was the image of Georgie in that Alley, fixed into Matt's mind. He held his hand up to his face, but he couldn't wipe the picture away. He just couldn't wipe it away.

"I can't," he said. "I can't."

Meryl Lee took a deep breath. "The bus driver is going to be coming back in a minute. You better be ready for what I'm going to do."

Matt looked up from his hood. "What are you going to do?"

She looked behind her and over the seat. The driver was already coming back up the aisle.

"You shouldn't imagine that this means anything more than it does," she said, and she leaned into Matt and kissed him again, and kissed him, until the driver, chuckling, had passed, and she leaned back up and they looked at each other and suddenly, Meryl Lee wondered if it had meant more than she thought it might.

She sat back against her seat, turned, and looked out at the snow. When she reached up to her face, she was surprised that she was crying.

"Are you okay?" Matt said.

She nodded.

He touched her shoulder. "Thanks," he said. "I mean it. Thanks."

She turned back to him. "You're in trouble."

"I guess you could say that."

"And you can't tell anyone what it is."

He shook his head. "Not unless I want to get them in trouble too."

"It can't be that bad."

Matt looked long and hard at Meryl Lee. He reached over and took her hand—and this time it wasn't just acting . . . though maybe his kiss hadn't all been just acting either.

She let her hand stay in his, and as the bus passed into Yarmouth, she told him about her parents, and the trial separation, and Philadelphia. And then, kind of stuttering, she said, "A-and . . . and then Holling."

He listened.

"He was in a car with his father. This car that he always wanted to drive. They were hit and when they got hit, Holling's head snapped back and they tried to get him to Syosset Hospital but there was nothing they could do."

Matt still listening.

"He loved baseball and especially the Yankees. And he loved Shakespeare. I know, can you believe it? Really, he loved Shakespeare. He once played Ariel, who was a fairy, but Holling said he was a warrior and I said . . . I never really said what I always wanted to say—that he was a warrior too. That I loved that he loved Shakespeare. That—"

She stopped.

"That you loved him too," whispered Matt.

"And I couldn't tell him goodbye. And I can't tell him how much I miss him."

"That everything afterward became sort of gray," said Matt.

"That sometimes, everything is a Blank," said Meryl Lee.

And they held each other's hands as Meryl Lee cried softly—softly because the lady with the full shopping bag was sort of watching them—and when she quieted up toward the turn to Bath, Matt did what he had not done for a very long time: he told her that his parents were gone, and that he had had one friend, Georgie, and that he was gone too.

"What do you mean, 'gone'?" she said.

The word was almost impossibly hard to say.

Matt shrugged. "I don't know what happened to my parents. And Georgie—they knifed him."

"Matt—"

"They killed him, Meryl Lee. That's why I ran. And that's all I can tell you, since—"

"It's all right," she said. "It's all right."

And Matt slumped farther down into his seat, and pulled his hood close over his face, and Meryl Lee glared over at the passenger with the full shopping bag until she turned away, and she put her head on Matt's shoulder, and he leaned his head against hers, and they each thought exactly the same thing: this is what I have right now, and maybe it won't last—or maybe it will—but it's what I have right now.

At the bus station in Bath, they waited until the driver got out to open the luggage bins beneath the bus—and they waited while the passenger with the full shopping bag pulled and tugged at the stupid shopping bag until she finally hefted it down—and when they got off, they scooted around the front of the bus and back down the other side so that the driver would not see them, and got into the station, where Mrs. Connolly was waiting for Meryl Lee.

She looked at her watch.

"You're almost fifteen minutes late," she said, as if this were somehow Meryl Lee's fault.

"I'm sorry," said Meryl Lee.

"Sorry doesn't bring back fifteen minutes. Come along."

"Your suitcase," whispered Matt.

"Oh." Meryl Lee stopped. "Mrs. Connolly, I'm so sorry, but I have to get—"

Mrs. Connolly waved her hand at her. "You should have thought about that when you got off the bus." She looked at Matt. "Perhaps you were otherwise occupied."

Meryl Lee ran to get her suitcase.

Matt stood with Mrs. Connolly in the Bath bus station.

They did not speak.

When Meryl Lee came back with the suitcase, Matt took it and lugged it to Mrs. Connolly's car. It really was snowing hard now, and by the time Matt had hefted the suitcase into the trunk, snow was already covering his hood.

"Mrs. Connolly, can we drive Matt to St. Elene's as well?" said Meryl Lee.

"We can when I am employed as a taxi service," said Mrs. Connolly. "Please get in. We're already much later than I had expected." She got into the car.

"I guess I'll see you around," said Matt.

"You okay?"

He nodded, and then he pulled back his hood, leaned over, and kissed her lightly on the cheek. "Okay," he said.

She put her hand up to her face, smiled at him, then got into the car with Mrs. Connolly.

Matt watched them drive away. He pulled his hood back up, though his face was warm enough.

Warmer than it had been for a long time.

"Matt Coffin," someone called.

He looked around quickly.

"Looks like you might need a lift," said Lieutenant Minot.

TWENTY-FOUR

THAT NIGHT, SNOW COVERED THE GROUNDS OF ST. Elene's Preparatory Academy for Girls, and the wind swept the drifts into sharp waves, sculpting small pagodas all along the poisoned wall. In the morning, ridges of snow bulged off the eaves of Putnam Library and along the ledges below the stained windows of Newell Chapel. Across the commons the snow was knee deep. Everything was white and bright and cold.

But at breakfast, the inside of Greater Hoxne Hall looked as cozy as you could possibly imagine, with its warm wood and yellow stained glass and deep red carpets and all the teachers gathered to greet their returning students, and all of them seemed happy, really happy, to have their students back. Mrs. Mott said, "So, Miss Kowalski, shall we see what mayhem we can foment in the new year?" (Meryl Lee hoped this was a joke.) Coach Rowlandson asked if Meryl Lee had been keeping up with her wind sprints, and when Meryl Lee looked a bit confused, Coach Rowlandson reminded her that spring meant *soccer season!* Mrs. Hibbard took Meryl Lee's face in her hands, hugged her, and didn't say anything at all. Mrs. Bellamy asked, "Are you ready to dissect a fetal pig or two this semester?" (Meryl Lee hoped this was a joke too.) Mrs. Wyss wore an apron splotched with powdered sugar. (Meryl Lee wondered if this was supposed to be some sort of signal to her, after her second quarter evaluation.) And the Awful Dignity was there, presiding—at least, for another few months.

She said, "Are you all right, Miss Kowalski?"

And Meryl Lee suddenly knew, suddenly and absolutely knew, that Dr. MacKnockater understood everything that had happened to her over Christmas vacation.

"I'm not sure," said Meryl Lee.

"No," said Dr. MacKnockater. "Of course you wouldn't be." She took Meryl Lee's hands in her own. "The biggest Obstacles are the ones that come closest to our hearts."

"How did you know?" she said.

"Your parents told me when you first came. One reason they brought you here was so you would not see firsthand what they did not want you to see. Not after your other loss."

Meryl Lee nodded. Suddenly, she wasn't sure she would be able to stop what was coming. She squeezed Dr. MacKnockater's hands, but it was still coming.

And then she couldn't stop it.

She couldn't.

Even though she was right there in the middle of Greater Hoxne Hall.

Dr. MacKnockater took her shoulders and led her to a little room, where they sat on little needlepointed chairs, by a little cherry table, in a little alcove with high windows that looked out over the commons. And Dr. MacKnockater gave her a tissue and she waited until Meryl Lee was still.

"Why didn't you tell me?" said Meryl Lee finally.

"It was not my place, Meryl Lee. Your parents were to tell you."

"But you could have prepared me for it."

Dr. MacKnockater leaned forward.

"That is exactly what we have been trying to do."

"How?"

Dr. MacKnockater leaned forward even more. "Resolution and Accomplishment, my dear."

"But I'm not Accomplished in anything."

"I would say you are already becoming quite Accomplished."

Meryl Lee looked at Dr. MacKnockater—sort of. It was a pretty watery look.

"In what?"

"If you have not discovered that for yourself by the end of the semester, I will tell you," said Dr. MacKnockater. "But perhaps this may lead you in the right direction: You gave Matthew Coffin a great gift yesterday."

"A gift?"

"You trusted him. That is a great gift, Meryl Lee. One of the greatest gifts anyone can give."

"He's in trouble, but he wouldn't tell me why."

"He could not trust you with knowledge . . . knowledge that he is hardly willing to share even with me. And yet, despite that, you helped him when he needed it."

"Dr. MacKnockater, anyone would."

But she shook her head. "Miss Kowalski, that is not so. It is the rather rare person who would. And now, I have told you enough. And I'm afraid that if I delay you any longer, you will either miss breakfast entirely or be late for Mrs. Connolly's American Literary Masterpieces class."

Meryl Lee didn't miss breakfast entirely, but she was almost late for American Literary Masterpieces. Mrs. Connolly was just closing the classroom door when Meryl Lee stopped her. She opened the door wide enough for her to come in, then shut it—decisively. "Miss Kow-alski," she said, "I'd like to see you in my office directly after class."

Meryl Lee nodded.

"Excuse me," said Mrs. Connolly. "I did not hear a proper response."

"I'm sorry, Mrs. Connolly. Yes, I'll come to your office after class."

She sat next to Marian, who whispered, "Is everything all right?"

Heidi leaned over. "You can borrow my field hockey stick if you need to."

"I'm not going to need your field hockey stick," said Meryl Lee.

"You never know," said Heidi.

Meryl Lee followed Mrs. Connolly to her office. Mrs. Connolly set her books down upon her glass-top desk and sat behind it.

"So, here we are again, Miss Kowalski," she said. "Sit down, please." A command.

Meryl Lee sat down. The chair was cold.

"As we are starting a new semester, it seems to me the appropriate time to suggest that you reconsider some elements of your conduct at this school. I say this to you with all goodwill and hope for your continued success at St. Elene's."

"My conduct?"

"I refer to your continued association with those who should be outside the orbit of a girl of character who is attending St. Elene's."

The temperature in the room dropped by about twenty-five degrees.

Meryl Lee felt herself fill with Resolution. She sensed that something was about to happen, something she had never done.

"Who do you mean?" she said.

"I might begin with the young man you were with when I picked you up at the bus station."

"I was with Matt on the bus, but we didn't meet on purpose."

"Perhaps, but this was the same young man who created mayhem at the Christmas soiree. Did you also not meet 'on purpose' then?"

"He was protecting me."

"That is not how the headmaster of St. Giles's imagines the episode."

"Then *imagines* is the right word."

Mrs. Connolly sighed and sat back in her chair.

"I have never once found verbal cleverness to be impressive, Miss Kowalski, particularly from a student. I am taking the time to warn you against unfortunate connections, connections that are not appropriate between you as a student at this school and those who are not part of the community. The repeated connection with this boy is one. The repeated association with kitchen workers at St. Elene's is another."

"Do you mean Bettye?"

"Bettye Buckminster is a servant at St. Elene's, not one of your peers."

"Mrs. Connolly," said Meryl Lee, "Bettye Buckminster is one of the only people here who talks to me."

"The solution to your perceived isolation is not a kitchen worker. It is reaching out to girls of a similar station to your own," said Mrs. Connolly.

"Who I choose for my friend isn't any of your business," said Meryl Lee.

"It is hardly for you to determine the business of a member of the faculty—and it is very much my business. An education at St. Elene's involves the entire girl, Miss Kowalski—not just the intellect but also social and moral and emotional spheres of experience."

Meryl Lee felt herself shaking. "I think I had better go," she said.

"And I point out that the result of your associations is that you have been leaving the grounds of St. Elene's without permission. Am I correct in this?"

"I guess I should have asked permission," said Meryl Lee.

"Yes, you should have." Mrs. Connolly adjusted herself in her seat. "I am not headmistress yet," she said. "But if I were, I would most certainly have denied the request. Leaving the grounds without permission is a violation of our expectations. Continued violations would eventually lead to expulsion."

"I'm sorry, Mrs. Connolly." Meryl Lee stood up to go.

"Sit down, please, Miss Kowalski."

They looked at each other across the glass desktop. *Obstacles,* Meryl Lee thought. *Obstacles.*

"Thank you, Mrs. Connolly," said Meryl Lee. "I really do think I had better go."

Mrs. Connolly stood.

Meryl Lee turned and left.

She wished she had been holding Heidi's field hockey stick— but it was a good thing for the glass desktop she wasn't.

The next day, Meryl Lee was called to the office of the headmistress.

She was starting to get used to being called to faculty offices.

Everything in Dr. MacKnockater's office was old—including Dr. MacKnockater, of course.

A flintlock hung above a brick fireplace, and the bricks were black from smoke. Someone had bound most of the books in Dr. MacKnockater's office with dark leather sometime before the American Revolution. Birch logs were heaped inside the old fireplace, and in front of them lay a long hinged box of very dark wood, ornately carved. The pine floorboards were almost two feet wide, and they were worn down in front of Dr. MacKnockater's desk—probably where centuries of students had stood before they were beheaded and impaled on the wall around St. Elene's. When she saw Meryl Lee looking at the desk, Dr. MacKnockater said that it had once belonged to Robespierre.

"Robespierre?" Meryl Lee said.

"He reigned in France during the Terror." Dr. MacKnockater ran her hand across the top. "I imagine he signed quite a few death warrants right here."

This was not a good beginning.

"Mrs. Connolly has written to me regarding your interview with her yesterday," Dr. MacKnockater said. "She complained of a certain arrogance. Do you know what Mrs. Connolly meant?"

Meryl Lee took a deep breath.

Dr. MacKnockater waited patiently.

"Dr. MacKnockater," she said, "in your Chapel talks, you encourage us to think independently and to have the courage to follow the path our reason and intelligence tell us to follow, especially when our hearts affirm the path. You say we should not let others decide for us and to test the world to see if we are meeting it in ways that are right and true and good. You say confronting Obstacles requires the courage of Resolution."

Dr. MacKnockater still waiting patiently.

"I'm trying to confront Obstacles," she said.

Still waiting.

"I don't mean to be arrogant."

Dr. MacKnockater leaned forward over Robespierre's desk.

"Miss Kowalski," she said, "next year, Mrs. Connolly will be headmistress of St. Elene's Preparatory Academy for Girls. It is unpleasant not to have a friend in the headmistress."

Meryl Lee nodded. She understood.

"However," Dr. MacKnockater said, "you have one now."

Meryl Lee understood that, too.

On Saturday, Marian and Heidi and Meryl Lee walked across the commons. Near Newell, a bunch of lower school kids were shrieking and throwing snowballs at one another, even though the snow was so powdery that the snowballs disintegrated in midair. Julia Chall, Barbara Rockcastle, and Elizabeth Koertge were trying to roll a snowman into existence, and laughing as it fell apart. And on the far side of the commons, Mrs. Hibbard was heading over to Putnam, carrying a bag bulging with bright yellow wool.

As they neared the gates in the poison-ivied wall, Marian asked if they had permission to leave the grounds of St. Elene's.

Meryl Lee paused.

"Did anyone tell us not to go for a walk?" said Heidi.

"I think we're not supposed to go without telling someone," said Marian.

They looked at Meryl Lee.

"Marian," said Meryl Lee, "I'm going off the grounds this morning."

"Um, okay," said Marian.

"Are you?"

"I guess," said Marian.

"Good," said Meryl Lee. "Now you and I have told someone, and the only one to get in trouble will be Heidi."

"Hey, wait . . ."

"Let's go," said Meryl Lee, feeling an Obstacle slip away.

They walked past the turnoff to Dr. MacKnockater's house—*I shouldn't visit without an invitation,* Meryl Lee thought, but she wondered what Matt was doing—and they turned down a street that headed toward the water, and soon they could see the docks and their moored boats, the masts bobbing in the bright air. It was cold, and Meryl Lee held her arms around herself as they stepped onto the pier. She was half looking for Matt—well, maybe more than half looking—and they passed several of the lobster boats until they came to *Affliction.* So when Matt Coffin looked up from winding the ropes, he was sort of startled to see her staring down at him.

And suddenly, there was Captain Hurd.

"Miss Kowalski," he said. "And you are . . ."

"Heidi Kidder," said Heidi.

"Marian Elders," said Marian.

"Elders, Kidder, and Kowalski," said Captain Hurd. "Sounds like a law firm."

Matt smiled a little and looked away.

It wasn't hard to figure out what he was smiling about.

When he looked back up, brushing his hair against the wind, the Captain reminded him to pay attention to the ropes he was winding.

"And how is Dr. MacKnockater these days?" asked the Captain.

"Did you know she isn't going to be headmistress next year?" said Meryl Lee.

Captain Hurd turned to help Matt with the ropes.

"Someone on the board of trustees doesn't like something she said in public. Maybe something political. So really, she's being forced to resign."

"You think she's resigning because the trustees want her to?" Captain Hurd said.

"Why else?" said Meryl Lee.

"You think that sounds like something that Nora MacKnockater would do?"

And it didn't take long for Meryl Lee to figure out that no, it didn't at all sound like something that Nora MacKnockater would do.

It didn't sound like her at all.

"So why else?" said Heidi.

"She would have her reasons," said Captain Hurd. "Do we know who the next headmistress will be?"

"Mrs. Connolly," said Marian.

"Mrs. Connolly?" said Captain Hurd. "Sharp-arsed Agatha Connolly?"

All three girls nodded. Heidi laughed.

"Heaven and all its holy angels defend thee," said Captain Hurd.

"What do you think we should do?" said Meryl Lee.

"Why would you think you could do anything?" said Captain Hurd.

"Because someone should," she said.

He looked at her. "Where were you thirty years ago when I needed you?"

"What happened thirty years ago?"

Captain Hurd bent down over Matt and hauled up the wound rope. Then he turned back to Meryl Lee. "Nora MacKnockater fired me," he said.

"Fired you? Why did she fire you?"

"Because it's impossible to have someone you love be your boss, too. So who's up for a quick sail around the bay?" he said.

"Someone you love?" said Heidi.

"Nora MacKnockater is not resigning as headmistress of St.

239

Elene's because she's intimidated by the board of trustees. So, are you coming aboard?"

They did.

Later, Meryl Lee wondered what it meant that Matt Coffin never spoke a word the whole time he steered them around the still waters of the inner islands.

On Monday, Mrs. Saunders asked Meryl Lee to wait after class for a moment, and when all the other girls had left, Mrs. Saunders said, "I wonder if you would care to walk around the commons," and they put their coats on and went out into air so cold, it was brittle.

Meryl Lee wondered if she was in trouble again.

"I think winter is my favorite season," Mrs. Saunders said. "My father was a great believer in cold, clean air. He said it made for healthy lungs."

Meryl Lee waited.

"And how lovely the campus looks, covered in snow."

Meryl Lee waited.

"I understand you've been leaving the school grounds without permission, but I didn't ask you to come for a walk about that. If Mrs. Connolly knew, however . . ."

"She knows," said Meryl Lee.

Mrs. Saunders nodded. "Few things escape Mrs. Connolly. Not even clandestine sea voyages." She looked at Meryl Lee meaningfully.

Meryl Lee nodded.

They passed by Putnam Library, its white clapboards so bright with the snow and sunlight that Mrs. Saunders and Meryl Lee put their hands over their eyes.

"I wanted to tell you how impressed I have been by your rapid growth as a student and as a young, mature woman, Miss Kowalski. It has been a delight to witness it."

Meryl Lee was a little bit surprised. "Thank you, Mrs. Saunders."

"And I am not the only one to notice. The headmistress speaks very highly of you. She looks for great things from you. So do we all."

"Dr. MacKnockater won't be headmistress next year."

"Perhaps not."

"I don't think the new headmistress will speak so highly of me."

"Some things are beyond our control, Miss Kowalski—and that is true both for you and for the new headmistress. But if Dr. Mac-Knockater is accurate in her assessment of your Accomplishment, you are likely to be surprised."

"Mrs. Saunders, what Accomplishment?"

Mrs. Saunders smiled—which didn't happen all that often. Then she looked over at Newell Chapel. "Won't the daffodils be lovely in the spring?"

TWENTY-FIVE

Matt had learned: never go back. Never, ever go back.

There could be someone watching for you. And that someone was not someone you wanted to find you.

Never, never, ever go back.

He was spending more and more time with Captain Hurd these days, as if staying off the land meant that only God could see him—God and Captain Hurd. But not Leonidas Shug. And not the guys from the Alley. Most mornings, he was on board *Affliction* even before Captain Hurd came down to the docks. Matt would stay there until the early January dusk, winding ropes, cleaning the bait buckets, stacking and restacking the traps, until he about drove Captain Hurd crazy, and at the day's end the Captain would clamber up onto the dock and stomp off, yelling back to Matt about checking the bowline one more time before he left.

And once it was full dark, Matt would head up toward home, where Mrs. MacKnockater would be watching from the window, and where, when he came in, the wood stove warmth of the house clasped him.

Then he would almost gasp at the thought of leaving and wonder if he could ever, ever go.

Mrs. MacKnockater would send him upstairs to wash off the

fishy smell, but he would stop by the wood stove to add a stick or two and check the draft, and by the time he came back down, she would have the table set for supper, and a candle lit, and a cup of chowder on his plate, and a casserole steaming in the center of the table. And they would talk about the book they were reading— Matt had tried *Kidnapped* but thought it was boring, and *Dracula* but thought it was dumb, and he'd finally settled on *Oliver Twist,* which he couldn't stop reading—and then about Matt's day on the water and Mrs. MacKnockater's at St. Elene's, and sometimes Captain Hurd would come by and grumble about the chowder but he'd eat it all anyway, and the night would end with Captain Hurd whomping Matt at checkers and then, sometimes, Mrs. MacKnockater whomping Matt at chess, and then Matt would go upstairs and work at *Oliver Twist* and think about how he never wanted to leave again.

Because you can never, ever go back.

This was not something, however, that Lieutenant Minot seemed to understand.

One night in the middle of January, he came between checkers and chess. He sat down on the rocking chair, across the coffee table from Matt and Mrs. MacKnockater. He asked how they all were. They were all fine. He asked if Matt's back had healed, and Matt stood, turned, pulled up his shirt, and showed him. It was fine. Lieutenant Minot had heard that Mrs. MacKnockater intended to retire at the end of the school year and he asked what she would do after that. She told him she'd be fine.

Then Lieutenant Minot took three photographs out of his pocket. He put the first down on the coffee table in front of them.

"Matt," he asked, "do you recognize this boy?"

Matt shook his head. He didn't.

"How about this one?"

"Nope. Why?"

"How about this one?"—and he laid Georgie's picture on the checkerboard.

Maybe you can't go back. But maybe what was back there can catch up to you.

Matt felt everything in him stop.

It was a young Georgie, younger than when Matt had known him. But there was so much that was exactly the same. His crooked smile, that one crooked tooth, the crooked way he stood.

"I thought you might know one of them," said Lieutenant Minot.

The way he stood with his left leg straight, his right always bent a little—as if it were a little too long. The squint of his eyes in the sun. The curl of his hair at the sides. The hook of his thumbs in his belt.

Matt shook his head. "I don't," he said.

Lieutenant Minot gathered up the first two pictures and put them in his pocket. "I told you, Matt—I'm good at this job. These pictures, they're all boys named George. They all went missing at different times somewhere near New York City."

"I'm from New Bedford."

"Like I said, they're all from New York. Like you are. No, don't lie. The accent always gives New Yorkers away, like they're wearing a label. So, tell me about Georgie."

"I don't know him."

"In this photo he's nine years old. He used to live in New Jersey. That's Asbury Park in the background. Sometime after this photo, his father and mother separated, and his father took Georgie up to New York City and disappeared for a while. Then the father was killed in crossfire six or eight months later, so Georgie was probably left on his own. But no one knows where he went after that."

"Like I said, I—"

"Sounds like someone else's story, too."

Matt looked at him.

"I think you can help us with Georgie's."

"I can't." Matt was starting to shake a little.

"His mother is still looking for him."

"I said—"

"Matt, his mother is still looking for him. You can imagine what that's like. I think you can help me give her some closure."

Matt looked at the photograph again. He picked it up.

Georgie.

The Alley.

He felt it all come back to him, back to him, back to him like a returning tide. He felt the breath leave his body, come back, leave, come back, leave.

"Matthew," said Mrs. MacKnockater quietly.

The Alley.

"She should stop looking," Matt whispered.

He breathed again, and then he looked at Mrs. MacKnockater. What had he done?

Lieutenant Minot sat back. "Tell me."

"It's all right," said Mrs. MacKnockater. "Matthew, it's all right." She took his hand. "It's all right."

And Matt turned to Lieutenant Minot, and he hated him. But he told him about the Big Guy, and the Small Guy. He told him about the Alley.

"Everything," said Lieutenant Minot. "Tell me everything."

So Matt told him about Leonidas Shug.

The wood stove didn't seem so warm anymore, and when the lieutenant left that night, not even Mrs. MacKnockater's ample self wrapped around him could stop Matt from shaking.

TWENTY-SIX

AFTER SHE GOT BACK TO ST. ELENE'S, MERYL LEE went to Putnam Library every day to read the papers about Vietnam.

Assaults against American positions by rocket attacks.

Mines.

Operation Rolling Thunder finishing up, with eight hundred and nineteen American pilots dead or missing.

Operation Dewey Canyon just beginning. Who knew how many American pilots this time?

After she began to feel the Blank hovering at the doors of Putnam, Meryl Lee stopped reading about Vietnam.

In Chapel a few days later, Dr. MacKnockater told the students of St. Elene's Preparatory Academy for Girls that they must resolve to define for themselves what they should become Accomplished in. They should not become Accomplished in something someone else wanted them to become Accomplished in, but in something that came from their truest selves. It was the Resolution to define their Accomplishment that mattered, she said. Not the skill, not even the Accomplishment itself—the decision.

Dr. MacKnockater's searchlight gaze lit up Meryl Lee four times during that Chapel.

So Meryl Lee decided to ask around, because if Dr. MacKnockater knew what her Accomplishment was, then maybe someone else did too—someone who would tell her.

When Meryl Lee asked Coach Rowlandson what she thought she should become Accomplished in, Coach Rowlandson said, "Probably not field hockey. I'm hoping soccer."

When Meryl Lee asked Mrs. Kellogg what she thought she should become Accomplished in, Mrs. Kellogg said, "You might think of public oration."

Meryl Lee considered this. "Wouldn't you need to have something that you really, really wanted to oration about?" she said.

Mrs. Kellogg looked at her. "Maybe I was wrong," she said.

Mrs. Wyss said a lady should always be Accomplished in household management. Meryl Lee pointed out that Mary Stuart, Queen of Scots, probably did not count this as her greatest Accomplishment. Mrs. Wyss pointed out that Mary Stuart, Queen of Scots, was beheaded. Twice.

She had a point.

Mrs. Mott said she herself had recently decided, given events in her Tea and Biscuit Conversations, to become Accomplished in the art of self-defense. Meryl Lee thought she was only kidding.

Later, she wasn't so sure.

When Meryl Lee asked Mrs. Hibbard what she thought she should become Accomplished in, Mrs. Hibbard considered for a while and then said, "Knitting."

"Knitting?" Meryl Lee said.

Mrs. Hibbard said, "What could be better than making useful things out of yarn? And you can never go wrong knitting for someone else."

Meryl Lee did not ask Mrs. Connolly what she thought she might become Accomplished in.

When Meryl Lee saw Dr. MacKnockater in Greater Hoxne Hall a few days later, she said her Chapel talk had been inspiring. "I'm glad you found it to be so," Dr. MacKnockater said. "I understand from some of the teachers that you have been making inquiries about Accomplishment."

"It would save me a lot of time if you would just tell me," said Meryl Lee.

"Patience, Miss Kowalski. You shall find out for yourself, or I shall tell you at the end of the school year—those are the only alternatives."

Just like a teacher. Or like Glinda, the Good Witch of the South—who, after all, could have just told Dorothy about the stupid shoes before she ever stepped foot on the yellow brick road.

But she didn't.

On Friday afternoon, Meryl Lee went over to Putnam Library and Mrs. Hibbard pulled out a bag of bright yellow yarn and taught Meryl Lee how to knit a scarf. Knitting did not take long to learn. *Maybe this is it,* thought Meryl Lee—and it did seem a good thing to know how to do, since it was really a cold January and knitting a scarf was probably more useful than needlepoint—even if Mary Stuart, Queen of Scots, wouldn't agree.

And after all, what would Mary Stuart, Queen of Scots, put her scarf around?

But still, Meryl Lee wondered what Dr. MacKnockater would tell her at the end of the school year.

That weekend, Alethea did not come to St. Elene's, and Bettye had to work alone, and she was a wreck—but not because of working alone. Jonathan had finally written. She showed the letter

to Meryl Lee. It began with "Do not let the Old Man read this."
Meryl Lee could understand why. It was awful. Two of Jonathan's
platoon were killed by land mines the third day after they landed.
Killed. Another had his leg blown off three days later. The blood
had blown into Jonathan's face, along with the kneecap.

Meryl Lee asked if Bettye knew where Jonathan was and she
said he couldn't tell her where he was but it was where there was
a lot of fighting. And probably land mines. She said her father
couldn't watch the *Evening News* with Walter Cronkite anymore,
since he kept looking for Jonathan in the pictures from Vietnam.
"He's terrified he's going to see him on a stretcher," Bettye said.
"Or worse."

Meryl Lee started to cry.

She hardly knew Bettye's brother. But she was crying anyway.
And the Blank . . .

The Blank stayed on the edge of her vision, a white blur that
promised it would slide across her whole vision if she let it.

And when she was all alone and she thought of Jonathan, and
Holling, it almost, almost did.

On Sunday night after Evening Meal, under a covering darkness, Meryl Lee met Bettye and together they went down to the
shore to watch the early stars. Heidi didn't go, since Mr. Wheelock
had said she was skating on the thin ice of Lake Catastrophe in
algebra, and so she stayed behind to work word problems and break
pencils in two. And Marian said that she was going to work on her
essay for Mrs. Connolly since, you know. So just Meryl Lee and
Bettye walked down to the shore, using the path behind Netley and
scooting quickly past the Main Gate.

At the side of the ocean, Meryl Lee and Bettye watched the
tide slide out, the waves gentle, hardly rustling the pebbles that

sloshed back and forth, back and forth. In the east, the first stars began to promise their light. A few snowflakes slid down.

Everything was soft and quiet. The air, the light, the snow. Bettye took Meryl Lee's hand and smiled at her. "Jonathan is going to be all right, isn't he?"

And there was the Blank. Right there. Oh, right there!

And here is what happened next: Meryl Lee turned her back to the Blank. She hugged Bettye Buckminster, and they held together for a long time above the gently sounding waves.

Later that night, Meryl Lee—who really was becoming an Accomplished knitter with Mrs. Hibbard's help—pulled out her scarf to show Heidi and Marian. She was knitting it from the bags of bright yellow yarn that, she explained, Mrs. Hibbard had bought for three cents a skein because the store figured no one would ever buy yarn brighter than any naturally occurring color.

When Meryl Lee brought out the scarf, Heidi and Marian cowered behind upraised arms.

"The light, it burns!" they cried. "Mercy, mercy!"

Heidi thought this was hysterically funny.

"Mary Stuart, Queen of Scots, never begged for mercy," Meryl Lee said.

"And she was beheaded," said Marian.

"It's for Jonathan," said Meryl Lee.

"Jonathan is in Vietnam," said Heidi.

"So?"

"Vietnam is tropical," said Marian.

"You never know," said Meryl Lee.

So Heidi put on dark glasses, and Meryl Lee knitted.

That day, she did nine inches.

Maybe she really could become an Accomplished knitter.

On the third Monday of January, Mrs. Mott's Tea and Biscuit Conversation did not go well. Meryl Lee did not think she was responsible.

When Mrs. Mott announced at the Tea and Biscuit Conversation that Spiro Agnew was coming to visit St. Elene's, Ashley said, "Isn't it great that we have a vice president who wants to finally wipe out all the commies?"

"Let's move on," said Mrs. Mott.

When Mrs. Mott asked Meryl Lee for her current event, she said, "Thank you, Mrs. Mott. I would like to discuss the opportunities for peace in Vietnam."

Ashley said, "You must be a commie too."

And before Mrs. Mott could say, "Let's move on," again, Meryl Lee had replied to Ashley.

Meryl Lee was sure that she was not responsible all by herself for what happened next, and she certainly was not the first one to stand in a huff and to spill her tea and to speculate on the patriotism or lack thereof of certain people like Meryl Lee and like some members of the faculty.

Meryl Lee was moved to use some words not usually heard in Tea and Biscuit Conversations, which led to Lois Tuthill covering her ears and running from Mrs. Mott's rooms, which led to Mrs. Mott asking Meryl Lee to please wait until the others had left.

When they were alone, Mrs. Mott described to Meryl Lee the virtue of a calm spirit, which apparently St. Elene was famous for.

Meryl Lee was absolutely sure she would not become Accomplished in the virtue of a calm spirit.

Mrs. Mott agreed that growth in this area might come only after a long process, but there would be plenty of opportunities for growth during her education at St. Elene's, and Mrs. Mott was confident that Meryl Lee would enlarge her capacities.

So the very next day, Meryl Lee tried to remember the virtue of a calm spirit in Life Sciences when Mrs. Bellamy announced that today they would be dissecting earthworms.

Meryl Lee hated earthworms. Who doesn't?

First, Mrs. Bellamy showed her class the earthworms. They were floating—kind of—in a gray glass jar filled with formaldehyde. They were much bigger than earthworms deserved to be. Bigger long and bigger round. Mrs. Bellamy said bloated earthworms were easier to dissect, but Meryl Lee thought bloated earthworms were easier to throw up because of. You want earthworms to be where they're supposed to be—in the dirt, with everything else that crawls and is slimy—like Jennifer, Ashley, and Charlotte from Charlotte.

Meryl Lee shook her head. She was resolved. She would try to practice the virtue of a calm spirit.

Then Mrs. Bellamy distributed metal forceps to use in removing an earthworm from the gray jar of formaldehyde. Earthworms in gray jars of formaldehyde are very slippery and very long and very hard to remove from their jar. And since Charlotte from Charlotte was Meryl Lee's lab partner and she wasn't helping because she absolutely could not would not risk the possibility of getting a drop of formaldehyde on her pale Charlotte, North Carolina, skin, Meryl Lee had to remove the bloated earthworm by herself. And when she finally flopped the thing onto their dissection tray, it wasn't her fault the earthworm spat a molecule of formaldehyde toward Charlotte from Charlotte and that Charlotte from Charlotte accused her of making the bloated earthworm do this on purpose.

Calm spirit. Calm spirit.

Then Mrs. Bellamy told the class they had to identify the anterior and the posterior. "You should be able to distinguish them because the anterior is round and fleshy and the posterior is small and pointed and has a small hole in it for evacuation."

Evacuation? thought Meryl Lee.

But when she tried to distinguish the anterior and the posterior, both ends looked pretty much the same. Actually, exactly the same. Bloated. And Charlotte from Charlotte was standing so far back, she would have needed binoculars to help. So Meryl Lee raised her hand and told Mrs. Bellamy they had some sort of mutant earthworm and Mrs. Bellamy came over and touched it—touched it!—and said that if they checked for the clitellum, they would see clearly which end was the anterior end. Then she took Meryl Lee's finger and pulled it—pulled it!—until she was touching—touching!—the clitellum and she said, "You see how this is thicker here?" and Meryl Lee nodded quickly because she was trying not to pass out. (Calm spirit. Calm spirit.) Then Mrs. Bellamy told Charlotte from Charlotte to come closer and she took her hand and pulled it toward the earthworm and Charlotte from Charlotte was leaning back as far as she could and all of her auburn flounces had suddenly wilted against the sides of her head and Mrs. Bellamy said, "Stop being silly," and she touched Charlotte from Charlotte's finger to the clitellum.

Meryl Lee thought Charlotte from Charlotte was going to evacuate all over the dissection tray.

It was great.

"Do you feel how this part is thicker?" said Mrs. Bellamy.

Charlotte from Charlotte tried to nod.

"What's the clitellum for?" Meryl Lee asked, and she really did ask because she wanted to know—mostly. Despite what Charlotte from Charlotte said later.

"Reproduction," said Mrs. Bellamy.

And Charlotte from Charlotte was gone. Meryl Lee was not sure anyone saw her leave the room, she was that fast.

That left Meryl Lee without a lab partner, but she swallowed hard, then pinned the bloated anterior and the bloated posterior to the tray, and opened the skin with a scalpel, and started looking for the organs Mrs. Bellamy was drawing on the board. It actually was amazing. The earthworm has five hearts—sort of. There are five dark loops wrapping around its esophagus. It has a crop where food is stored, and on top of the crop is another long dark vessel that carries the blood. From the crop, the food goes down to the gizzard and then to the intestines. And below the intestines is a white nerve that runs the whole length of the earthworm.

It really was amazing. Even Holling would have said it was amazing.

By the time Meryl Lee was done, the earthworm was completely splayed out on the dissection tray. It looked pretty mutilated, but Mrs. Bellamy said Meryl Lee had done fine for her first dissection. Maybe someday she would make an Accomplished biologist.

Then Mrs. Bellamy asked Meryl Lee if she thought Charlotte from Charlotte would like to see the earthworm completely splayed out.

"I'm sure she would," said Meryl Lee. "I'd be happy to take it up to her."

So together they flipped the whole dissected earthworm onto wax paper, and some of the guts spilled out and the wax paper got sort of streaky, but Meryl Lee took it anyway.

She put it under her bed until after she got back from Famous Women of History.

Then she left it outside Charlotte from Charlotte's door.

The scream came about twenty minutes later.

Meryl Lee didn't know if it was from Ashley or Charlotte from Charlotte.

Didn't matter.

TWENTY-SEVEN

On the last Monday of January 1969, when clouds thick with snow were gathering in the west and an hour after Mrs. Connolly had drafted her formal complaint regarding Dr. MacKnockater's outrageous decision to break the oldest tradition of St. Elene's Preparatory Academy *for Girls,* Matt Coffin was enrolled as a student, and something like a million years of precedent shattered.

Some precedents between Matt Coffin and Dr. MacKnockater had shattered too, as his enrollment was, Dr. MacKnockater understood, one of the very few times she would win with this boy.

But it had not been easy. She told him that she had taken him as far as she could in mathematics and the life sciences and that he needed teachers like Mr. Wheelock, who could introduce him to the pleasures of algebra, and Mrs. Bellamy, who could fascinate him with the wonders of invertebrate and vertebrate biology.

He told her that he would never need algebra and that even if he did, he doubted there were many pleasures in it, and he doubted there was a whole lot of wonder in verte-something biology, either.

She told him that he would need algebra and invertebrate and vertebrate biology for college.

He laughed at her.

She told him that the first day, perhaps they could start slowly—with just one class. Say, algebra. Then, if he liked it, they could move on from there.

He said he had been in classrooms before and he knew he wouldn't like it.

She told him that the classrooms of St. Elene's were nothing like the classrooms of Harpswell Junior High.

"You're right," he said. "Because they only have girls."

"Miss Kowalski would be in your classroom," she pointed out.

"Oh," he said, after a minute. "Okay."

The night before, while Mrs. MacKnockater was in the kitchen looking for the lemons she had quartered, Captain Hurd had told Matt that there were certain times when Nora MacKnockater was a godlike force that could not be denied and he was wise not to try. "It's like trying to hold back the tide," he said.

"So, how often have you tried to hold back the tide?" said Matt.

"Twice," he said. Once when he tried to get her onto *Affliction* for a sail around the islands. She had made it quite clear she wasn't taking a single step off land.

"And the other time?"

"When she told me she wouldn't marry me."

Matt looked at him.

"Love is a tough business," said Captain Hurd, and then Mrs. MacKnockater came back in with the lemons.

And so, on that last Monday, while the snow clouds gathered, Matt Coffin and Mrs. Nora MacKnockater walked through the high gates of St. Elene's Preparatory Academy for Girls, hurrying across the commons because they were a little late.

"Bagheera," said Matt, "you're the headmistress. They'll wait for you."

She looked at him. She realized she was resisting the urge to take hold of his hand.

"Matthew," she said, "perhaps it is best if on the grounds of the school, you should call me Dr. MacKnockater."

"Why?"

"Propriety."

"What's that?"

"It is why I call Captain Hurd 'Captain.'"

"You know, he wants you to call him something else."

"Yes, he does. Now, here we are. This is Lesser Hoxne Hall. Do you want me to go up with you to the class?"

"I can handle it from here, Dr. MacKnockater."

She looked at him again. "You *are* going to the class, correct?"

"For you, Dr. MacKnockater."

"Stop that."

"Okay, Dr. MacKnockater. I'll see you back at the house."

She watched him climb the stairs toward Mr. Wheelock's classroom, and she thought how sweet it would be to hear those words—"I'll see you back at the house"—every day for a very long time.

And smiling, she also thought, *Why can't he ever keep his shirt tucked in?*

Matt hung his coat on one of the hooks in the hall. When he opened the door, Mr. Wheelock was already handing out a stack of dittos. Matt, who had never been in a classroom he liked, was surprised at how immediately he liked this one. Plants that filled the bay window—a bay window as long as the classroom was wide—gathered what sunlight there was, grabbed hold of it, and blossomed. Purple and white flowers were shouting on the ledge, some hidden by long vines, their leaves shielding the pink flowers that blushed behind them. Matt thought that he had never seen anything so beautiful off the water.

There was no desk in front, only a long table on which was an open math book, a black mug, an ashtray with a box of matches sitting in it, a pipe, and a square box filled with yellow pencils—all sticking up their perfectly sharpened points. There were also no desks in the classroom, just long tables of two or three girls—every single one of whom was looking at him.

Every single one.

He almost turned around, but he had promised Bagheera.

Mr. Wheelock, whose red cheeks made him look as if he had just come in from the cold, turned to the class. "Students of St. Elene's, please welcome Mr. Matthew Coffin, who has today made history just by his entry into the room as the first young man to take classes at this academy. Mr. Coffin, you are most welcome here, and though we two are vastly outnumbered, I hope that you will help me uphold the honor of our gender as strangers in this strange land"—and he gave a slight bow.

"I guess," said Matt.

Mr. Wheelock smiled, handed Matt a ditto, then picked up his pipe and pointed at a table toward the back of the classroom. "A chair beside the lovely Miss Truro awaits," and Matt—still knowing that everyone in the room hadn't stopped watching him—walked back toward the table with the lovely Miss Truro, where a new *The World of Algebra!* book and a new *The World of Algebra and You!* workbook were waiting too.

When he sat down, the lovely Miss Truro scooted her chair just a little bit closer to him.

Two tables up and to the left, Meryl Lee Kowalski was

sitting with her *The World of Algebra and You!* workbook open. He watched the back of her head and how she sometimes reached up and pulled the hair behind her right ear. When he'd sat down, she had turned toward him and smiled and now he was waiting for her to do that again. He wanted to ask her if she remembered how they had kissed on the bus and how that felt and was he familiar with algebraic word problems?

Matt looked up.

Mr. Wheelock standing between the tables, not so far from him.

"What?" said Matt.

"Are you familiar with algebraic word problems?" said Mr. Wheelock.

"Algebraic word problems?"

"Probably not," said Mr. Wheelock. "So let me introduce you to their pleasures." He really said that. Then he turned to the whole class. "Please note the problem I have just handed out, which you see here mapped clearly for your visual delectation."

Really, he said that.

So Mr. Wheelock told the class to imagine Mr. Jones, who was driving west from the tip of Harpswell Peninsula, through Harpswell proper, and then past Bath and down to Sebasco on Popham Peninsula, a distance of thirty-six miles, we'll say for the sake of argument. Mr. Smith, meanwhile, was driving from Sebasco to the tip of Harpswell Peninsula. Mr. Jones was a reckless driver and was going fifty-five miles per hour. Mr. Smith, on the other hand, was a careful driver and was traveling at twenty-five miles per hour. At what point on the arc from the tip of Harpswell Peninsula to Sebasco would they pass each other?

He turned to Matt. "Let's try this intuitively to start off. Where might the two cars meet, Mr. Coffin? Halfway?"

Matt shook his head.

"Exactly right. Not halfway, as Mr. Jones is traveling more than twice as fast as Mr. Smith. So how might we calculate where exactly they might cross?"

Matt had absolutely no idea.

"It depends on the traffic," he said.

"There is no traffic," said Mr. Wheelock.

"There's always traffic," said Matt.

"It's early on a Sunday morning. There is no traffic."

"Suppose Mr. Jones hits a traffic light and Mr. Smith doesn't?"

"For the sake of argument, let us say that they are traveling uninterrupted at a constant speed, and there are no traffic lights on this route in Harpswell."

"Isn't that sort of unlikely? And there are two traffic lights on this route in Harpswell."

"Exactly right again. It is unlikely, and perhaps impossible in the real world, to maintain an exact constant speed. But I think you are wrong about the two traffic lights."

Matt pointed at the dittoed map. "One here, the other here."

Mr. Wheelock considered this. "Right again, Mr. Coffin." He looked up at the class. "When we tie any ideal problem to the real world, we are faced with the fact that the ideal, by definition, cannot exist. So, Miss Kowalski, in the face of that dilemma, what options do we have?"

"We could pretend that the ideal could exist."

"And though pretense is not often used in mathematics, I think Miss Kowalski is on to something. We either must adapt the problem to reality, or we suspend our disbelief and work as if the ideal could exist." He looked back at Matt. "So let's follow Miss Kowalski's advice and pretend."

"Okay, but wouldn't it be better for them to take a boat from Harpswell to Sebasco?"

"There are no boats."

"There's always boats for rent down at the docks."

"Not on Sunday mornings."

"I think you might be wrong about that, too," said Matt.

"Given your previous correction, I would tend to trust you on this matter. But remember, we are suspending disbelief. Pretend. Two men, two cars, two constant speeds."

Matt looked down at the ditto. "Then I guess they would meet somewhere around Bath."

Mr. Wheelock smiled. "Yes, I guess they would. Good. So now let me show you how close to Bath they would be. Come up to the board with me. Miss Kowalski, you come too, please. Miss Truro, there is no need to decorate your ditto with penciled flora."

So Matt and Meryl Lee went to the board with Mr. Wheelock, and as Mr. Wheelock drew the map and the routes of Mr. Jones and Mr. Smith, Matt felt sweat running down his sides and his mouth start to go dry, and he said again that it was pretty dumb to drive all that way from Harpswell to Sebasco when all you needed was four bucks to rent a stupid boat for a couple of hours, but Mr. Wheelock said, "Let's have velocity represented by the letter V. And so the velocity of Mr. Jones is V^1 and the velocity of Mr. Smith is V^2. Are we together so far? Good. Now, distance is measured by velocity multiplied by time, and we know that the time in which they travel is the same, since they will meet. So V^1 multiplied by t—which will stand for *time*—plus V^2 multiplied by t will equal thirty-six, the distance they will travel. Correct? Let us write that equation on the board." Mr. Wheelock wrote the equation with his tongue sticking out a little bit: "55t + 25t = 36. Divide both sides by t and we have what, Miss Kowalski?"

"55 + 25 = 36/t."

"Exactly right. So, Matthew, let us see if we can solve for t now."

And they did, and it wasn't long before they figured that Mr. Jones was driving 24.75 miles and Mr. Smith was driving 11.25 miles, and as they walked back from the board, Matt and Meryl Lee looked at each other and Matt thought it was pretty cool to stand there with Meryl Lee and watch Mr. Wheelock work the solution and then to hear Meryl Lee say, "I get it," at the very same moment when he did too.

And you know what else was satisfying? Matt, for the first time in any school he had ever been in—and okay, there hadn't been that many, but still—Matt knew that Mr. Wheelock was not going to make him feel stupid.

Matt looked at Meryl Lee and wished he could tell her that.

He looked at Mr. Wheelock and wished he could tell *him* that—except Matt figured that he already knew.

He went back to his table, sat next to the lovely Miss Truro, and watched Meryl Lee pull the hair behind her right ear as the class worked a new problem of Mr. Jones and Mr. Smith on their way back and forth between Brunswick and Bath.

Very cool.

TWENTY-EIGHT

Later that week, Meryl Lee met Matt in the
lobby of Lesser Hoxne on the way to Mrs. Bellamy's class. He whispered to her in the hall, "Are you going to kiss me again?" and she
whispered, "Only if you see a dangerous bus driver," and Matt whispered, "Is that the only way it's going to happen?" and Meryl Lee
whispered, "The only way," and so they came to Lesser Hoxne 213,
where Mrs. Bellamy assigned them to be dissection partners since
Charlotte had sent a note that she would be ill that day.

"Ill?" said Meryl Lee.

"That we are to dissect locusts may have something to do with
her absence," said Mrs. Bellamy.

To start, they had to pluck a locust from a large gray glass jar
swarming with living specimens. "Aren't they just splendid?" Mrs.
Bellamy said. She almost clapped her hands at their splendidness.

When it was her turn, Meryl Lee rolled up her sleeves, since
Matt had said there was no way that he was going to reach into a
gray glass jar of living specimens.

"But you're a boy," said Meryl Lee.

"You must have already taken some advanced science classes,"
said Matt.

Meryl Lee looked at him with her eyes narrowed.

"I hate insects," he said.

So Meryl Lee reached in and the locusts swarmed over her arm and up toward her sleeves. She shook her arm and shook her sleeves and locusts fell back into the jar.

Matt took one or two steps away.

"Don't be squeamish," said Mrs. Bellamy. "Simply pluck one from the jar."

"Yeah," said Matt. "Just pluck one."

Meryl Lee's kick went past his right shin.

So Meryl Lee plucked at one—and the one she plucked at was not only swarming but positively jumpy in her hand.

Meryl Lee closed her eyes and pulled it out.

The living specimen's wings buzzed against her palm. Meryl Lee's eyebrows got pretty high.

"Take the specimen to your lab table," said Mrs. Bellamy.

Meryl Lee held the living specimen as far from her as she could while she walked toward the lab table. Its wings still buzzing. Meryl Lee walking a little faster now. A lot faster now. She wondered if the locust's jaws were already snapping above some critical vein in her hand. She wondered if locusts excreted venom. Green insect venom. She closed her eyes.

"Matt!" she said.

No answer.

Meryl Lee opened her eyes.

Matt was standing by the classroom windows.

Meryl Lee picked up the test tube on the lab table, opened her hand, and tried to shove the living specimen inside. But the living specimen held on to the edge for dear life. "Matt!" Meryl Lee said again.

Matt still standing by the classroom windows, moving a little closer to the classroom door.

Meryl Lee gritted her teeth and tried not to think of insect jaws and green insect venom. She shoved, and the living specimen went inside. She covered the top of the test tube with her palm, and the living specimen whirred against it, angrily. She grabbed the wad of cotton, shook the test tube sort of desperately so that the living specimen fell to the bottom, and then, before it could shake itself upright and figure out which way was her flesh, Meryl Lee stuffed the cotton into the opening.

The living specimen glared at her venomously.

Which is when Mrs. Bellamy came over with Matt, her hand behind his back. "Matthew," she said, "Meryl Lee is your lab partner, and part of this procedure is learning how to work together with your lab partner."

Matt looked as if he would not mind at all learning how to work together with his lab partner. But he wasn't interested at all in the living specimen.

Meryl Lee handed Matt the test tube. "You hold this, and I'll pour in the ethanol."

Matt took the test tube.

"That's right," said Mrs. Bellamy.

And even though he closed his eyes, Matt held the test tube mostly steady, and when Meryl Lee was ready, she said, "Okay, Matt . . . Matt, you have to open your eyes," and Matt did and she began to pull out the cotton a little bit—and the living specimen saw its chance. It waited, poised, and when Meryl Lee pulled the cotton out more than a little bit, it leaped and snapped its jaws and excreted disgusting green insect venom and Matt dropped the test tube and the locust was suddenly on Meryl Lee's face and ethanol was infusing the classroom air.

"Open the windows," cried Mrs. Bellamy—maybe because of the ethanol, but that's not how the living specimen saw it. The locust made its escape.

This time, Meryl Lee made Matt reach into the locust jar for a new living specimen—even though the escape hadn't been his fault, he said.

"It isn't that big a deal," she said when he began to reach in.

"He won't bite you," she said when he grabbed one.

"It's not like he's poisonous," she said when Matt tried to shove him into the test tube.

"Push him in with your finger," she said when the locust wouldn't drop down.

"Be sure you—"

"He's in, all right? He's in. So get the cotton," Matt said.

So Mrs. Bellamy poured in the ethanol and when the locust was quiet, they tapped it out of the test tube—examining its abdomen for holes through which air could pass, and making sure it was not dead—and pinned it to the wax slab in their lab tray.

Actually, Meryl Lee did the tapping and the pinning.

Matt was back by the classroom windows again.

"Next," said Mrs. Bellamy, "slice off the wings with your scalpel, then cut through the exoskeleton with your scissors."

Meryl Lee did the slicing and the cutting, and every time she slid the scalpel or closed the scissors, Matt made a noise from somewhere deep inside him that sounded like a hurt animal.

This did not give Meryl Lee a steady hand.

"Next you will identify and remove the esophagus, the gizzard, the Malpighian tubules, and the colon," said Mrs. Bellamy. "Please note their positions in the sketch on the board. The partner who did not cut through the exoskeleton should perform this task."

Meryl Lee handed the scalpel to Matt.

Matt looked at the pinned locust. He looked at Meryl Lee. He looked at the scalpel's blade.

"It's okay," said Meryl Lee.

But it was not okay with Matt. It was definitely not okay.

Because suddenly all Matt saw was the knife the Big Guy was wiping off on the Small Guy's shirt. The way he laughed while he wiped it off.

Matt handed the scalpel back to Meryl Lee.

It was not okay.

So Meryl Lee removed the esophagus, the gizzard, the Malpighian tubules, and the colon, and Matt held his breath. But when Meryl Lee unpinned the locust and it started to move as if it was trying to whir its missing wings, Matt was out the door, and nothing Mrs. Bellamy could do would bring Meryl Lee's lab partner back.

Again.

And Meryl Lee went to the classroom windows and watched Matt cross the campus lawn at a run, and she almost saw the Blank running after him, until falling snow hid them both from view.

Snow sheeted the grounds of St. Elene's during Algebra (which Matt did not come for) and Domestic Economy, so by the time Meryl Lee walked back to Netley, the commons was already covered in a couple of inches, and the walkway up to Newell, and the sidewalks between Sherbourne, and, well, everyplace else was already starting to cover up as well. Meryl Lee could feel the flakes decking her hair, and gathering in her eyebrows, and lowering onto her shoulders. Around her, girls were hurrying and sliding and pulling hoods over themselves. On the other side of the commons, sharp-ars—Mrs. Connolly walked stiffly and quickly, as if she wasn't going to be intimidated.

By Evening Meal there must have been five or maybe even six inches everywhere—not counting the drifts blowing up between the buildings. Towels were spread all over Greater Hoxne lobby to catch the snowfall from the girls when they came in, and Bettye was rolling up the wettest ones and throwing down new ones as fast as she could.

"Bettye," said Meryl Lee, "how are you going to get home?"

Bettye looked around behind her, and then she said, "I'll stay here tonight if I have to."

"Where?"

"There's a cot in the basement."

"Come to our room."

"I can't."

"Bettye, you . . ."

Bettye looked around quickly again. "Meryl Lee, I can't." She took the rolled-up towels, dripping wet, and lugged them back across the lobby.

Bettye served Meryl Lee's table again that night.

Meryl Lee did not ask for another glass of water.

Afterward, she walked back from Greater Hoxne in snow that kept falling as though it had something to make up for. There must have been seven or eight inches, maybe more, and the fantastic billows beside Putnam—not to mention those bulging in front of Newell—were well past Meryl Lee's waist.

She and Jennifer watched out their dorm windows through

the evening as it snowed and snowed and snowed, and Meryl Lee thought of Holling, and what he would do with those drifts, and she wondered if Matt was looking out his window too.

Nine o'clock, and still snowing hard.

Ten o'clock, and still snowing hard. Mrs. Kellogg walking through the halls of Netley, shutting off lights, checking the windows, tidying here, straightening there, then going down to the lobby to lock the outside doors.

Eleven o'clock, and Meryl Lee lying in her bed, Jennifer asleep, and everything quiet, and Meryl Lee realized that she no longer heard the wind, or the light taps of snow against glass. She looked: the moonlight was coming bright, almost bright as day, through the window. She got up—of course—and looked over the grounds of St. Elene's Preparatory Academy for Girls, where the long folds of snowy down sparkled like a thousand slivers of mirrors in the moonlight.

Meryl Lee got dressed.

She found her Camillo Junior High sweatshirt.

She found her coat.

She crossed the room in the dark, opened the door as slightly as she could, and listened for a prowling Mrs. Kellogg. No sound. She walked out into the hall.

And Charlotte from Charlotte came out of the bathroom.

She had on a hairnet over her auburn curls.

They looked at each other.

"What are you doing?" said Charlotte.

"It stopped snowing."

"So—"

"And the moon is bright."

In the half-lit hallway, Charlotte looked out the window.

"I'm going out," said Meryl Lee.

"You are?"

Meryl Lee nodded.

"Me too," said Charlotte.

It was not what Meryl Lee had expected.

"Wait for me," said Charlotte.

Meryl Lee waited, and a few minutes later Charlotte was back without the hairnet and they were sneaking through the halls of Netley, still watching for Mrs. Kellogg, but she wasn't in sight and they got to the bottom of the stairs and crossed the lobby and tried the front door.

Locked.

Back across the lobby and down a hall to the rear door.

Locked.

Back to the lobby to figure out what to do and guess who was standing by the door?

"You girls are up awfully late," Mrs. Kellogg said.

What could they say?

"Since there is a ten o'clock curfew, I have to assume that—despite the coats—you are sleepwalking."

They waited.

"I see," Mrs. Kellogg said. She began to smile, and nodded a little bit, as if she had made up her mind about something. "Years ago," she said, "when I was a girl here, there was once a beautiful, enchanting snow. It fell deep and thick before the full moon came out. It was lovely. So that night, Nora Thaxter—your current headmistress—and I snuck out after curfew and walked all around the campus."

Meryl Lee and Charlotte stood absolutely still.

"It's a night I've never forgotten." Mrs. Kellogg walked across the lobby, took a key from around her neck, unlocked the front door, and turned around and walked up the stairs. "Sleep well, girls," she called back.

Meryl Lee and Charlotte looked at each other, and then they laughed quietly—giggled, almost—and went out.

It was a night they would never forget, either. The hush of everything, the way a gleam of light coming from Sherbourne House reflected on Newell Chapel, snow piled like phantasms all over, a million reflections of the moonlight—so bright they prismed.

Things can be different, in the bright darkness, in the deep snow, at night, everything looking new. Things can be different, in the close and deep cold, alone together, hand in hand. Things can be different.

For a long time, they didn't say anything. But when they got all the way down to the main gate, Charlotte suddenly said, "You're so brave in Mrs. Bellamy's lab."

"Not really," said Meryl Lee.

"No, you are. I could never do what you do."

"Charlotte," said Meryl Lee, "yes, you could."

"Ashley says I'm afraid of everything."

"You're not."

"How do you know?" And Meryl Lee saw Charlotte looking at her as if this was really an important question. Like she really, really wanted to know.

"You're out here with me," said Meryl Lee.

Charlotte looked at her. Then she looked away. "Ashley says I spend too much time on my looks. Do you think I spend too much time on my looks?"

"Yes," Meryl Lee said.

Charlotte was quiet for a long time. "You don't know what it's like, growing up without any real friends."

"You've been living with the same girls at St. Elene's for forever."

"You're not listening," she said. "I mean *real* friends. Like when you and Heidi and Marian and even that girl Bettye leave St. Elene's. I've seen you. I wanted you to ask me to come."

"I didn't think you would come."

"You were wrong."

"I thought you didn't like me."

"You were wrong about that, too."

They walked by the wall, where snow covered all the poison ivy vines.

"I thought," Meryl Lee said slowly, "maybe I might go down to the shore tomorrow. Right after classes. It will be beautiful in the snow."

Charlotte quiet.

"Would you like to—"

"Yes," Charlotte said. "I really would."

"It may be against the rules."

"So is this," said Charlotte.

And that, just like that, is how things begin again—because poison ivy looks a whole lot nicer when it's covered with white snow sparkling in the moonlight.

It really was lovely.

At breakfast the next morning, Mrs. Mott reminded the student body of St. Elene's that young ladies do not wander the grounds of the school at night—most particularly during a nor'easter—and those who might violate this rule should be aware that they are within easy sight of Sherbourne House. She would be more attentive in the future, she promised.

The whole time, Meryl Lee and Charlotte were trying not to look at each other, because if they had, they would have burst out laughing.

Meanwhile, Mrs. Kellogg was carefully buttering her English muffin.

Mrs. Kellogg might really be a good egg, thought Meryl Lee.

Maybe Charlotte, too.

The night that Meryl Lee and Charlotte were wandering the grounds of St. Elene's during a nor'easter and within easy sight of Sherbourne House, Matt was looking out the bay window in the parlor of Mrs. MacKnockater's house, watching the swirls of snow, listening to the wind curl around the cornices and push against the clapboards. The heat of the wood stove was solid and hot, but still he could feel the draft come right through the panes of glass, and he put his hand out to the window to hold the glass from rattling.

He wondered if he might one day really be a part of St. Elene's. Mr. Wheelock was okay, and he was kind of interested in algebra—maybe even figuring out the pleasures. He'd finished the homework—and all the makeup homework for the quarter—in just a couple of hours. And once they cut out the dissection stuff, maybe he'd like Mrs. Bellamy, too. So even though it was a girls' school, maybe he'd be a part of it.

What would Georgie say to that?

He moved closer to the window, because he could, since not even Leonidas Shug would be out on a night like this, and it was safe.

Captain Hurd had come for supper that night. He'd asked how school had gone, and Matt told him what he'd told Bagheera: it was fine. The Captain had asked if Matt would come out in *Affliction* on Saturday, and Bagheera said he might be busy with homework, but Matt said he'd be down to the docks before sunup. Captain Hurd asked if he was learning anything important, and Matt told him about Mr. Smith and Mr. Jones.

"Why didn't they just take a boat across?" said Captain Hurd.

"Hush, you old fool," said Mrs. MacKnockater.

"Well, why didn't they?"

Matt listened to them happily. And now, as he thought about Captain Hurd and Bagheera, he wondered again if maybe he could be a part of that, too.

Later, Matt banked the wood stove for the night, and Bagheera sent him upstairs with a couple of rough towels to lay against the drafty windowsills, but they didn't do much to keep out the cold. He undressed shivering, and shivering scuttled between the cold, very cold sheets, pulling two woolen blankets and a down quilt over him and feeling their lovely weight on his chest and legs.

If Myrna Two had been there, it would have been perfect.

He put his hands behind his head and stared at the ladder that led up the chute to the roof. It had stopped snowing. Maybe there would be stars.

Suppose he didn't run?

Suppose he stayed after all?

TWENTY-NINE

FEBRUARY HAD A BRUISED SKY THAT NEVER SEEMED to heal, and it was all the more dismal in Meryl Lee's room because Alden, sweet Alden, had written to say how heartbroken he was that his father insisted on his taking up some of the charitable responsibilities of the family and so he would be appearing at the opening of several museums and concerts to represent the estate but all the while, he knew Jennifer understood that his heart was with her on St. Valentine's Day—and on every day.

So Valentine's Day had passed with tears and darkness.

But on this Saturday, the sun was finally out and warm, the sky a blue that reminded you of spring, and in the distance, the sea cozied around the islands and Meryl Lee wondered if Matt was out there with Captain Hurd and she sort of wished she was too.

That afternoon, the air got warm enough that Heidi and Marian told Meryl Lee they needed to go for a walk—which was a big deal, since Mr. Wheelock had threatened Heidi with no spring soccer if things didn't start going a whole lot better quadratically, and they stopped by Charlotte's room and she came out too. Heidi told Meryl Lee to wear her knitted yellow scarf, which was now thirty-four inches long, and she looped it around her neck, careful not to drop the stitches. When they got outside, it was so warm that Meryl Lee said, "Why did you want me to wear my scarf?"

"Because it might get dark out," Heidi said, and they all began to laugh.

And just then, a car turned its very expensive self through the gates of St. Elene's and up the drive. It stopped, and the window rolled down.

"I wonder," the driver asked, "if you could point the way to Nestle Dormitory?"

"Do you mean Netley Dormitory?" said Heidi.

"I suppose," said the driver.

Meryl Lee pointed. "Keep going on the drive, and when it forks, take the left road. Netley will be a little ways up on your left."

The window rolled up. The car moved on.

Meryl Lee drew the scarf tightly around herself.

When they got back to Netley later, Jennifer was standing in the lobby with the driver and, Meryl Lee supposed, his wife. When he saw Meryl Lee, he threw up his arms. "Our guide in our hour of distress," he said. "We are Mr. and Mrs. Truro. And you are . . ."

"Meryl Lee Kowalski," she said. "I'm Jennifer's roommate."

"Perfect. We're going out to dinner. We haven't seen our little girl since last June, and it's time to celebrate."

Meryl Lee wanted to say, "You haven't seen Jennifer since last June?" but she didn't. She said, "Maybe you want to be alone together?"

"Yes," Jennifer said.

"Nonsense," said Mr. Truro. "Of course your roommate must come." He looked at Heidi and Marian and Charlotte.

"I've got algebra," said Heidi.

"Of course you do," Mr. Truro said. He looked at Meryl Lee and then at his watch. "You better hurry and get ready."

Meryl Lee figured he meant she shouldn't be wearing her Camillo Junior High sweatshirt and her ratty red sneakers.

She changed and made sure the Woolworth's tag did not show. She added a sweater from Marian, a scarf from Charlotte. Heidi offered her field hockey stick, but Meryl Lee said she'd have to do without it this time.

When she came back down into Netley lobby, Jennifer looked away and played with her pearls.

In the car, Mr. and Mrs. Truro gave Jennifer the family news: Aunt Doris had been bothered by her arthritis but was better now. Cousin Andrew had found a new job in the Berkshires. Bertram was still trying to find himself out in Washington State, and he'd been taking some art courses—so he'd probably live on the estate's allowance for the rest of his life. Oh, and they had found an upstairs apartment in a two-story in Provincetown that was a little nicer for John and Sue, so they were finally out of the house, which was a relief. Alden could have a room of his own and not have to sleep on the couch.

"Alden?" Meryl Lee said.

Mr. Truro looked at her in the rearview mirror.

"Do you know John and Sue?"

"No, but I thought Alden lived in Scotland."

"Alden lives on the Cape," said Mr. Truro. "John and Sue live in Wellfleet. Why would you think he lived in Scotland?"

They looked at Jennifer, who looked at Meryl Lee the way the executioner of Mary Stuart, Queen of Scots, had probably looked at her.

"I thought he was from Scotland," Meryl Lee said.

Her parents looked at Meryl Lee, then at Jennifer again, then back at Meryl Lee.

"Alden is our gardener's son," said Mrs. Truro.

"He's never been to Scotland," Mr. Truro said. "I'm not sure he's ever been anywhere. Maybe Canada once?"

"Are we almost at the restaurant?" Jennifer said.

Jennifer and Meryl Lee were very quiet at the restaurant. They both had scrod, and they both said it was fine when Mrs. Truro asked if they liked it. They both said the baked potato was fine. And the sorbet was, well, fine. Mr. and Mrs. Truro sipped crème de menthe and were glad the sorbet was fine. They had decided to spend this summer in Hyannis. Had they told Jennifer about Hyannis? Maybe they hadn't. Perhaps things could be arranged so she could come down from St. Elene's for a week, since it wasn't far. It would make up for missing her at Christmas, which couldn't be helped, but Charles said she seemed to have enjoyed the run of the house. Had she?

Jennifer and Meryl Lee were very, very quiet at the restaurant.

That night, when they got back to Netley and the Truros had driven off to New York City—and they certainly would try to remember to arrange Hyannis for a week this summer and if they couldn't remember Charles would and maybe Mary Ann could join Jennifer?—that night, Jennifer stood in front of her green satin duveted bed with her arms crossed, strands of her long blond hair tangled in her fingers.

"So are you going to tell everyone?" she said.

"Tell everyone what?" Meryl Lee said.

"About Alden. Are you that stupid you couldn't figure it out before this?"

Meryl Lee had to admit, she was tempted to tell everyone. She was really tempted. She was really, really tempted.

But she said, "I guess I was that stupid."

Jennifer watched her. "What does that mean?" she said.

"My parents are separated. My father lives in New York and my mother lives in Philadelphia," said Meryl Lee.

Jennifer still watched her.

"It stinks for both of us," Meryl Lee said.

Jennifer's arms tightening around herself.

Meryl Lee hearing Holling. Oh, hearing exactly what he would say. No Blank.

"Let's go find a Coke," she said.

They went downstairs to the refrigerator in Netley's kitchen and did. And they opened the Cokes and heard that fizz that only a cold open Coke can give, and they went back to their room, and they sat on Jennifer's green satin duvet and talked about Jennifer's parents and how she never ever saw them, not even at Thanksgiving or Christmas, and they never ever saw her even in summer and Hyannis would never happen, and about Meryl Lee's parents living in two different cities, and Jennifer said maybe they sent her to St. Elene's so she wouldn't see them splitting up in front of her eyes, and then both of them crying on the green satin duvet, and crying, and crying. And suddenly, holding each other. The way friends do.

Things really can start over again, thought Meryl Lee. *And when they do . . . well, when they do.*

In the morning, it was misting and the temperature right about freezing when Meryl Lee and Jennifer walked to Morning Chapel.

They sat together in Newell. Next to Heidi, who was a little surprised.

And while the girls of St. Elene's listened to Words of Accomplishment, the morning mist coated the brick walk in thin ice and slicked it with a sheen of freezing water on top. When the girls and the teachers came out, the walk was so slippery that they were trapped on the porch, and none of the upper school girls would move.

Until Heidi came out and saw the icy bricks . . .

Heidi stepped onto the walk, balanced, then pushed off and started to slide down, and she put her arms out, and she bent her knees, and because Heidi had balance like Richard M. Nixon had Republican, she began going faster and faster, and faster and faster, all the way to the bottom of the walk. Just like that! And at the bottom, she twirled and curtsied—sort of like Dorothy might do—and the girls all clapped, and then Heidi hollered and waved.

Meryl Lee looked at Jennifer.

Ashley said, "Jennifer, what are you doing?"

Jennifer took Meryl Lee's hand—which is what new friends do. She took her hand, and they stepped onto the brick walk. They balanced, and then pushed off and started to slide down, and they put their arms out, and bent their knees, and began going faster and faster—but because Jennifer did not have balance like Richard M. Nixon has Republican—and neither did Meryl Lee—and because they were laughing their guts out, they did not make it all the way to the bottom.

But they made it pretty far.

Then some of the other girls started to slide too—and you really couldn't help it, the walk was that slippery—and some of them even stayed up on their feet most of the way.

Marian and Charlotte did not stay up on their feet even a little of the way, but they were laughing so hard, who cared? Who cared if their regulation St. Elene's uniforms were a little muddy? Who cared if they were more than a little wet?

But when Mrs. Connolly came out of Newell Chapel, she cared, and she stepped out onto the brick walk to *stop all this!* and Meryl Lee thought that wasn't the best thing to do, and she was right, because when Mrs. Connolly stepped onto the slick bricks, she started to slide down too. She waved her arms and turned around to try to get back to the chapel, but she couldn't. And now she was sliding downhill facing backwards, and since she was sort of bending over, the sharp-ars— the skinny wrong part of her was in the lead.

She did not reach the bottom.

She might have given what was in the lead a large and uncomfortable bruise.

In the late afternoon, the sun low, Meryl Lee was coming around the corner of Lesser Hoxne, heading past Newell Chapel on the way to Putnam Library before Evening Meal. No one else was around—except Dr. MacKnockater and Matt, who were up at the top of the hill on the chapel steps. Meryl Lee watched Dr. Mac-Knockater peer across the commons—probably to see if anyone was watching—and Matt said something to her, and then she stepped onto the brick walk and started to slide down. Meryl Lee could hardly believe it. Dr. MacKnockater sliding down the brick walk! She didn't wave her arms or bend her knees. She slid slowly and with Awful Dignity all the way to the bottom, and after she slowed, she stepped onto the grass, sort of adjusted herself, and looked back up.

Meryl Lee watched her. *I hope,* she thought, *that when I am a hundred years old like she is, I will slide down an icy walk too.*

Then Matt pushed off. He bent his legs so he was low to the bricks, and it was as if he were flying—his arms out like wings, his cap blown off and his hair blown back, his legs adjusting easily to the shallows of the bricks, slowing down just a bit toward the bottom and then sliding right into the open arms of Dr. MacKnockater.

Right into her arms.

Meryl Lee could not, could not, believe it.

Right into her arms.

Meryl Lee watched Matt do this two, three, four times—sliding down from the chapel into the arms of the Awful Dignity. But she didn't look like the Awful Dignity then. She looked like . . . she looked like a mother.

Like a mother.

Then, after four times, Matt looked over her shoulder, and he saw Meryl Lee.

Smiled.

Held out his hand.

Dr. MacKnockater watched from the bottom while Matt and Meryl Lee held hands and slid down together, and she thought they looked as if . . . they looked as if they had found what the Tin Woodman had lost.

And maybe what she had lost once too.

She thought of Captain Hurd, and she began to wonder, to really wonder, whether she shouldn't lose it again.

THIRTY

THE SNOW CONTINUED. THE COLD CONTINUED.
Though the days were about to pass into March, it seemed that the
sun had forgotten that it needed to shine a little bit longer. It still
got dark before Evening Meal.

On the last day of February, Meryl Lee was knitting a couple
more inches of bright yellow while sitting next to Jennifer on her
green satin duvet, when there was a knock on the door. Jennifer
opened it.

Bettye stood in the hall with a coconut cream pie.

Really. A whole coconut pie.

"My father watched the *Evening News* with Walter Cronkite
last night," she said. "Mostly about Vietnam. He bakes whenever he
gets nervous, so he made six of these. Would you like one?"

Jennifer looked at Bettye, and then she looked at Meryl Lee,
then she looked at Bettye again. "Won't you come in?" she said.

Bettye looked at Jennifer and she shook her head. "I only . . ."

"Please," said Jennifer.

This is what it looks like when things start over again.

They all sat on the green satin duvet, eating coconut cream pie,
and Bettye told stories about Jonathan.

About how Jonathan kissed Melinda DuChenney when he was

eleven and the slap she gave him that everyone heard even though they were in the church basement when she slapped him.

About how Jonathan fell into the Christmas tree when he wouldn't let Bettye put on the star, and how when he fell, he knocked down every Christmas ornament. Not a single one left.

About how Jonathan once met Willie Mays and Willie Mays said Jonathan was a better hitter than he was when he was Jonathan's age.

About how Jonathan asked Reverend Buckminster—his grandfather, not his father—how Lazarus got out of his tomb if he was all wound around with sheets and bandages so he couldn't move his legs or his arms or even see, and how his grandfather told him to try it his own self and so Jonathan did, and he fell two flights down the stairs, and the next Sunday his grandfather preached on "The Perils of Unbelief" while Jonathan stood by the pulpit of First Congregational as a sermon illustration with a black eye and a broken arm and how he smiled like he was the star the whole time.

And Jennifer and Bettye and Meryl Lee were laughing so hard that Heidi came in with Marian, and then Charlotte came in, and most of the pie was gone pretty quickly.

That's really what it looks like when things start over.

But not everything starts over.

Late the next afternoon, when Meryl Lee was heading to Putnam, she saw Ashley walking out of Lesser Hoxne. Ashley saw her, hesitated, then came toward Meryl Lee.

Meryl Lee waited—even though she wanted to run into Putnam.

Maybe she should have.

"I want to ask you something," said Ashley.

"Okay," said Meryl Lee.

"Who do you think you are?"

Meryl Lee was pretty sure Ashley didn't expect an answer.

"Do you really think you're someone who should even speak to Jennifer Truro? Really? You're nobody. You're nobody at all."

Meryl Lee stepped back, as if something had collided against her.

"We're just friends," Meryl Lee said.

Ashley put her hands on her hips. "Is that what you think you are?" she said. "Friends?"

"Yes."

"*We're* friends—Jennifer, Charlotte, and me. *We're* friends."

"Can't we—"

"No, you can't. Not when she's what she is and you're what you are. Someday she's going to marry Alden Windsor Leighton, from one of the best families in Scotland. You have no idea what that means, do you? You're just someone trying to worm your way into being friends with someone whose life you wish you had."

"You don't understand," Meryl Lee said. "It doesn't matter that—"

"And maybe that works with someone as stupid as Charlotte. But don't think it's going to work for a minute with Jennifer Truro. And don't think for a minute it's going to work with me, because"— she leaned in close—"I hate you. I hate the way you have to have everyone to yourself."

"That's not fair," said Meryl Lee.

Ashley—who suddenly looked as if she was about to cry— turned and headed back to Netley.

———— ⤐⤐ ————

That night, Matt settled in with *Oliver Twist,* while Mrs. Mac-Knockater enjoyed Edna St. Vincent Millay. She tried to get him to listen to "Passer Mortuus Est," but Matt wasn't interested. "It's poetry," he said, and got up to stoke the wood stove.

Mrs. MacKnockater drew an afghan over her legs and turned the pages.

She read. She nodded. She closed her eyes, opened them, closed them. Her mouth opened a little.

And Matt watched Mrs. MacKnockater fall into sleep, still holding the poetry of Edna St. Vincent Millay, him holding *Oliver Twist,* and he imagined many nights doing that, again and again. If only . . .

The next week in Mr. Wheelock's class, Matt asked Meryl Lee if she wanted to go down to the shore with him on Saturday and maybe out with Captain Hurd, and she said yes, and Matt went home that night praying for fair weather. Praying, praying, praying for fair weather. And probably because of that, Saturday dawned with sunlight that began to heal the bruised sky and melt the icicles around Netley and Newell and sweat the piles of snow that bulked around Greater Hoxne and beside the great wall of St. Elene's Preparatory Academy. Matt and Meryl Lee met at the main gate and together they walked down toward the docks, as quiet and still as the low waves between the tides, and the Captain was waiting at dockside—"Miss Kowalski!" he called—and he helped her board *Affliction* as the waves chucked the boat under its chin, and Matt jumped in afterward, easy as coconut cream pie (the last two pieces of which Meryl Lee had brought with her), and they were out into the bay.

Captain Hurd and Matt laid out only one string of traps—"Just to say we did something," said the Captain—and Matt warned her not to step too close or get her hand tangled in the lines—"You can't believe how quick you can get drawn overboard if you get your hand tangled"—and then they began to chug around the islands. Captain Hurd took the wheel and told Matt to go up front with Meryl Lee so she didn't fall over the bow, and he did, and they stood there together in the cold off the ocean, wiping at their teary eyes and holding on to each other when *Affliction* chunked into a wave, and Captain Hurd felt something between happiness and envy. *Their whole lives,* he thought. *They have their whole lives ahead of them.*

And they did.

And maybe that's what Matt was thinking when he took Meryl Lee's hand and did not let go, and he looked at her and wondered, *Suppose two people start out at very different places, and one heads in a small boat to a small cove in a small harbor from one direction and he's running because he has to, and the other heads to that same small boat and that same cove in the same harbor from a completely different direction and she's not running but she goes anyway. How long will it be before they find each other?*

The answer?

It didn't matter, as long as they found each other.

And he thought, *Could that really be the answer?*

And Meryl Lee closed her eyes against the wind and she listened to the thrumming of the engine, the *chunk chunk* of the waves, the churning seawater at the stern, the gulls whose calls came and faded as they yawed into the wind. When she opened her eyes, she pushed her hair back—all to no good at all.

When they came down from the bow, Captain Hurd asked if she'd been out on the water much.

"Only with you," she said.

Captain Hurd pointed at Matt. "You'd do well to watch this one, then," he said. "He was born to be on the water."

Meryl Lee looked at Matt.

"How come you were born to be on the water?" she said.

Matt shrugged. "I guess I don't stay in one place very long."

And, for the first time in what felt like a long time, Meryl Lee felt the Blank rush upon her, as real and as solid as a wave rearing up over the boat.

"You okay?" said Matt.

"Why . . ." she began, "why can't anything stay in one place?"

And Matt suddenly, fiercely, completely, wanted more than anything to say, "I will now."

And just as suddenly, fiercely, completely, he wanted to kiss her again—right there in front of Captain Hurd, who had decided to lay out another line of traps after all and Matt should stop fooling around with Miss Kowalski and get to the stern if he was going to be any help.

Matt went back to the stern.

But he'd decided. He was going to stay in Harpswell for as long as he could. Especially if Meryl Lee would be . . . Well, he was going to stay in Harpswell.

That evening, deep in the South Bronx, certain elements of the FBI closed in on a beat-up apartment house that no one in the neighborhood ever went near. They moved in pairs, some gathering by the back entrances, some by the ruined front entrance, and some along the alley that ran beneath the first-floor windows and ended in an abrupt and high rear wall. At exactly 8:05 p.m., they stormed inside.

The exchange of gunfire lasted less than two minutes, though well over a hundred bullets sparked the air.

Three of those bullets found a huge guy that the FBI had identified as one of the ringleaders. One bullet in his left calf spun him around. One in his right shoulder blade blew him upright against a wall. One in his left ear flew into his brain. His body fell, his eyes went dark, his heart thumped on for twelve seconds, and his consciousness ceased entirely—just like that.

Soon after the two minutes, the FBI men opened the door to the upstairs loft, where eighteen boys had backed into a corner. The littlest ones were crying. Some of the older ones, too.

By midnight, most of the identifications had been made—both at Family Services and at the morgue.

A phone call woke Lieutenant Minot not long after.

He asked one question.

"No," said the FBI man. "No one we can ID as Shug."

THIRTY-ONE

AND SO, THE COLD GAVE WAY AND THE SUN CAME
up earlier and the snow pulled itself back at the edges to show the
grass that was already greening underneath. And Matt finished
Oliver Twist and the Captain suggested one of the Horatio Hornblower books and Matt read three of them. And at night he watched
Mrs. MacKnockater slowly fall into sleep while he figured out Mr.
Wheelock's algebra and wrote up Mrs. Bellamy's science labs, and
when he finished he would read until the wood stove was low, and
he would bank it and turn out the lights and then he would wake
up Mrs. MacKnockater and she would startle and say she was only
just napping, and he would head up to bed while she went to turn
on the lamp in the front hall.

And that's how his nights were, again and again, and how wonderful they were. He wished that Georgie could have had one night
like this. Just one night like every night was now for Matt.

For Matt, it was sort of like being out on the water, moving
with the waves around the islands, moving with the wind and the
waves, with nothing but water and gulls and clouds and sky out in
front of you.

That's what it was like.

Now when Captain Hurd looked at him, he thought that the
boy had changed somehow. Maybe he'd suddenly gotten taller. And

when Mrs. MacKnockater looked at him, she thought that Matt had gotten . . . Oh, she didn't know how to put it. *Brighter.* Maybe brighter, like the sky was brighter after a long winter.

After long grief, she thought, Matt was happy.

March grew warmer and warmer, bringing in an early spring— which, after a flannel-gray February, made exactly no one unhappy. Robins and their worms, trees pushing out those red-gold buds, that first afternoon when the air feels warm, the purple crocuses passing quickly and the first pushes of Mr. Wheelock's daffodils, the tendrils of ferns unrolling a little over the dark soil.

And spring brought open windows, and so the high whistles and low coos of birds outside Newell Chapel, peepers in the morning outside Mrs. Bellamy's lab, the buzzing of quick insects. Spring brought light, so the sun was fully up now when Meryl Lee went to Greater Hoxne for breakfast, and it was still up when she came back from helping Matt and Captain Hurd stow away gear on *Affliction,* and she could even see a little bit left in the sky when she sat down to write Mrs. Connolly's two-hundred-and-fifty-word explications of Renaissance sonnets—as if anyone could figure out a Shakespeare couplet.

Spring brought Mrs. Saunders's announcement that she hadn't been working her Famous Women of History class hard enough. She gave them two days to write "extensive timelines" for their subjects, which she would assign.

Meryl Lee's subject was Florence Nightingale—who at least hadn't been beheaded.

And then one warm morning, so warm she could hardly imagine working on Jonathan's scarf, she thought the Yankees would be into spring training now and Opening Day wouldn't be far away and Holling would have loved to be at Yankee Stadium on Opening

Day—and suddenly, she realized that the Blank had not come. She had thought of Holling, and the Blank had not come.

For a moment, she almost felt . . . guilt.

Or something like it.

As if the Blank should come.

As if the Blank should always come.

But it hadn't, and in the warm and blue day, guilt faded.

Holling would have loved to be at Yankee Stadium on Opening Day, and Meryl Lee smiled.

But spring did bring one other thing to Meryl Lee. It came when she felt Coach Rowlandson lean over her after dinner one day: "Are you planning on playing spring soccer?" she asked.

"Umm," said Meryl Lee.

Coach Rowlandson looked at her. "The skills are different from those of field hockey, so don't let your past . . . experiences . . . influence you."

"I'm not sure I'd be any good at it," said Meryl Lee.

"I'm not sure either," said Coach Rowlandson.

"So why ask . . ."

"Because Julia Chall has decided not to play this spring—don't ask me why—and I need to put together a team if we have any chance of competing with St. Scholastica's and that means bodies out on the field. Sticks down, Kowalski."

"St. Scholastica's?"

"Can I count on you?"

"Coach Rowlandson, I was really—"

"Did you know Mrs. Connolly is looking for an assistant during the transition to headmistress? That girl will type, file, sort correspondence, and run errands for Mrs. Connolly. I understand the position will require two to three hours most days in

Mrs. Connolly's office. I was thinking of recommending you," said Coach Rowlandson.

A long pause. All the sounds of spring stopped.

"You wouldn't do that," said Meryl Lee.

Coach Rowlandson leaned forward. "In a single short heartbeat," she said quietly.

Meryl Lee's eyebrows rose to chipmunk-y heights.

"I would be happy to play soccer for St. Elene's this spring," Meryl Lee said.

"Practice begins a week from today," said Coach Rowlandson. "It won't matter if there is snow on the ground or not. You are the backup goalie."

"What does the backup goalie do?"

"Hope the first-string goalie doesn't get hurt. Now, have you been keeping up your wind sprints and . . ."

Later, Heidi, who was planning on playing first-string goalie, said Meryl Lee had made the right decision.

But Meryl Lee wasn't so sure—because it was a little hard to imagine Heidi playing first-string goalie, since Heidi had an epic cold. She was sneezing all the time and sniffling all the time and then coming in to sit on Jennifer's green satin duvet because it was so soft and filling up their wastebaskets with crumpled tissues and then wheezing some and tearing at the eyes and hacking up . . . Well, her cold was really epic.

And if Heidi couldn't practice, that meant . . .

So Meryl Lee asked Heidi how goalies practiced. And Heidi said, "It's great." She wheezed. "The goalie stands in the middle of the net." She coughed. Her face grew red. "Then the players kick soccer balls right at her." She blew her nose hard. Twice. "As hard as they can." Coughed. "And the goalie has to catch them or flick them over the bar or"—three quick coughs from deep in her chest—"dive for them." Blew her nose.

"Dive for them?" said Meryl Lee.

"And after the goalie handles a couple hundred shots—"

"A couple hundred shots?"

"After that, players kick lots of soccer balls as hard as they can into the corners of the net"—wheezing, wheezing, a cough, a hack—"and the goalie has to dive after those, too."

"How many?"

"A lot"—cough, hack—"and after that there's the scrimmage."

Meryl Lee was not sure that spring soccer was something at which she cared to be Accomplished.

Coach Rowlandson stopped by Netley three times that week to check on Heidi because the first practice was coming soon, very soon. And afterward, all three times, she stopped at Meryl Lee's room, opened the door, and looked at her with Significant Eyes.

"Why do you think she keeps doing that?" said Jennifer after the third time.

"I think I'll go make Heidi some herbal tea," said Meryl Lee.

Heidi was not at the first practice because of her epic cold. In fact, she was not even at St. Elene's Preparatory Academy for Girls because of her epic cold, since Miss Ames had called her parents and she went home to Rutland for a few days, which led to Heidi swinging her field hockey stick dangerously close to several Netley Dormitory windows when she found out Miss Ames had done that.

So Heidi wasn't on the field when Coach Rowlandson made

the Lasses run something like two hundred miles and then sprint inside the gym to dribble soccer balls around orange cones five thousand times and then run up and down the gym bleachers a million times.

But Meryl Lee was.

And Heidi, who would have loved all of this, wasn't on the field when Coach Rowlandson took the Lasses back outside and told them it wasn't so cold and they should stop complaining and now they were going to practice shooting balls at the net. She looked around for her backup goalie, who, as it turns out, was hiding behind Marian Elders.

"Sticks down, Kowalski," said Coach Rowlandson.

Heidi is in big trouble, thought Meryl Lee.

So she stood at the net, tired from running the length of Massachusetts, freezing, hating Heidi's cold, hating spring soccer, wondering why Matt was there . . .

Wait. Was that Matt? That was Matt.

"Hold up your hands," shouted Coach Rowlandson.

Meryl Lee held up her hands.

Coach Rowlandson took the first shot.

"You're supposed to stop it from going into the net," shouted Matt.

"Good advice," said Coach Rowlandson, as the rest of the Lasses lined up behind her.

"How am I supposed to do that?" said Meryl Lee.

"Anticipate," said Coach Rowlandson.

"Pay them off," shouted Matt Coffin.

Then the Lasses began.

A billion kicks toward the goalie.

Afterward, while Meryl Lee and Matt were gathering up the billion soccer balls in the back of the net, Coach Rowlandson said Meryl Lee hadn't done so badly standing in for Heidi.

"That is a lie," said Meryl Lee.

"Only a little one," said Coach Rowlandson—another lie.

"Don't you think being a goalie jeopardizes my knitting?" said Meryl Lee.

Coach Rowlandson considered this. "Kowalski," she said, "becoming Accomplished in knitting and becoming Accomplished in spring soccer are both fine and honorable pursuits. But since we're not competing against St. Scholastica's in Knitting Studies, if we have to sacrifice your fingers for the good of the school, so be it."

"She was kidding," Meryl Lee said to Matt on the way back to Netley.

"How do you know?"

"Because if I play goalie, we'll lose every game. By triple digits."

"It won't be that bad," said Matt.

She looked at him.

"I mean, it won't be triple digits probably."

Meryl Lee thought about how many balls had flown, run, scooted, flipped, bounced, leaped past her into the net during the first practice.

"It will be triple digits," said Meryl Lee.

And then, because sometimes the world is like this, losing by triple digits didn't matter much anymore, since Matt leaned forward and kissed her lightly on her cheek.

She put her hand up and touched the place. "Why did you do that?" she said.

He shrugged.

She took his hand.

That night at Greater Hoxne Dining Hall, when Meryl Lee sat down at her table and Bettye set the scrod casserole in front of her, she heard Ashley at her table say, "Did you know that Meryl Lee played goalie today?"

"Really?" said someone.

"I heard she couldn't stop a single ball, but no one could be that bad, could she?" said Ashley.

Not even Florence Nightingale, Meryl Lee thought, not even Florence Nightingale, angel of mercy though she might have been, could have put up with Ashley Higginson. If Florence Nightingale had found Ashley Higginson wounded on the battlefield, bloody and broken and murmuring, "No one could be that bad, could she?" then Florence Nightingale would have said, "I think I'll leave you here to die," and walked away.

Mary Stuart, Queen of Scots, would have beheaded Ashley. She would have let it take three tries.

Then Meryl Lee smiled and put her hand to her cheek.

Three soccer practices later—three very long soccer practices later—Heidi came back to St. Elene's Preparatory Academy for Girls. Coach Rowlandson had called Heidi's house every day to check up on her, probably because Coach Rowlandson wanted to beat St. Scholastica's more than she wanted the sun to rise in the morning, and the Lasses would not be beating St. Scholastica's with their backup goalie.

The Lasses would probably lose by quadruple digits.

After a week and a half, Heidi returned to St. Elene's. The first thing she did in Meryl Lee's room was look at Jonathan's scarf.

"How long is that?" she said.

Meryl Lee unscrolled its length. "Fifty-three inches," Meryl Lee said.

"How are you doing as backup goalie?"

"Umm."

Heidi took the sun-bright yellow scarf, folded it quickly, and stuffed it under Meryl Lee's bed.

"What are you doing?" Meryl Lee said.

"I need my eyes for soccer," she said.

The third quarter evaluations at the end of March did not include comments upon Meryl Lee's knitting skills, comments that might have included words like "remarkable" and "nimble." The third quarter evaluations did include comments on her algebraic skills (with words like "adept" and "proficient"), on her writing technique ("at times clumsy, but showing promise of a pleasing style"), on her dissection technique ("bold and incisive"), on her culinary abilities ("inventive"), and on her historical analysis ("sometimes spotty, but often discerning").

Overall, not as bad as she thought they might have been.

THIRTY-TWO

Heidi was getting fed up.

Meryl Lee was driving her crazy.

It wasn't her fault, Meryl Lee said. She hadn't asked to be part of the vice-presidential luncheon. And she hadn't known when she said yes that the vice-presidential luncheon had a very long history at St. Elene's Preparatory Academy. A very, very long history, said Dr. MacKnockater. A very, very, very long history, said Mrs. Connolly.

She hadn't known that so much was at stake.

So Meryl Lee was nervous.

Heidi said she was acting as nervous as a cat in its eighth life and she was driving her crazy.

So maybe that is why what happened during the vice-presidential luncheon happened.

Even though Dr. MacKnockater—sort of with the help of Meryl Lee and Heidi—had planned the schedule for the luncheon to the minute.

Ashley and Charlotte and Lois Tuthill and Elizabeth Koertge were supposed to meet the vice president when he stepped out of his car. (Ashley said her father had close ties to Mr. Agnew—Mr. Higginson was even on the security detail—so she should be the one to meet him first.) Ashley and Charlotte would together present the vice president with a bouquet of tulips and then escort him into Newell Chapel, where all the girls would be waiting. They would pause at the door until the organ began, and the girls would stand, and while they were singing hails to St. Elene's, Ashley and Charlotte would process in front of the vice president and so bring him to his seat on the platform, where Mrs. Kellogg and Dr. Mac-Knockater and Mr. Lloyd C. Allen, head of the St. Elene's board of trustees, would be waiting.

While everyone was still standing, Mrs. Kellogg would lead the school in the Pledge of Allegiance. Then Dr. MacKnockater would step forward and read a short but uplifting passage from the classics about the calling of good government. Following that, everyone would sit down.

Meryl Lee would then rise to introduce the vice president. (Ashley said *she* should be the one to introduce Vice President Spiro Agnew since he knew her family so well, but Dr. MacKnockater said they would spread the responsibilities among several girls.) Mrs. Kellogg said that Meryl Lee should be sure to look at the vice president before she began. "You must always make eye contact with your guest of honor before and after you introduce him," she said.

After Meryl Lee's introduction, Vice President Agnew would give his address. Following his address, Jennifer and Heidi and Julia Chall and Barbara Rockcastle would follow the vice president down the center aisle and escort him to Sherbourne House for the vice-presidential luncheon with the teachers and the organizing committee. Mrs. Wyss was planning the menu—which meant that everything would be perfect.

That was the schedule for the vice-presidential luncheon. Planned to the minute.

What could go wrong?

Except that three days before the vice president came, Mrs. Connolly, on behalf of St. Elene's Preparatory Academy for Girls, invited students from St. Giles's Preparatory Academy for Boys to attend. So on the day, when Meryl Lee came onto the platform to await the vice president's procession with Ashley and Charlotte, those four boys from St. Giles's were sitting right on the end of the first aisle.

The same four boys whose blood was now permanently in the grout between the tiles in the lobby of Greater Hoxne Hall.

Meryl Lee looked at them.

She was very glad that Matt had decided to go out with Captain Hurd on the day.

But that didn't stop the Disaster.

The organ began, and everyone stood, and Ashley and Charlotte walked in, followed by Vice President Spiro Agnew holding his bouquet of tulips and smiling and shaking hands with all the teachers and saying something to each one. His Secret Service guys moved behind him—the ones who really do wear dark glasses. The agent right next to the vice president slid beside him like a ghoul, close and looming and long-armed and watchful. Meryl Lee couldn't take her eyes off his creepy self, even when everyone in Newell Chapel was watching the vice president slowly walking down the aisle, moving back and forth across the long carpet, making his way forward little by little in grand style, his perfect shoes shining, his perfect smile beaming, his hair perfectly parted, his step always a little ahead of the ghoul on his right.

The vice president reached the platform, slowly stepped up to it, and he shook Mr. Lloyd C. Allen's hand and he sat down and crossed his legs and got all relaxed as though he'd done this a million times and it was no big deal.

Then Mrs. Kellogg went off script a little and she said how privileged St. Elene's was to host the newly inaugurated vice president of the United States and how he had come to the north shore only to visit with the students of St. Elene's Preparatory Academy for Girls and St. Giles's Preparatory Academy for Boys and how he had to be back in Washington that evening for a slide presentation by the astronauts of *Apollo* 8 and she looked toward him and the vice president smiled his big vice-presidential smile.

Then Mrs. Kellogg stood beside him and put her right hand over her heart. The vice president stood up quickly and put his hand over his heart too. They all pledged allegiance to the flag of the United States of America. And when they finished pledging, Dr. MacKnockater, in Awful Dignity, stepped forward and read from Plato's *Republic*.

In Greek.

The vice president looked as if he did not understand a single word.

Then, when the Awful Dignity had finished her Plato and all the girls were sitting in their pews and those on the platform were sitting in their chairs and everyone seemed to be looking at her—especially the ghoul on the vice president's right—Meryl Lee walked behind the podium.

She turned toward the seated guest of honor. She looked at the ghoul first, who was smiling.

Then she looked at the seated guest of honor.

And that's when she noticed that the newly inaugurated vice president of the United States of America had his zipper down.

And a corner of his white shirt was sticking through.

A very large corner.

You couldn't miss that his zipper was down.

So what was she supposed to do? It's not like you can lean over to the newly inaugurated vice president of the United States and say, "Hey, your zipper is down," while the ghoul is smiling at you.

Then Meryl Lee heard Mr. Lloyd C. Allen cough behind her.

Meryl Lee looked out across Newell Chapel.

This is how she was supposed to begin:

"On behalf of the students at St. Elene's Preparatory Academy for Girls, I would like to welcome Vice President Spiro Agnew."

This is how Meryl Lee began:

"On behalf of the students at St. Elene's Preparatory Academy for Girls, I would like to welcome Vice Principal Spiral Agnew."

She heard Mr. Lloyd C. Allen cough behind her again.

But honestly, *Spiro* was a name almost as weird as *Holling,* and it wasn't as if someone else probably hadn't made the same mistake before, and *principal* sounded so much like *president* (didn't it?), and there was this white corner of the vice president's shirt showing, and his zipper really needed uplifting.

And there was this ghoul smiling at her—and it wasn't a happy smile.

Then Mrs. Kellogg coughed behind her.

And suddenly, absolutely everything she was going to say vanished somewhere into space where the *Apollo 8* astronauts had been.

There was a very long silence, and Mrs. Kellogg coughed again.

So Meryl Lee said how very glad the students of St. Elene's were to host the vice president when he was so busy during wartimes—except she didn't say *wartimes*, she said *war crimes*.

Mr. Lloyd C. Allen stood up.

And then Meryl Lee remembered how she was supposed to end: "Please join me in welcoming Vice President Spiro Agnew," and she was supposed to start the clapping—except she said, "Please join me in welcoming Vice President Zipper Agnew"—she really said that—and so no one clapped when she started to.

And she could suddenly hear the vice president behind her, trying to uplift his zipper, but he must have gotten it caught on the very large corner of his white shirt, since when she turned around to make eye contact again, the guest of honor wasn't smiling anymore and he didn't seem as relaxed.

Mr. Lloyd C. Allen wasn't smiling either.

The vice president's address was very short and he stayed carefully behind the podium. He apologized, but he had to get back to Washington immediately, he said. He regretted that he could not attend the vice-presidential luncheon, but such emergencies were not unusual, only frustrating because he was drawn away from lovely events like this lovely event on the . . . um . . . lovely coast of Massachusetts. "Thank you for having me," he said.

He left by the side door, closely surrounded by his big Secret Service guys.

It all happened in sort of a rush.

The organ began to play the school song, and the students of St. Elene's Preparatory Academy for Girls and the St. Giles's Preparatory Academy for Boys processed out. Meryl Lee turned to join the line of procession, but Mrs. Connolly was standing right nearby, standing with her hands on her hips, looking at Meryl Lee, and it really did not seem that she was listening to the school song at all.

After the vice president's car had pulled away and was speeding out of St. Elene's Preparatory Academy for Girls, the ghoul from the Secret Service retinue turned back toward the chapel. He saw the girl who had mangled the vice president's name scurrying away toward the dormitories.

He wished for a moment he could have mangled her.

But then he laughed. Who cared? It was just the vice president. He sort of hoped the name would stick. Zipper Agnew! Really. Zipper Agnew!

Then he walked around the chapel to meet his daughter by the chapel's front porch.

"Dad!" Ashley Higginson called.

He took her into a hug.

"How's my girl?" said the ghoul.

"Okay," she said.

"Just okay?"

"Better than okay. But I haven't seen you in a long time."

"You know how busy I am, girlie. Merchandise comes in and I have to find a way to move it. It's not an easy job—especially when some people aren't as cooperative as they could be."

"I get it. You know that girl who introduced the vice president?"

"Yeah. 'Zipper Agnew.' That was great."

"She's not cooperative either. She's been a problem the whole year."

"Who is she?"

"No one. She's from Hicksville. Can you believe that? Hicksville.

She really doesn't know anyone here so she's trying to be a big shot. And she hangs around with this guy."

"'This guy'? I thought this was a girls' school."

"So did I. But there's this new guy who came after Christmas who lives with the Knock and he's taking classes too."

"What's his name?"

"Matt something."

"Matt?"

"Did you bring the pearls like you said?"

"Huh?"

"The pearls?"

"Oh, yeah." He pulled a string from his pocket and dropped them into her hand. Ashley tried to put them on, but she couldn't get the clasp to work.

"Matt something, you said?"

"Yeah. Could you help me with . . ."

The ghoul smiled and turned to look across the commons. "Bingo," he said.

The next morning, Dr. MacKnockater sent a note asking Meryl Lee to come to the headmistress's office after classes. They were to speak about her recent introduction of Vice President Spiro Agnew. There were some concerns, explained the note.

Meryl Lee figured this meant she was going to be expelled, which in September wouldn't have been so bad, but now . . .

Marian said it had been an honest mistake. Meryl Lee wasn't going to be expelled.

Heidi said he had his zipper down, for heaven's sakes. She wasn't going to be expelled.

Jennifer said the vice president probably hadn't even noticed. She wasn't going to be expelled.

Charlotte said Dr. MacKnockater probably wanted to congratulate her. Expelling wouldn't even be on her mind.

When Ashley, who was wearing a string of pearls, saw her in the hall, she said, "I hear you're going to be expelled."

Meryl Lee thought, *Calm spirit, calm spirit, like St. Elene, calm spirit.*

None of this helped.

That afternoon, when Meryl Lee sat down in front of Robespierre's desk, Dr. MacKnockater was holding a letter.

She looked very serious, as if something dreadful beyond belief had happened.

Meryl Lee wondered how long it would take to pack her suitcase. She wondered if she had kept the two shopping bags.

"Miss Kowalski," Dr. MacKnockater said, "this is a letter regarding your introduction of the vice president yesterday. Do you have any idea who has written it?"

Meryl Lee did. "Mrs. Connolly," she said.

"No. It was written by Mr. Lloyd C. Allen on behalf of the entire board of trustees. I have kept Mrs. Connolly's letter for another time."

That did it. Definitely expulsion.

"The letter uses strong language," said Dr. MacKnockater. "In fact, some of the strongest language I have ever read in academic correspondence."

Meryl Lee felt the anterior and posterior parts of her digestive system begin to collapse.

"I have to agree with Mr. Allen," said Dr. MacKnockater, "that mangling the vice president's name while demoting him to vice principal was impolite. And certainly ascribing war crimes to the gentleman is vexatious."

There was a long pause. Meryl Lee closed her eyes. She wondered how many students had been expelled in the history of St. Elene's Preparatory Academy for Girls. Or had their decapitated heads impaled on the wall.

"But I must disagree heartily with Mr. Allen when he complains about your reference to the vice president's attire."

And then, this is what happened next: Dr. MacKnockater started to laugh. Really. She started to laugh, and she couldn't stop, even though she tried. She laughed until she cried, and even then she couldn't stop laughing.

When she finally calmed down, Meryl Lee said, "Would you like me to write to Mr. Allen?"

"I have already done so," she said, and then she began to laugh again. It took a few more minutes before she could speak. "I told him we would be talking and I was certain you were very sorry for any missteps in the chapel. And I told him you did not intend to poke fun at the vice president or accuse him of war crimes— though, as I suggested to him, someone who leaves his zipper down certainly runs the risk of the first, and someone in an administration that proposes to drop bombs on grass huts may run the risk of the second. But I told him you did not intend this at all and there was no damage done to the goodly reputation of St. Elene's."

Meryl Lee said, "Would you like me to write to the vice president to apologize?"

"No, no," Dr. MacKnockater said. "Do not write to"—and she started to laugh again, and she laughed and laughed and laughed until she caught her breath and was able to choke out—"do not write to Vice President Zipper Agnew." And then she began laughing again, and that was pretty much the end of the meeting.

Meryl Lee left Sherbourne House, first peering out the doorway for Mrs. Connolly, then hurrying back to Netley.

Late that night in her room, Meryl Lee read about the Good Witch in *The Wonderful Wizard of Oz* and how she kissed Dorothy's forehead to leave a mark before she sent her off to the Emerald City.

The Good Witch reminded her of someone, and she set the book down and smiled before she turned out the light to go to sleep.

At almost that same moment, at Mrs. MacKnockater's house, after Matt had already gone upstairs, Mrs. MacKnockater's telephone rang just as she was lighting the lamp in the front hall. The annoyed Mrs. MacKnockater answered it—"Dr. MacKnockater," she said sort of grimly—and then she waited for a long time, hearing absolutely nothing on the other end of the line, but still sensing that someone was there.

She laid down the phone slowly, looked up the stairs, and then went to check that the doors were locked and the downstairs windows all fastened.

She left the lights on in the parlor.

She turned on the porch lights.

She almost called Captain Hurd, but decided not to.

Then she climbed the stairs to her room.

THIRTY-THREE

THE FUNERAL SERVICE FOR ALETHEA'S BROTHER WAS held two days after his flag-draped body had been flown home.

Alethea came back to St. Elene's two days after that, and she served at Evening Meal. She could hardly bear to look at anyone— even if she had been allowed to. She couldn't even look at Ashley, who was wearing her pearls to every meal and fingering them so obviously that you almost had to look at them. But Alethea did not.

But she did look at Meryl Lee, who, before the meal started, stood beside her and said, "Alethea, I am so, so sorry about your brother. I am so sorry." Then Meryl Lee wrapped Alethea in her arms and held her tightly, and she felt Alethea's back and shoulders stiffen and harden—at first—and then release. She felt Alethea's arms tighten around her. And when, after a long time, they leaned back and looked at each other eye to eye, something new had happened, and Alethea held up her hand and wiped the tears from Meryl Lee's eyes.

Afterward, Bettye brought Alethea to Netley and to Meryl Lee's room, and Alethea and then Bettye began to cry. And Meryl Lee too. They cried and cried, holding one another. And Meryl Lee remembered this: she knew, she knew, she knew, the Blank that Alethea had found.

Meryl Lee wanted to say to Alethea that everything was going to be better.

She wanted to say to Alethea that her brother had sacrificed himself for all of us, and America was safer, and the world better, because of what he had done.

She wanted to say to Alethea that her brother's death was worth it.

But no matter what words she used, she could not make Alethea's loss feel worth it. Alethea wanted to have her brother home— and no words could give her that.

There are times when words can't do what you want them to do, no matter how much you wish they could.

Meryl Lee knew that.

They sat there for a long time, but not alone. First Jennifer, and then Marian and Heidi and Charlotte were there too, holding Alethea's hands, rubbing her shoulders. They were mostly crying too. And Meryl Lee thought, *I wonder how this happens. You live side by side for a while, and suddenly you realize you like living side by side, and you can't imagine not living side by side because you've become friends. And then your friends become friends with one another, and they sit beside one another and cry. How does that happen?*

But isn't it good that it does?

Alethea said her brother was a painter. He liked to paint storm clouds—really wicked dark ones with lightning bolts flickering and throwing themselves over the landscape and everything beneath them huddling and waiting to be smothered by the thunder and rain and wind. She said he was a soccer goalie too, so he and Meryl Lee had something in common—"Not really," said Meryl Lee. And he liked to fish, and he said nothing could compare to eating a fresh trout you've just caught and cleaned and fried in butter and salt and pepper on the shore of a river. And he liked checkers and won all the time, except with her—he always let their games end up in a tie. Her parents could hardly speak these days. They had sent Alethea back to work at St. Elene's for a new start, they'd said.

She's not going to have a new start, thought Meryl Lee. *There is no new start. There's only what's next.*

"I don't know if I can do this," said Alethea.

"Yes you can," said Meryl Lee.

"How do you know?"

And Meryl Lee thought of the Scarecrow, and the Tin Woodman, and the Lion, and Dorothy, and said, "Because all of us have to."

On Monday, Meryl Lee dissected a gross gross gross leech with Matt, while Marian dissected a gross gross gross leech with Charlotte—and Charlotte did the best she could. Matt too. Neither would cut into the leech, but they were standing by the lab table when Marian and Meryl Lee did. So Charlotte might have squealed when a drop of formaldehyde squirted onto her lab coat, but she didn't pass out and she even laughed a little when Mrs. Bellamy said that squirting formaldehyde was an occupational hazard and by the time the class was finished, they'd all smell like dead leeches. Really. Charlotte laughed at that.

But afterward, she took a shower that used up most of Margaret B. Netley Dormitory's hot water.

On Monday, in Famous Women of History, Mrs. Saunders announced that they had all done so well on their reports the previous week that they would all now be writing a report on a famous female artist and creating a work of art in her style.

"Will we have to have partners again?" Ashley asked, and she looked at Meryl Lee.

Mrs. Saunders said these might or might not be individual projects.

"Thank goodness," said Ashley, and she rubbed her pearls slowly against her chin.

Marian partnered with Meryl Lee.

Mrs. Saunders took her class to Putnam, where Mrs. Hibbard had already laid big-paged art books on all the long tables, and Meryl Lee looked for female artists—of whom there are fewer than you might think. Finally Meryl Lee opened a little book called *The Drawings of Kate Greenaway,* and she thought, *This is it.* It was sort of dark in Putnam, but even so, Kate Greenaway's pictures were full of sun. Everything was lovely and delicate. Children in perfect clothes, running around on perfect lawns—and you knew they were never going to get a grass stain on anything they were wearing. Milkmaids with pretty red lips, and white fences, and ivy-covered cottages, and flowers everywhere—mostly roses.

It looked like a gentle world where Vietnam could never happen.

Meryl Lee and Marian decided that Kate Greenaway would be their project.

On Monday afternoon, during an extra soccer practice because, Coach Rowlandson said, they needed it, Coach Rowlandson told Meryl Lee that playing goalie could possibly be Meryl Lee's Accomplishment. "Certainly you're moving your hands a whole lot more quickly"—which, Meryl Lee figured, was true, since you want to move your hands very quickly whenever a soccer ball is hurtling toward your face.

But Meryl Lee said, "Coach Rowlandson, Heidi's back."

"I've spoken with Heidi," said Coach Rowlandson. "You've done well as the backup goalie. Heidi thinks so too."

Meryl Lee felt suspicion cloak her.

"And Heidi has never had an opportunity to play forward and score goals—which would be very nice for the Lasses to do now and then."

"If you're saying that . . ."

"So I'd like you to play first-string goalie for the season."

Meryl Lee looked at her. "I am not happy about this," she said.

"You're doing fine," said Coach Rowlandson.

"I'm not doing fine."

"Kowalski," said Coach Rowlandson, "one week from tomorrow—eight days, or one hundred and ninety-two hours—St. Elene's Preparatory Academy for Girls has its first soccer match of the spring season. We need you in the goal."

What Coach Rowlandson did not say was "Kowalski, one week from tomorrow, St. Elene's Preparatory Academy for Girls is playing St. Scholastica's Academy for Girls, which has won at least the regional championship every year since Dwight D. Eisenhower was president of the United States. It is rumored that their shots on goal are cannonballs. It is rumored that they always fire their first cannonballs directly at the goalie's face to intimidate her. Last season, three goalies from other teams who played St. Scholastica's Academy lost teeth. And their school mascot is a dragon rampant."

That is what Coach Rowlandson was really saying.

Meryl Lee told Coach Rowlandson she was going to be deathly sick next Tuesday.

"What are you coming down with?" she said.

"Something as yet unknown to modern science. Something not even Florence Nightingale would be able to cure."

"You would still be goalie," said Coach Rowlandson.

"I might die in front of the net," said Meryl Lee.

"I'll take my chances," said Coach Rowlandson.

"Coach Rowlandson, I really do want to keep all my teeth through eighth grade."

Coach Rowlandson said, "I'll take my chances with that, too. Sticks down, Kowalski."

The game wasn't for one hundred and ninety-two hours. Perhaps, Meryl Lee thought, something would happen by then so she wouldn't have to play first-string goalie.

Maybe the Apocalypse, which is not something Kate Greenaway would ever have painted.

And on Monday, after soccer practice and before Evening Meal, Meryl Lee and Charlotte and Marian and Jennifer and Heidi walked down to the docks with Alethea and Bettye and together they squeezed onto the bench by the bait house, where the sun was shining and it was warm—though sort of fishy. They watched the waves come in as the tide rose. Together, they held on to Jonathan's scarf, draped across their knees.

That was Monday, when Alethea did what she had to.

On Monday night, Matt also did what he had to—because it was too late to do anything else.

That night, while Mrs. MacKnockater slept with the afghan on her lap, and while the fire in the wood stove fell to embers, and while the sound of a low wind in the pines mingled with the sound of the rising tide and the buoys out on the bay rolled their bells and Captain Hornblower blew up the French supply train heading toward Napoleon's army to bloody bits, Matt—half asleep himself—heard the sound of the porch creaking beneath what sounded like slowly moving, stealthy feet.

Everything in Matt rose to attention. He knew he should run.

He knew he should run.

But he looked over at Bagheera. Asleep.

He looked across to the door. Unlocked.

He looked back at Bagheera.

He got up slowly and yawned, and stretched his arms, and looked around for a place to set the book down, and stretched again, as if he were just sort of tired and logy. He moved toward the front door and, as if nothing at all was wrong, he turned the lock quietly. He reached for the light switch and turned off the overhead. Then he moved to the lamps in the room and turned them off one by one, listening—all the time listening.

Bagheera woke up when he turned off the last one.

"Why is it so dark in here?" she said.

"Bagheera," whispered Matt, "shut up."

It was probably the first time in her life that Dr. Nora Mac-Knockater had ever been told to shut up—and it didn't matter that it was only a whisper.

"I will most certainly not shut up in my own house."

Matt knelt beside her.

"I think we're in trouble," he said. "Go back to the kitchen and make sure the door is locked."

She looked at him.

"Move like you're getting ready to go to bed."

"How do I do that?"

"Bagheera, just do it."

Mrs. MacKnockater pulled the afghan off her lap, stood slowly, and walked into the kitchen. Matt heard her turn the lock in the back door, then lift the receiver off the hook and begin to dial.

Now the only light in the front room came from the wood stove—and there wasn't much. Little enough that Matt could look out through the windows and see the silhouettes of pines and—if there was anyone—the shadow of someone on the porch.

He listened to everything: the sigh of the wind through branches, the way it stroked its palms across the clapboards, the low thrash of the waves below the ridge, the dull bells of the buoys, the footsteps of Bagheera as she came back in and sat down.

"I've made some phone calls," she whispered.

Matt nodded, even though she probably couldn't see him.

He knelt by the bay window and watched.

Nothing.

Nothing for five minutes.

For eight minutes.

And nothing until Lieutenant Minot's black-and-white rolled across the gravel and into the front yard—a few minutes before Captain Hurd showed up.

And Matt could not be sure if he really had seen something—someone—rush away into the dark woods at the sound of the siren.

But that night, after Lieutenant Minot had checked the outside and found nothing, and after Mrs. MacKnockater had finally gone to bed, and after Matt had gone upstairs and then snuck back downstairs with his hatchet, he did not fall asleep, thinking about how some things only God can see—but he wished he could too.

However, he did see Captain Hurd walk past the house three times that night, holding his gleaming lantern high to shove back the darkness.

THIRTY-FOUR

DURING ANNOUNCEMENTS AT DINNER IN THE SECOND week of April, Mrs. Mott invited the students of St. Elene's to join the newly constituted St. Elene's Literary Society, which was now open to anyone connected to St. Elene's Preparatory Academy for Girls. This was an initiative that Mrs. Connolly would be leading in anticipation of her new role at the school, and it was replacing the traditional Tea and Biscuit Conversations. All a student needed to do to show interest and commitment was to submit a Shakespearean sonnet for the first meeting.

Meryl Lee, unfortunately, laughed out loud at the thought of spending more time with Mrs. Connolly than she absolutely had to.

She should not have laughed out loud.

When she did, Mrs. Connolly turned and left Greater Hoxne Dining Hall, and Meryl Lee could see that Mrs. Mott was disappointed in her.

After dinner, Mrs. Mott told Meryl Lee that she had something she needed to see to.

Meryl Lee knew she did.

For a little while she wondered if she should volunteer to be the office assistant for Mrs. Connolly—but she couldn't go that far. So she went to Mrs. Connolly's office to apologize—but Mrs. Connolly wasn't there. Either that, or she would not open her door.

That afternoon, Meryl Lee went to Putnam Library to read about Kate Greenaway.

Dr. MacKnockater was sitting at the table right by the door.

She held out the book she was reading: *The Grapes of Wrath*. "Have you read Mr. Steinbeck, Miss Kowalski?" she said.

Meryl Lee nodded.

"I'm told that this novel is lewd, but I fail to see it. A reader such as yourself might be interested to know that Mrs. Connolly is forming a literary society at St. Elene's."

"I heard about the literary society," said Meryl Lee.

"It would be too bad if not enough girls attended Friday's first meeting, don't you think?"

"I guess," said Meryl Lee.

"Will you be going?"

"Mrs. Connolly is really angry with me right now," said Meryl Lee.

"All the more reason to attend," said Dr. MacKnockater.

"But . . ."

"Would you have her hold the meeting alone?"

Meryl Lee thought about Mrs. Connolly—how whenever she saw her, she was alone.

Life is a lot easier when all you have to do is snatch the broomstick of the Wicked Witch of the West. There's only the one thing you have to do. And the Wicked Witch of the West is wicked, so she deserves to have her broomstick snatched.

But suppose the Wicked Witch of the West isn't just wicked.

Suppose, deep inside her dark castle, the Wicked Witch of the West is lonely.

Or hurt.

Or maybe wanting to be your friend, even if she doesn't know how.

It's after you've snatched the broomstick that things get complicated.

"All right," said Meryl Lee.

"Good," said Dr. MacKnockater. She closed her book.

"Dr. MacKnockater," said Meryl Lee.

"Yes, Miss Kowalski."

"You weren't sitting here waiting for me, were you?"

Dr. MacKnockater handed *The Grapes of Wrath* to Meryl Lee. "If there is a flaw in this splendid book," she said, "it's that Tom leaves the narrative action before he should. I don't think it's lewd, but one should never leave the narrative action before she should."

Matt Coffin did not feel obliged to join the St. Elene's Literary Society—though Mrs. MacKnockater asked if he would be interested.

He just looked at her.

"I'm not insisting," she said.

"Good," said Matt.

"Still and all, it might be enlightening for you to . . ."

"Because if you were insisting, Bagheera, then . . ."

"I think I see Captain Hurd at the door."

And that was the end of their conversation about the St. Elene's Literary Society.

These spring days, Matt was doing his best—his very, very best—to not get up at first light, eat quickly, and head down to the docks. The stars were fading earlier and earlier, and the days were warmer and warmer, and the sea was blue blue blue—and Captain Hurd never suggested that he might go to the St. Elene's Literary Society instead of going out with him on the ocean.

During breakfast, Mrs. MacKnockater watched him when he wasn't looking. It was so good to have him in the house. All those rooms, and so little life—until now. She watched him as he looked out at the sea, and she knew how much of his heart was already on the water. She wondered how he got himself to classes at all.

Maybe because he knew that Mrs. Bellamy and Mr. Wheelock would give him heck if he missed.

Or maybe Matt's decision to go to classes was actually about a certain Miss Kowalski.

And Mrs. MacKnockater wondered if she really did want to take him away to Edinburgh.

Some afternoons, after classes, Matt went down to the shore and skipped stones and thought about Pastor Darius and Sophia Malcolm, about Mr. Tush and the Myrnas. About Georgie. Sometimes he'd go to old Captain Cobb's shack and sweep out the cigarette butts left by the St. Giles's boys and remember those cold months alone. That felt like a lifetime ago, as though it had been taken out by a tide that had never come back in.

And when he came back home, he would open the windows to let in the sea breeze, and it rushed indoors, twisting and frolicking, rustling the papers that Mrs. MacKnockater had laid out for Matt's language arts assignments and baffling them to the floor, and he would gather them and—usually with a sigh—sit beside the wood stove and begin.

But he had not forgotten the sounds on the porch, and more than one night, he lay awake in his bed, listening. Sometimes he stood at his window, watching. Sometimes he stayed downstairs after they turned out all the lights and Mrs. MacKnockater had gone up to her bedroom, and in the darkness, Matt watched the porch windows for passing shadows, his hatchet at the ready. But as time went by, he wondered more and more if he had been mistaken, if he had really heard anything at all.

Though he was pretty sure he hadn't been mistaken.

After the afternoon at Putnam, Meryl Lee was beginning to rethink her project choice for Mrs. Saunders. Marian was writing the report, but Meryl Lee was composing a painting in the style of Kate Greenaway—who was probably a very nice person and a lovely artist, but Meryl Lee was getting tired of all those roses.

And Alethea's brother had died in Vietnam.

And Holling was—

And Bettye's brother was still over there.

And her parents were—

And suppose Matt went to Vietnam? Suppose he had to go too?

Meryl Lee decided she did not want to draw anything like Kate Greenaway right now. She asked Mrs. Saunders if she and Marian could switch to a different artist.

Mrs. Saunders said no.

So that second week of April—except for a little time off for Jonathan's scarf, which was now sixty-five inches—Meryl Lee worked on a painting in the style of Kate Greenaway.

After a few days, she hated Kate Greenaway.

But that wasn't all she was working on, because on Friday, Mrs. Connolly was holding the first meeting of the St. Elene's Literary Society and Meryl Lee had to submit a Shakespearean sonnet to show her interest and commitment, and since Meryl Lee figured Mrs. Connolly did not like her very much, she worked like Shakespeare himself were going to read her Shakespearean sonnet.

"Do you know how hard it is to write a Shakespearean sonnet?" she said Thursday night.

"How many did Shakespeare write?" said Heidi.

"I think he wrote a hundred and fifty or something like that," said Meryl Lee.

"Then how hard can it be?" said Heidi.

"That's it," said Meryl Lee. "If I'm going, then you're going too."

"I don't write poetry," said Heidi.

"It looks like you will now," said Jennifer.

Heidi looked at Jennifer. "Then so will you."

"I've never written a poem," said Jennifer.

"Sticks down," said Heidi.

"Let's go find Marian and Charlotte," said Meryl Lee.

On Friday morning, Meryl Lee finished her Shakespearean sonnet. So did Jennifer, Heidi, Charlotte, and Marian.

Then on Friday afternoon, after classes, feeling as if this was going to be a disaster, going mostly because of Dr. MacKnockater because she sure did not want to go herself, Meryl Lee appeared in Putnam Library to join the St. Elene's Literary Society, led by the sharp-ars— by the beloved Mrs. Connolly and open to anyone connected to St. Elene's Preparatory Academy for Girls.

There were only six girls there from the eighth grade: Meryl Lee, Jennifer, Heidi, Charlotte, Marian—and Ashley, who sat in the back, behind them all, rubbing the string of pearls against her chin. Four girls had come from the seventh grade, and two from the sixth—and they sat sort of fearfully in the front row.

It did not help their cause that when Mrs. Connolly asked what had inspired them to come and participate in the new literary society, one whispered, "Mrs. Felch is giving extra credit."

When Mrs. Connolly stood straight and told the sixth graders that extra credit was poor motivation for joining a literary society, it seemed as if gravity had suddenly come upon them, and their bodies shrank and collapsed into their seats.

Mrs. Connolly began the first meeting of the St. Elene's Literary Society by reading one of Shakespeare's sonnets aloud.

Meryl Lee had no idea what the whole "if this be error and upon me proved" thing was about.

"Now," Mrs. Connolly said, "I will read the submitted sonnets written in the style of the master." She gave a significant look at the sixth graders—which led to more collapsing. "We will begin with the eighth-grade girls."

She first read Jennifer's sonnet about St. Elene's Arm and its rings and then said to her, "I welcome you formally into the Literary Society of St. Elene's Preparatory Academy for Girls." Everyone clapped politely.

Then she read Marian's sonnet about a garden scene on a remote island, and by the time she was done, Meryl Lee could smell the petunias in the salt air.

Mrs. Connolly welcomed Marian formally into the Literary Society of St. Elene's Preparatory Academy for Girls.

Then she read Heidi's sonnet about scoring a soccer goal, and Charlotte's about the ocean, and everyone clapped politely, and Mrs. Connolly welcomed them formally into the Literary Society of St. Elene's Preparatory Academy for Girls, even if, she said, soccer might not be an altogether appropriate subject for a Shakespearean sonnet.

Then she read Ashley's sonnet about cats, and even though

Meryl Lee thought a sonnet that had a whole lot of lines that ended with *cat, mat, hat, sat,* and *rat* might not be altogether appropriate for a Shakespearean sonnet, Mrs. Connolly said to Ashley, "I welcome you formally into the Literary Society of St. Elene's Preparatory Academy for Girls." Everyone clapped politely again.

Then Mrs. Connolly came to Meryl Lee's sonnet. And after she finished reading it, she put it down on the desk beside her. "Miss Kowalski," she said, "you have not fulfilled the assignment."

And Meryl Lee said, "I thought I did."

"The assignment was to write a Shakespearean sonnet. You have not written a Shakespearean sonnet."

And Meryl Lee said, "I think I did."

"Miss Kowalski, what must the final two lines do in a Shakespearean sonnet?"

"Rhyme."

"Do your final two lines rhyme?"

"Yes."

"Obviously they do not, since *slain* and *again* do not rhyme."

"Mrs. Connolly, I have been studying the sonnets of William Shakespeare, and he rhymed *slain* and *again*."

"*Slain* and *again* might have rhymed in the English language during the Renaissance, but they do not rhyme now. And you should have chosen a subject more suitable to the sonnet form than the Vietnam War."

Meryl Lee stood up.

"Meryl Lee," said Jennifer.

"Maybe I should have picked something like cats," said Meryl Lee.

"Cats would have been more appropriate," said Mrs. Connolly.

"Obviously," said Ashley.

"I think poetry should deal with something more significant than cats," said Meryl Lee.

"And I think not every student at St. Elene's is suited to this literary society," said Mrs. Connolly. "You are accepted provisionally. Sit down, please."

By then, gravity had collapsed the four seventh graders into their chairs too.

Meryl Lee sat for the rest of the literary society meeting:

> And hockey stick she wished she bravely held
> To scatter her foes, and Connolly fell.

And she didn't care that *held* and *fell* didn't exactly rhyme.

Saturday night, midnight, raining hard. Meryl Lee was still awake, still trying to figure out how to compose a Kate Greenaway painting. The wind was coming up and the rain blasted against the windows—and suddenly a flash of lightning, then thunder that rattled the pencils on her desk.

Jennifer did not wake up, but Meryl Lee almost jumped out of bed.

Then, as if the lightning had gone off inside her, she understood why she couldn't figure out how to do a Kate Greenaway painting. Kate Greenaway paintings made the whole world into a greeting card with pretty people and pretty places and everything pretty pretty pretty.

But that wasn't the world.

Holling. Alethea's brother. Jonathan. Her mother and father. Maybe Matt off to war someday.

Then another flash of lightning and more thunder. More rattling pencils.

She knew exactly what to do.

Monday afternoon, soon after Meryl Lee turned in her painting, Mrs. Saunders sent a note, asking her to come to her rooms in Sherbourne. Meryl Lee was a little nervous about this. She had never been to Mrs. Saunders's rooms, and when she got there, the rooms weren't exactly what she'd expected. There were books everywhere, on everything. Every bookcase was stuffed double-thick. Piles of books teetered in the corners. Rows of books ran along the windowsills. Books leaned against the couch and against the paisley chairs. It looked as if the round table in the middle of the room hadn't been empty of books since, oh, the turn of the century.

But Meryl Lee didn't look at the books for very long, because her painting was leaning on the couch.

Mrs. Saunders offered her a cup of tea. They sat down in the paisley chairs. Then Mrs. Saunders looked at Meryl Lee's painting.

"Not exactly Kate Greenaway," Mrs. Saunders said.

"No," said Meryl Lee.

"It is not what I expected," Mrs. Saunders said.

"No," said Meryl Lee. "But isn't that what art is supposed to be? Not what you expect?"

"Sometimes," she said. "So tell me about this piece."

So Meryl Lee did. How the painting was in the style of Justin Browning—who she understood was not a female artist, but he liked to draw really wicked storm clouds ready to throw themselves down to smother everything below them.

"And this element here?" Mrs. Saunders pointed to a flower—sort of like a Kate Greenaway rose.

"It's a chrysanthemum," said Meryl Lee. "It's what's not going to be smothered."

"Have you shown the painting to Alethea?" Mrs. Saunders asked.

"No," she said.

"I think she might like to see it," she said.

When Meryl Lee left, she still didn't know if Mrs. Saunders liked her painting or not.

She thought she might.

On Tuesday, the Lasses of St. Elene's Preparatory Academy for Girls played the Rampant Dragons of St. Scholastica's. Heidi could not wait for the first whistle. She ran up and down the field, pumping her legs, stretching her legs, pumping her legs, stretching her legs, shouting defiance, leaping into a string of jumping jacks, throwing down a couple dozen pushups, getting up and shouting defiance again.

The goalie for the St. Elene's Lasses was not quite as eager, even though Matt Coffin stood beside the net to cheer her on.

The goalie for the St. Elene's Lasses watched the Rampant Dragons warming up. "You know," she said to Heidi, "we could forfeit if we wanted to."

Heidi looked at her.

"It's just a game," said the goalie for the St. Elene's Lasses.

Heidi narrowed her eyes. "Tiddlywinks is just a game," she said.

Which may explain why Heidi was so unhappy that night at Evening Meal, since even though she had scored seven goals— and she would have scored eight except she was called offsides when she wasn't and what she said to the ref when she got called offsides made Coach Rowlandson have her sit out the rest of the game—so even though they scored seven goals, the St. Elene's Lasses had lost.

Because the goalie for the St. Elene's Lasses had let in ten goals. Eleven if you counted the penalty kick that came after Heidi said what she said, but no one was saying that that was Meryl Lee's fault.

Meryl Lee pointed out to Coach Rowlandson that four of those ten had been on St. Scholastica's corner kicks, which the Lasses had never practiced and which Coach Rowlandson said they would start practicing a whole lot now. And three shots were way above her head so what was she supposed to do? And the other three were right at her face and she thought the St. Scholastica's Rampant Dragons did that on purpose and remember how she wanted to keep her teeth through eighth grade? If Godzilla were on the team, he would be tall enough that . . .

Godzilla was not on the team, Coach Rowlandson pointed out, but Meryl Lee was. "We work with what we have. And," she said, "I'm pretty proud of what we have."

That made the goalie for the St. Elene's Lasses a little bit happier—even if it didn't do a thing for Heidi.

And truth to tell, it also helped the goalie for the St. Elene's Lasses when, on the way back to Netley, Matt Coffin leaned down to her just before he left and kissed her and told her she was a heck of a goalie.

And maybe she really wasn't unhappy at all at the end of Evening Meal, when Mrs. Mott stood to announce that the girls were all to pay very special attention to what had been hung on the north wall of Greater Hoxne lobby as they exited the dining hall that night.

So they all did.

Hanging on the wall was a painting in a large oval gold frame: a wicked dark sky, and lightning, and a chrysanthemum that looked a little bit like a Kate Greenaway rose. Mrs. Mott stood beside it, adjusting it to the level. The picture looked like it was painted by an Accomplished artist—mostly because of the frame, but still.

Maybe, Meryl Lee thought, Mrs. Saunders liked it after all.

Maybe Mrs. Mott did too.

So all the girls gathered around—not Ashley, of course—and then Alethea and Bettye came out and saw the painting.

Alethea looked at it, and she looked at it, and then she turned to Meryl Lee and she took her in her arms and she started to cry. And it wasn't a bad cry. It was like . . . like relief. At least a little.

When Mrs. Saunders came out of the dining hall, Meryl Lee told her that what she did was one of the nicest things anyone had ever done for her.

"I doubt that very much, Miss Kowalski," she said.

"No, really."

"I think," said Mrs. Saunders, "that you should consult *Funk and Wagnalls* for the word *hyperbole*."

"It isn't a hyperbole," said Meryl Lee.

And Mrs. Saunders, flinty old Mrs. Saunders, reached out her hand and touched Meryl Lee's cheek. "My dear, Dr. MacKnockater has been right about you all along," she said.

"Dr. MacKnockater?" said Meryl Lee. "Right about what?"

If April had been blue cotton, the beginning of May was yellow gingham, with Mr. Wheelock's daffodils blowing and waving and the first dandelions bright-spotting the green lawns of St. Elene's Preparatory Academy for Girls. The air was warm, and the first yellow bees hummed because the clover was open for business.

At the end of April, Meryl Lee and Charlotte and Matt had

been waiting for Heidi and Jennifer and Marian when a white van pulled up beside Newell and the driver got out and called to them. "Do you know a Mrs. Bellamy?" he said. They did. "Do you mind? I'm way behind schedule," he said, and he got out, opened the back doors, and handed them two plastic pails filled with frogs. Big frogs. Big croaking frogs. "These have to be delivered to Mrs. Bellamy," he said.

Between them, they had carried the two pails of croaking frogs to Lesser Hoxne, Meryl Lee and Charlotte taking one, Matt the other. Carrying them was not easy, since the pails were pretty heavy and they were holding them about as far away from their bodies as they could.

When they got the pails to Mrs. Bellamy's classroom, she had been delighted. "At last!" she said, and she took the pail from Matt and she looked down at the frogs and she said, "In a little while, you'll all be pinned to lab tablets. You won't be croaking so loudly then."

Meryl Lee thought Charlotte would faint right there.

"I hope I have enough pins," said Mrs. Bellamy.

Charlotte had put their pail down and run.

Matt had looked at the two pails sort of sadly.

But May being what it was—yellow gingham—it brought about the exciting and mysterious Great Escape, when the frogs destined for dissection—something not a single eighth-grade student at St. Elene's Preparatory Academy for Girls wanted to be a part of—made their inexplicable getaway. After the girls—and Matt—had come to class and put on their lab coats, Mrs. Bellamy had emerged from her prep room, holding two empty pails, and she said she was terribly sorry, but all of the frogs were gone. She couldn't understand it. Somehow the pails had fallen on their sides and the frogs had escaped out the windows—which she didn't even remember leaving open and which she couldn't even figure out how the frogs had gotten to.

Charlotte was ready to stand on her lab stool and dance.

Meryl Lee was pretty sure that Charlotte's delight had something to do with how grateful she was that what Mrs. Bellamy drew on the blackboard for them to copy was not something they were seeing in real life, splayed out on lab tablets and held down by long pins.

And Meryl Lee was also pretty sure that Matt's delight—and he didn't smile all that often—was also a sign of something.

"So, what did you have to do with this?" she whispered while they were drawing.

"With what?"

"The Great Escape."

"I don't know what you're talking about."

She looked at Matt. "You are a terrible liar."

"Actually," said Matt, "I'm a very good liar—but I still don't know what you're talking about."

"Okay, so try lying to me right now."

"You really want me to lie to you?"

"Yes. Say whatever you want and I'll tell you if you're lying."

"Really?"

"Go ahead."

"Okay. Here goes. Meryl Lee, I don't want to kiss you right now."

Meryl Lee was more than a little surprised. "Um . . ."

"I thought you said you'd be able to tell."

"I usually can."

"I told you I was good."

She looked at him.

He leaned over and kissed her.

Mrs. Bellamy cleared her throat loudly.

"*That* wasn't a lie," whispered Matt.

That was the same day Coach Rowlandson told Meryl Lee that, as she was now the first-string goalie for the St. Elene's Lasses, her coach would be expecting her to exert strong leadership skills in the next match.

"Leadership skills?"

"St. Margaret's School for Girls lost every game last spring and, so far, every game this season," said Coach Rowlandson.

"So have we," said Meryl Lee.

Coach Rowlandson shook her head. "A team that's lost that many games in a row is hungry," she said.

"So we should be hungry too," said Meryl Lee.

"Yes we should. Sticks down, Kowalski."

"Sticks down, Coach Rowlandson."

Heidi helped Meryl Lee practice the whole week:

"Midfielder back! Midfielder back!"

"Forward! Move forward, dang it!"

"I don't care if you have hemorrhoids!"

Meryl Lee practiced yelling stuff like that.

But even though she was prepared to exert leadership skills, the goalie for the St. Elene's Lasses was a sieve that day, and St. Margaret's left the field having broken their long losing streak.

The Lasses were pretty devastated.

Heidi walked back to Netley alone, and Meryl Lee was very glad that she was not carrying her field hockey stick.

Meanwhile, Mr. Wheelock's daffodils bowed and waved, holding their yellow selves this way and that to show off, and trumpeting for attention to anyone who came in sight of Newell Chapel, announcing, "Spring! Spring! Spring!"—the way they do.

When Meryl Lee saw them, a loss to St. Margaret's School for Girls didn't seem all that big a deal.

And maybe it didn't seem like all that big a deal to Heidi, either, since at Evening Meal that night, she came over to Meryl Lee's table as Alethea was laying out the dessert, hugged Meryl Lee from the back, and told her that the goalie for the St. Elene's Lasses had done as well as she could, and that was a lot. "Besides, how can I be mad at you when I know you have to spend your nights writing poetry for the St. Elene's Literary Society—which is sort of like having the Wicked Witch of the West do root canal work on your back molars."

"It's not so bad," said Meryl Lee. "But you have to write too."

Heidi shook her head. "All done," she said. "You want to hear it?"

"Go ahead."

Heidi straightened up.

> "Ball toward goalie—
> She curls, leaps, knocks it away.
> Grass stain on her shirt."

"Not terrible," said Meryl Lee.

"What do you mean, 'not terrible'?"

"Poetry?" said Alethea. "Bettye writes poetry."

THIRTY-FIVE

On the second friday of may, the st. elene's Literary Society was to meet again. They were all to write a haiku—or a villanelle if they were particularly ambitious.

On that day, Meryl Lee decided that Mrs. Connolly was evil.

Mrs. Connolly was really really really evil.

Bettye came to the meeting. She sat between Meryl Lee and Charlotte. Two of the seventh graders and one of the sixth graders had fled the literary society, but Mrs. Connolly welcomed the rest of the members—provisional or otherwise—and repeated that she and she alone would be in charge of the society. Then she read aloud all the haiku and all the villanelles that had been sent to her—except Bettye's.

Every single one except Bettye's.

"Now that I have read the submissions aloud," said Mrs. Connolly, "let's begin by discussing—"

But Meryl Lee raised her hand and asked if Mrs. Connolly had forgotten to read Bettye Buckminster's villanelle.

And Ashley said, "Is Bettye Buckminster a member of the literary society?"

And Mrs. Connolly said, "Bettye Buckminster is neither a student nor a teacher at St. Elene's. She is a kitchen worker. She is ineligible for this society."

Long silence. Bettye pushing her chair back.

Meryl Lee raised her hand again. "The invitation said everyone from St. Elene's was invited."

"The invitation was not meant to include the junior staff," said Mrs. Connolly.

"The invitation said 'everyone,'" said Meryl Lee.

But Mrs. Connolly looked at Bettye Buckminster. "As I said, the invitation was not meant to include the junior staff."

Bettye got up and, looking at the floor, left.

Another long silence.

Then Mrs. Connolly said, "So, let's begin our discussion."

But they didn't begin, because Meryl Lee stood up.

"Mrs. Connolly," said Meryl Lee.

Mrs. Connolly's eyes rose from the collected poetry.

"I can't attend the next meeting if Bettye is not invited."

And Mrs. Connolly did that breathing thing with her nose and said, "Miss Kowalski, do not be influenced by misguided sentiment."

And Meryl Lee said, "That's exactly what I'm trying to do, Mrs. Connolly—not be influenced by misguided sentiment."

Then Charlotte stood up too.

"Miss Dobrée," said Mrs. Connolly, sort of warningly.

And Charlotte said, "Bettye Buckminster deserves to be a part of the literary society."

"Bettye Buckminster is not part of the literary society," said Mrs. Connolly.

"Then neither are we," said Meryl Lee.

They left together. Jennifer and Marian and Heidi went behind them.

They found Bettye in the kitchen. She was trying not to cry. They told her to ignore Mrs. Connolly. Anyone associated with St. Elene's was supposed to be eligible, and she was associated with St. Elene's. They told her to come again next time. Okay?

"Bettye," Meryl Lee said, "you are an Accomplished poet."

"Maybe so," Bettye said, "but I need this job."

And Charlotte said, "Your villanelle is amazing. I'm glad I wrote mine before I read yours, or I wouldn't have even tried. And it doesn't matter that Mrs. Connolly didn't read yours aloud. It is still better than anyone else's."

Then Bettye and Charlotte hugged.

That's a sign of how things are going to be someday, thought Meryl Lee.

After Evening Meal, the eighth-grade members of St. Elene's Literary Society—provisional and otherwise—each got a letter from Mrs. Connolly. The goal of the literary society, the note said, was the development of a keen and discerning understanding of literary forms and expression, and this development was limited to the academic members of the St. Elene's community. Those girls who did not wish to proceed under these conditions should think about following other extracurricular pursuits.

Meryl Lee first thought about what Dr. MacKnockater would say. Then she thought about following other extracurricular pursuits.

Spring soccer looked as if it would be the one and only.

Monday morning, in history class, Mrs. Saunders was absent with a cold, so Dr. MacKnockater came in to teach. They were supposed to start a unit on Eleanor Roosevelt, but instead Dr. MacKnockater began to talk about women's suffrage, and how women got the vote, and how they had to demonstrate and go to prison before they got the vote, and how her friend Ella was the first woman to vote in Flushing, New York, where she grew up. Then Dr. MacKnockater began singing the lyrics for *Votes for Women!* songs from a hundred years ago in her old lady warble, and then she decided to have the girls sing the old *Votes for Women!* songs in their young sopranos, and pretty soon they were all singing—"To the tune of 'The Battle Hymn of the Republic,' girls!"

> Ye men who wrong your mothers,
> And your wives and sisters, too,
> How dare you rob companions
> Who are always brave and true?
> How dare you make them servants
> Who are all the world to you?
> As they go marching on?
> Men and brothers, dare you do it?
> Men and brothers, dare you do it?
> Men and brothers, dare you do it
> As we go marching on?

The songs were pretty rousing, and Dr. MacKnockater gave them her full mezzo warble. And Meryl Lee had to admit, singing "Votes for Women!" was a whole lot more fun than studying Eleanor Roosevelt.

But when they were finished and class was almost over, Dr. MacKnockater said, "Girls, we've had a good time with these songs, but let's remember this: The women who sang them, sang them during sit-ins that brought about justice. They sang them during sit-ins that brought about change. They sang them from their hearts."

Then Dr. MacKnockater looked right at Meryl Lee. "What are you going to sing from your heart?"

On Wednesday morning, Meryl Lee stood by Mr. Wheelock's daffodils as the teachers and students of St. Elene's Preparatory Academy for Girls, lower school and upper school, walked into Newell Chapel. She held a sign in her left hand—

OPEN THE LITERARY SOCIETY TO ALL!

and she held a sign in her right hand—

FREEDOM TO ASSEMBLE

FREEDOM OF SPEECH

and she did feel sort of . . . conspicuous.

When Mrs. Connolly saw Meryl Lee and her signs, she turned away and looked straight ahead as she processed into Newell.

When Mrs. Saunders saw Meryl Lee, she smiled and processed in, blowing her nose.

When Mrs. Hibbard saw Meryl Lee, she stepped out of line and kissed her on the cheek.

When Coach Rowlandson saw Meryl Lee, she mouthed, *Sticks down, Kowalski!*

When Dr. MacKnockater saw Meryl Lee, she nodded and went in.

Meryl Lee stood by the daffodils through Chapel.

She stood by the daffodils through morning classes.

She stood by the daffodils during dinner.

She stood by the daffodils during afternoon classes—when Jennifer came to stand next to her.

She stood by the daffodils during Evening Meal, when Heidi came with two plates of Chicken à la King and mugs of hot tea. Heidi held the signs while Meryl Lee and Jennifer ate, and when they finished, Heidi took the OPEN THE LITERARY SOCIETY TO ALL! sign and said she'd stay with them.

A little while later, Charlotte came with some blankets, and she stood with them as it got dark and cold.

Mrs. Kellogg came around eight o'clock.

"Girls," she said, "you need to come back to the dorm now."

Heidi and Charlotte looked at Meryl Lee.

"Will Bettye Buckminster be allowed into the literary society?" Meryl Lee said.

"I am not part of that decision," said Mrs. Kellogg.

"Then we'll stay," said Charlotte.

Mrs. Kellogg hesitated. "I won't compel you to come to the dorm," she said.

"Thank you," said Heidi.

A little while after Mrs. Kellogg left, Marian came with mugs filled with very hot tea and lemon. When they'd all finished drinking, Marian said she would stay too.

And in the morning, when the teachers and students of St. Elene's Preparatory Academy for Girls processed into Newell Chapel, Meryl Lee and Jennifer and Heidi and Charlotte and Marian were still by the daffodils, holding their signs. They were looking a little bit bedraggled. Charlotte's hair was positively uncurled.

But they stayed all day.

And after Evening Meal, Mrs. Kellogg brought them more blankets and thermoses of hot chocolate and hot tomato soup.

They stayed all night, again.

And on Friday morning, when the teachers and students of St. Elene's Preparatory Academy for Girls processed into Newell Chapel, Mrs. Hibbard got out of the line and stood with them. She took the OPEN THE LITERARY SOCIETY TO ALL! sign and held it high.

Then Mrs. Saunders got out of the line and stood with them too. She took the other sign.

And then Lois Tuthill got out of line, and Julia Chall and Barbara Rockcastle and Elizabeth Koertge, too.

And during Chapel, Bettye came.

And then, Alethea. She looked at Meryl Lee for a long time.

"You know, you were right," she said.

"About what?"

"I didn't know you." Then Alethea folded her arms across her chest and it looked as if it would have taken three trawlers to move her away from the front of Newell Chapel.

Which was good, because Meryl Lee was exhausted. Two nights sleeping outside of Newell Chapel with just blankets?

On Friday afternoon, Dr. MacKnockater came to Newell Chapel. Marian was asleep.

"Ladies," she said, "Mrs. Connolly has resigned from the literary society, which is now, for lack of a mentoring teacher, disbanded."

They looked at each other.

"What does that mean?" Meryl Lee asked.

"It means, Miss Kowalski, that if there is to be a literary society open to participation by all, it will need to be reconstituted with a new mentoring teacher."

"I am free on Friday afternoons," said Mrs. Hibbard.

Dr. MacKnockater nodded.

But Meryl Lee still didn't understand. Perhaps her brain had fallen asleep.

"Meryl Lee," Dr. MacKnockater said, "you can go back to your room. You have been brave and true. And you have won. Maybe you have changed the world a little bit."

That Meryl Lee understood—in a drowsy, underslept sort of way. "Now we'll see what happens," she said.

"Yes, we will," said Dr. MacKnockater.

Meryl Lee went back to Netley.

Jennifer spread her green duvet over the two of them, and she and Meryl Lee slept, and slept, and slept.

They slept all through the night, and then through breakfast, and they would have slept through Morning Chapel if Mrs. Mott had not shaken them awake. Even so, Meryl Lee was barely conscious when she processed into Newell with all the students of St. Elene's Preparatory Academy—the one boy being absent, as usual—and she felt herself nodding dangerously close to the pew in front of her, yawning and yawning, and her eyes closing, and so she only half understood what Mrs. Kellogg announced from the front: that Dr. Nora MacKnockater had been found that morning in her Sherbourne House rooms, unconscious. She had fallen and struck her head against the floor, causing a presumed concussion that the doctors feared might be dangerous in the extreme.

It took a few seconds until the words meant anything at all to Meryl Lee.

She sat up.

She turned to Heidi.

"What?" Meryl Lee said.

THIRTY-SIX

Captain Hurd picked up Meryl Lee the next morning to take her to the Downeast Medical Center.

When they got there, Dr. MacKnockater was still unconscious.

Matt had stayed all night—and he looked like it. Together they watched the nurse on the new shift come in to check Dr. Mac-Knockater's vitals. "Are you relations?" she asked.

"Yes," said Matt.

Dr. MacKnockater was so still. The white of the bandage wrapped around the top of her head seemed no whiter than her skin, which looked thin and dry. Her eyelids fluttered now and again, but they did not open, and the tubes of oxygen that ran into her nose seemed . . . violating.

She looked old.

After the nurse left, Matt stood over Mrs. MacKnockater and he whispered, so quietly that only Meryl Lee could hear, "Bagheera." He leaned over her. "Bagheera," he whispered again. "I'm so sorry. I'm so sorry."

Nothing.

He could not even see her breathe.

And then, suddenly, he was in the Alley again. And Georgie was on the ground. His eyes were open, but he wasn't seeing anything. His mouth was open too, but he wasn't breathing.

Meryl Lee rose and took Matt's hand.

She didn't need to look at his face to know he was crying.

The doctor came in, and he looked at the chart, then at his watch. He took out a flashlight, lifted Mrs. MacKnockater's eyelids, and shone the light onto her pupils.

"Her concussion is severe," they heard the doctor say to the Captain. "We don't know what precipitated it. A heart event, perhaps. A stroke. Maybe something as innocuous as a stumble against a chair leg."

Matt leaned down closer. "Bagheera," he whispered. "Don't go."

"The unexplained oddity," said the doctor, "is that in addition to the blow to the forehead, there is also a blow to the back of the head."

"How did that happen?" said the Captain.

"We don't know," said the doctor. "It seems unlikely that both blows would come from a single fall."

Matt stood up. He looked at Meryl Lee. "They didn't," he whispered.

He let go of Meryl Lee's hand.

"In any case, one such wound in a woman her age is dangerous. Two . . ."

"I've got to go back to the house," said Matt.

The doctor and Captain Hurd looked at him.

"You're staying with me tonight," said the Captain.

"No," said Matt. "I'm staying at the house."

"Then I'll stay with you."

"I'll be fine," said Matt.

"I don't care if you think—"

"Can we go now?" said Matt.

Quiet in the room—though even in that quiet, they could not hear Mrs. MacKnockater breathing.

"Okay," said the Captain.

Silently they drove to Mrs. MacKnockater's house. Silently Matt got out. He closed the door. He did not look at them. He said nothing. He walked up onto the porch, pulled the door open, and slammed it shut behind him.

As they drove away, they did not see him look through the front room window and watch them drive out of his life.

And they did not see him go back outside, sit on the porch steps with his pea jacket hunched around his shoulders, and wait through the day as the sun began to slide down toward the incoming tide and paint everything a dark yellow.

Captain Hurd dropped Meryl Lee off at St. Elene's. She sat through dinner, then wandered over to Putnam, waved at Mrs. Hibbard, sat down to work at quadratic equations—which seemed to take forever. She fussed with the next poem for the literary society but couldn't get any of the lines right, then wandered the stacks until she found a book of Edgar Allan Poe poems that she thought might help—but after a few of those, she knew that anything she wrote that day would sound like "Annabel Lee." So she gave up, gathered her books, waved at Mrs. Hibbard, and walked back outside. But she did not go back to Netley. She wandered beyond the dorm out to the soccer field, and she stood beside the goal. The air was colder than she expected for May, and she drew her jacket tightly around her. Already the sun was down and it was quickly getting darker. The light shining on the steeple of Newell suddenly came on, and in the blue-black air it seemed almost a beacon.

She walked around the goal and leaned back against one of the posts.

Matt was going to run, she thought. She knew he was going to run. And he would be gone.

Across the field, the Blank seemed to gather itself.

He'd be gone not like Holling, but still gone. She'd never see him again.

Gone not like her father, but still gone.

Gone just as much, in a way, as Alethea's brother was gone.

The Blank began to rise.

Gone like Jonathan had gone when he went off to war—leaving home and going someplace Bettye had never been, would never go.

Gone to war.

Like Matt—sprinting down the stairs in his red boxers as if he were going to war.

Meryl Lee suddenly stood straighter.

Sprinting down the stairs in his boxers as if he were going to war.

As if he were going to war.

Across the field, the Blank disappeared. Stars shone through where it had been.

She knew suddenly with an absolute and complete knowing that Matt was not going to run.

She began to sprint across the soccer field.

Matt was going to war.

Matt sat on the porch steps as the stars began to prick through the darkness. The wind blew high through the pines, and they bowed their heads to one another slowly and shed their scent beneath them. The sounds of the waves chucking the chins of the sharp rocks down on the shoreline. The shrieks of the late gulls swooping down for mussels. The slosh and splash of the water pulled out by the tide, receding from around the rocks, leaving the clam holes quietly popping.

The absolutely dark house looming behind him.

The moon not yet up, and some clouds coming in like gloves wiping the stars away.

And Matt thought about all those he had left behind, and who had been hurt because they had cared about him.

He couldn't keep leaving people behind to get hurt.

He began to count them, starting with Georgie.

And Pastor . . .

But he didn't have time to go through his list. It was too late. He stood at the shadow that came toward him.

"I know why you're here," Matt said slowly.

The shadow coming closer.

Matt waited.

"I know why you're here too," said Meryl Lee.

Matt's heart stopped.

"What are you doing?" said Matt.

"You just said you knew."

"You have to get out of here," he said.

"It's a free country," she said.

"You don't understand. He's coming. He's coming and he doesn't care . . ."

"Who's coming?"

Matt took a step toward her. "Listen, I'm not kidding. You have to get out of here."

"He's been coming ever since I've known you, hasn't he?" She reached out and took both of Matt's hands, and Matt closed his eyes. It felt so good to hold her hands.

But Leonidas Shug was coming.

He took his hands back.

"Get away from me," he said. "Just, get away from me."

"No," said Meryl Lee.

"Listen, this guy, he kills people, Meryl Lee. He killed . . . Georgie. He killed him. And whatever happened to Mrs. MacKnockater, he did it. He wants me back, and the only way he's going to stop is if I go with him. And if he comes here and finds you . . ."

Meryl Lee turned toward the shadows. "Here I am," she hollered. "Meryl Lee Kowalski. Right here."

Matt grabbed her in an agony. "Shut up!"

"Anybody out there who wants Matt, you can't have him!"

"Meryl Lee!"

"He belongs here. It may be weird that he's a student at St. Elene's, but he is. He's not going anywhere."

Matt spun her around.

"I'm not going to stop, Matt. I'm not going to let anyone hurt you. I'm—"

And Matt put his hands upon her cold cheeks, and his mouth upon hers, and he kissed her. He kissed her for a long time. And when he pulled back a little, she said, "Did you do that to shut me up?"

"Maybe," he said.

"You really are a terrible liar."

"And you," started Matt—but he did not finish. He looked over her shoulder at the moon rising over the islands, and the pale light it threw from behind the thin clouds hit the silhouette standing not far from them underneath the pines.

He drew Meryl Lee behind him. "Run," he whispered.

She looked at the silhouette, stepping toward them quickly.

"Run," whispered Matt again.

She hesitated only a moment. Then she ran.

He felt her go out of his life—again.

"Good to see you, Matt. It's been a long time."

The air around him grew colder, even frosty. The moon rose higher to backlight the silhouette, as if this were all a play, carefully staged.

"I'm coming with you," said Matt. "You don't need to do anything. I'm coming with you."

"Smart," said the silhouette. "Real smart. I knew it from the beginning. 'That one, he's smart,' I told my associates. 'We may have to kill him someday, he's so smart.' That's what I said."

"You killed Georgie."

"He wasn't so smart. You still have what you took from me?"

"Most of it."

"Where is it?"

"Inside."

"You know I've already cut the phone lines."

"And the power line, too. I figured that."

The silhouette nodded. "See what I mean? Always one step ahead." Then he looked at Matt. "But you made a mistake with her. A boy going to a girls' school. You had to know that would get around."

"Maybe I wanted it to get around."

"No," said the silhouette slowly. "It was a mistake. You probably let yourself care, right? Always a mistake. You can't let yourself care. Look where it got you. Cornered, Matt. You're cornered. That's what giving your heart away will do to you every time."

Captain Hurd hung up the phone. Three times, and no signal at all? Maybe just a problem with the line. But maybe . . . He looked through the trees toward Nora's house. No lights, either?

He put on his coat. Those high clouds meant a cold front. Maybe he'd walk by Nora's house one more time, just to see that the kid was okay. Then, before he left the house, he almost made one more phone call. To Lieutenant Minot. But no. No reason to get people all riled and upset. Probably the phone line. And maybe a fuse. He'd fix it in no time.

"I told you I'd go with you," said Matt.

The silhouette shook his head. "I don't need you anymore, Matt. I'm legitimate. I work for the freaking Secret Service. No kidding. Didn't I teach you how important it is to keep friends in high places?"

Leonidas Shug took a step toward him and drew something out from his pocket. He opened it. It glinted even in the moon's light.

"But times being what they are, I need to keep my options open. You understand. I can't go looking soft. So, first things first. Where's the money?"

"First things first," said Matt. "I need to know that once you get the money, you're gone. Forever."

Shug took a step closer. "You know, Matt, I did Georgie myself. That's why it was a little bit messier. Those guys I hired, they're professionals. They can stick a knife into you and pull it out, and hardly a drop of blood shows. That's professional. That's high class. But they watched when I did Georgie, and even though I'm not high class, they were impressed. The kid couldn't even scream because of where I stuck him first. He just sort of looked at me and gurgled the whole time I did him."

"You—"

"Careful, Matt. Remember what I taught you? Bad language

only draws attention to yourself. And you know, I've already given you a couple of passes. I didn't stick the old lady, and I didn't stick your girlfriend, did I? And I could have. You know I could have."

"Yeah, you're a real humanitarian."

"That's me: a humanitarian. But two passes is all you get, Matt. You're going to have to buy the next one with what you stole from me. Understand? So let's go find the money. Then we'll talk about what happens next."

But Leonidas Shug did not expect what happened next. Matt, either.

With a roar like the sea in his mouth, Captain Willis Hurd, of the lobster boat *Affliction,* smashed into Shug's back. It was like a rogue wave catching a boat hull up, and Shug fell to the ground like a drowning man. The Captain lifted his fist and brought it down once, twice, on Shug's head.

"Get out of here!" the Captain screamed to Matt.

Meryl Lee had reached the main road to St. Elene's—and with all the wind sprints she had done, she reached it quickly. She ran to the first house with lights on, pounded up the porch, pounded at the door, and, when it opened, pounded out her words: "The police. Call the police."

Matt did not get out of there. The slash of Shug's knife through his upper thigh took him down before he could do a thing.

"No!" cried Captain Hurd.

Then the Captain was on his back in the grass, suddenly quiet.

"Get up," said Shug.

Matt felt himself about to throw up.

Shug grabbed Matt by the hair and forced him to his knees, then his feet.

Matt held his hand to his upper thigh, already sticky with blood.

"Inside," said Shug.

They went into the house.

"The Captain," said Matt.

"The money," said Shug.

The darkness inside made everything close, as if even the ceiling could topple down upon them. Not even a glow from the wood stove. So Matt moved with one hand held out in front, and he followed the thick hall carpet to the stairs and began to climb, with Shug right behind him; he could almost feel the knife at his back. They climbed the stairs that Matt had once bounded down in his boxers—twelve steps, Matt counted, then a turn to the left and two more—and Shug so close behind him he could hear his breathing.

"How is the old lady, anyway?"

"Like you care," said Matt.

"I don't," said Shug, "but it's good to keep account of what resources I have available."

Down the hall, and Matt stopping to open his door. He listened to the familiar catch of the hinges, and walked in slowly.

Then suddenly swung around.

Kicked as hard as he could where he figured Shug's left knee would be.

Connected. Almost unplugged the kneecap.

Shug screaming and slashing ahead with his knife.

Matt slamming the bedroom door and Shug slumped in the hallway, howling.

Matt reaching for the lock, reaching for it, feeling Shug's sudden weight against the door, reaching for the lock until he found it and twisted the bolt across.

The heavy thump of Shug's fist against the door panels.

Lieutenant Minot had decided to stay close to Harpswell that night. He was pretty sure what happened to Dr. MacKnockater had more to it than a fall.

He was just cruising past the Gate of St. Elene's when the report came over the radio.

The bedroom door strained against the terrible pounding as Matt pulled out the bottom dresser drawer. He grabbed the hatchet and slipped it through his belt loop. Then he went to the ladder and began to hoist himself up through the darkness of the chute, one hand on the rungs, the other clutching his thigh. Below the skylight, he opened the cabinet and took out the pillowcase. He held that clenched in his teeth.

Splintering behind him.

On the single-lane ridge road, Lieutenant Minot came up behind August Haviland's 1952 Ford pickup, which, under August's foot, traveled about fifteen miles an hour. Lieutenant Minot put on his siren and every single light in the car, but there was no room for August to pull off.

Then August slowed down to ten.

Matt fumbled for the latch to the skylight.

More splintering below.

He pulled the latch back and scrambled up the ladder. With the pillowcase and the hatchet, he didn't seem to have enough hands.

The sound of the bedroom door below being slammed open against the wall.

Matt climbed out onto the level roof and closed the skylight. It was darker than he thought it would be. The stars had all succumbed to the thickening clouds, and though he could hear the waves, he could not see them cracking white below him—probably because he had no intention of leaning out too far.

"You think you're going anywhere?" he heard Shug yell. "You think you can get away?"

Matt stood on the level roof, knees bent a little. And when the skylight popped up, Matt drove his heel down onto the frame, forcing it down.

It didn't matter.

The glass shattered, and Shug reached through, swinging the knife.

Matt, as hard as he could, threw the hatchet down into the chute. Then he crossed the level roof and reached the sharp angle that led up to the dormer.

And that's when Matt's leg gave out.

He fell to the roof, holding his hand to his thigh—aflame with pain. His hand filled with the stickiness of blood.

He looked back at the smashed skylight and saw the frame jerk upward.

Crawling, Matt hefted himself up onto the angle of the dormer and started up, grasping where he could, sliding back a bit, and then struggling up again. But the slickness of the slate gave him nothing to hold on to, and he slid straight back onto the level roof, and there was Shug, standing close, the knife in one hand, the hatchet in the other.

"Bingo," Shug said.

Lieutenant Minot curled off the ridge road, figuring that he'd see the lights of the MacKnockater house—but they were all off. They were never all off. She always left the downstairs lamp by the front window on.

But now the house was dark.

He took the drive onto the property and scattered the gravel well into the woods. What he did to the rhododendrons was not something that Nora MacKnockater would let him forget.

The siren screamed at the house.

Shug pointed to the pillowcase. "That my money?"

Matt stood up—it wasn't easy. "You know what that siren's all about, right? You don't have much time."

"I have enough."

Matt hobbled to the edge of the roof and held the pillowcase over the edge. Far below, the rocks and the waves and the sea.

"Be smart, kid. You know you're in trouble. Hand it over and maybe you'll come out of this okay."

"You're a really bad liar."

Shug held up his knife. "Then go ahead. Drop it. After that, I'll drop you. Looks like a pretty long fall. Then I'll go back down and pick up my money. But I won't go away. Maybe I'll go visit your girlfriend."

"I can throw it past the ridge."

"Nice try, kid."

"Go down and I'll throw it to you. Otherwise it goes into the sea."

"No deal."

Matt pulled the pillowcase behind his back and cocked his arm. "Think again," he said.

And Shug threw the hatchet.

Lieutenant Minot ran up the front porch steps. The door swung loosely, and he could tell immediately that the lock had been forced and the doorjamb wrenched away. He drew a flashlight and went inside. "Matt," called Lieutenant Minot. "Matt Coffin, you here?"

Matt lay on the slate roof, holding his shin where the hatchet had clipped him. He could hardly see, it hurt so much.

Shug took a step toward him. "I always liked you, Matt. I was going to let you come with me. I really was. It could have been like the old times used to be. But look at you. Pathetic. You're about to start bawling. So just hand over the money. Do it now, and maybe I won't visit your girlfriend after this."

"Go to hell."

And Shug shifted his knife to his left hand, and lunged in the darkness.

But he stepped against the sharp angle that led up to the dormer.

His left foot twisted on the slick slate, and his leg folded, and he fell heavily on the level, rolled, and started over the edge of the roof, clutching at air.

Matt heaved out the pillowcase and Shug grabbed for it, holding on as the rest of him slid over into the air.

"Don't let go!" cried Shug, but with his weight, the pillowcase began to tear.

Flat on the roof and his hand twisted in the pillowcase, Matt began to slide to the edge.

And money spilled out from the pillowcase. Hundred-dollar

bills blew past Shug and out toward the ocean. Dozens of bills, and dozens of bills, and Shug watched them. Dozens.

And he reached for them. Dozens.

"No No No," yelled Matt.

But Shug reached anyway, and the new angle tore the pillow-case even more, and more, and as the hundred-dollar bills came out in a rush and covered Shug before they flew off, the pillowcase gave way entirely.

Leonidas Shug fell, striking the granite ridge, then tumbling over and over and over down to the rocks and the waves, as surprised seagulls, disturbed from sleep, rose up into the air, screaming, screaming, screaming their anger and fear.

And then the night was dark—night darkness so deep that only God could see Matt Coffin lying on the slate roof, crying.

THIRTY-SEVEN

For THREE DAYS THERE WERE POLICE REPORTS WITH Lieutenant Minot.

There were police reports with agents from New York City.

There were meetings, many meetings between Lieutenant Minot and the New York City Police that ended with a decision to rule any involvement by Mr. Matthew Coffin (minor) in the death of Mr. Leonidas Shug as "accidental" and not subject to indictment.

There were phone calls—lots of phone calls—to New York and Philadelphia, with long accounts to anxious Kowalskis.

There were explanatory visits to Mrs. Connolly, acting headmistress of St. Elene's Preparatory Academy for Girls.

There was a visit by Mrs. Connolly and Mrs. Kellogg to Ashley Higginson, and later, a visit between Mrs. Connolly and Ashley's aunt and uncle, who took Ashley home with them, "until arrangements could be made."

There were hospital visits to Dr. Nora MacKnockater from Meryl Lee and a limping Matt. For two of the three days she remained unconscious. On the third she was groggy. On the fourth, she was flat-out ornery.

And there were hospital visits to Captain Willis Hurd by Matt and Meryl Lee as well. He was unconscious all the way through

Mrs. MacKnockater's ornery day, and when he finally woke up, the first thing he said was "Nora okay?"—and then "And you?"—and then "And *Affliction?*"

When Captain Hurd was released several days later, he was brought to Mrs. MacKnockater's house, where a hospital bed was waiting for him in the front room.

"I have my own house," he said.

"You need more care than you'd get there."

"You think I can't—"

"Willis, just be quiet for once and do as you're told," said Mrs. MacKnockater.

He was. He did.

And back at St. Elene's Preparatory Academy for Girls, Mrs. Connolly, the acting headmistress, assigned Bettye Buckminster the morning shift, and Alethea Browning the afternoon shift, and Miss Ames the evening shift at Dr. MacKnockater's house. And when Dr. MacKnockater complained that she didn't need any help, Mrs. Connolly explained that she should just be quiet for once and do as she was told.

She was. She did.

On the day before the Lasses played their last game of the season against St. Anne's, Coach Rowlandson made the team practice defense against corner kicks until dark. But the goalie for the St. Elene's Lasses was not quite as sharp as she needed to be, so even though Matt and Heidi were hollering back and forth the next day when peppy St. Anne's ran onto the field, and Charlotte and Jennifer were clapping on the sidelines and yelling stupid St. Elene's chants, the Lasses' goalie let in nine goals—which was eight more than the St. Elene's Lasses scored. Three of the goals were off corner kicks.

Goaltending was not Meryl Lee's Accomplishment.

When the game was finally over, Meryl Lee and Matt walked—or limped—quietly back to Netley, then down to the shore, where they skipped stones into the waves before Mrs. MacKnockater—who was only pretending to use the cane that she was supposed to be using all the time—called them up for chowder and corn bread.

"Miss Ames is a wonderful nurse," Mrs. MacKnockater whispered to them after dinner, "but she makes chowder as if she grew up in Illinois. Bettye and Alethea, however—"

It was late May, and the skies grew even bluer and the sunlight warmer. The grass on the commons greened and greened and the buds on the trees split open into fresh leaves and the yellow daffodils were still waving while the tulips were thinking they should be catching up to the daffodils and the poison ivy on the wall was perking up.

The final Tuesday of May, Meryl Lee and Matt and Charlotte and Marian worked together to dissect the horrible fetal pig in Mrs. Bellamy's class. They all almost gagged—this little sort of pink-mostly-puke-gray body sitting on a dissection board with its tiny feet and snout and ears and tail and everything. "Turn it onto its back and cut it open from chin to tail," said Mrs. Bellamy. "You can't imagine what wonders you'll discover."

Meryl Lee and Marian did not want to imagine.

Matt and Charlotte really did not want to imagine.

Meryl Lee—who after all had done the locust—handed the scalpel to Matt. Matt took a deep breath. He approached the pink-mostly-puke-gray pig. He lowered the scalpel. It touched the skin . . .

That was more than enough for Matt.

He gave Marian the scalpel.

Marian approached the pink-mostly-puke-gray pig. She lowered the scalpel. It touched the skin.

Charlotte started to whimper.

And then Marian plunged in and cut open the whole pink-mostly-puke-gray pig in kind of a hurry.

She kept her eyes closed the whole time.

Which later was a problem, since for homework they were all supposed to draw the unimaginable wonders that spilled completely out of the much-too-deep incision and which Marian and then Meryl Lee and even Matt a little bit tried to push back into place—Charlotte being no help at all with this—so they could observe the unimaginable wonders in the positions they were supposed to be in, and when they failed at pushing the unimaginable wonders in with forceps and then Mrs. Bellamy used her thumbs to shove everything back inside in a big mush, Charlotte, Marian, Meryl Lee, Matt, and even Mrs. Bellamy all turned sort of grim around the mouth and felt suddenly that there was not quite enough air inside the room—perhaps it was the effect of the formaldehyde.

But you know what? Later, when they all sat down in Putnam to try to draw the unimaginable wonders, Meryl Lee looked around and there was no Blank. There was Charlotte trying not to laugh, and Matt focusing with his tongue at the side of his mouth, and Marian bearing down with her pencil, and Mrs. Hibbard knitting, and the fiction shelf where *The Grapes of Wrath* was supposed to be but Mrs. Mott was in an easy chair scanning the pages of the book, and there was no Blank.

Meryl Lee had been wondering, so the next day, after Chapel, she asked Dr. MacKnockater—who was back at St. Elene's now, because no one could stop her, and she wasn't even pretending to use the cane—if she had read *The Wonderful Wizard of Oz* that spring after all.

"I have," she said. "In fact, I have been thinking about the Lion."

"The Lion?"

"I've been wondering if he always had courage inside himself and only needed to find a way to recognize it, or if he had to resolve to put on courage as something utterly new to him."

"I don't think it matters," said Meryl Lee.

"Why?"

"What matters is that he became courageous."

Dr. MacKnockater nodded.

Meryl Lee looked at her. "This is about Mrs. Connolly," she said. "Isn't it?"

Dr. MacKnockater nodded again.

And that was why, later that afternoon, after another day of American Literary Masterpieces when Mrs. Connolly had been oh so coldly polite to all the girls but especially one Meryl Lee Kowalski, Meryl Lee stood outside Mrs. Connolly's office door, knocking.

Sort of hoping no one would answer, but wondering what would happen if . . .

Mrs. Connolly opened the door. She looked at Meryl Lee and she said, "Yes?"

"May I come in?" said Meryl Lee.

"I'm busy, Miss Kowalski."

"I won't be long."

Mrs. Connolly considered this, then turned and went back to her glass-top desk. She sat down behind it and poised a red pen over a stack of exams.

Meryl Lee sat down.

"How are you?" said Meryl Lee.

"Busy, as I said," said Mrs. Connolly.

"I know. Mrs. Connolly, I'm sorry that—"

Mrs. Connolly put her red pen down.

"Miss Kowalski, this isn't going to be a scene, is it? I don't have time for scenes, and if you're thinking of staging one now, I'm going to ask you to leave."

"I'm here to ask you to come back to the literary society," said Meryl Lee.

Silence in the cold office.

Long silence.

"We can start again, Mrs. Connolly," said Meryl Lee, almost in a whisper.

Mrs. Connolly waited a long time. Then she said, "I'm considering leaving St. Elene's, Miss Kowalski. I'm afraid it's too late."

"Leaving? You'll be headmistress next year."

She shook her head. "No, I will not. I'm sure it will be all over campus soon enough, so there's no harm in telling you. My son Thomas, who is a senior at St. Giles's, was filmed by a local news crew burning his draft card, swearing he would head to Canada to escape this imperialist nation of ours. He always has been articulate, and he was on this occasion as well. His speech was replayed on several more prominent newscasts, and he has since crossed the border."

"I don't understand what this has to do with—"

"Mr. Allen has declared that the headmistress of St. Elene's Preparatory Academy for Girls cannot be a woman whose son is a" —she paused—"draft dodger."

"I'm sorry, Mrs. Connolly."

"I have been asked to remove my name from consideration. That's the way things are done." She stood and turned away from Meryl Lee. "No loss, I suppose. None of the girls, and few of the faculty, would have been glad to see me as headmistress."

"That's not true," said Meryl Lee.

Mrs. Connolly turned back to her. "Miss Kowalski, you have just uttered what you know to be a prevarication."

"A . . . ?"

"Look it up in Mrs. Saunders's *Funk and Wagnalls* tonight."

"Where's Thomas?" Meryl Lee asked.

Mrs. Connolly sat back down. She looked at her hands. "I don't know," she said finally. "I hope he's . . ." She didn't finish.

Meryl Lee reached down into her notebook and pulled out a sheet of paper. "We had to write haiku again for the next literary society. Bettye gave me hers."

"Bettye Buckminster? Are you trying to be annoying, Miss Kowalski?"

"She wrote it about her brother Jonathan, thinking about him in Vietnam. May I read it to you?"

"I told you I was—"

Meryl Lee read it:

> "Brother far away.
> Light, stars through my dark branches:
> The same moon he sees."

Mrs. Connolly sat silently for a long time. Then she reached across the glass-top desk and took Bettye Buckminster's poem. She read it again. And again. Then she turned in her chair and looked out the window, her back to Meryl Lee.

"I'll think about the literary society," she said finally.

She did not turn around again, and Meryl Lee, after a little while, left.

Three days later, the Literary Society of St. Elene's Preparatory Academy for Girls met under the guidance of Mrs. Hibbard. Mrs. Connolly came and sat in the back row.

Ashley had left a poem to be read at the literary society, but clearly she thought Mrs. Hibbard had said "limerick" instead of "haiku." But after Mrs. Hibbard had read Ashley's limerick about daffodils, which Ashley made *pink* to rhyme with *stink,* everyone clapped politely anyway.

Then Marian read her haiku about sitting in a small parish church when she was thirteen. They all felt a kind of holy quiet about it. And they all clapped—for real, this time—and Marian said her images weren't nearly as good as Ashley's, and everyone could imagine Ashley smiling and fingering her pearls—but no one mentioned that.

Then Bettye read hers, and they clapped again, and Mrs. Hibbard said Bettye had caught the longing we all have felt for someone we love who is far away.

Then sharp-ars— Mrs. Connolly told Mrs. Hibbard that no, she didn't want to read because she had only a sonnet and not a haiku, but Mrs. Hibbard said she should, and finally Mrs. Connolly stood up and went to the front of the room and smoothed out the poem on the lectern, and she looked right at Meryl Lee, and then she began to read.

Here are the first two lines. It's all Meryl Lee remembered. Everything else was sound and sadness and longing.

The night dark your shoulders, moon glow your hair,
Dim stars your eyes, and all else your despise.

The poem was about Thomas crossing into Canada, leaving behind everything he ever loved, leaving behind everyone who loved him. Meryl Lee wished she could remember more—it was so beautiful, and sad, and by the end she was crying.

And then Mrs. Connolly left the lectern and went to sit back down. But before she sat down, Bettye walked over to her, and they looked at each other, and Mrs. Connolly took Bettye's hands, and she said something only to her, and after that, they sat side by side, holding hands, like they both knew something—the same thing.

On campus the next day, Meryl Lee told Mrs. Connolly she thought her sonnet was beautiful.

And Mrs. Connolly said, "Thank you, Miss Kowalski."

That was all.

But it was enough to begin again.

THIRTY-EIGHT

ON THE NEXT WEDNESDAY, DR. MACKNOCKATER WAS waiting for Meryl Lee on the steps of Newell when she came out. They walked together, and Dr. MacKnockater nodded to the wilted daffodils. "The site of your sit-in," she said. "I suspect it will not be your last."

"Maybe not," Meryl Lee said.

"Mrs. Connolly has rejoined the literary society, I understand."

"And she is not going to be headmistress next year. Does that mean that you'll—"

"I'm wondering how Meryl Lee Kowalski is doing."

"She's fine," Meryl Lee said.

"Is she?"

"Sometimes."

"'Sometimes' is a good answer, Meryl Lee. You've had a terrifying experience. And you've lost a great deal this year."

Meryl Lee nodded.

"And have you found much?"

Meryl Lee thought about that. "I think I have," she said.

"I think you have too. The world can be such an ugly place. It takes a special person, a truly Accomplished person, to make it a beautiful place."

Meryl Lee felt herself trembling. She seemed about to understand something. Or maybe she seemed about to believe something.

But what?

On Saturday, an early morning rain cleared away and a rainbow bobbed on top of distant waves as the eighth-grade girls of St. Elene's Preparatory Academy went down to Popham Beach for the June Lobster Fest. They couldn't stop staring at the rainbow until Dr. MacKnockater called for help. Heidi and Charlotte and Barbara Rockcastle were in charge of making up two fires, Meryl Lee and Elizabeth Koertge and Lois Tuthill were in charge of setting the tables, Marian and Jennifer and Julia Chall were in charge of fixing the salads, and Bettye and Alethea were in charge of the lobsters, since aside from Mrs. Wyss, they were the only ones who knew something about domestic economy and boiling lobsters.

Ashley Higginson, who had come back the night before for the end-of-the-year ceremonies and who was not wearing her pearls, was in charge of looking sour and gloomy.

Mr. Wheelock had the lobsters in the back of his station wagon, and one by one he and Matt carried the crates down to the water and the girls covered them in seaweed, which even Charlotte did, and only one crate got knocked over and Mr. Wheelock had to recapture those lobsters frantically trying to get themselves back into the ocean, and some had lost the bands around their claws so they were snapping at him and you do not want to go after a snapping lobster in shallow water.

Some earned their freedom.

For the others, Mr. Wheelock put two huge lobster pots on the fires to boil seawater, and some of the girls peeled hard-boiled eggs and some stirred lemonade, and Mrs. Wyss flustered happily. It was a perfect blue day by the sea, with the water calm and bright and smooth, and the sand a little damp but still warm, and only a couple of clouds puffing on the horizon, and everyone fussing by the tables— except Ashley, who walked out to sit on the rocks alone, looking as tragic as Mary Stuart, Queen of Scots waiting for her execution.

Meryl Lee supposed that lobster was fine to eat—if you didn't see the lobster being lowered to its death in boiling water, or hear it scream, or mind ripping red shells apart and sucking meat out of little tentacles, or legs, or whatever they were. Jennifer and Charlotte and Heidi and Marian and Matt each ate a whole lobster. Meryl Lee tasted one, and then ate some of the fried chicken Mrs. Wyss had brought along for Mr. Wheelock, who said he didn't eat anything with that many legs.

And though Meryl Lee asked her to come to the tables, Ashley said she was a dope to think that she could eat lobster at a time like this.

Or chicken.

On Sunday, Meryl Lee wrote to her mother about the eighth-grade graduation.

> I hope you are able to come. It's going to be a lot of fun. The girls from the upper school are decorating the chapel with white flowers and white ribbons, and we're going to be wearing white corsages. When everyone has been seated and Mrs. Mott has offered a prayer for the day, Dr. MacKnockater will give a speech, and we'll read a litany together, and then we receive our eighth-grade diplomas from St. Elene's Preparatory Academy for Girls.

There's a dinner afterward where the families sit together. Heidi and I and Charlotte and Jennifer and Marian have it all planned out—there will be just enough seats at one long table—so we have it reserved.

I hope you're coming! I'll see you in less than two weeks.

That's what she wrote.
Then she wrote her father.

I hope you are able to come. It's going to be a lot of fun. The girls from the upper school are decorating the chapel with white flowers and white ribbons, and we're going to be wearing white corsages. When everyone has been seated and Mrs. Mott has offered a prayer for the day, Dr. MacKnockater will give a speech, and we'll read a litany together, and then we receive our eighth-grade diplomas from St. Elene's Preparatory Academy for Girls.

There's a dinner afterward where the families sit together. Heidi and I and Charlotte and Jennifer and Marian have it all planned out—there will be just enough seats at one long table—so we have it reserved.

I hope you're coming! I'll see you in less than two weeks.

She mailed both the letters the next day on the way to the headmistress's office to meet with Dr. MacKnockater about housing for next year.

"I'm assuming, of course, that you will be here next year, Miss Kowalski."

Meryl Lee looked around Dr. MacKnockater's office—Robespierre's desk, the shelves of books, the long dark carved box in front of the fireplace. Then she looked outside onto the lovely commons, where a breeze was puffing at the new leaves. "There's no place like home," she said.

Dr. MacKnockater looked out the window with her. "Indeed," she said softly. The sun came out suddenly and light dappled the slate roof of Newell. "And have you thought about your living arrangements?"

Meryl Lee nodded. "We've figured it all out. Heidi had her heart set on Grafton Regis, since that dorm looks over the field hockey field—of course. But in Malvern they have suites with two bedrooms for three girls each. That means that Heidi and Marian and Charlotte and Jennifer and me and one other girl can all live together. We just have to find one more girl to complete the suite."

"I see," said Dr. MacKnockater. "Have you considered who the sixth girl might be?"

"Not really," said Meryl Lee.

Dr. MacKnockater smiled. "I think you may have," she said. "You know someone else who needs a home."

Meryl Lee looked down at the fireplace. "Dr. MacKnockater," she said, "what's in the box?"

"A relic," she said.

Meryl Lee looked at her.

"When I need a great deal of patience, it helps me to look at the box and remember . . ."

"Dr. MacKnockater, it's not . . ."

Dr. MacKnockater looked at her.

"Not really," said Meryl Lee.

Dr. MacKnockater still looking at her.

"I'll talk to Ashley," said Meryl Lee.

"There's no place like home," said Dr. MacKnockater.

On Tuesday morning, Meryl Lee looked for Ashley at breakfast to ask her if she would room with her next year. But Ashley wasn't at breakfast.

Or Chapel.

Or any of her morning classes.

Or dinner.

So Meryl Lee left Greater Hoxne Dining Hall early to run back to Netley to see if she was sick.

She knocked at her door, and when Ashley didn't answer, Meryl Lee tried the door and it was open so she looked in.

Ashley's side of the room was bare. She was gone.

Meryl Lee asked Mrs. Kellogg why Ashley's room was bare.

"Last night, her aunt and uncle came to take her home," said Mrs. Kellogg.

"Is she coming back for graduation?" said Meryl Lee.

"We had hoped so, but it seems she felt she could no longer stay," said Mrs. Kellogg.

"Is she coming back in the fall?"

Mrs. Kellogg shook her head. "Miss Kowalski, life is hardly a Victorian novel where all must be revealed. Sometimes personal stories should remain personal."

The rest of that week, Meryl Lee couldn't stop thinking about Ashley.

Friendships start in different ways, Meryl Lee thought. *Some-*

times they start right away. Sometimes they start slowly. And some-times, maybe sometimes they don't have any chance at all.

On the last day of the semester, when classes were over and finals were done and Heidi had passed algebra and all that remained was graduation, Meryl Lee walked down to the wall, where three gardeners under the supervision of Dr. MacKnockater were ripping up the poison ivy vines! They were wearing plastic protective suits so they wouldn't be contaminated, and they had saws and shovels and even a backhoe. Dr. MacKnockater stood by the main gate and when she saw Meryl Lee, she asked what she thought.

"Any time you can rip up poison ivy, it's probably a good idea," Meryl Lee said.

"Just so. Have you heard back from your parents?"

Meryl Lee very quiet.

"Oh," said Dr. MacKnockater, "I'm so sorry."

"I'll be riding back to New York with Marian and her parents," said Meryl Lee.

"Very good."

"Dr. MacKnockater," Meryl Lee said, "there are some rumors going around."

"Miss Kowalski, it's a prep school. There are always rumors going around."

"There's a rumor you're going to stay on as headmistress."

Dr. MacKnockater spread a smile as happy as the blue spring day. "I'm thinking of having the entire wall taken down this summer," she said.

"But hasn't it been around for, like, a couple of centuries?"

Dr. MacKnockater looked at Meryl Lee.

"Miss Kowalski, perhaps what you have shown St. Elene's

Preparatory Academy for Girls this year is that any time you can take down a wall, no matter how long it's been around, it's probably a good idea."

Meryl Lee looked at Dr. MacKnockater.

"We could plant something instead," Meryl Lee said.

"What would we plant?"

"Chrysanthemums."

"That will do nicely."

They watched together as the gardeners ripped out the poison ivy, handful by handful.

The fourth quarter evaluations of Miss Meryl Lee Kowalski were waiting for her in her mailbox the next morning. There were comments from Coach Rowlandson: "shows the effort of a true athlete—if not a natural one." From Mrs. Saunders: "developed surprising artistic skills as she honed her oral presentation style." From Mrs. Bellamy: "evidence of a focused scientific mind that may flourish into real expertise." From Mrs. Connolly: "the heart of a sensitive and perceptive writer." From Mr. Wheelock: "as dependable and determined as an axiom." From Mrs. Wyss: "as lemon is to scrod."

From Dr. MacKnockater: "Accomplished."

THIRTY-NINE

In THE LAST WEEK OF MAY AND THE BEGINNING OF June 1969—the month when Meryl Lee Kowalski would graduate from eighth grade at St. Elene's Preparatory Academy for Girls—two hundred and forty-two young Americans died in the Vietnam War. *Life* magazine published all their names and pictures together for a nation to say goodbye.

In June 1969, President Nixon announced that the number of American soldiers in Vietnam would be sharply reduced. When he made that announcement, there were more than half a million Americans at war. Many of them were not sure why they were fighting.

In June 1969, Dr. MacKnockater named Miss Bettye Buckminster and Miss Alethea Browning to be instructors in the new Culinary Arts Program of St. Elene's Preparatory Academy for Girls. As part of their remuneration, Bettye and Alethea would each receive a St. Elene's scholarship to cover all of their St. Elene's costs, as well as all future college tuition costs.

Maybe, Meryl Lee thought, if Alethea's brother had been there right then, maybe he'd say this was what he had really been fighting for.

————»«————

In June 1969, Coach Rowlandson said Meryl Lee should be proud of what she had accomplished in her short career as goalie for the Lasses this spring. She said Meryl Lee should try out for goalie on the freshman team next year.

Meryl Lee thought that this was Coach Rowlandson's way of telling her that life doesn't stop even when horrible horrible things happen.

Meryl Lee told Coach Rowlandson she wasn't sure about spring soccer, since she'd be pretty busy with Life Sciences. Mrs. Bellamy had asked her to think about becoming her lab assistant. And besides, Heidi might want to play first-string goalie again.

"But won't you have to dissect things as a lab assistant?" said Coach Rowlandson.

Meryl Lee nodded.

"Ick," said Coach Rowlandson, and shuddered.

"Sticks down, Coach," said Meryl Lee.

In June 1969, on graduation day, Mrs. Connolly congratulated Meryl Lee on completing her first year at St. Elene's. "I hope you continue to write your poetry over the summer," she said. "You don't want to waste all those days."

"I won't," said Meryl Lee. "I think I may be in New York for a few days, then in Philadelphia for most of the summer."

"A fascinating city," said Mrs. Connolly.

"Will you stay here?" said Meryl Lee.

Mrs. Connolly looked across the campus. "St. Elene's is lovely in July and August, but I think I may be spending some time in Montreal. I'll look forward to seeing you next fall, perhaps in the next edition of the St. Elene's Literary Society."

"I'll be there," said Meryl Lee.

"We'll start with Spenserian stanzas," said Mrs. Connolly. "Do you know what a Spenserian stanza is, Miss Kowalski?"

Meryl Lee shook her head.

"Then you have your first summer assignment," said Mrs. Connolly.

"My first?"

"Others to follow at regular intervals," said Mrs. Connolly. "Poetry is a demanding mistress."

On graduation day, Dr. MacKnockater asked Meryl Lee to pose for a graduation Polaroid, and Meryl Lee had an idea. She ran to her room for Jonathan's yellow scarf. Then she ran back to Newell, gathering girls along the way. "Maybe this is going to look silly," she said, "but . . ." No one thought it would look silly. She wound the end of Jonathan's scarf around her neck, and then Charlotte wound the scarf around her neck, and by then, it had momentum.

"For posterity," said Dr. MacKnockater. And there they were in a row: Meryl Lee, then Charlotte, then Jennifer, then Marian, then Heidi, then Bettye, then Alethea, who pointed out that even with all that winding, there was more than enough scarf for the rest of the eighth grade of St. Elene's Preparatory Academy for Girls.

What there wasn't enough room for, Meryl Lee thought, was the Blank.

When Meryl Lee went to help Dr. MacKnockater figure out how to develop the Polaroid, she reminded her about her promise.

"My promise?" said Dr. MacKnockater.

"You said you'd tell me what I had become Accomplished in."

Dr. MacKnockater smiled. "Oh, Miss Kowalski," she said, and

she pointed at the group of girls who were still getting themselves untied from the scarf, with Bettye winding it around her left arm.

"There is your Accomplishment," Dr. MacKnockater said.

"What do you mean?"

And she took Meryl Lee's face in her two hands and she said very very quietly, "Meryl Lee Kowalski, look."

And Meryl Lee saw Marian and Alethea laughing as they tried to untangle Jennifer, and Bettye laughing, and Heidi and Charlotte hugging each other.

And she saw Mrs. Connolly watching them and laughing. Mrs. Connolly—whose son was now so far away.

And Matt! There was Matt, still with his limp, coming up the walk.

"You are the Tin Woodman," said Dr. MacKnockater, "who lost your heart, and despite the Obstacles, found it again in the only way that you can find it: by giving it away." She leaned in close. "And I suspect that you will give it away again and again, and that you will find it again and again. Meryl Lee Kowalski, that is your Accomplishment. And believe me, it is a very rare one indeed."

Meryl Lee looked around again.

"It didn't work with my parents," she said.

"The future is always in motion," said Dr. MacKnockater. And just like that, Meryl Lee felt herself hurtle into Resolution.

Summer 1969

FORTY

Matt, down on the shore, below Bagheera's
house, a blue June day, the waves calm enough that he could skip
seven, eight times easy, the sun bright and warm on his chest, his
toes digging into the cooler strip of sand.

And then the memory.

The sea breeze brought it to him like a gift, like something that
had been released.

He was on the beach.

He was on the beach, sitting on a blanket and digging his toes
into the sand, and his mother said, "Let's put some of this lotion on
you." She squirted it into her hand and rubbed it on his shoulders,
on his back, on his chest, on his cheeks, and then, with a laugh, on
the very tip of his nose.

His father came up from the water. He let himself collapse
beside the blanket, laughing. Then he rolled and got sand all over
himself, and Matt laughed and started to pile sand on his back.

"Make Daddy into a sandcastle?" said his mother.

He remembered.

She handed them both paper cups filled with mixed lemonade
and grape juice from a red thermos and it was so cold it almost
hurt. But he drank it anyway. So did Daddy. Then he showed Matt
his purple tongue, and Matt showed him his.

He remembered.

Then his father handed some guy his camera, and the guy took a picture of the three of them scrunching together on the blanket on the beach.

It was all there: the sound of the waves, the gulls, the drying salt water on his shins, the smell of lemonade and grape juice, the sand, his mother and his father sitting on the blanket, and the cool lotion on the tip of his nose.

It was all there.

And he knew what he would do now that he was free of Leonidas Shug. He would look for his mother and his father. He would ask Lieutenant Minot to help—since he was pretty good at what he did. Dr. MacKnockater would help too. Maybe he would find out what had happened to them. Maybe he would find them.

Maybe.

As it turned out, Meryl Lee came back to St. Elene's sooner than she had imagined—in mid-July. Matt met her at the bus station, and together they walked the long way to Dr. MacKnockater's house—Matt still limping a little bit. Down at the docks the next day, Matt helped Dr. MacKnockater step on board Captain Hurd's lobster boat—she would not use her cane—and then Matt and Meryl Lee stood at the stern beside Bettye while Reverend Turner Buckminster officiated at the wedding of Captain Willis Hurd and Dr. Nora MacKnockater on the slow and gentle waves of the bay.

Afterward, Matt had Meryl Lee look over the stern at the newly painted lettering for the newly christened boat—now renamed *The Tin Woodman*.

"Is that a good name for a lobster boat?" said Meryl Lee.

"It is for this one," said Matt.

That afternoon, the newlyweds left for a honeymoon in Edinburgh. "Take care of things," they told Matt.

He promised the Captain and Bagheera he would.

In the evening, after securing *The Tin Woodman*, Matt and Meryl Lee climbed through the chute in Matt's room and up to the slate roof. They watched the tide run out and the moon run up and the stars run all about. Below them, the front room was picked up and the kitchen was clean enough and the lamp by the window lit. The red embers were banked in the wood stove, since it had been a coolish evening. They'd pulled the east windows halfway down against the damp.

Meryl Lee sat close to Matt, and Matt draped an afghan around their shoulders. They held hands, and they looked out at all that the bright moon had lit: the shore ridge, the pines, the moving tide, the white-cresting waves, the distant islands.

"We can see everything," Meryl Lee said.

"Safe and secure from all alarms," said Matt.

She looked at him.

"For now," he said.

Meryl Lee closed her eyes. The sea breeze came up and swirled around them, and she drew the afghan a little closer, then leaned into Matt. "For now," she said.

And far away, the buoys belled and belled and belled their ocean lullaby while the waves rolled in and broke upon the eternal shoreline as they always do—just like that.

Gary D. Schmidt is the beloved and best-selling author of *The Wednesday Wars*, a Newbery Honor book; *Okay for Now*, a National Book Award finalist; and *Lizzie Bright and the Buckminster Boy*, a Newbery Honor and Printz Honor book. He is a professor of English at Calvin University in Grand Rapids, and lives in rural Michigan.